MW00633001

# More Canterbury Tales

## A novel by JD Sedlack

### Book 1 of the More Conversations Series

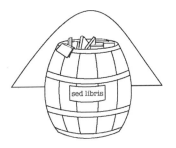

sed libris

Copyright 2019, sedlibris, LLC

*As with all things in my life, this book is dedicated to Maryann with love.*

*Special thanks to Dean Rudolph Weingartner and Professor Lacey Baldwin Smith who taught a young man to look beyond.*

# Table of Contents

It occurred to the Lord Chancellor that he had been in constant conversation with himself for as long as he could remember. The conversation had begun with his earliest memory, waking up in his little room in the house on Milk Street when he was four or five years old. The dawn had just broken, though the buildings around, and the smoke in the air from surrounding chimneys, kept his room in a deep twilight. Only a hint of smoky rose' was becoming apparent in the small patch of sky Thomas could see from his bed. Thomas knew it was dawn, though, from the dairymen, who had just begun loudly hawking their wares in the street below.

Thomas's room was on the third floor of the More house, and was small, filled with shadows cast by the near-light through the single, small, sooty, port hole window. With the proper angle, standing on a chair, Thomas could peer through the tiny irregular glass down on the garden of the house, or up at the eaves and chimneys of the buildings all around. In the early London morning, the shadows of the curling smoke of a dozen rekindled coal fires danced indolently across the walls, purple, magenta, and black. The flaws in the glass cast these dark rainbows every which way around Thomas's awakening form.

"*Well, it's morning,*" said a deep, reassuring voice inside his head. Without thinking, Thomas replied that he wanted to sleep a while longer. With that, Thomas had begun his life-long conversation.

Secretly, the adult Thomas would wish those first remembered words had been pithier, but he would always be pleased that he could remember them, and, over time, the conversation had indeed grown progressively more dense and more involved. On occasion, Thomas would indulge himself with attempts to impress the voice in his head with his erudition. On those occasions the voice would act as a kind of grader, or judge, commenting on the latest thought – a quick *"good job,"* or *"be clearer in your thoughts,"* or, on blissful occasions Thomas could achieve a deep rolling laugh from the voice. That laugh was joyous, proud, and loving all at once.

The nice feature of this internal conversation, Thomas had often thought, was that it changed the goals of conversations with others. In Thomas's mind, these private internal dialogues elevated him, and elevated his own conversation. Now, seated at the Chancery Bench in the Great Hall at Westminster, Thomas More, the Lord Chancellor of England, engaged in his own private reverie while the arguments over some particularly uninteresting land dispute played out in front of him.

Thomas's mind wandered around the Great Hall of Westminster Palace. The immense beige stone walls, thick with centuries of soot; the massive dark oak hammer beam roof, sturdy as England itself, meticulously polished. The great hall radiating the impression of stability and power. Of Authority. Of the overarching Will of the King himself. And seated in the center, at the high table, along the long wall. was the King's Lord Chancellor.

The Great Hall of Westminster Palace was divided into three sections, each portion housing a significant Court; the King's Bench, the Chancery, and the Court of Common Pleas. Having the three main Judicial bodies of the land in one hall, however large, led to a magnificent din, as lawyers spoke their pieces, as litigants emoted, and as judges tried, mostly successfully, to maintain order and decorum. The constant coughing in the room, with so many people stuffed into the Hall there seemed to constantly be someone coughing, sometimes irritated Thomas in the center court. Mostly, though, Thomas viewed this room as his home, and the many people there his family.

Thomas looked over from his own seat, atop the Chancery Court towards the King's Bench. He stared sadly at the seat on that Court that his father had occupied until he had died, two years before. He ached with longing to see old John More still sitting there, red, fleshy, and happy, wisps of flyaway white hair, smiling proudly at him… but such was not to be. Instead, seated at his father's place was the new Justice, John Spelman, whom Thomas himself had sworn in only a month before. The new judge still looked uncomfortable seated alongside his father's two great friends, Humphrey Coningsby and John Port.

Thomas smiled wistfully, and turned his attention back to his own Court, thinking, "at least the lawyers are arguing in English. I accomplished that."

The voice in Thomas's head responded stoutly, *"God's blood, yes, but listen to that idiot Northerner lawyer with the eye patch go on with his accent. I wonder sometimes if that northern drivel really is better than the Norman French."*

Thomas smiled inwardly, thinking, "I always hated Norman French. I hated learning it. I hated speaking it. This is better, even if byrred.

His voice replied, *""At least he comes to a quick point and stops talking."*

"True," thought Thomas, noticing that his court had gone silent and was looking at him.

The silence was broken when a Herald, in full Royal regalia, bright red tunic with a blue dragon emblazoned on the chest, attempted the impossible; slipping unnoticed along the side of the court, past the bar, and along to the right of Thomas's dark wooden Bench. The lawyer's attention on Thomas waned as their eyes fixed on the Herald. The messenger bowed slightly and silently handed Thomas a rolled-up parchment, the King's wax seal obvious in the middle.

Thomas took the message without acknowledging the messenger, and broke the seal, unfurling the parchment letter. In the King's small, meandering handwriting the letter said simply, "My Lord Chancellor, come to dinner with me today. Richmond Palace."

Thomas looked now at the Herald, who surprisingly, instead of backing away had remained standing at Thomas's side. Thomas asked, "did His Grace, the King, say what this was about?"

The Herald kept his face a mask, both to Thomas and to the now staring lawyers. He responded stiffly, "no, My Lord Chancellor."

Thomas coughed, then gave a slight pound with his fist on the bench, as a gavel, and, looking at the curious attorneys, said, "Gentlemen, I am going to have to stop you there for the day. We can reconvene tomorrow, if you please."

Thomas abruptly stood, his gold Esses chain clinking lightly as he stood before falling heavily on his chest. The hair shirt Thomas wore under his robes scratched violently on his flank, causing the Lord Chancellor to twist a bit as he stood, a flash of pain in his eyes. The Herald remained impassive.

Now erect, the Herald and the Lord Chancellor eyed each other suspiciously, before Thomas broke the impasse with a laugh and a smile.

Thomas said, "It is late morning already. His Majesty certainly did not leave much time."

The Herald finally smiled thinly, saying "No my Lord Chancellor."

Thomas grinned winningly, replying "Well then, pray, lead on Herald. Let us go sup with our good Lord, the King."

"I wonder what all this is about," thought Thomas.

Oddly, silence from the voice in his mind.

## Chapter 1 - April, 1483

The house on Milk Street was, and as far as anyone was concerned, had always been, a part of the Cripplegate Ward. The upper section of the Street had, until 300 years before, been the district of the wealthy Jews. They, first among Londoners, had build expansive stone homes when the typical London home was build of wood. Stone, particularly the lovely Kentish ragstone, lent a real air of permanence to these London structures that Thomas enjoyed and that gave him a foundation in life.

For Thomas, a feeling of permanence in buildings lent feelings of security to an otherwise insecure life. In fact, Thomas often thought one's true childhood home to be the home most deeply remembered, an impression he based upon his memories of the Milk Street house. Even grown, Thomas and his sister Elizabeth would occasionally look at their large, elegant homes, then look at each other, laugh, and say simultaneously, "Ah…. Milk Street!"

Milk Street was lined at the street level with shops. Between the shops were entrances to the Great Halls of some rather nice homes. It was rumored among the children of the street that several of the foundations of the buildings went back to Roman times. There were tantalizing hints of old Roman mosaics in the undercrofts of several houses, and, as the Street had risen, these Roman entrances had become basements, in fact, several of the buildings in the area had remained excavated at the original level. In these very old buildings, the original ground floor was accessed by damp, musty, incredibly worn stairs going down six or seven feet. As a young man, Thomas discovered to his delight that some of the best taverns in London existed in these old Roman ground-floors, now cellars.

At the entrance of the More home, halfway up the ancient narrow street on the left-hand side, there were, in fact, old stone steps going down to an ancient basement, and a narrow set of wooden stairs that led upwards a few feet from the entrance to what was now the ground floor of the home. The real entrance to the residence was achieved, however, by passing to the right of these stairs into a high arched stone passageway, wide enough for a man and a horse, then down a gently ramped walk, into a courtyard. This central courtyard was surrounded by stone and brick buildings, and had ornate doors to the left of the passageway that led first to a great hall, and then, on the left side, doors leading up into a dark, narrow stairway to the apartments and solars of the upper floors.

The courtyard of Thomas's home was small, only about twenty feet square. Thomas's mother, Agnes, an avid gardener, had brought in plants and flowers and had created a garden around the edge of the courtyard. In deference to his wife, Thomas's father, John, a rising young London lawyer, had arranged for the stables to be reached around the back of the house, off Wood Street, instead of through the courtyard, leaving his beloved Agnes her own private oasis.

As a small boy, Thomas enjoyed sitting in the courtyard with his mother. She would teach him the names of the various plants that she had brought. Agnes knew the Latin names for each of the plants, and Thomas thus began his Latin studies at a very young age, as he and his mother would make jokes and puns using the Latin and English names of the plants. Thomas's favorite was that the Latin name for the Mulberry bush was Morus, and that the Latinized version of the family name was also Morus. There, Thomas thought, "the mulberry is my tree." In time, he also had discovered that the Greek version of his name, Morae, meant "silliness." Thomas and his mother could sit for hours saying "More's silly mulberry," laughing each time he ran through "More's morae Morus."

Since gardening was Agnes's main preoccupation, Thomas enjoyed a steady stream of plants coming and then going as the seasons dictated. The garden itself was surrounded, extending up three stories by the walls of the houses and on apartments of the mansion. The five-year-old Thomas often said to his mother, "when I grow up I am going to be very rich, and I am going to get you the best garden in the whole world!"

Agnes would always respond with a gentle, "that's lovely, Thomas," and she would return dreamily to pruning or smelling her flowers.

If one turned back from the garden and went up the narrow stairs, they would reach the solar, or the second-floor main living room of the house. This room was in many ways a kind of great hall; the ceilings were about 12 feet high, and the walls were wainscoted with a lovely dark English oak. There were bookcases with Johns law books, and other volumes of interest to the family. As a novelty, Thomas's father, John, had recently acquired a few copies of books that the Queen's brother, Earl Rivers had funded Caxton to print in Westminster. The first two were the Canterbury Tales, and Mallory's *King Arthur*. These two carefully bound volumes were given pride of place in the solar on their own pedestals, the red dyed leather covers gleaming with care and love.

Also, new in this room, were the fireplaces on either end. As his career as a London lawyer had progressed, John More had added these modern fireplaces to the house as a form of central heating. He loved to sit in this room reading, or looking at the fires, content and happy in his world.

The solar room had cased lead windows that projected about five feet out over Milk Street, and which peered across the street into the houses on the opposite side of Milk street, which also had solars projecting out over the street. These projections left only a few feet between the buildings. As a result, Milk Street below was in nearly perpetual darkness from the projections of each rising floor, until the buildings, nearly touching created a dark and damp block long archway over the cobbling and the shops below.

A positive side of these kissing buildings, though, was that it was very easy for children to make friends with any other children living on the other side of the street. The well-to-do children of London, it seemed, spent much of their early years smiling and waving at each other across the narrow divides. As they became older, the cleverer ones would devise ways of opening the windows to speak or with increasing sophistication, use strings and pulleys to send treasures back and forth. Obviously, part of the joy of these channels of communication lay simply in keeping ahead of parents and servants.

Thomas often wondered if they should just connect the buildings and complete the archway over the street, as the city was slowly doing at ground level with the rivers of London. Thomas had seen a picture in a book of the archways between buildings in Venice. Citing fire hazards, the ordinances in London prohibited building any further projections out over the Street. But the street was dark enough as it was, and the occasional torches at street level enhanced the ever-present fire risk.

From the solar of the More home, one went out the north door and entered a paneled passageway which led to John's office and study, which were small connected rooms. The south door led through another dark hallway, past rooms for John and Agnes, to stairs going up to the third floor, which contained chambers for servants and guests. The third-floor hallway extended all the way around the courtyard. Many of the rooms on the second and third floor had small leaded glass windows overlooking Thomas and Agnes's garden. Servants retainers and guests all stayed in these chambers, or just camped out in the great hall.

When he was four or five, Thomas had been given a tiny room, tucked in the back corner of the north side of the home. Thomas would later recall it as being more of a broom closet, but is was private, had great light, and, even as a young boy, it allowed Thomas the unusual luxury of being alone with his thoughts and with his interior voice. The greatest feature of this room, as far as Thomas was concerned, though, was its small window, and its view of his mother in her garden.

Another advantage of Thomas's little room was that at night he could look out of his little window and see the stars if the thick London smoke had cleared enough. Thomas loved looking at the stars. The millions of shimmering points of light always inspired him to think of great things.

The ground floor and the old Roman undercrofts of the houses on Milk Street were all of stone, but by the third story, stone had given way to traditional open timbered whitewashed wattle and daub. The beams had been inserted directly into holes cut into the original stone façade of the building. The solars and projecting rooms of the third floor had been built on these projections and finished outside as half-timber. The whitewash was a lime plaster mixed into, and coating the horsehair and straw filling of the wall, leading to great insulation and warmth for the whole house. The disadvantage of this material was that the smooth whiteness of the neighborhood had been greatly stained by the heavy smoke of all the coal fires of London, leaving the white lime messily grey-black.

The roof of the house was finished with green glazed tiles which had been installed all over London. These large ceramic plates were the favorite, fashionable roofing material of the Burghers of the City. The rooftops of London in 1483 were also sprouting increasing numbers of large heavy clay ornamental chimney pots as the newer invention of a wall based fireplace, like

John More's, had become popular. Venting fire smoke through a chimney was quickly replacing the central firepit of a smoky medieval Great Hall, which vented smoke lazily through louvers in the roof.

Unfortunately, all the roof work and the chimney and chimney pot installation in the More house had left a small leak in the room in Thomas's room which was never fixed. His father promised that eventually it would be fixed, but never, while they lived there, fulfilled that promise. When asked a few more times about it, John would tersely respond, "Only God is perfect."

Encircling Thomas's domestic womb on Milk Street was the great City of London. To Thomas the City was a great, persistent miracle that enveloped his entire being like a loud, smelly security blanket.

Milk Street, Thomas found as he grew, was but a small side street that lay just north of Cheapside, the great market street of London. If Thomas came out of his home and turned a quick right, he would pass the diary shops of Osgood Cheeseman, a rotund, mustachioed bear of a man, with dark, wavy hair that was beginning to gray at the temples. He was a northerner who had come to London from the outpost city of Carlisle on the dangerous frontier with the Scots, to seek his fortune making and selling cheese. He spoke with a heavy burr, and had decayed, blackened stumps of teeth. He was unfailingly kind to Thomas and his friends, slipping them freshly cheddared curds that were lovely and salty and that squeaked when you bit down on them.

Across Milk Street from the More house was the mansion of Edward Stafford. He was a round faced boy with blue eyes and red hair. Edward nearly always had a friendly smile on his face. Thomas and Edward were from very different classes – Edward's father being the Duke of

Buckingham, great-grandson of King Edward the Third. Edward's mother was a Woodville, sister of the Queen. Despite this, Edward and Thomas had become fast friends, meeting first through the glass of their nearly kissing solars.

The boys had then progressed rapidly to regular adventures, always great fun. Usually they involved going down to the Cheape, soaking in the sights and sounds of London – examining all the costumes, things for sale, all the oddities wandering the streets – overwhelming for five-year-old boys, who believed themselves escapees, not realizing they were discreetly followed by usually amused servants or retainers at discreet distance.

On one occasion Edward had seemed distracted and upset since they had started, but instead of his usual bluster about Kings and Dukes, Edward winced at the gentle punch and began to sob. Thomas quickly went to put his arm around his friend, asking what was wrong.

"My father…" Edward sobbed. "Mother says I can't talk about it. Can't say anything."

Thomas was upset for his friend, and thought about pushing him for more information.

*"Leave him be, Thomas. Just be his friend."*

Thomas and Edward looked at each other, and Edward said simply, "My father and the King have fallen out. My mother is crying, saying we must flee London."

"Is your father well," Thomas asked.

"No," replied Edward after a pause. "I think he is to be killed."

Edward started crying again. A few passersby paused to look at the two young boys, one crying, but no one stopped. Edwards watchers came close and Edward saw them. Recognizing them, he immediately stopped crying and rolled a bit out from under Thomas's arm. With an effort of will, he composed himself, and gave a steadied wave of his hand to the watchers.

Forcing a smile, and sniffing, he said, "we must go onward, Thomas. I might not be able to do this again."

Proceeding west on the Cheape, the boys came to the corner of St. Paul's Churchyard. There was a magnificent speaker's platform built there, and as they passed, there was an oddly deranged looking speaker present in the pulpit, exhorting the crown on some aspect of their defective Christianity. The boys stopped to listen for only a moment, briefly taken in by the passion of the speaker, but both quickly unnerved and disappointed by his insanity, and before any noblemen were mentioned.

Beside the outdoor pulpit, the massive piers of St. Paul's loomed ahead, Gothic and white, though heavily smoke stained. Of Portland stone. Sturdy and solid. The church rose upwards into the sky, out the the comprehension of the small boys. With a little luck, and hidden by their small statures, the boys slipped into the Cathedral and into a busy, loud world fanning up the aisles.

The interior of the now 400-year-old church was breathtaking. There were so many interesting things to look at that the boys simply stopped and stared, quickly moving from one fascinating site to another. High in the sky of the inside of the church were old, dirty bishop's miters, stained with age and use, and from the dripping of pitch from the hammer beamed roof above them. There were delicately carved statues everywhere. Gargoyles and saints. The stone buttresses and flying buttresses. And, contrary to the Scripture, the inside of the massive St. Paul's, the largest and tallest cathedral in Europe, the inside of the church had become a great place to do business, sheltered from the weather. A corrupt and broke clergy had allowed market stalls into the aisles, where goods remained dry and sellers warm in winter.

With one object foremost in mind, the two boys would slip sideways in an obscure side corridor and up into the north side of the choir. There were massive furnishings of wood, elegantly carved with the insignia of wearers of the garter, the King's favorites. Edward pointed up at his father's golden knot.

The boys moved around the choir stalls to the north wall where John of Gaunt, the Duke of Lancaster, was entombed. There was a fine marble carving of the Duke, along with his first wife, Blanche, next to him for all eternity, but---treasure!! John's lance and shield were leaned up against the tomb. There was, as there frequently was, a small crowd of furtive looking boys there, testing the ancient shield and sword, lifting them, or at least trying not to let the tip of the lance dip in its heaviness to clack on the floor, risking bringing adults to the scene, or trouble.

The shield was an old wooden one, with the Duke's arms emblazoned in colorful paint, little boxes of red with golden castles, white boxes with red lions, and blue boxes with golden lilies. The leather straps were worn and the shield was heavy. Generations of boys had come to sneak into Paul's to play with the lance, and the handle of the lance was well worn from small hands attempting to lift it.

The clergy of the Cathedral had a traditional secret watching place in the gallery above the choir. They could watch the boys play, a very enjoyable pastime. Occasionally, one of the young sub-deacons, not from London, and not yet initiated into this old tradition, would find the boys, and would drag the young offenders out by reddened, twisted ears. Watching the dragging off of a young boy was also a very enjoyable sport. When these sub-deacons grew older and were initiated, they would often burn with embarrassment watching a newer generation repeat this ritual, their elders reminding them of their own behavior years before. And so it had been for hundreds of years in St. Paul's Cathedral.

Thomas and Edward were soon joined by a sneaky little group of six and seven-year-old boys, cautiously touching and admiring the lance. Eventually the group swelled as Henry Percy, age 7, and Thomas Boleyn, age 9, and one or two others joined in. Thomas Howard, age 10, red hair aflame, was soon seen peeking around a carved pillar, enviously watching the younger boys, wishing he could still join in. They soon reached a critical mass of whispers, however, then giggles, and a young deacon came around the corner.

Thomas Howard slid quickly away, making a little warning whistle. Boleyn and Percy and a few of the others heard the warning and melted quickly into the shadows of the choir. The warning was slightly too late for Thomas and Edward, however, as their ears were pinched, turning their heads painfully towards the young cleric.

The young deacon had a thin face and very lively eyes. He seemed amused rather than angry as he diffidently rocked his head rightward, swinging a lock of straight, black hair out of his eyes. His cassock was of black wool, but was, like his white surplice, clean, very well tailored, and expensive looking, but not gaudy.

"Who…are..you?" the deacon asked quietly, moving slightly, as to shield the boys from the view in the gallery.

The two boys stood their ground. The deacon was startled by this reaction. Usually the boys just wriggled free and scampered. These two just stood there looking at him inquisitively. The dark-haired boy calmly studying him, the red-haired boy just stood blank faced.

Making a decision, the deacon looked at Thomas. "What is your name, boy?" he asked.

"I am Thomas More, of Milk Street, London, Deacon John Colet," replied Thomas composedly, eyes still darting towards his friend.

John Colet smiled, "You know me then, Master More?"

Every Londoner knows you, Sir," replied Thomas. "Your father was Lord Mayor. You lost twenty-one brothers and sisters in the fevers." Then softly, "You were the only one to survive."

Deacon Colet regarded the little boy very sadly, but with curiosity, then abruptly shifted his attention to Edward, who had abruptly stiffened and turned pale.

"Boy, are you alright?" asked Colet, with concern.

"Father..." murmured Edward, looking past Thomas and John Colet.

"Yes?" replied John Colet reflexively before realizing his error.

From behind the choir, a person emerged, flanked by several others, all in black cloaks, the cowls pulled over their faces. The man in the center had pulled back his hood, revealing a round face, with an avuncular expression, yet somehow quite sad. Thomas noticed his red face and hair, and that as he was looking at Edward, a gentle smile came over the stranger's sad face.

"Father," Edward said again, louder.

John Colet stood aside and bowed, as Thomas's friend Edward ran to his father.

Edward's Father, the Duke of Buckingham, knelt and held his son's small hands in his. He looked furtively at the still hooded men on either side. Edward began to cry. Thomas strained to hear the Duke's low words, whispered to his son's ear, but couldn't. Edward cried harder, wrapping his arms around his father's neck.

John Colet simply stood there, tears at his eyes, unable to move or speak.

Suddenly, two older priests came darting around the corner. They slipped a bit on the smooth marble floor in their haste.

"John Colet," the oldest of the two called quickly. "You need not concern yourself with these two. We saw the whole thing."

Thomas looked confusedly at the scene. The voice in his mind as confused as he, *"what is going on?"*

Thomas caught snatches of whispers between the priests.

"..the boy…his father…Duke of Buckingham…"

"…to be executed….King Richard…treason…"

"….no wonder….terrified…"

"..allowed to say goodbye to his son…."

The men on either side of the Duke were gently starting to pull the Duke to his feet as the priests were gently prying Edward's grip from his father's neck. Father and son were openly sobbing, but then the Duke gently removed his son's arms and held the boy's small hands in his own.

Loud enough for Thomas to hear, the Duke said to Edward, "Son, I love you. Pay no attention to what you hear of me. Take care of your mother. I am so very proud of you."

With that last, the Duke backed up a few paces, still looking at his son's teared face, Edward still gently held by the priests. When he had backed into his own attendants, the Duke smiled and winked kindly at his son, then masking his shaking, turned into his attendants and was taken quietly off through the choir.

Colet gently extricated Edward from the older priests, and brought him over to Thomas. He then returned to the priests, who had continued their low conversation.

Thomas put a small arm around Edward, who looked longingly for his father to return tears in his eyes, but composing himself with a great effort.

As the priests were speaking, and appeared to have forgotten the boys, Thomas quietly leaned a bit and nudged Edward with his foot. "Edward," Thomas whispered, "we've got to get out of here. Come on."

Edward sniffed and glanced at the clergy. He moved stiffly with Thomas as Thomas stealthily backed away. They edged around a corner, then ran for all they were worth out of the Cathedral. To Milk Street. Home

"Come in here, Thomas, and sit down," said John More, kindly.

Thomas was a little nervous. His father rarely asked him into his library to sit down. In addition, the chairs were tall, so sitting down with his father meant jumping into a chair, then dangling feet which nearly, but not quite touched the ground.

Thomas's father was always genial and kind, but rarely warm with Thomas. John looked concerned. This caused Thomas to look concerned.

*What does he know? Does he know about Edward's father?*

John More was a rising lawyer in the City. He had even done some legal work for the late King Edward. It was said that he was marked to Sergeant at Law, or even Judge. He had a brown hair that was starting to thin and grey, a round happy face with a full jaw, and a middle that was expanding. John was still wearing his black law robes, but now, Thomas could see, he was wearing red felt slippers, as well. He was seated in his favorite chair in his library, made from ornately carved walnut., and completed with a green velvet upholstery on the seat and back. On a small table next to him were several law books, as well as some parchment and a quill. A gentle afternoon light streamed in through the leaded, diamond shaped windows.

Mirroring his father's pose, Thomas sad down in a nearby chair and crossed his legs, though his feet still dangled. Thomas put his chin in his right hand, and put his right elbow into his cupped left hand. He pursed his eyes, and looked seriously at John, who refrained from laughing, only out of the current concern he felt.

Thomas leaned forward apprehensively. Finally, John laughed, "Thomas. Relax. It's not an execution," he said.

On hearing the word execution, Thomas's composure crumbled and he began crying. He popped out of his chair and began to pace with anxiety.

John was overwhelmed and concerned by this reaction. He stood and gathered Thomas in his arms and brought him to his chair on his lap. Thomas continued crying, but not saying why.

"Thomas," John repeated, continuing, "I heard a report that you and your…you and the boys you play with…" John More was careful not to use the word "friends," "were playing with the lance at John of Gaunt's tomb."

Thomas was taken aback, *"How had he known that,"* came the voice

Pulling himself together, Thomas said, "yes father," evenly, not sure where this was going.

"Thomas," John continue. "Thomas, you are only five, and I don't expect you to understand this, but the boys you were there with, and you, really shouldn't be playing at the tomb of Duke John. Not with what's going on in the world today."

Thomas looked up at his father and said simply, "I don't understand."

"Thomas," John answered, "as you know, the nobility of this country has spent the last hundred years killing each other off. That includes all those boys' fathers, and grandfathers and great-grandfathers."

Thomas stiffened, and John noticed. John looked curiously at his son, wondering if he had heard the news yet about his friend, Edward's father. John decided to continue.

"These noble men and families," John continued, "have been fighting for one of two sides, the House of York, and the House of Lancaster. Sometimes a nobleman would shift sides, or fight for no sides. Allegiances shifted."

"Yes," said Thomas, feeling confused, still working out the meeting between Edward and his father.

"That boy, Edward Stafford," John continued, a little flustered, "who lives across the street."

"Yes," said Thomas, stifling a sob.

"You and he are particularly close," continued John, cautiously. Each word carefully picked, and precisely pronounced. John watched Thomas's reaction.

Thomas started, sobs barely suppressed. Tears welling at eyes.

Thomas managed to squeak out, "we like to play together."

"And that's fine," said John, "but do you know why is father is not at home?"

"Yes," sobbed Thomas, relieved that his father knew about the Duke. He blurted out, "the King is going to kill him…"

"It's not as simple as that," said John, surprised. "Edward's father led an uprising against the King."

"Edward's father would never do that!" Thomas said passionately.

"Its true," John said quickly, surprised at Thomas's heat, "King Richard thought Edward's father wanted to be King himself, so Richard has no choice but to execute him."

"Edward's father wouldn't do that," Thomas repeated. "He said not to believe what we might hear."

"Who said not to believe?" asked John, "Edward?"

Thomas's turn to be puzzled, "No, Edward's father, the Duke. He was at St. Paul's to see Edward. He was wearing a cloak. He came around the choir and talked to Edward." Thomas began to speak more rapidly, unloading his visions and thoughts. "He seemed nice, but sad. At the end, he kissed Edward and told him he loved him, and to not believe everything he heard."

There was a pause, and Thomas and his father looked at one another, each seeing new things in the other that were unexpected.

John marveled at Thomas, and this turn of events.

"There is no real reason that Edward would see his father as anything other than simply his father," said John, gently. "Not as a man who wanted or didn't want to be king, but as his father who suddenly disappeared."

"I don't understand," Thomas repeated.

"Good," said John, with real passion. "The reason that I am telling you this is that you boys were seen at St. Paul's, and by that, I mean you, and Thomas Boleyn, and Thomas Howard, and Edward Stafford, and all the rest were seen playing at the tomb of Duke John."

"But it's really interesting," Thomas burst forth. "there's a real lance, and you can pick it up, and a real shield, with straps on the back, and they're not attached to anything."

"I know," smiled John.

"How do you know?" asked Thomas.

"Duke John died a hundred years ago, and I was once five," replied John.

"You played there?" asked Thomas.

"Yes, as did my father before me. It IS fun to play with a real lance," John said wistfully, adding, "but that's not important. The boys… you… play… with…. the… boys... well, they're all noble born."

"Oh, boy. Do I know that," said Thomas. "They tell me all the time."

John smiled, "Yes. I imagine that they do." He paused, and picked his words carefully. "Thomas, you know of all the wars of the last few years?....."

"Yes," Thomas interjected.

"Brave knights, like the statue of Duke John?" John continued. "Yes…Well, wars also involve killings," John said, continuing, "the nobles of England have spent the last hundred years killing one another over… well, no one really knows what… At least I'm not sure any more… Over who's going to be the King, I suppose. But now the nobility and the priests that ran this country are being replaced by men who can actually do the job." John went along, unconsciously becoming more proud as he gazed at the son in his lap, "men of talent, who's merit comes from accomplishment rather than from an accident of birth…"

"Yes, father," Thomas replied expectantly, looking up.

Well," said John, "the noblemen are divided now between two main gangs, or teams. Currently, the teams are the House of Lancaster and the House of York."

Thomas held his father's gaze.

John continued, a little slower, and a little softer, "So, your… the boy you play with, Edward Stafford… his father, the Duke." John's voice trailed off noticing his son's tears coming back.

"Yes, father," said Thomas very quietly with a sniff. "He is to be killed."

"Yes, Thomas, he is to be killed," said John sadly. "And who is ordering it?"

"King Richard," Thomas said a little hotly.

"Right," said John. "and in these wars, do you know what side King Richard is on?"

"York," said Thomas, proud to know the answer.

"And the other gang is?" asked John precisely.

"Lancaster," said Thomas definitively.

"Excellent," said John. "Now, let's see how observant you are. On Duke John's tomb, do you know what the inscription says?"

"Yes, I heard the other boys reading it," replied Thomas, his mind wandering to how interesting that funeral must have been.

"Alright," continued John, pleased, "let's see how clever you are. What was the Royal Duke John, the Duke of?"

Thomas paused, puzzled for a second, recalling the conversation about the tomb and the lance and Duke John. It came to him suddenly. "He was the Duke of Lancaster," he said excitedly.

"Excellent!" said John proudly, beaming at his precocious son, then pausing to gaze at Thomas, wondering if the five-year-old boy would make the connection.

Thomas already had, but was confused. Speaking hesitantly, Thomas said to his father, "And so by being at the Duke of Lancaster's tomb, we are showing a preference for one side in the war?"

"Well, not so much you," said John, kindly. "The concern would be that by the other boys being at the tomb, that people will think that their parents are going with a side that is not with the King."

Thomas paused, and pursed his lips in thought, then blew out, puzzled, trying to work it out. Finally, "we are children, why would anyone care?" he asked.

"That's a very fair question," laughed John. Then seriously, "what is happening to Edward's father, the Duke, again?" he asked gently.

"He is having his head cut off," Thomas answered again.

"Right," said John. "Why? What does the King want?"

"He wants to take care of Englishmen," Thomas answered innocently, happy to have an easy question at last.

"In an ideal world," said John, "but this is not an ideal world. This is England in 1483. A King wants, above all, to live. King Richard is engaged, completely and totally, in a struggle for his own survival. All Kings probably are. The late King Edward perhaps wore it a little better, and let others do his dirty work for him. He thought his popularity would help keep him safe. In fact, he had his brother Richard do a lot of his dirty work for him."

John paused for a moment to let that sink in, then continued quietly, "now Edward is gone, rest his soul, and Richard has become King. Alone and friendless Richard. With no one to do his dirty work for him. The King doesn't know whom he can trust. The Duke of Buckingham, Edward's father, was a very good friend of King Richard, helped to keep him safe after King Edward died, and then betrayed him. But no one knows how he betrayed him…. There are rumors, of course, but no one knows for sure. Some say Margaret Beufort, others say Bishop Morton. I suppose it doesn't matter. Buckingham is an adult and a Duke, so the responsibility and the risk lie with him. So Richard will kill him."

Thomas looked aghast, and John, noticing, added hastily, "you see, Thomas, King Richard has no earthly idea who he can trust, and so he is always on the lookout for the next small betrayal, worried that it will turn into a larger treason. The treason that will kill him."

"And, Thomas," he continued, " and I'm sorry that I need to explain this, that you need to understand this at so young an age, that those…boys you were playing with at the tomb of Juke John of Lancaster, might be seen by the King as a warning that one of their parents might be about to betray him."

Thomas's mouth went dry. He understood. He wished he didn't. It has been so much fun. What should I do, father?" Thomas asked.

John leaned back in his chair, studying and pondering his son. Making a decision he leaned forward and took Thomas's two smaller hands in his. Looking his son straight in the eyes, he said seriously, "I want you to do two things for me. I want you to be careful with nobility. It is easy to get caught up in their lives, and their little dilemmas, all that seems very big and grand. I want you to be careful with nobility. Remember, what the grown-up nobleman wants most of all is to live. He may seem to want money, or women, or power, but most of all he wants to live. In my experience, to find someone who wants to do the right thing more than he wants to live or die; someone for whom the most important thing is to try to please God, is very unusual."

John paused, impressed by the thoughtful look on his young son's face.

"Which leads me to the second request I have of you. I want you to promise me," John continued, "that you lead your life in such a way as you know pleases God; to make God's pleasure more important than your own. Thomas, remember that you are a Londoner through and through. A nobleman wants to survive, maybe pass his money on to a son. A Londoner thinks in the longer term. We are more of a clan, like the Scots. We Londoners want our great-grandchildren to be important and wealthy. And their great grandchildren. We think of family and connections. We help each other."

Thomas nodded gravely, chewing over these requests.

"And now, Thomas," John continued, now smiling, "is the handle of the lance still a different color than the rest?" John leaned towards his son with a look of conspiratorial anticipation on his face. His smile widening, causing his son's smile to break at last.

Thomas said, in his little boy stage whisper, "the paint's all worn down on the handle. The wood on the handle is really smooth and shiny"

"That's from boys touching it for a hundred years," John added solemnly, remembering the lance, how it felt in his hand.

A few days later, Thomas set out across the street to where Edward was waiting for him at a shop stall. He looked particularly sad. His thick and heavy features were thicker and heavier than usual. He had clearly been crying.

"How are you Edward?" asked Thomas gently.

"I've upset my mother," said Edward, wiping away a tear. "She's inside crying now," he added, jerking his head back towards the door of their mansion. Thomas noticed that there was only one soldier outside Edward's door, instead of the usual ten. In addition, the soldiers uniform had been stripped of the Stafford knot, leaving behind the unfaded fabric that had been underneath showing what had been.

The soldier eyed Thomas and Edward warily but did not move.

"Is it about Duke John," asked Thomas, knowing the answer, his stomach sinking.

"Among many other things, yes," said Edward. "How did you know?"

"My father spoke to me last night," responded Thomas. "Somehow Duke John ties into everything."

Edward looked even more miserable at Thomas's mention of his father. "My mother asked me if I wanted her to he killed as well," said Edward, pausing to sniffle.

Thomas asked softly, "a King wouldn't kill a woman, would he?"

"I wouldn't be so sure," whispered Edward. "My mother's sister was King Edward's Queen. Richard hates them. He already killed their brother, Lord Rivers" Edward looked darkly at the ground, then added in a small voice, "do you have any idea what happened to my cousins, Prince Edward and Prince Richard? Edward was to be King."

"No," replied Thomas. "No one does since the end of summer." Thomas had seen them briefly, and had heard that once Richard had taken power he had placed the boys in the Tower so that they would be safe.

"My mother told me that my father and King Richard were doing something with my cousins, and that's why her sister the Queen went into sanctuary at the church," said Edward. "Then, my father and King Richard fell out, and that's why King Richard is killing my father."

Edward looked stricken and confused, starting then stifling a sob. Thomas stepped forward and put his small hand on Edward's shoulder.

Edward looked up at Thomas and asked, "Do you think the King would ever kill me?" he asked.

"No," answered Thomas resolutely, "you are way too good a boy!"

"I don't understand…don't understand any of it," said Edward, sitting down disconsolately on a step. "Mother says that after Father is executed we must flee London. Go to friends in the country. 'Lie low,' she said. That or hide in a church like her sister."

"I know," consoled Thomas, "neither do I. My fa…" Thomas stopped as Edward looked up at the word. He continued, carefully, "tried to explain it to me. I think I understood a little, but it has to do with Lancaster and York, and Duke John, and that I should be careful around you noble people."

Edward looked up, brightening a bit. "Be careful of us?" he asked, looking up at Thomas. "Maybe I'm dangerous?" Edward made little fang V's with his fingers in front of his mouth and swayed his head goofily at Thomas.

"Well…I don't think just yet," smiled Thomas, happy at cheering up his friend a bit. "Except maybe your farts."

Edward laughed and stood up. "Dangerous," he pondered softly, puffing his small chest a bit.

"You are really kind of a goof," Thomas said seriously. "And I am sorry about your father." He put his arm around his friend's shoulder and the two friends just stood in the shadows on Milk street, letting London pass them by.

Edward and his family had moved out of their mansion on Milk Street shortly after Edward's father's execution in November 1483. The family had been stripped of the Duchy and much of their family money. For a while the family had escaped to relations in the countryside, but, oddly, a fanciful tale had circulated widely of Edward's narrow escape, disguised as a girl, moving from household retainers through the country, breathtakingly just ahead of Richard's soldiers.

No one really knew of his whereabouts, a cause of ongoing anxiety for Thomas on behalf of his friend. When out and about Thomas scanned crowds for Edward, and occasionally thought he had seen his friend, and would wave. Edward remained a mystery for Thomas, much as the fate of the Princes remained a popular mystery in London.

Thomas and the More family remained on Milk Street, as John More still steadily ascended in the legal community in London. John remained well liked by all, and Thomas had remained a popular figure on Milk Street as he reached seven years of age.

On occasional mornings Thomas's father would awaken him with a gentle pull on his shoulder. Leaning over Thomas as the child opened his eyes, John would smile kindly and ask, "want to go run errands, Thomas?"

Thomas would nod enthusiastically and climb out of bed, quickly wash his face, and put on a pair of breeches. John would gently take his hand, and the two would together descend the narrow steps to the yard, and then out through the old gate into Milk Street. Thomas waved cheerily to Mr. Cheeseman, who always smiled and waved back. A sidelong glance at the empty Stafford mansion across the street, then John and Thomas would always first head north the three blocks to St. Lawrence Jewry, the family church.

Like so many of the buildings of this, the old Jewish Quarter of London, the Church of St. Lawrence had been elegantly built of stone some two hundred years before. This building had, in fact, originally been a Jewish Temple, and then, after the bloody expulsion of the Jews by King Richard the First, had been converted into a church.

The building had a smallish entryway, overshadowed by a large iron grating, or gridiron, eight feet across, that was left hanging over the door. St. Lawrence had been roasted alive by the Romans, and had died, a barbecued martyr for the faith. Rumor had it that this hanging iron grill was the actual grating upon which Lawrence had been cooked. Lawrence had become the patron saint of comedians for suggesting, half-way through his own execution that he be turned over, "for that side is done."

Thomas loved that particular rumor.

As always, as John and Thomas quickly passed the grisly relic, Thomas scanned the grating for any signs of truth to its rumored authenticity. Occasionally, his pulse would quicken at the sight of a bit of string or some such that had been caught by the wind on the grill.

"Nothing today," thought Thomas resignedly.

"*Maybe tomorrow*"

"Turn me over. He couldn't have really said that."

"*Why?*"

"He was being executed. You can't make a joke while you're being executed."

"*Why not? How will the outcome change? And besides who would remember him if he hadn't made the joke? He became the patron saint of comedians for that joke?*"

"I don't know."

Thomas was pulled forward, through the door of the church by his father's insistent tug at his hand. The pair headed up the right side of the church, past several nondescript and thoroughly uninteresting tombs. They approached the altar and its carved, wooden rood. John would routinely kneel at the side of the altar and pray, his eyes closed, mouthing words in Latin.

Thomas, being a fairly active seven year old, looked avidly around the old church.

"Pater Noster…" Thomas prayed idly, mimicking his father's prayers.

*"Yes?"*

"What"

*"Nothing, sorry."*

After a few moments of enforced quiet at the altar, Thomas was allowed to wander the church.

Thomas was especially fond of nosing around the ornate sepulcher, or mock tomb, where the Eucharist had been kept between the Good Friday vigil, and its jubilant emergence on Easter Sunday. Thomas remembered two months before how he and his father had joined the other parishioners, the first time he had been allowed, in attending Jesus during his entombment, keeping watch during a long night's vigil. Thomas had, of course, fallen asleep, then been mortified to awaken with the dawn, curled up in a pew, with his father's cloak covering him. He felt as though he had been tested, and had failed.

As Thomas looked again at the sepulcher he thought for the thousandth time, "I'm sorry about falling asleep."

After visiting St. Lawrence, the pair had a typical routine. From the church, they would walk east from the church, past the massive courtyard of the Guildhall, on Lad Lane, until they reached Basinghall Street. They would then head north on Basinghall until they reached the Wall.

The London Wall fascinated Thomas throughout his entire life. The Romans had build the first wall as a defense after the ravages of Boudicca, the mad, fierce, warrior Queen. The WALL, always thought of in uppercase given its imposing bulk, and its definition of the geographic outline of the CITY, also uppercase, had been rebuild, repaired, or enhanced over the ensuing 1400 years, but still remained. Twenty and even thirty feet high in many places, with five imposing gates, the square mile of London was, Thomas felt, a marvelous island of endless fascination surrounded by an often frightening wildness outside. The WALL, on approach, created a feeling of security for Thomas that was unmatched by anything else in his life.

Now, as a seven year old child, Thomas approached the WALL, touching it reverently. Messages were occasionally left in chinks in the WALL, small rolled up papers. Seeing none today, Thomas looked at some of the plaques that had been placed to commemorate persons, or guilds that had financed one repair or another, the timeless cry, "I existed," displayed on the most permanent structure in England.

Stalls and carts had been brought up against the WALL as usual, and the narrow lane separating it from nearby buildings turned the avenue into a large, open air market. In the early summer sun, the WALL heated up and gave, it seemed to Thomas, a marvelous shimmer to the entire confabulation of noise, colors, and smells.

Occasionally on these errands Johns would stop and buy something from one of the stalls, a treat for Thomas, perhaps, or a present for Thomas's mother or one of his sisters. When this happened, John and Thomas had a routine: John and the vendor would agree on a price, and

John would look at Thomas and say, "All right Thomas, the price here is tuppence, and I am giving the man a silver groat. What will I receive in change?"

Thomas would furiously calculate the various coins, subtracting the price from whatever coin his father had used that day and would then give his answer to his father. If he was correct (2 pence), he and his father would split the change. If Thomas was incorrect, his father would cluck, "no Thomas, sorry. Better luck next time," and would pocket the change himself.

Continuing their walk, Thomas and John passed east along the wall, looking at the stalls, and past the crowded street of Moorgate. As they were approaching the street leading to the gate, John More would always cry, "Our gate, the family gate!" while making a sweeping gesture towards the gate with his left arm.

Thomas laughed and ran to the gate, the newest of the gates in the WALL. There was a massive iron portcullis drawn up on the far side. The gate building itself was four stories tall, with leaded glass windows and apartments.  On either side of the large passageway leading through the building to the gate itself there were arched doorways, above which were circular stained glass windows and then two stories of rectangular windows. The building was cast in yellow ragstone with white marble accents.

Through the gate, Thomas could see the road heading past the great, smelly ditch of London into the Moorfields beyond, where he hoped to be old enough to go ice skating this winter when the swampy moors had frozen over. Thomas was enchanted by the windmills, slowly turning in the June breeze, continually pumping the water out from the moors into the remaining rivers to the Thames. Centuries of pumping and landfill in the moors seemed, to John, to be finally making a difference in the marsh.

Once past Moorgate, the two would continue to hug the inside of the Wall until they reached Bishopsgate. This much older gate was rumored to have been built by the Romans, then later rebuilt by a Bishop. It followed the general pattern of the gates, having a central tunnel with a large iron gate on the far side, and two arched entryways on either side of the tunnel for access to the building above. Instead of the rectangular windows of Moorgate, there were vaulted apses, with statues of the great Bishops of London. The road here, Bishopsgate Street, turned outside of the city into the Great Northern Road, one of the five great roads built by the Romans. In fact, their original pavers, Thomas knew, could still be seen.

At Bishopsgate Street, John and Thomas would turn right, and head south for two blocks. They, like all the rest of Londoners would pause and marvel at Crosby Hall, the largest and grandest mansion of the City that was not a palace, that took up a square block across from St. Helen's Church. The house itself was larger than the church, and its yellow stone walls, bricked building, and great gothic arched windows with stained glass scenes in the center of many panes of leaded glass, always gave Thomas chills.

Apart from its size, the other attraction of the house was that it had been the home of the King while he was Duke of Gloucester up until his own coronation. The King had kept the house, as he loved it as much or more than any of his palaces in London, and he was occasionally seen still going in through the giant oak doors of the Great Hall.

Father and son would then walk small hand in big hand down Bishopsgate to Threadneedle, and down Threadneedle past St. Anthony's school, where Thomas would be attending in the fall. John and Thomas stopped to look at the non-descript building. There were, oddly, pigs moving freely in the surrounding street. John laughed and cried "St. Anthony's pigs!" then made pig noises at Thomas until Thomas laughed. The pigs were the property of the school, and were licensed to wander the streets of London eating refuse and tended by harried students. John pointed at a student and said to Thomas, "That'll be you soon."

Thomas's smile was a mixture of confusion and concern. Nevertheless, he marked the location in his memory for when he started school in the Fall.

Threadneedle Street would take them past tailor shops. Occasionally Thomas and John would stop in for new robes or doublets for John, or breeches for Thomas. This day, they just watched the clothes being made. Eventually, they reached the Poultry, a madhouse street of chicken vendors, with birds in all states, from egg to plucked, dead, and hanging by a bloody comb from a hook in a stall. Feathers, and portions of feathers filled the air, and Thomas would bat the down away from his face. The smell in the Poultry was just horrific, and it was a warm June day, which only made the smell worse.

Thankfully, John sped the two through the Poultry to Ironmonger's lane, where they would take a side trip to the Mercer's Hall. John was a proud member of this guild, and there was always food and a place for them to sit and rest a bit in the Great Hall of the Guild. John greeted men by name as they came and went. Most of the men stopped to speak with Thomas as well, asking him when he would be joining the Guild.

After their rest at the Mercer's, the pair picked themselves up and trudged heavily back to Milk Street, taking care to walk around Eleanor's Cross in Cheapside. John More had told his son that there was a small carving of Daniel and the Lion in the Cross, and that sometimes coins could be found jammed behind. So father and son always concluded their jaunts with a peek behind Daniel in the cross. Sometimes there was even a ha'pence!

Finally, they would arrive home exhausted, and flop into chairs in the Solar, in John' favorite place in the world, happily retelling the events of the day to Thomas's mother and sisters. Thomas always finished the story of the day with a furtive look through the windows of the library across Milk Street to the now empty rooms of Edward's home across the street, wondering when he would next see his friend.

One morning in June, Thomas was pleased to be gently shaken awake by his father. His mind registered the look of concern on his father's face, but he put it aside in his delight at another "errand day."

Thomas and John reached St. Lawrence Church in their usual fashion. John was less talkative than usual, but there was still no evidence of St. Lawrence on the grill. At the altar rail, John seemed to be especially intent on his prayers, and Thomas noticed that his father had a small copy of Augustine's *Civitas Dei* tucked into a pocket of his cloak. Idly, Thomas let his finger trace the carvings on the raised pulpit.

"Thomas," John whispered abruptly, "come on."

Thomas turned to see that his father had risen and was now gesturing from the aisle that it was time to leave. Thomas looked reluctantly again at the wooden cross over the altar, and inhaled the perfume of the beeswax candles, the polished wood, and the burning incense of the church.

He turned to the sepulcher and quickly thought, "sorry I fell asleep."

*"You can always come back, Thomas."*

"All right."

Thomas returned to his father's side, and, together, holding hands again, they stepped out into the bright sunshine. It was warmer outside, and the shift in temperatures from the cool inside to the warm outside caused Thomas to shiver a bit.

They turned left, as usual, but then, suddenly , John turned into the courtyard of the Guildhall, and headed straight to the Gothic porch of the central government building of the City. Thomas had never been in the Guildhall before, and was desperate to question his father about the change in routine, but John's genial face had been replaced with a distracted, hard stare. Thomas clutched his father's hand tightly.

*"Don't be frightened,"* said the voice. *"You are going into one of the most interesting and important buildings of the world."*

"Not frightened," thought Thomas, "just curious about why father seems so upset."

*"All in due time. For now, look at the statues."*

On either side of the porch entrance to the Hall were two giant plaster and wicker statues of, well, giants. Gog and Magog. They appeared to Thomas to be enormous, bearded Celtic creatures, with the woodlands in their wicker hair. They were crowned and holding spears. There were metal chains on their legs, fixing them to their posts on either side of the entrance. Thomas knew the story…John had told him many times. Brutus, the son of Aeneas had escaped the destruction of the fall of Troy and had traveled by sea to Britain where he had conquered and ruled the land, founding the City of London. Brutus's greatest act had been vanquishing the twin Celtic giants, Gog and Magog, whom he had chained to the gates of the city.

"I'm a lot more impressed with Brutus now," thought Thomas, "if these are Gog and Magog."

*"You're funny.*

*" Careful, Gog is moving his lance.*

*"Made you look"*

Thomas and John walked through the porch, Thomas's slight hand gripping so tightly that John's fingers paled. As they moved, Thomas rapidly turned his head right and left at the giants, lest they move. Once past, Thomas relaxed a bit, and they passed the large entry door into the magnificent Great Hall of the City.

The first thing Thomas noticed in the room was the white carved stone walls, with five enormous arches along each long wall. There were oaken doors at the bottom of each arch. About a third of the way up each arch were stunning balconies, created out of oak, lightly stained and beautifully carved. At the far end of the Hall was an arched stained glass window with beautiful stone tracery and mullions. The stained glass in the morning sun cast lovely colors on the creamy stone walls. Thomas's breath was taken away the the Hall's wonderful feeling of light and air.

The arches of the walls further added to the sense of space by extending through the balconies into beautiful buttressed roof arches, over which a ceiling of lead and wood had been created. In all the interior of the Great Hall of the Guildhall was four stories high.

John had softened a bid at seeing Thomas's awe at entering the Great Hall for the first time. His usual genial self and caring father reemerged, and he relaxed from his troubles a bit, to bend over and point out interesting features of the Hall to Thomas.

"There, Thomas," John said, pointing to one of the window's opposite, "is the window that has in it the names of all the Mayors of London."

John pointed in the opposite direction. "Over there is a statue of Dick Whittington, thrice Mayor of London," And then he sang a bit of the old pageant song, "turn around Dick Whittington, turn around."

He continued, "That's where the Lord Mayor keeps his court…"

There were, it seemed to Thomas, an unusual number of people in the Hall, and they all seemed excited, or nervous. John's eye caught something Thomas could not see, and he abruptly stooped his tour and stood nervously upright. Then Thomas saw a tall thin man, with a serious angular face, approaching the pair rapidly. The man was wearing bright crimson robes, and he had a large golden chain draped around his shoulders. His serious expression relaxed a bit as he looked at Thomas, and he smiled and greeted John warmly.

John, however, tensed at the approach of the man Thomas recognized as Henry Colet, the Lord Mayor of London. "My Lord Mayor," Johns said, as he bowed his head in deference. Thomas, not sure what he was to do, bowed deeply, with a sweeping wave of his right arm. An exaggerated imitation of his father. Thomas bowed so low, in fact, that his hair seemed to brush the ground. The Lord Mayor smiled at Thomas.

"Thank you for coming, John," said the Lord Mayor. He had a thin face with brown eyes and jet black, longish hair just touching the collar of his red Mayoral livery and chain of office. "We are at a crisis here with the King."

Thomas's ears pricked up.

"The King?" he thought.

*"Shh..don't speak. They might make you leave."*

The Lord Mayor looked again at Thomas, who was standing unobtrusively behind his father. Colet tousled Thomas's hair with his hand. He kindly offered, "Thomas, you've grown!"

"Yes my Lord Mayor," Thomas sort of squeaked. "Nearly four feet now!"

The Lord Mayor looked at Thomas, smiling sadly. He clearly loved children, but Thomas remembered that twenty-one of his twenty-two children had died while small, leaving his only son John, formerly a sub-deacon at St. Paul's, and now studying at Oxford.

Henry Colet recollected himself. He straightened and looked directly at John More. "John," he whispered, "the King…he's in the old Library. He's asked for both you and for Thomas."

"Why?" asked John, in what seemed to Thomas, a surprisingly fierce whisper.

"Wait," thought Thomas…."The King asked for me?"

*"Hold very still Thomas."*

Thomas stiffened, his entire body willed to stillness, all senses on alert. Heart racing.

Colet replied, "it's a couple of things, John." He paused for a second, organizing his thoughts. "First, it's those damned bonds he's been trying to sell for two months. But it's more than that. His wife is dead. His son is dead. For all intents and purposes he has no heir. Henry Tudor is massing troops. To give the King credit, he is trying to raise money without going back on his promises of not extorting money the way every other King has done. So, Richard is hemmed in on all sides. Now he is here, he says, to find out why Londoners haven't been buying his war bonds. He wants to know what he can do for London."

"The King wants to talk about London?" John asked with astonishment. "The great man from the North?"

"You're my Solicitor," said Henry, "so let us go in and talk with the King about London. In we go." The Lord Mayor turned to move, but John stayed him by holding his elbow as he turned.

"Wait," said John, "You said a few things."

The Lord Mayor stopped then looked oddly at John. "That's an odd one," he said. "He said he wanted you to bring young Master Thomas, but wouldn't say why."

Until that moment Thomas had been forgotten, which suited him fine. Now, though, the Lord Mayor and John More stared at Thomas.

"Henry," John said gravely, "I brought Thomas along because you asked me to. But I didn't agree to bring Thomas to the King without knowing the particulars." As he spoke, John's face flushed a bit.

The Lord Mayor immediately moved closer to John, placing a hand on his shoulder. "John," he said quietly, "I'm sorry about that. The King requested, but also requested that I not tell you more. "In fact," he added hastily, "he wouldn't tell me any more either."

John, still flushed, moved rapidly in an indecisive manner, clearly weighing what he should do. He looked at Thomas.

"The King wants to see me?" Thomas thought.

*"take a peek inside the room."*

Thomas looked into the room the Lord Mayor had been heading. At the door frame were two soldiers in the multicolored Royal livery, red and blue alternating quadrants on the tunic, three red outlined crouching golden lions on the front, a steel helmet, and each of them with a halberd in hand.

"*HALBERDS!,*" screamed the voice.

Thomas moved towards the room, pulling his fathers undecided hand a bit. "Father," Thomas said gently, urgently, "I am fine, and it will be all right."

Henry Colet, the Lord Mayor, looked at Thomas inquiringly, then laughed. "My son John was right about you," he said.

John also regarded his son, then conceded, "All right, Thomas." Then he added with a little laugh, "let's go see the King.

The Lord Mayor and John More strode, Thomas between them, east through the Great Hall, crowds parting before them. Thomas nodded gravely at the soldiers with their halberds.

They stepped on the large, stone dais, raised about a foot from the floor of the rest of the hall, then walked purposefully across to the carved wooden façade covering the lower third of the whole wall. Thomas, his heart racing, tried unsuccessfully to insert himself into the folds of his Father and the Lord Mayor's robes.

The soldiers nodded sternly to the Lord Mayor and parted their weapons, allowing the doors to be opened. One of the soldiers winked at Thomas as the three of them entered the Library of the Guildhall.

This room had been build a hundred years before by Dick Whittington, the Lord Mayor, and, Thomas had heard, the richest man in the history of England. Whittington had been friends with Kings, and had endowed countless charities in and around London. And, in this library, he had built a smaller, lighter, and airier version of the Great Hall, this time lined with shelves containing hundreds of books, most from his personal collection.

Thomas's heart leapt! At the far side of the room, there was a large chair, and there sat Richard the Third, King of England. Henry and John approached as they were beckoned by pages on either side of the King. Thomas decided to continue his unlikely strategy of hiding in the folds of the two men's gowns as they walked.

Richard was sitting, yet not nearly in repose. He was smaller in stature than Thomas had expected. Very thin, and wasted in the temples. He had dark, stormy eyes, and a strong pointed chin. His jet black hair was longish, and straight, parted in the middle. Atop his striking hair was a black velvet bonnet cap, adorned with an enameled brooch of a white rose. He was wearing a black velvet doublet with puffed arms, black tight hose, and high black leather boots. The darkness of his clothes was magnificently offset by a golden tunic, and a thick golden chain.

Thomas noticed that though the King's body seemed to be in constant, gentle and small motion, his eyes were still and quiet, and seemed to bore in on Thomas alone. His physical agitation combined with his still eyes, dark complexion and clothes, made him appear to be nothing less than a very worrisome thundercloud.

King Richard wore a large ring on the fourth finger of his right hand. Thomas could see the large, deep blue stone set in the gold.

*"The Coronation Ring!"* came the voice, "much better than a halberd."

Thomas recognized a few of the attendants standing behind the ring. To the King's right was John Howard, the Duke of Norfolk, and the grandfather of his friend Thomas Howard. Howard's long black moustache and short black hair fringing a balding pate, giving a vaguely sinister, oily air to his presence.

As John More and Henry Colet approached, the King stopped talking to John Howard, keeping his wary eyes on the Londoners. Thomas abruptly bowed to the King as the gowns on either side of him crinkled as his father and the Lord Mayor bowed to the King.

Another few steps, and another bow. The King continued to watch.

Another few steps, and a third, deeper bow, completing their approach to the King. The King nodded back, acknowledging their courtesy as he reflexively spun the large coronation ring on his delicate appearing finger. He then gave them a slight, shy smile, and said, "My Lord Mayor of London, and his Solicitor, John More. Thank you for attending upon me."

When the King spoke, it was in an unexpectedly soft and gentle voice, with more than a trace of a Northern accent.

The Lord Mayor smiled and replied evenly, "we are at Your Highness's service."

"I wish that I could count on that," said Richard seriously.

"Your Highness?" said Henry, taken aback.

"Not a personal criticism," said Richard, with sadness, "but I've found very few persons in the Kingdom, upon whose service I may absolutely trust

"The King does not trust his subjects?" said Henry, worried at the direction this conversation was taking. Richard had a known history of interviews such as this ending badly. Hastings, for example… "We are your servants," Henry continued.

John tried and failed to unobtrusively shoo Thomas into the protective folds of his gown.

"The King must trust no one," said Richard resolutely, as if still trying to convince himself. With that, he sat up and looked sadly at Henry saying, "My Lord Mayor, I should like to perform some good works for this city. None of us knows how long we shall be on this Earth. I would never have expected my son or my wife, the Queen, to be carried off so young. So, while I am able, I want to do something for this City that has been my off and on home for so long. I should like to be remembered for good, rather than evil.

"Edward Stafford told me that he thought King Richard killed the little Princes in the Tower," Thomas thought.

*"Does he look like the sort of man that would kill children?"*

"No.. He looks sad. But what about Edward having to run for his life dressed as a girl."

"He looks defeated.*"*

"He doesn't look afraid."

*"No. You can be defeated and unafraid of the consequences of defeat."*

Thomas came out of his reverie to hear the King say, "I would like to serve God in some meaningful way in the time that I have. My good wife, Anne, would have wanted it that way…" The King's voice trailed off into mist.

Thomas had been slowly, and to his mind, invisibly, peeking out from his father's robes. Richard caught sight of Thomas's small head, the angle of the brown eye and hair emerging from the black wool folds. The King suddenly smiled.

"John More," King Richard said, laughing. "You seem to have sprouted an additional, very shy, head from your side."

John More started, as the King continued kindly, "and who is that back there?"

John More answered deferentially, "Your Highness, it is my son, Thomas." John then reached his arm around behind Thomas's shoulders and, gently, pushed him forward towards the King.

Completely at a loss for what to do, Thomas put his put his left foot forward, then bowed low with a theatrical sweep of his right arm, and said loudly, "Thomas More, your Highness, I am the King's good servant."

This was met by stunned silence from the room, except for a giggle from behind the King. The King himself at first had a small startled reaction, then a suppressed smile.

John More and Henry Colet simply looked stunned.

Thomas remained in his sweeping bow, feeling quite naked in front of the King.

The King sat up then leaned forward towards Thomas and said in his quiet voice, "we shall see. Come closer to me Thomas."

Thomas did as he was told, stood and approached the King, hands clasped together in front of him, knees locked and feet moving in a shy little shuffle step, propelled forth mostly by rocking the hips.

King Richard laughed, saying, "So this is the famous Thomas More, of whom I have heard so much!"

Thomas was too frightened to speak.

*"He is a King. He is also a man. Speak to him Thomas as you would any other man."* Came the voice.

"My Lord King," Thomas stammered, starting to feel confidence return.

*"Good start!"*

Thomas felt his fear suddenly melt away, and he nodded his head again to the King, and said, perhaps a little too loudly and quickly, "Yes, My Lord King. I am Thomas More, and I am happy you have heard of me, but I beg to ask from whom?"

Richard laughed out loud, as did the other men in the room. Looking happily at Thomas's father, the King said, "your boy seems to have relaxed in a hurry, John More!"

John More had relaxed as well.

"Before I answer your question, young Thomas," said the King, "let me ask you one."

Thomas nodded seriously, in a thoughtful pose.

The King continued, "Tell me. What do you think makes a good King?"

Thomas thought for a moment, scrunching up his face and putting his chin in one hand as he studied Richard. Finally he said, "Wanting to serve more than to be served, My Lord King."

Richard sat up completely, exhaled through pursed lips, and looked at Thomas with a surprised face. "I could not have said that better myself, Thomas," said the King.

The King looked at John Howard and asked, "Norfolk. What do you think of this?" He pointed at Thomas and continued, "the mouths of babes, and all?"

John Howard replied, "I know young Thomas as well. He used to play sometimes with my grandson. My Thomas Howard is a little older, but this Thomas More…He holds his own."

Richard's for relaxed a bit. "Will ye be a soldier, young Thomas?" he asked.

Thomas responded seriously, "honestly, I do not know what I will be. It is for God to decide."

"No, Thomas," corrected the King, gently, "it is for you to decide. If is for you to decide how to live in accordance with what God wants. How your life may best serve God."

Thomas thought on that. Finally, with a smile and a bow, he said, "Your Grace. I think that God wants me to be a child for a while longer."

Richard laughed uproariously. "The mouths of babes!" he cried, "John Howard, the mouths of babes!"

The crowd around the King also laughed with the King. Some of them had mirth in their eyes, some did not. John More appeared delighted with his son, and amused by his response. Henry Colet was more thoughtful.

The King then tilted his head slightly as if making a decision. John Howard was looking at him intently.

Making his decision, the King leaned forward, and said in a conspiratorial voice, not loud enough for John and Henry to hear, "May I confide in you, young Thomas, a Royal secret?"

Thomas looked very seriously at the King, leaned in a bit, and whispered, "of course, sir."

The nodded a bit, and continued, "and I have your absolute word that you will never reveal what I am going to tell you?"

Thomas's eyes widened a bit, his heart racing. The King had leaned in so close to Thomas that Thomas thought he could smell his breakfast. Thomas nodded, biting his lip.

The King looked at Thomas and said kindly, "Thomas, I need you to say it, to swear a solemn oath to God that you will never reveal to anyone what I, the King of England, tell you today, as my good servant."

Thomas stared into the King's dark eyes, and the two of them reached an understanding, and Thomas said quietly, "Your Highness, I swear my solemn oath to God that I will never reveal the King's secret."

King Richard smiled, and clapped Thomas on the shoulder. "Good man, Thomas," he said happily. Then he looked at Thomas and said solemnly, "The Royal secret is this, Thomas..."

Thomas and the King leaned a little closer together. "The King of England protects children," he said with finality.

Thomas reeled back a bit, confused. "But...," he stammered, "but..."

The King smiled, and said, "but what of the little princes?...but what of Edward Stafford?"

Thomas looked at the King, their eyes continuing to meet. "yes," Thomas said simply.

Looking up at John More and Henry Colet, and raising up his right arm and giving a little wave of the hand, the King asked, "from whence do you think I have heard of little else but the name of Thomas More?" He smiled broadly.

With that the small knot of courtiers behind the King parted a bit, and Edward Stafford, taller and a little plumper than since last seen, stepped forward.

Thomas and Edward stood and looked briefly at each other. Thomas's mouth moving in search of words, then with simultaneous and enthusiastic lunges at each other. Completely unmindful of the reactions of the adults around them, the two seven year olds embraced in an enthusiastic bear hug.

John More stood alone in the room, confused and quite torn. He felt a seeping anger, thinking that he had been used. The King noticed the look on More's face as he turned, smiling, from watching the two boys.

"John More," cried the King, "you good father and solicitor. I owe you an explanation."

The King stood, and with a gentle smile he walked slowly towards John. Thomas and Edward had stopped hugging to turn to watch the King. The King was lean, and of average height. His walk seemed a little painful and his back had a scoliotic bend that rendered the right shoulder higher than the left. As he approached John More, the King raised his right arm, causing the sleeve of his cloak to fall back, revealing a muscular forearm with a number of visible scars. With a casual grace, the King placed his hand on John's shoulder. John and the King's eyes met.

"Solicitor More," said the King gently, "I could not tell you the reasons for asking you to bring your son here today. I appreciate your bravery and loyalty in bringing him. How are you doing in deciphering what is happening?"

John's anger was abating, melting away in fact as the nearby King aimed his charm at him.

Thomas also was working on the problem.

"Edward is supposedly in hiding from a King that wants to kill him," Thomas thought.

"*And yet, here he is, with the King,*" replied the voice.

Thomas saw his father kneel at the feet of the King and bow his head. The King's hand remained on his shoulder. Henry Colet stood by impassively.

"I swear an oath to you my King," Thomas heard his father say clearly, and loudly, "that I will never betray the King's secret, and will, for all my life pledge my troth to furthering the King's sacred venture."

The King gently gestured for John More to rise. He took John's two hands in his, and said, "thank ye," in his quiet, gentle northern burr. Thomas watched intently as the King and his father separated, and the King returned to his chair.

Once seated, the King announced to the room in a happy voice, "now that we have the estimable Mores in our company, I would ask two others to join us."

The soldiers at a side door banged their halberd stems on the ground, and opened the door to admit two teenage boys. Edward, smiling broadly, clapped Thomas on the back and whispered, "well, Thomas, now you're in for it."

Thomas looked confused, but his father took a step back and exhaled with deep surprise. "Edward and Richard," John More gasped. "The Princes…..the, the King." And he bowed.

Thomas bowed reflexively with his father.

"The Princes!" Thomas thought.

*"yes, Thomas, the Princes!" came the voice.*

"But King Richard supposedly had them killed?"

*"and yet here they are, with the King. And all while the King was also hunting Edward, who is also here."*

"So what does that mean?"

At that moment, John More was asking the King and his assembled group including the sons of his brother, the late King Edward the fourth.

"The Princes are alive?" John asked quietly, continuing directly to King Richard, "the country believes them dead, and many believe that you were responsible for their deaths."

"Yes," replied King Richard, allowing John More to continue processing.

"You never correct those rumors," said John.

"Correct," said the King.

"Before your brother, King Edward, may he rest in peace, died, he named you Protector of his sons," John went on. "You swore to the King that you would protect his children."

"Yes," answered Richard quietly and solemnly with a small nod of his head.

"And yet you removed Edward from his rightful Crown," continued John, still sorting.

"Yes, for now," replied the King.

"You have the Princes here with you now, and the people think they have died, and you are blamed for their deaths" reiterated John.

"Yes," said King Richard, with a small smile

"You saved them," said John More with finality, "and are hiding them in the open." He whistled softly, finally looking up at the King with respect.

Thomas was still processing this, but then espied his friend, Edward, from the corner of his eye. "But you did kill Edward's father," Thomas blurted out.

Edward shrank, and Thomas immediately felt badly, that he had betrayed his friend. He looked up fearfully at the King, who was looking at him intently, neither angry, nor happy. Simply neutral.

John moved to Thomas, reaching out to him, saying warningly, "Thomas…"

"Nay, John More," interrupted the King. "Young Thomas is correct. I did execute the Duke of Buckingham. His crimes against the crown were significant, and his punishment was just. Edward and I have discussed his father, and that conversation is between he and I. If, at some time Edward chooses to share that conversation with you, that is his business, and I give him my leave to do so. Edward has shared much with me about his remarkable friend, Thomas More. He even shared with me that you were present when he spoke with his father the last time at the tomb of…his ancestor John, the Duke of Lancaster."

The King smiled benignly at Thomas, who had given a start.

"Thomas More," the King continued, "you are a kind and loyal friend to my cousin Edward. You are also an impressive boy." Thomas bowed a little, still uncomfortable. "Remember always," the King continued, "that things are not always as they seem. Remember also always, 'my good servant,' the vow you made with me today. You and your father are sworn to help me protect my nephews the Princes. If they are protected by people being convinced that I have killed them, then so be it."

With that, the King stood abruptly. The others in the room bowed, including Thomas and his father.

The King turned to leave, but had a thought, and held, before turning back to Thomas and saying, "Oh and Thomas.." Thomas looked up from his bow. "I made the same promise to Edward's father about Edward." The King winked at Thomas, who stood, and smiled at the King as the King turned and departed the room, followed by the princes, Edward, and their entourage, leaving only Thomas, his father and the Lord Mayor in the echoing Guildhall library.

John More had smiled benignly and bowed respectfully towards the departing Royal party until a few seconds after the exiting doors had been closed. He then turned to the Lord Mayor and acidly hissed, "Thank you so much, Henry."

Henry Colet raised his hands in a warding motion towards John. "John," he said softly, "I do owe you and Thomas and explanation."

"How…dare…you…" John stammered, "bring my innocent seven year old son into this Royal mess? It's bad enough that you have now made me solicitor to one King in the effort to deny the crown to another, whose claim to the throne is entirely valid. Many, if not most would say is actually the legitimate claim. In effect, Henry, you and King Richard have conspired to involve my son and I in treason."

John had become progressively more red faced during this, but his voice remained measured and calm. Thomas looked at his father with pride.

"Father is angry, but calm," he thought.

"*A lawyer,*" replied the voice. "*he is not letting his anger get in the way of his argument.*"

"Treason, though?"

"*I suppose that could be argued. But on the other hand, Richard is crowned.*"

Henry Colet was making a similar argument with John, but had continued, "look John, Richard is the annointed King, confirmed by the Parliament. He faced a shitty set of choices after his brother, the King, swore him to the protection of his children. We know through bitter experience how a child King fares with poor King Henry the sixth. And with the second Richard before him.  A hundred years of civil war. Two Kings deposed and murdered.:

"One on the orders of Richard's brother, King Edward," John retorted.

"Yes, but," replied Henry calmly, "with full judicial review. And besides that, John, who better to know and understand the fate of a child King than Edward?"

John, breathing through his nose and exhaling through his mouth, like he did when he was trying to calm himself.

Henry continued, calmly, "Edward was ill. He was dying. There were men circling his body, and his son, to take advantage of the young Edward. The father knew, from bitter experience, how much jeopardy both of his sons were in."

"So, Lord Protector status until adulthood," John replied.

"Yes John, but don't forget that the Queen's family immediately strove to take control of the Prince. Richard, who had legally been named Protector, was almost immediately moved against by Rivers."

"The Queen's brother, Lord Rivers?" John replied incredulously. "He was too busy with his books."

"Yes, him," Henry replied drily. "Turned out he was ambitious."

Henry and John both laughed at the memory of the imperious and arrogant Lord Rivers, whom Richard had dispatched after assuming control of the Prince.

"John," Colet added gently, "if it helps, I believe that King Richard was acting to protect the boys. I think that he relieved them from being boy Kings, subject to all kinds of treachery and pain, and assumed the Crown himself.

"That can't justify…." John interjected before Henry cut him off.

"That is not your place, John More," Henry Colet cut him off impatiently. "King Richard needed to make a decision. It was a bad decision either way, but he made it. Then took upon himself the onus of protecting the very boys whom he was accused of usurping. Their own mother went into sanctuary. Buckingham…."

Thomas's ears pricked up

"Buckingham didn't agree and moved on Richard." Colet continued with some heat. "Threatened to expose the whole thing. Tried to raise an army. Worked with Morton. King Richard arrested him, but then let him go say goodbye to his son," he gestured towards Thomas, "your Thomas's friend Edward. Then swears to Buckingham that he will take care of Edward as he had taken care of the Princes."

John worked this all through his mind. Thomas was reeling.

"The King allows himself to be accused of murder, and of trying to kill Edward Stafford because he assumes that if people think that he has killed these children, then it will be much easier to hide and protect them until they are grown."

"And he chooses to keep *that* fact a secret?!?" asked John, incredulously.

"yes," replied Henry definitively. "He does. And *we*," gesturing to Thomas and John, "are going to help him."

"How?" asked both father and son simultaneously, though Thomas asked excitedly and John resignedly.

Henry smiled. He had won. "John," he said quietly, "this effort desperately needs an attorney. The King needs new identities for the Princes, and maybe for Edward. They need to be prestigious enough not to pinch, but not so prominent as to cause questions. The King will want to settle enough income on both of them for comfort, but again, not enough to be conspicuous."

"False identity is a crime," said John, but already working out how to do it.

Henry ignored him. "and you, Thomas More…." He hesitated, looking at Thomas. Thomas looked at him expectantly. "Thomas, Edward Stafford needs a friend. He needs someone he can talk to and play with. But he also needs a friend who will never, ever tell anyone else, not his mother, not his other friends, about Edward, that he is anything but in hiding from a ruthless, possibly evil King."

"King Richard seems like a good man," said Thomas, but the Lord Mayor cut him off.

"Thomas and John. Both of you. It is critically important for the lives of the Princes that no one ever hear that from either of you. From this day forward, the people need to believe that King Richard is a dark man, who usurped the throne from his nephew, Edward, and then to save himself, saw to the Princes' deaths. And, Thomas, that he is hunting your friend Edward Stafford, with the idea of killing him as well."

"So no one will ever know the best part of him?" asked Thomas.

John shook his head, finally understanding. "No, son," he said gently, "no one must ever know."

"The King has assured me," Colet continued, "that when the Princes have grown to manhood and can protect themselves and the Realm, that they will be discovered alive, and ready to assume their duties. He will stand aside."

"What about Henry Tudor?" John asked.

"What about him?" Colet replied, "He can't raise enough troops to be a serious threat."

John shook his head gravely, worried, then said, "all right, Henry. I can do what you ask. What the King requests. Some parts might be a little expensive, particularly the specifications of the estates for the Princes – 'generous enough, but not so generous as to attract attention' –

sometimes I think a farthing would attract attention. But it can be done. Where will the money come from, and are you my contact for this?"

"Yes, John," the Lord Mayor replied, happy that John More had willingly signed on. "you are my solicitor, and so therefore you and I speaking will attract no attention. Similarly, I am the Lord Mayor, and my speaking to the King when he is in London will also not attract attention."

"What shall I do," asked Thomas anxiously.

"For now, Thomas, how are your letters?" asked Colet.

"Pretty good," replied Thomas bashfully.

"Then for now, Thomas," Colet replied genially, "I want you to write Edward Stafford a letter every week. You are to sit with your father and no one else to write the letter, and you are to give that letter to your father, who will deliver it to me. I will give it to the King of England, who will pass it along to Edward. How is that for a start?"

Colet smiled at Thomas and John. "I thank you both, as, I know, does the King." Then he winked at Thomas and added conspiratorially, "and Edward Stafford as well."

Thomas felt pleased with himself, and he gratefully and proudly stepped next to his father and took his big hand in his much smaller one.

The meeting concluded with a façade agreement issued between the Lord Mayor and King Richard for the London Guilds to purchase more of Richard's war bonds, and for Richard to endow a few more charities in the city, and to commit to the completion of the Saint Mary Barking Church in the All Hallows priory at the base of the Tower of London.

Thomas and his father left the Guildhall and headed home. Thomas practically skipped the entire way, never slowing his talking. "We spoke with the King!" Thomas cried, though trying to maintain a low voice at the same time, " I'm helping Edward. I made the King laugh, Father!"

As they made their way past Saint Lawrence church at the top of Milk Street, John abruptly maneuvered Thomas through the front door of the church, and found a small alcove to the right of the altar. Checking to ensure they were alone, John leaned in to his son's ear and whispered, "Thomas, we need to talk before we get home."

As they had reached Saint Lawrence, Thomas had been about to effusively express more thoughts about the whole morning, but as they passed quickly under the grate over the door, Thomas became quiet. Now, emotions under control, he simply looked quietly at his father before him.

John debated what to say, and then finally started with, "You were a very good boy today, my son, and I am so proud of you."

Thomas smiled, and was about to become ebullient again, when John raised his hand to calm him and continued. "Thomas, today puts you and I into a tough position. We are helping the King to do what he feels very strongly is the right course of action, but that course of action involves both deceit and a very significant amount of risk."

Thomas nodded seriously.

John continued, "The nobles, they fight to the death over the crown, one side against another, and they betray each other quite easily. What we saw today was a King with a plan, but also a number of people who are in on the plan, and who are, at this particular moment, on the King's side. But that could easily change. For example, your friend Edward Stafford's father, the Duke of Buckingham. He was with King Richard until, very suddenly, he wasn't."

Thomas interrupted in a whisper, looking around the empty church, "But King Richard swore to take care of Edward!"

John responded softly, sadly, in a whisper, "after he executed his father for treason. Thomas, the Duke of Buckingham was a friend, a peer of King Richard, a cousin. And he killed him. If this King, or any King, is unhappy with a commoner such as you or I, how much hesitation do you think there would be before a similar, but more gruesome fate?"

Thomas's ebullience was replaced by visions of hangings in the square that he had heard of. His mother had successfully kept him from public executions, so Thomas's ample imagination came to full, awful flower in a moment.

Thomas was brought back though by his father continuing, "we do have protections though, Thomas. We have the law. And we have the church. These two institutions are England, every bit as much as the person of the King."

Thomas looked confused, not sure how this worked. John went on, "Thomas, the King is not a God. He is a man, and, as the saying goes, 'no man is above the law.' I… we… will do what the King asks of us, but always within the bounds of the law. When I create protected identities for the Princes, or, if need be, for Edward, I will create them, and establish their lives and finances within the strict constraints of the law. If anyone tries to prosecute us for having done this, our defense is, and will always be, 'this was done within the constraints of the law.'"

Thomas was curious, and asked, "father, will you be able to create safe identities for the Princes?"

John smiled broadly, and replied, "Oh, yes Thomas, I will. For you see, I am a very very good lawyer."

Thomas stepped forward with a serious look and replied, "I believe you father."

Still holding hands, father and son left Saint Lawrence church and walked down Milk Street. Since it wasn't yet noon, the shops were still busy, and Mr. Cheeseman said hello to John and Thomas.

John stopped at the stall, and said, "Mr. Cheeseman, my son and I have had a very busy morning, and, if you please, we could do with some of your curds."

Mr. Cheeseman laughed, and in his northern accent replied, "for the Mores, anything."

Laughing and eating curds, and enjoying the salty squeak as they bit down, the two went into the house.

As they entered the door, Thomas turned and looked back at Edwards empty home, and said quietly to himself, "hopefully soon, Edward."

As he went into the cool dark house, Thomas thought, "I thought the King was very nice."

The voice replied, *"I liked him, and I think he could be a great King."*

## Chapter 5 - August, 1485

Some of Thomas's earliest and best memories were of being with his mother, Agnes. She had brown hair and eyes and was, in Thomas's eyes at least, very beautiful. Agnes wrote left handed, which was unusual, but not so unusual as a woman writing. She didn't care about the ignorant whispers, and used to declare that she needed to use her left hand, as her right hand "might as well be a dolphin's flipper." Agnes provided an excellent foil to Thomas's father, John; she sometimes provided the necessary ballast as the true adult of the house.

Thomas's father, John, apart from the errands with Thomas, could be aloof with his children, being very busy as a rising London lawyer. Agnes, by contrast, was actively involved in all aspects of their childhoods, from virtually the moments of awakening, until they fell asleep. Contrary to fashion and common wisdom, Agnes did not believe that you could spoil a child by holding them, and she and Thomas had developed a special bond, different and deeper than the bond between Thomas's sister, Elizabeth, and mother.

Unlike many of the upper middle class women of the time, Thomas's mother could read, and she loved reading to Thomas. When she was not otherwise occupied running the house, she would call Thomas over to where she was sitting in a small alcove of her garden. Agnes would smooth out her dress and tell Thomas to climb up. Thomas would clamber up onto her lap, sing to him, or they would just talk. Like John, Agnes never spoke down to children.

And then Thomas's mother would read. They thrilled together with a copy of Malory's stories of King Arthur and the Knights of the Round Table. She read him Chaucer's tales, heavily edited, of course. She read him the Bible. And she told Thomas the stories of London. Agnes's father was a London merchant, and alderman, and Agnes was a London girl, through and through, loving every nook and cranny of her home.

Agnes had a surprisingly thorough knowledge of the City's history. As a seven year old boy, Thomas was particularly taken with the story of William Walworth, the Lord Mayor of London, stabbing Wat Tyler in the neck during the Peasant Revolt a hundred years before. Other favorites of Thomas included the arrival of Julius Caesar, the Romans and the Celts. Agnes particularly loved telling the story of Queen Boadicca and the revolt against the Romans. She spoke of the building of the windmills in the Moorfields. And she told, and retold the life of Thomas a' Becket, the patron Saint of London, who had been born in a little house on Wood Street, one block over from their home on Milk Street. Thomas a' Becket had grown to be Lord Chancellor of England and Archbishop of Canterbury, only to be slaughtered in Canterbury Cathedral by a gang of non-London Knights and the behest of the non-London King, Henry the Second. The outrage was palpable in her voice when she spoke.

Two years before, when Thomas was five years old, she had seemed to Thomas to be genuinely sad when she spoke of the death of old King Edward the Fourth. Agnes had taken Thomas to Cheapside to see the funeral procession on its way to Windsor. She had held Thomas's little hand while they watched the funeral bier process down the wide street, standing just near the white stone of Eleanor's cross. Thomas had been awed by the ceremony as the coffin and caisson bearing the King passed, followed by all of the Knights and members of the Guilds, in full livery, including John More with the Mercer's guild, all bright and colorful, passing solemnly by.

Agnes possessed a lively sense of gossip, and Thomas had, until a month before, been outraged as Agnes shared stories of the young King Edward, and his brother the Prince Richard, Duke of York, cousins of Edward Stafford, being held in the Tower. He had been alarmed as his mother described the Princes' Uncle Richard taking the throne for himself. Then the execution of

Edward's father, the Duke of Buckingham, and the disappearance of the Princes, and Edward Stafford's flight.

Thomas had remained faithful to his vows to his father and to the King not to share what he had learned. But this was difficult with his mother, his adored mother, talking about Henry Tudor moving against the King, and how Tudor could help right the wrong done to England with the murder of the Princes.

King Richard still presented an enormous puzzle to Thomas, and he turned it over in his mind as his mother went on about the Princes. This interior conversation was hampered by a lack of any new information since the meeting with the King a month before. Thomas had dutifully written a short weekly note to Edward Stafford, which he had given to his father for delivery to the Lord Mayor. Thomas's father had had several meetings with the Lord Mayor, but had not shared any information with Thomas. Thomas's head hurt a little as he turned the problem over in his head again.

"Who is Henry Tudor?" Thomas abruptly asked his mother, first to focus his mind on his mother's voice, second to convince her that he was listening, as she had started to look at him the way she did when he was daydreaming, and finally, out of a guilty conscience at not sharing his news about the King and the Princes with his mother.

Agnes stopped, and looked warmly at Thomas, "Thomas, I've told you about him. It's a little dangerous to mention him though since he is trying to invade England to become King." Mother leaned in conspiratorially to son and continued in a mock whisper, "He is the remaining Lancastrian claimant to the throne, even though his claim may be weak. He's really a Welshman. Though he is a half-nephew to the old King Henry the Sixth through his grandmother, the Queen

Catherine, may that lovely Frenchwoman rest in peace." At that she nodded her head in the late Queen's memory.

Thomas was alarmed, and stammered out a "..but what about King Richard?" before realizing his error.

"King Richard?" asked Agnes with surprise and a little anger. "King Richard is a usurper who killed the Princes in the Tower. He has a bent back and is more Northman than English." She paused, perhaps realizing that in her surprise she had been disloyal in front of her son, who was now looked ashamed and red-faced, looking solidly at the floor instead of her. So she changed the subject. "So Thomas, are you ready for school?" she asked. "You start at St. Anthony's in only two weeks."

Relieved at the change, but unable to look his mother completely in the eye, the true cause of his embarrassment still unperceived, Thomas leapt at the chance to move onto something easier, "I am very excited about it, mother," he replied quickly. "I am a little concerned about the pigs, though." And he laughed.

His mother laughed as well, and, relieved, she proceeded to tell Thomas the story of St. Anthony's pigs.

Two weeks later Thomas was awakened by a servant with the news, "Thomas, wake up. Your parents need you."

"What the problem?" Thomas sleepily asked, but the servant had already moved from his little room.

Obediently, Thomas rose and padded into his parent's room. His mother was sitting quietly in a corner of the room. Thomas noticed that she had a flushed thin face, and looked tense and nervous. His older sister, Joan, aged 10, and youngest sister, Elizabeth, age 3 were already there. Oddly, there was no sign of his sister Agatha, age 5, or brother Edward, age 4. Probably still asleep.

"Children," Agnes More began, his voice odd, "the King will be coming down Cheape on his way to be crowned this morning."

Thomas simply asked, "I thought Richard was crowned a long time ago."

His sister Elizabeth gave him an exasperated look, "Thomas, there is a new King Henry today. King Richard is dead." She looked a little superior. "Killed at Bosworth."

Thomas recoiled, quickly thinking, "King Richard is dead?" he thought.

*"He was just alive," the voice.*

"A battle at Bosworth. A new King."

*"I liked the old King. I made him laugh."*

He was sad. Maybe the new King will be happy."

Thomas suddenly noticed his mother's flushed face. "Why are you crying, Mother?" he asked.

Agnes straightened, and smiled thinly at her son., "I'm just a little overtired this morning, Thomas," she said, glancing towards where the younger children were sleeping. Agatha and Edward weren't feeling well last night, and I might be coming down with something.

"Are they alright this morning?" Thomas asked.

She ignored the question, instead responding, "you and Joan should go to the parade on Cheap. Your father will be in it. Your friends will certainly be there."

Sensing that further questions would be unwelcome by mother, Thomas said "fine," a little more shortly than absolutely necessary, turned on his heel, and put on a coat and some short trousers, and went down to the door of their house on Milk Street.

Thomas looked across the street reflexively at his friend's home, but his attention quickly focused on the front door, where there was activity like he had not seen since before Edward's father's execution two years before. Soldiers in red livery were bustling in and out of the entry. Hopefully, Thomas looked up towards the solar window of Edwards house, but did not see his friend, Edward, there.

Thomas turned to his right, towards the Cheape. Crowds of people were gathering in the street. He moved towards them, but had only taken a few steps when he spied several of his friends, including Edward, coming north on Milk street, towards Thomas but on the opposite side.

As the other boys pulled closer, Thomas More made out several boys that he knew, including parts of their old St. Paul's haunts, all about the same age, including, of course, Edward Stafford, but also Thomas Boleyn, son of a previous Lord Mayor, and Thomas Howard, of the line of the Dukes of Norfolk. Thomas Howard's face was red, and he appeared to have been crying.

"Howard's crying too," Thomas thought.

*"Why does it seem everyone is crying?"*

"New King….change….fear."

Thomas Howard had been a page to his father, and he had boastfully shown off his bright red uniform only a few days before. The boys were all now wearing brightly colored clothes, and, when they saw Thomas More, the boys' laughed at Thomas's simple breeches and shirt.

"You'll not be going to the King's parade dressed like a farmhand, Thomas More," said Thomas Howard, angrily, his red face matching his spectacular red hair, "at least not standing anywhere near us."

Thomas looked at his clothes. He thought they were fine, but the Lord Howard was four years older, much more knowledgeable in the ways of the world, at age eleven.

Thinking quickly, Thomas asked, "what do you suggest?"

*"Watch out, Thomas,"* the voice warned.

The other boys conferred conspiratorially, with Thomas More off to the side, temporarily excluded from their group. Agreeing, they turned back to Thomas, and Edward Stafford said, "look Thomas, we want you to be with us, but you need to be dressed better to see the new king. Come to my house and we will bet you dressed appropriately. But we've got to hurry. The King's party will be in the Cheape soon."

Thomas agreed, and after being hurriedly dressed by the other boys, the group set out towards the Cheap and Eleanor's Cross.

As Thomas went down Milk Street, he saw Mr. Cheeseman pointing at him, calling out, and waving. Thomas waved back quickly as he hurried to keep up, nearly tripping over the pointy curled tips of these unfamiliar shoes with the effort.

"I like Mr. Cheeseman," Thomas thought.

*"He was nice to point and wave,"* came the voice, *"but he wasn't smiling like he usually is."*

The Coronation parade was everything that a seven year old boy could have hoped for. There were large poles set up on either side of the street, hung with streamers. Thomas had a little difficulty, but with some help, and a boost from the other boys, he was able to shinny up the pole a ways to get a better view.

The new King, Henry Tudor, had spared nothing for the procession, and there were animals from the Tower zoo, still caged, but moved up on carts. There were two leopards, the

Royal lions, and walking behind to the astonished gasps of the crown, an Oliphant, the larges

animal Thomas had ever seen.

Behind the tower animals came the Lord Mayor and the Guilds in full regalia, gleaming

in the August sun. Thomas waved at the Lord Mayor and called out. Thomas saw the Lord

Mayor look in his direction, then trip a little over some unseen debris on the street before

continuing on. The guilds came next, in order of precedence. There was a loud whoop from the

nearby guildhall of the Mercer's guild as they walked by, as they always did, first in precedence.

Each member of the livery company wore a bright red cape, with a little piece of fox fur on the

lapel, and a black wool hat. Thomas knew and admired many of these men, his father's friends.

In the front row, hobbling a bit, was the bent figure of William Caxton, the printer. In the second

row was John More, looking to be in serious thought, waving absently as he passed.

Thomas waved confidently at his father who took notice of him and stumbled, then,

collecting himself, proceeded onward. In one of the later companies, the tallow chandlers,

Thomas caught sight of his mother's father, Thomas Graunger, normally a smiling, happy man,

but today looking oddly pinched and serious. Other livery companies passed, and then musicians,

and jugglers. Then there were soldiers, wielding axes and halberds, gleaming in the August sun.

Some walked alongside their horses. Some of the armor was dented. Thomas looked in vain for

evidence of blood from the great battle, but saw none. He could not decide if he was

disappointed.

Finally, as his arms and legs ached from the strain of holding onto the pole, Thomas saw

the new King. He was riding a white horse, and had on his battle armor, though it had been

cleaned. His face was pinched and straight, and carried a sour, distant look as he took in the sight of the crowds, his new subjects. Thomas waved vigorously at the King, and thought the new King nodded in acknowledgement of him.

After the King had passed, Thomas climbed down the pole, and was discussing the events, particularly the soldiers and the Oliphant, with the other boys. Even Thomas Howard seemed to be coming out of his funk. The gaiety was disturbed by Mr. Cheeseman, who came huffing down the street, his stained white apron flapping at the near breeze his moving bulk created.

"Thomas More," he called out to Thomas, who turned.

Mr. Cheeseman's face was still red from the effort of the run, but his breathing was slowing, and he crouched, hands on knees, down to Thomas, and said, "Thomas More, you must come with me. It's your mother."

"Mother?" Thomas asked, "Why?"

Ignoring the question, Mr. Cheeseman simply replied, "Come along, Thomas." The big man then grasped Thomas's hand, and led him, tripping and fumbling in his overlarge, borrowed pointy toed shoes, hurrying up Milk Street, and the entry passage to the More house.

At the parade, Thomas had heard rumors of a sweating sickness that had accompanied the new King to London. It had been only two weeks since Bosworth, and this illness had arrived, it seemed, in London the day before, as a new plague. People at the Cheape were saying that there were quite a few ill people down by the docks, and out in the surrounding country-side.

Thomas became increasingly concerned by seeing his grandfather and father, both crying, conversing quietly to the side of the hallway outside John and Agnes's room. The two stopped when they saw Thomas, and straightened their backs. They were about to speak, when Thomas heard his mother calling for he and his sister, crying out for them really, in a wildly delirious voice.

Thomas would always remember his father trying to keep the children out of the sick room, as a kind of quarantine had been placed on Agnes. Thomas ran quickly around his father's legs before the bedroom door was closed again, and came to his mother's side.

There were Doctors in attendance doing what they knew how to do. Thomas noticed his mother's blood in a small brass bowl at her side, with pressure being applied to the crook of her elbow, where the vein had been opened. Thomas's mother was ghastly white, but she recognized Thomas, seemed to quickly clear and calm, and said, "Thomas, More's Morae, Morus, be good for me."

With that, Thomas was bodily lifted by his father, and taken screaming hysterically from the room. John More deposited Thomas at the feet of his grandfather, and then hurried back into their room and his wife, closing the door behind him.

Agnes's mother, arrived shortly after, stopped to give Thomas and her other grandchildren a peck, before sweeping worriedly through the door and closing it after.

A short time later, Thomas heard his father let out a great sob. A little bit after that, John More emerged to tell Thomas and his sisters and brother that their mother, sister Agatha, and brother Edward had died of the fever sweeping through the City that day.

Thomas made his goodbyes at Westminster, heading out the large doors on the side of the palace. There was a wide dirt road that lead up along to the Whitehall palace that intersected with a brick path going to the right along the soiled, muddy bank of the Tyburn to the boat landings for the Palace on the Thames. The noonday sun was hot, and Thomas, still in his woolen judicial robes and hat felt quite stifled by the heat.

"It would," he thought, "be cooler at Richmond."

*"Even cooler and more pleasant in the garden in Chelsea, under the Mulberry tree.."*
*Returned the voice.*

Thomas loved to sit in the shade under the mulberry tree in his garden. He could be blessedly alone there – that was know as his space and the family made sure to leave him to his thoughts there.

*"Mores, morus, morae…More's funny Mulberry."*

"remember how mother taught that?"

*"even on that day."*

That day, August 30, 1485 was forever known as "that day" – the day Thomas's mother, brother and sister had all died within a few hours of becoming ill with a disease that had not been known in England until a week before, when Henry Tudor had invaded with French mercenaries.

Thomas had later learned that this fever epidemic had in the space of a week killed nearly one out every ten inhabitants of London. Such widespread death had created real fear of Henry's assumption of the throne. The plague also had the effect of causing the postponement of Henry VII's coronation to October, when the cold weather made the City safer.

Thomas came back to attention. One needed to be very careful of all the animal traffic in the road, and Thomas snapped back out of the way of a horse ridden by a nobleman. Thomas reflexively bowed his head, but then heard a familiar voice cry out, "My Lord Chancellor! How are you!"

Thomas smiled, because he knew the voice. Looking up cheerily at the young noble on the magnificent brown horse, Thomas cried, "Henry Stafford! So very good to see you."

Henry Stafford was the about to be 30 year old first born son of his old friend Edward Stafford. Thomas loved Henry as if he were a son, and they had a common passion for collecting books.

"What new treasures, have you Henry?" Thomas asked cheerily.

Henry gave a happy "whoop!" and swung down from the saddle and alit near Thomas. Henry was a little taller, but still possessed the Buckingham girth and jowls. He greedily took a woolen bag from a hook on his saddle, and produced a smallish but thick book with a white calfskin cover. There was no writing on the soft, beautiful cover. The book was about six by eight inches and about 3 inches thick.

"It seems well disguised, Henry," Thomas joked.

Henry laughed and flipped the cover open to show Thomas.

"it a copy of Ludolph's '*life of Christ*'," the younger man said excitedly. Printed in Lyon by Barthelmey Buyer in 1480."

"You found one?!?" Thomas demanded happily.

"Yes," then he hedged, grinding his toe coquettishly at Thomas, "though I do suppose that I could have settled for another copy of Utopia."

"Thomas laughed at the tease, "your father was my biggest customer," he said, "I'd be surprised if there were any left."

"Maybe, my Lord Chancellor," Henry said with a bow. "I would like for you to have this. A gift."

Thomas bowed, gratefully accepting the book, placing it in a side pocket of his robes.

"How us your sister, Elizabeth?" Thomas asked mildly, immediately regretting the question

Henry looked pained, and replied, "still quite stormy. And still with… that Duke… Thomas Howard… but you would know that better than me."

It was Thomas's turn to look uncomfortable. Edward Stafford had married his daughter Elizabeth off to Thomas Howard when she was fifteen and he was thirty-five. It was a marriage of two Ducal households, and had been very stormy. Further, Elizabeth had remained loyal and in the household of the Queen, Catherine of Aragon, and her husband was the loving uncle of the King's mistress Anne Boleyn.

"Henry," Thomas said earnestly, "I love you as if you were my own family, and I would never cause you pain. I'm sorry that I asked."

Henry straightened and brightened a bit. "At least there are still wonderful books to find, my friend."

Thomas smiled kindly, "there are indeed."

St. Anthony's School on Threadneedle Street had become a place of refuge over the five years Thomas had been in attendance. John More had become withdrawn and angry after the death of his wife. He had remarried to have someone to care for the children, but then, once that responsibility had been attended to, had retreated into his work. To his fellow lawyers, John More was a genial fellow with a brilliant mind. To his children, he was like a beautifully wrapped Christmas box with no gift inside; endless excitement and promise on the outside, and disappointment within.

The errands with Thomas were also gone, and the stern face that John presented to Thomas reminded him acutely of the loss of his mother. John had remarried a lovely woman named Joan. She was the widow of a friend of the elder More, named John Marshall, and, while she was nothing but kind to Thomas, she would never be his mother.

Two weeks after the death of his mother, Thomas had begun his studies at St. Anthony's The term normally started on St. Bartholomew's day, August 24, but there had been so much turmoil, with the death of the King at Bosworth on August 22, and then the death's of so many prominent Londoners from the sweating sickness, that the opening of the school had been delayed to give time to bury the dead. It had long been rumored that, since the plague had reached London with the new King that it was God's judgment on the City for not being more supportive of King Richard. This feeling had passed, as King Henry had made good on his promise to marry Elizabeth of York, Edward IV's daughter, sister to the now missing Princes, and, nine months later, blessed the country with the birth of a young Prince, Arthur.

The morning of the start of the delayed term, the seven year old, very sleepy Thomas was awakened by a servant at five in the morning and fed. Thomas was then put out into the street to find his way to school. His father had never emerged from his room, still sick with grief. Thomas stood at the gate, the September morning air still cool and damp. The sun had barely risen. Thomas carried a leather satchel that was nearly as big as he, and that threatened to use its weight to pull the carrier onto his back like some upended turtle. The bag contained two wooden writing tablets, pencils, a little paper, and a few grammar and song books. There was also a loaf of bread, and some butter wrapped in a cloth.

Frightened and unsure, Thomas stood tentatively at the gate. Mr. Cheeseman approached. "Thomas," he boomed, unable to switch between street hawking and normal conversation, "what are ye doing up so early?"

Thomas fidgeted. "It's my first day of school today," he replied timidly.

"Well, who is taking you?" the dairyman asked, concerned.

"No one," Thomas answered plaintively. He began to cry.

"There, there, Thomas," Mr. Cheeseman said, stooping to cup a massive hand on Thomas's shoulder. "I can get you to school. We can walk the way, like. That way tomorrow you'll know it."

Thomas brightened and looked into the kind, bearded face. "I think I know the way," Thomas said. "It's Saint Anthony's, on Threadneedle. I've walked back a hundred times with my father, but never there alone."

Mr. Cheeseman laughed, his loud, rolling expanse that began deep within him like some distant thunder, then, clap, was upon you, taking your breath away. Cheeseman wiped his hands on his apron, then said to his son, only a little older than Thomas, "Matthew, I'll be back in a bit. I'm running young Thomas off to school." He then took a long white staff from inside the door of his shop.

Matthew, twelve years old, and as chubby as if he were in competition with his father, came out, rubbing his pink hands together, his face oddly distraught and red. "Hurry, father," he called out in a sad voice, "don't be too long. The curds are about ready."

"I could stay here with you," Thomas volunteered, thinking of the tasty curds.

"Did you eat breakfast, Thomas?" Mathew asked, clearly looking up and down at Thomas and judging him too skinny by half.

"Yes," said Thomas, surprised at the question.

"Then we'd better get you off to school before you get hungry again and eat up all our curds!" laughed Mr. Cheeseman, who then gently grasped Thomas's hand and steered him down Milk Street towards the Cheap. But not before grabbing a little paper wrap of curds and slipping it to Thomas conspiratorially, while Matthew was looking away.

"For the road, Thomas," Cheeseman said under his voice and with a little wink at Thomas. He picked up a white stick that had been propped. He laughed sadly again, then gently grasped Thomas's hand and steered him down Milk Street towards the Cheape. "Threadneedle, ya say?" he asked.

Thomas nodded.

The walk only took about five minutes, and Thomas was delighted to be walking with so big a figure as Mr. Cheeseman. It seemed that everyone knew the kind dairyman. Everyone nodded gravely. A few of the passersby, also carrying white sticks like Mr. Cheeseman, were given wide berths. Thomas began to chatter as he relaxed, and the older man let him talk. He stopped abruptly when Thomas asked, "Mr. Cheeseman, where is your wife? I haven't seen her for a while."

"Madge died with the sweats," Cheeseman said, very quietly, "just like your mum and brother and sister."

Thomas stopped and looked anew at Mr. Cheeseman. Biting his upper lip, "So she's in heaven," he said very hesitantly, as if afraid of the answer.

"Without doubt, Thomas, without doubt," the older man said, confidently, but with a look of infinite sadness on his face.

"But you've been in your shop every day," observed Thomas.

"If ye believe," said Mr. Cheeseman with a slow sniff, "then death is nothing to be sad about…." A tiny smile pulled at the corner of his lip. "I have my son, Matthew with me still, and I will be with her again someday." He sniffed. "Besides, milk don't wait for me, either curds or curdled, as Madge used to say."

"Why do you have the white stick?" asked Thomas.

"It tells people that the sweats have been in your house," answered Cheeseman, "so they can take precautions if they want to."

"Why don't I or my father have one then?" asked Thomas.

Mr. Cheeseman was preoccupied and appeared not to hear the question over the general din of the city. The Cheape gave way to the appalling smell of the aptly named "Poultry," with its stalls of hanging slaughtered birds. A few quick steps, a left turn and onto Threadneedle, the pigs, and St. Anthony's school.

With a reassuring smile, Mr. Cheeseman waved towards the school and said, "There it is, Thomas, and I will leave you here. – 'curds or curdled,' as Madge would say." He then backed off, waving at Thomas, and gesturing with sideways scooping motions towards the school building. Thomas laughed and waved, adjusted his satchel into what he hoped was a jaunty, confident position, and made his way across the crowded street and into the school.

Entering St. Anthony's, Thomas was swept into a swirl of activity that helped him to cope with the physical loss of his mother and the emotional loss of his father. The school building foyer was dark, and going through the door, entering St. Anthony's was always for Thomas, like crossing into another world entirely – one of preadolescent boys and their smells, of their laughs and carryings-on.

The school was a timbered building with exposed rafters. All five years of students, a hundred or so, were in one long large hall together. The rules of the school were strict, but no amount of rules or restraint could ever really harness the energies of that many seven to twelve year old boys packed into that small a space. The headmaster, Nicholas Holt, was young enough yet to realize this and, instead, strove for an 'ordered chaos" in the school that suited Thomas very well.

There was a progression of the educational activities through the years, the younger students learning music through plainsong, and the older students, those bound for University, concentrating on polishing their Latin and Rhetoric, while also scribbling out math on the laptop chalk boards, or choking on the Aristotle that the so called "new learning" had inflicted on the young. The Saint Anthony's students were famous debaters, known for their wit in argument. Over time, Thomas, with his quickness, facility for language, and unparalleled memory, became the star of the school.

Every day for five years, then, Thomas would rocket from bed at five in the morning, race through breakfast, and run out of the house to school. Thomas always stopped on Milk Street to give Mr. Cheeseman and Matthew little waves, but then off running, heavy bag dangling, down Milk, up Cheape, through Poultry, then a jog onto Threadneedle to school. Coming home was a more leisurely affair, as Thomas would stop and gawk at the rich gold in the goldsmith's shops on the Cheape, or, if it was hot out, get some water from the Standard, a large imposing marble water fountain in the Cheape, across from the Bow Bells tower. The water was piped in from a well north of London, and was clean, cool, and safe.

Occasionally Thomas would stop at Eleanor's Cross and check to see if Daniel had been moved. He e rarely saw Edward Stafford, since Edward had been taken into the new King's household "for safekeeping."

On a few occasions, John More had taken Thomas with him to Westminster for a trial or other business. John had tried to emerge from his grief over the loss of his wife and two children, and to reestablish his relationship with Thomas.

On a few occasions, waiting in an anteroom at Westminster Palace while John conducted some business in the hall, Thomas and Edward had met.

Thomas and Edward's friendship remained close and easygoing, and Edward had retained in his round face an outgoing, friendly nature. On the rare occasions that the two boys could be alone, though, there was a gulf between them that was surmountable, but took a lot of effort on Thomas's part since Edward had been remade Duke of Buckingham, which he enjoyed very much, and spoke of frequently, and at length. Thomas found that he had a natural ability to make allowances for friends, and to simply enjoy Edward's company, no matter how insufferable he could be. He did, however, decline to fetch for his friend, or to agree with him when he did not in fact agree.

Edward was hungry for news from outside the castle and the King's orbit. Thomas had learned that although the King and the Queen were generally kind to Edward, the King was suspicious of the young boy's ambitions and genetics, jealous of his large holdings and income, and therefore kept him a virtual prisoner in the Royal Court. The King had made Edward his ward, and, under feudal law, had taken complete control of his finances to his own benefit. After assuming control, though, the King had generally ignored Edward, shuttling the young Duke into various ceremonial positions where he would be visible but non-threatening and out of the way.

The Queen, Elizabeth, was another matter. She took and active, abiding, and loving interest in Edward. She was only twelve years older than Edward and Thomas. She was the eldest daughter of Edward IV, and through mothers, Edward Stafford's first cousin. She had married King Henry as part of an arrangement to unite the houses of York and Lancaster, the red and white roses, By all reports she had come to love her strange and quiet husband..

Thomas caught a glimpse of the Queen occasionally in these meetings. Thomas loved her from the moment he laid eyes on her. She was beautiful and kind, with a lilting, happy laugh. Her bright red Plantagenet hair flamed like the sun, matched by lively auburn eyes. Thomas thought the Queen the most beautiful woman he had ever seen and was completely smitten with her.

There was one area in particular in which Edward always craved information - Thomas's experiences with the famous St. Anthony's pigs. Thomas was delighted to help in this regard. After five years at St. Anthony's, now twelve year old Thomas was increasingly confident as a raconteur. And all the St. Anthony's boys were given ample ammunition in funny stories by the school's attitude towards pigs.

St. Anthony's took their pigs very seriously. The pig was the symbol of St. Anthony himself. The school used these pigs for eating, of course, and the St. Anthony's pigs were used by the city to clean the troughs and the gutters of the frequently disgusting streets of London –

the pigs were both effective and non-discriminating in providing some degree of hygiene to the City. In fact, as a matter of public policy any pig deemed inedible at the slaughters in Smithfield had its ear cut, was spared, and was let loose in the City to eat refuse. The cut ear thus marked the pig for St. Anthony's, and it was illegal for any Londoner to touch a St. Anthony's pig. In course, those pigs grown fat on their diets of London refuse were collected and eaten by the monks of Saint Anthony.

The students of St. Anthony's school were the swineherds. The boys all grew close to the pigs, grieving when one fattened up enough to be slaughtered. And the boys grew close to one another while attending to the pigs. And so, there they were, a bunch of boys ages seven to twelve, spending their days singing, declaiming in Latin, and nurturing undersized pigs. All, boys and swine, grew so close and so similar that after a while it wasn't clear whom was being referred to by the phrase "St. Anthony's pigs."

Five years to the day after Thomas's mother had died, August 24th, was St. Bartholomew's day in London, and that meant the opening of the St. Bartholomew's fair.

The annual fair was held in the square in front of the very old St. Bartholomew's church, at the edge of Smithfield, just outside the city walls at Aldersgate, just north of St. Paul's on St. Martin's lane. The square was large and spacious, and lay between the lovely old church, built of dark grey stone, and the imposing edifice of St. Bart's hospital, equally old. For fair days, the area was festooned with colorful banners and pendants.

Thomas was always thrilled to be in this square because of its importance in the history of London, in that the peasant's revolt had ended in this very spot only a hundred years before when Wat Tyler, a leader of the rebellion had been stabbed in the neck by the Lord Mayor of London himself for a perceived disrespect to the King. The wounded Tyler had been dragged to the hospital but had died quickly. The Lord Mayor was hailed as a great hero, mostly by the nobility so threatened by the rebellion. The dagger used to stab Tyler had ever since been on proud display in the Fishmonger's Hall.

Edward Stafford and Thomas had made several trips to view the knife. Edward had been especially keen to rail against Tyler and the mob of the revolt, since a particular object of the ire of the rebellion had been the excesses of his ancestor, John of Gaunt. They had even, to Edward's ongoing outrage, burned to the ground John's London mansion, the Savoy Palace. The destruction of the building had been passionate and savage and now, a century later, the ruins remained, the property useless, a jarring contrast on the Thames between London and Westminster surrounded by large, intact palaces.

The St. Bartholomew's fair had followed a proscribed course for time out of mind. After the initial pageant, the fair opened with a debating contest amongst the boys of the schools of London. The debates were conducted in Latin, and the teams of four or five boys from each school went on stage and conducted a formal debate on whatever topic interested the Judge that day. For this day the Judge was the Archbishop of Canterbury, the Lord Chancellor of England, John Morton.

The Archbishop had a thin, sallow face and bulbous eyes. He wore green robes that day with a white stole that complemented his white miter. The neck of his robes were loose, and the swelling in his lower neck moved when he swallowed. For all that, he unexpectedly wore a broad smile that happily crinkled his eyes at their edges. His eyes were sharp and intelligent, Thomas noticed immediately, and appeared to miss nothing. As the crowds entered the grounds, the Archbishop stood from his seat repeatedly and waved at the crowds, and this motion emphasized his long, angular limbs.

Thomas peeked around a curtain in the church that offered a look at the grounds.

*"There's the Archbishop,"* the voice.

"He looks like a giant crane," Thomas thought.

*"Unkind, but apt. Concentrate on your Latin. And don't forget to smile."*

"There's father."

*"And his wife."*

"Oh, yes. Her too."

*"Thomas, she loves you. She came out to see you. She will never be your mother, but she could be your friend."*

"I don't need her as a friend."

*"Yes, you do. People around you love you. You, dear Thomas, need to let them. Part of you died with your mother, but that dishonors her, and limits you. Your mother wouldn't...doesn't want that for you. Let the anger go, Thomas. Love and Trust."*

"Love whom?"

*"Everyone, Thomas, but especially those who love you. And enjoy yourself too. Big day for you. Be happy...especially for your mother's sake."*

Thomas looked out from behind a drape set on the stage, first at the Archbishop, and then at his Father, seated a few rows down. Looking closely, Thomas noticed that John's genial face had returned, as he gazed happily at his new wife, Joan, at his other children, and then, proudly up at the stage. Thomas's head may have been protruding a little far from the drape, because Thomas realized that his father had seen him, and had begun happily waving to him. With a start, Thomas dropped the drape, retreating behind.

Thomas looked around happily. The sky was blue and the air warm and friendly. The banners seemed more brightly colored than Thomas had remembered him. The stalls and tables around the courtyard were already laden with wool cloth, and hawkers were already hollering for attention.

Thomas decided to sneak another peek at his family around the drape. As soon as he did, his whole family, stepmother included, were ready, and called his name, waving excitedly.

*"Look at that, Thomas. They are all here to see you because they love you...Remember to smile."*

A trumpet played, and boys emerged from respective curtains on either side of the stage. For this debate, Saint Anthony's was pitted against Holy Trinity, all clearly nervous. When they had reached their spots on the stage, the Chancellor's Herald in red and green livery, called for silence from the exuberant crowd. When that peace was, against all odds, achieved, John Morton, the Lord Chancellor and Archbishop of Canterbury, rose ceremoniously and smiled at the crowd. Another small burst of enthusiasm, a smattering of applause.

The Lord Chancellor spoke in a high, reedy voice, announcing, "Welcome to the St. Bartholomew's Day School debate."

The crowd, a lot of parents present, cheered, naming their child's school. The More's cried out "St. Anthony's!" as one.

When the crowd quieted, the Archbishop continued, "We have two schools here to compete for the prize. I will judge the quality of the arguments, which will be in Latin. For those who do not have Latin, don't worry, we have a translator for the crowd."

John Morton smiled genially at the crowd which cheered the news of the translator. An astute politician, he waited for quiet, then waved his hand for the young cleric seated next to him to rise, saying, "and I have the distinct pleasure of bringing a wonderful young clark today as translator. A true Londoner. Son of a Lord Mayor… Father John Colet!"

Thomas watched as John Colet, instantly recognizeable, stood and waved fondly at the crowd. Loud cheers and smiles from the Londoners took a bit to die down, to allow the Archbishop, now with a radiant happy face, to continue, "I will also offer the question. The boys of Holy Trinity School will argue for the question, and the boys of Saint Anthony's will argue against. So, boys," he stopped to smile benignly at the debators, "if you are ready, the question: Certus: S est mairbus consonant."

John Colet, cried out dramatically, "Londoners, My Lord Archbishop, the question for debate today is: 'Affirmed - *S" is the greatest Consonant'*"

There were giggles from some of the boys on either side, as well as a few sick looks.

"Lucian, he's referencing Lucian." Thomas quickly thought. "'which is the greatest consonant, Sigma or Tau.'"

*"The jury was consonants,"* came the voice.

"Which one won? Why did it win?"

*"Does it make any difference?"*

While Thomas was thinking, the Holy Trinity boys were making a valiant effort at arguing in favor of the letter S, something about the Holy Spirit, *spiritus sanctus,* and the great theological benefits attached to sanctity.

John Colet was keeping up with the boys easily translating the twelve year old's Latin

Soon, too soon, it was Thomas's turn.

"What is the greatest consonant," he thought madly.

Thomas looked at St. Bartholomew's church, at the great porch in front. On either side of the door were mulberry bushes, their black fruit hanging in the August sun.

*"More's Morae Morus."* More's silly mulberry.

Thomas thought another word in quick succession, "mother."

*"your mother, Thomas,"* said the voice quietly.

Thomas knew what to do. He smiled confidently, and his shoulders relaxed. Just before being called to speak, Thomas leaned to a friend behind the curtain and whispered some instructions to him. The boy nodded and ran off to the stalls of the fair.

In a loud voice, shifting octaves with nerves, and a twelve year old's voice changes, Thomas began. His inner voice coaxing and coaching him.

"Dominus meus Archepiscopus," Thomas began.

*"My Lord Archbishop."*

Thomas paused, and nodded at John Morton, who gravely nodded in return. Thomas licked his lips and stole a glimpse at his father. Colet stopped and looked kindly at Thomas.

"Ego sum postulo ut reverenter discrepo per meus philogus collegium Sanctus Trinity."

*"I must respectfully disagree with my learned colleagues of the Holy Trinity."*

Thomas nodded at his opponents, taking the moment to try to regain some control of the timber of his voice.

"Mairibus consonant non 'S' est."

*"The greatest consonant is not 'S'."*

"Dum 'S' bonus consonant est, 'S' non valde consonant est."

*"While 'S' is a good consonant, it is not a great consonant."*

There was a small titter from the crowd. From the corner of his eye, Thomas saw his father beaming. He did not dare to turn his head, but looked directly at the Archbishop Lord Chancellor.

"In argumento mihi siscipet, EGO dedi sequens items."

*"In support of my argument, I offer the following items:"*

"Cuspis prothoplastus: Spritus Sanctus Trinitarius tertius est, ut meus philogus colleagues meus libere sinet."

*"Point the First: The Holy spirit is the third of the Holy Trinity, as my learned colleagues should freely admit."*

There were more giggles in the crowd, but the boys from Holy Trinity looked shocked that Thomas would turn their own name against them.

"Cuspis alter: sub valde Lucian un jury sub vowels sentio 't' ut exsisto majoribus quam 's'."

*"Point the second: Under the great Lucian, a jury of vowels judged t to be greater than s."*

"Cuspis tertius: In deferentius ut Archepiscopus Canterburius, et meo patre didicit, ego propono ut 'M' est quantum consonant."

*"Point the third: in deference to the Archbishop of Canterbury, and my learned father, I would propose that 'M' is the greatest consonant."*

A gasp in the crowd at the twelve year old's audacity. Thomas smiled inwardly, and said "Thank you," to his inner voice. *"you're welcome."*

Thomas then stalled a bit in Latin for a while, quoting Cicero on the nature of consonants versus vowels, and what made a good consonant, and how, under Cicero's rules, 'M' was ideally suited to greatness. He knew that he was running a narrow space between cute and irritating. Colet and the Archbishop smiled blandly at him.

The boy reappeared near the Archbishop, holding a potted plant.

Thomas nodded at him, and then turned and gave his father a nod and then a big grin.

The Archbishop was staring at Thomas, now with amusement on his face, as Thomas continued:

"Ita, meus senior Archepiscopus, in propinquus ego precor vestry clementia ut ego tendo vos per-"

*"And so, my Lord Archbishop, in closing, I beg your indulgence as I present you with-"*

"Mortonis Morae Morus!! Quod Erat Demonstrantum!"

*"Morton's silly mulberry! Thus it is proven!"*

The crowd clapped, Morton laughed uproariously, John More's face was flushed with delight as he wiped away tears. With a theatrical bow, the underclassman placed the small potted mulberry in front of the Lord Chancellor.

*"'M' stands for other things as well, Thomas."*

"You don't say."

*"I've always liked you, Thomas."*

Thomas smiled broadly and then bowed deeply to the Lord Chancellor. The crowd now erupted with laughter. Several of the St. Anthony's boys were making pig grunting noises and clapping Thomas on the back. The Headmaster, Nicholas Holt, stood off to the side, arms crossed over his chest grinning broadly and nodding.

Thomas looked at his father, who was beaming proudly at him. His new wife, Joan, was clapping happily. Thomas engaged her eyes, smiled directly at her, and made a little bow of respect.

After a bit, the crowd dispersed to walk about the fair. The Archbishop stood, and motioned Thomas towards him. Thomas approached, head bowed.

The Archbishop eyed Thomas appraisingly, then said, 'what are you doing next year, Master More?"

"I have been accepted at Eton to finish my education," said Thomas nervously.

The Archbishop waved that off with his head, "I would like for you to come into my service as a Page," he said, smiling at Thomas. "I know your father," he turned his head and nodded at John More, who had approached. "Who knows, you might be an Archbishop, maybe even Lord Chancellor some day."

John More started, and looked at the Archbishop with a surprised look of mild horror on his face, and said, "Clergy, My Lord?"

"Maybe, John," Morton said, "if the boy, and England, and the Church are all lucky."

"I'd planned on him entering the law," said John.

Thomas looked back and forth at the two men, saying nothing. The Archbishop smiled at John More, and said, "only if felons and the moneylenders are fortunate. Your boy could absolve their crimes." He smiled broadly at John More, and added, "Let time decide, John More, my friend. Let him be my Page for a while."

"Of course, your Lordship," said John, bowing his head to the prelate.

And so it was decided.

While the King was conferring with his Lord Chancellor, Archbishop Morton, the Pages for both men had nothing to do. The dinner had finished at Lambeth Palace. The scraps had been taken away, and the tables taken down. In the Great Hall, the young squires had separated into two opposing teams, King's and Archbishop's.

There were a few independents or stragglers, not affiliated with either Archbishop or King. These unaffiliated pages typically wore the livery of the house they were serving, and at large parties, their uniforms meant feeding the lesser guests and trying not to get food or wine spilled. One boy, whom Thomas knew to be William Blount, the young Baron Mountjoy, for example, was resplendent in the noble family's gold and black clothing, but not so self assured as to approach the boys.

Glaring at each other, most in both groups had known each other since infancy. Henry Percy and Thomas Boleyn gingerly stepped forward, and like magnets drew pages from both camps towards them.

There were a few other boys their age off to the side, and Thomas waved in a friendly way to them, though they were not part of "the London set," – the group of boys raised in London in close proximity who shared a special bond.

The young squire, Thomas Howard, a few years older than the pages, was also standing shyly in the corner. He and his family were still mostly out of favor with the King and so, he was in service to no Knight, as there was no Knight who would risk offending the King by taking him on. His grandfather had been killed, and his father wounded fighting for Richard at Bosworth. His father had been taken with his fresh wounds and locked directly in the Tower of London. To add insult, shortly after his coronation, King Henry had taken the unusual step of requiring

Parliament to declare his rule to have started the day before Bosworth, so that technically everyone who had fought for Richard at that field was a traitor to the King.

The Howard family was having a tough time getting around all those barriers, but with steady patience, the family, Thomas and his father, were slowly re-climbing the ladder to their hereditary Duchy and prominence.

"Thomas Howard!" called out Edward Stafford, the young Duke of Buckingham. "Come over here and join us." Edward, wearing the livery of the King of England, a red tunic with a golden lion on the front, motioned from amidst a group of the King's pages for Thomas Howard to join him in the group, including Percy and Boleyn. Edward thought for a second, then also added, "Thomas More," calling to the group of the Archbishop's pages in blue and silver, "you too!"

Smiling broadly, the old friends converged on Percy, Stafford and Boleyn.

Upon meeting, Thomas Howard bowed slightly and nervously to the younger Edward, and said, "Your Grace honors me."

Edward cut him off, "Oh stop that Thomas. We are old friends, all of us. It's just Henry, and Edward, and Thomas, and Thomas, and Thomas. By God, quite a lot of Thomas's. Was Becket really that powerful?" As they all were laughing, Edward winked at Thomas More, recalling an old debate. Edward continued with a yawn and an exaggerated stretch of his arms, "Saint Thomas protect me but I am bored. What do we do? We have the whole afternoon."

Turning to Thomas More, Edward asked slyly, "So Thomas, has Morton made you a priest yet?"

"No," Thomas More laughed, "not yet. Though I admit, I've thought about it."

"Well," Edward guffawed, "what does your father say?"

"He isn't happy," responded Thomas with a wince.

"No, I imagine not," joined in Howard.

"The Archbishop wants me to go to Oxford next year," More added hesitantly, unsure of the reaction this would receive.

"Oh, you are the proper little priest," Boleyn jeered.

"Well, father says he won't support it," Thomas said sadly.

"Your father is a smart man, Thomas," Henry Percy said in his usual gruff, Northern manner, "you should listen to him."

The conversation stalled there a bit, and the boys sort of milled there a bit.

Thomas Boleyn sidled up greasily in his white tunic of the Earl Stanley. "Edward," he said, "have you met the King's little sons yet?"

A guffaw from Henry Percy and Edward reddened, "Never miss a trick, Boleyn."

"All I'm asking," Boleyn replied calmly to the taunt, smiling, "is if the young Princes are well, but, now that I'm thinking of it…"

"Here it comes," said Edward softly."

Boleyn went on as if he hadn't noticed, "Buckingham here, you should see him at table. He can't pour water without spilling it."

Everybody, including Edward, laughed. "once…. I spilled water….ONCE." Then he softened, and smiled sweetly, "of course, it just had to be on the Archbishop."

The entire group looked incredulously at Thomas Boleyn. How had he known that? Boleyn was, by that point mimicking Edward dumping a pail of water on the Archbishop, who was swearing in Latin. Boleyn could be funny, and he was a wonderful linguist.

Edward laughed the loudest, "Thomas Boleyn, I swear that you have the soul of a pimp."

Thomas More looked around a little nervously to be sure the Archbishop had not exercised his uncanny ability to materialize out of thin air. He decided to change the subject. "Howard," he asked genuinely, "how, and what are you doing?" His smile was genuine.

Thomas Howard shifted, a little nervously, but then returned More's smile and replied, "My father is in command in the North. I am joining him soon. I am to be a soldier."

"A General!" replied Henry and Edward at once. "You will be brilliant at it too!" continued Edward.

Thomas Howard looked down nervously, and softly said "My father says 'it remains to be seen. The only way to know the true measure of a man is in battle." He paused and looked nervously around the room before adding, "after what happened to my father and grandfather..." he lowered his voice to a barely heard whisper, "at Bosworth," rising voice again, "I'm not so sure about being a soldier."

Thomas More remembered Howard's grandfather, his black coiled moustache, standing next to his King, Richard. He looked at Edward smiling happily.

"I wonder what happened to the Princes," he thought idly, for the thousandth time in the past seven years.

*"Why don't you ask your father?"* the voice.

"You know why. He told me to never bring it up again. Said it was safer that way."

*"That's probably true. Cardinal Morton and the Queen have made sidelong attempts to feel you out for information."*

"And it's probably best that I don't actually know anything beyond what I learned when I was seven years old."

*"You are a marvelous fellow, but a terrible liar."*

"Thanks. What about Edward, though. He must know more."

*"Ask him, sometime."*

"It's hard to get him alone."

*"The others are staring."*

The other boys had stopped talking and were looking at More. Just a pause. Thomas shook his head ruefully, and muttered, "Sorry." By now they were all used to that little stare from him.

Having an idea, and wanting to divert, Thomas More brightened and asked, "Do you fellows have anything to do this afternoon?"

Howard replied immediately, "Do you have anything in mind?"

"Shooting the Bridge," said Thomas emphatically.

The others rocked back a bit. "Oooh, Thomas," said Edward, "when did you decide to die?"

"I've seen it done," replied Thomas, "and it's a rite of passage for all true London men."

"Bad idea," said Henry, "very bad idea...I've seen them fishing bodies from the Thames."

"How's that, Henry Percy from the North?" replied More, sweetly.

"For starters," said Edward, "I'm the only one here who knows how to swim."

"Well," replied Thomas, "that's what the boat's for."

King Henry the Second had commissioned the rebuilding of a sturdy and stable London Bride in 1209 as partial penance for his influence in the murder of Thomas Becket. In building the bridge the engineers had driven piles of elm trees deep into the riverbed in the shape of sharpened ellipses up to 34 feet wide. The engineers had then filled in the ellipses with stone and gravel to create small islands crossing the river like giant stepping stones. On these islands, or starlings, the massive piers of the bridge had been built supporting the arches.

Almost immediately after construction had been completed, and in true London fashion, commerce had taken over and houses and shops, always shops, had been built the whole length of the bridge. The bridge had houses from one end to the other, following the City with shops on the ground floor, and living areas above. Over time these homes had extended out over the water with each added story. Toilets were generally placed in these over-water extensions, allowing for direct discharge into the Thames.

On the Southwarke side of the bridge, opposite the main body of the City, there was a massive gate house, built of yellowed, ragstone. This, well, castle, had a crenelated top, and housed the gatekeepers, who were responsible for the timbered portcullis and gates that had, to Thomas's constant amazement, actually repelled invaders during the Peasant Revolt, and, more recently, during Jack Cade's rebellion. Also, and Thomas More was never entirely sure how he felt about this, as a constant reminder of the authority of the King, the parboiled heads of traitors were prominently displayed atop the gatehouse, speared on long poles.

"Bridge dwellers," those who lived in the houses built on the bridge, were a group of Londoners all their own. At the peak of bridge living, there were 124 homes on the 900 foot bridge. They had their own ward and alderman, and, as nearly as Thomas could tell, rarely left the bridge for anything. They had eagle eyes for trouble as well. They were always on the lookout for fire, of course, and they watched the water below for trouble, such as a boy making a rash attempt on the rapids below their homes.

They also kept a lookout on the starlings, upon which their homes and livelihoods depended. These small islands suffered the constant erosions of the river flow around them, and they required continual maintenance. One of the engineering drawbacks of this manner of spanning a river was that the islands had the effect of creating a significant narrowing, and then turbulence of the flow of the river, particularly during high flow periods, such as the ebbing tide.

At London Bridge, the starlings were impressive, but the number, nineteen, and size of these islands narrowed by three quarters the available width of the Thames at that sole point for water to flow. Under normal conditions this would create rapids. But add in that the Thames was tidal, and the rapids created at an ebbing tide at the bridge could be truly terrifying. So naturally young men would want to take a boat and "shoot the rapids" to prove their manhood. There was a valid reason that the watermen had divided into above the bridge and below the bridge specialists and had landing points so people could walk around the bridge safely.

Therein lay the fun of shooting London Bridge in small boats. Shooting the bridge involved taking a small boat and poling it down the Thames, and then riding the boat in the violent rapids between the starlings. Arms were broken; people drowned; boats were overturned; lacerations; cuts. Despite, or perhaps because of, these risks, shooting the bridge remained a steadfast rite of passage for young London men, who would ride these rapids to prove their fearlessness, to exult in a very fast ride, really as quickly as anyone could travel. If they survived the passage, they would emerge from the Thames a true Londoner.

Because shooting the bridge was so dangerous, it was very much frowned upon by civic authorities, which meant, of course, that it was both a more attractive feat, and that it needed to be planned stealthily, and executed quickly, impetuously. Obviously these competing needs required skillful coordination, or, more frequently, dumb luck to achieve a successful run.

The five boys stood still, comprehending what Thomas More was proposing.

"Shoot the bridge?" asked Thomas Boleyn, incredulously. "Today?"

"It will be ebb tide in about two hours," replied Thomas More, with greater confidence in his voice that he felt.

"I'm not sure we're old enough," remarked Henry Percy nervously.

"Oh, come on," said Thomas More, as he laughed, saying, "fellows, this will be fun!"

"If we live," commented Boleyn.

"And if we don't, people will tell stories of our courage forever," said More. "What's life without a little risk?"

"Life preserved," said Howard.

"Well, then, who wants to live forever?" asked Thomas exuberantly.

"I do," the other boys replied quickly and in unison.

"Well, I'll tell you what," said More, "I will do it, and you guys watch. Then, if you decide you want to do it, I will do it with you again. How about that?"

He paused as the other boys absorbed that. Boleyn, in particular appeared to be doing an in depth risk calculation on the prospect. Edward Stafford appeared conflicted, genuine concern for his friend on his face.

Henry Percy snorted, "I am not a Londoner, and if taking a boat past a bridge is what qualifies for manhood down here, I'm content with Northern bravery."

Thomas More ignored that, and added reasonably, "You lot can watch from the foot of St. Thomas's Chapel. That seems fitting since so many of us are named Thomas. Maybe, then, while you are all sitting there on your arses, you can see what it means to be a real Londoner." He paused for a second and looked at Percy before finishing, "and with more respect." He nodded and smiled at the others.

In the center of London Bridge was St. Thomas's Chapel, dedicated to the Patron Saint, and lifelong Londoner, Thomas Becket, from Wood Street. One block west of the Milk street homes of both the More's and the Staffords. It was built on the central pier, and this chapel in particular was very important, because chapel donations paid a good portion of the maintenance costs of the bridge, through the bridge corporation of the City. Descending the chapel stairs after entering at the level of the deck of the bridge, one exited through a small door out onto the starling itself. Watermen had been known for years to use this door and the chapel during the day, when the tide and flow were right, to get a little physical as well as spiritual refreshment.

It was important, though, that the tidal flow be right, because the water rapids of the bridge at peak flows were also fastest at that point, and it took a very skillful waterman to be able to dock at that point. Generally, what they would do is get out of the channel and try to swing their boat around by that lead point of the ellipse of the starling. If they missed that point, the current would sweep them through the channel and, if they didn't capsize, they could swing out of the current and dock at the opposite point. Two chances to dock.

Since the chapel starling was the largest of the bridge, and in the relative center, the currents were fastest there. Thomas had already decided to attempt the bridge at that channel. He had also already acquired a small boat from a friend in the Cardinal's service. Giving the other boys a chance to get out to the bridge, Thomas slowly made his way out to his hidden boat at the side of the Lambeth Palace pier. He climbed gingerly into the small, tippy boat and slowly began to paddle to the center of the river.

The other boys had set off at a run from Lambeth Palace, along Harbor Wall Road, through the Paris Garden and its fields, onto Maid Lane, and through the Borough of Southward and its stews. They had just entered the courtyard of St. Mary Overy when Thomas Boleyn suddenly stopped, panting, and looking at the narrow door of a brothel. He reflexively felt his purse along the left side of his belt. Grinning sheepishly, he left the three other boys and made his way to a girl, dressed in garish rags, smeared makeup on her pock marked face, who was leaning suggestively against the door jam. He turned from the girl back to the boys, and gave a little shrug, then disappeared into the rundown building.

Howard, Percy, and Stafford, panting heavily, stared in disbelief at Boleyn.

"Well, that was unusual," said Stafford. "And still in Stanley livery."

"just like him," said Thomas Howard, red in the face both from running and from blushing about Boleyn.

Henry Percy just grunted, rubbed his tongue between his upper lip and teeth. His thick eyes squinted towards the now empty doorway.

"We've got to get to the bridge!" said Edward, catching his breath.

The three remaining boys started off again, and after exiting the western gate of St. Mary Overy churchyard and going up a little hill, past the Tabard Inn, they entered Bridge Street. They went through the large, open portcullis, under the severed heads. Edward gave a shiver, remembering his father's head on a pole to the left of the gate. Today there were, thankfully, no faces any of the boys recognized. They continued along the narrow alley between three and four story houses, shop stalls open, around groups of people. They reached the door of the Chapel, pushed through, ran down the stairs around two startled priests in black cassocks. They pushed another door open and passed back outside onto the starling and its surface of white stone covered with moss. The tide was ebbing and the Thames water rushed past them, heaving and churning noisily about three feet below the stones upon which they stood.

They were just in time. Thomas More was about 200 yards upriver of their channel, and was picking up speed. He was clad in a leather jerkin and a black shirt. He had, thankfully, remembered to remove and hide the Archbishop's livery. There were small crowds on either shore, that had noticed the attempt, and were pointing excitedly.

Thomas Howard looked out at Thomas More in his little boat and muttered, "This is a really bad idea.

More's boat continued to pick up speed, and he waved unsteadily from his small, accelerating boat. He had an enormous smile on his face. When the main current of this particular break in the starlings securely caught the boat, Thomas stood up and, balancing delicately, he raised his arms into the air and yelled joyously, "I am Thomas More, son of John More. I am London born and bred, and I claim this bridge!"

Forgetting worry, the other boys on the starling laughed and clapped. Thomas continued to balance, his feet now spread apart, in a little crouch, arms out, as the boat passed the lead point of the starling. Thomas was still whooping as the boat whipped through the channel, past then. The boys held their breaths. All was going well until just as he was about to exit the channel, a reflected wave hit the boat on the right side, and the boat flipped sideways, pitching Thomas into the rough water at the exit.

"Oh, damn," said Edward as he moved quickly down the starling.

Thomas's head bopped up once as he splashed and thrashed. The current carried him and the overturned boat down into the calmer water. Thomas sank again under the water.

Edward was off in a flash, ripping off his red tunic and kicking off his boots. He dove into the water, and swam straight to where Thomas had just gone under. Grabbing him by the hair, he pulled More's sputtering head to the surface, released the hair, and grabbed him by the upper arm, holding his head out of the water.

"Kick your feet you stupid git," hissed Edward.

Thomas, his breathing slowing as he relaxed a bit in his friend's grip, developed a wide smile. As they reached the overturned boat, he turned to his back a little, learning, in a way to swim. Thomas exhaled and stated simply, "that was great."

"Well, you'd be fish food right now if a merciful God hadn't intervened," Edward sputtered through the last chops on the river.

"I'd be fish food right now if you hadn't intervened," Thomas replied. "Thank you Edward."

The other boys left the starling, scrambling back up through the chapel. They had managed to remember to grab Edward's boots and Royal tunic before departing.

Thomas laughed as they floated gently downstream, holding onto the boat. Edward, with the sure strokes of a confident swimmer began to cut across the stream to the Southwarke side of the river. Already, the houses on that side of the river were thinning out, leaving a green field. Across the river, the white turrets of the Tower of London loomed over the river, traitor's gate, the opening in the river wall of the tower that was the last port of entry for traitors to the tower, could be seen.

Thomas involuntarily shuddered at that view and floundered a bit. Edward notices, and said kindly, "Relax and you'll float better," adding, "though personally, I think the river believes you too stupid to want to drag under."

"Perhaps," Thomas grinned, "but I did it! I shot the bridge."

With a grunt, Edward pushed Thomas up onto the hull of the boat. A small crowd had gathered on the bridge, watching, and they broke into applause when Thomas was safely on the boat.

"If you attempt to bow, I believe that I will kill you," said Edward, with a happy smile on his face. He waved at the crowd. The crowd, realizing that the drama was over began to disperse.

Edward and Thomas began to lazily kick from the boat towards the Southwarke side of the river. The sky was a beautiful, cloudless blue and the air was warm. Thomas asked gingerly, "Edward, my friend, how are you doing?"

Edward, surprised, immediately answered, "fine." He softened immediately upon looking at Thomas, and said softly, "I'm really fine, Thomas. Thank you for asking me. The Queen is kind to me, and I am slowly getting a grasp of my family situation. My mother doesn't help all that much, but since she married the King's uncle, at least there is some…some family protection for me."

Edward's face broke a bit. "The King keeps taking my money. I'm a minor and his ward, so I can do nothing. He married me off to Alinor Percy two years ago when I was 12. He took the Percy dowry, and then made me pay the scutage, but since she she and Henry's father was killed, they are the King's wards as well, so he took their money too. So basically, at age 12 I paid five thousand pounds, a king's ransom, to be married to a girl I hardly knew. I don't actually care about the money, but it bothers me. I'm worried that he tries to push me into making a mistake. So he can hurt me, hurt my family.  So I let him do what he wants" He shuddered a bit, and stole a small glance at the unfamiliar heads on the pikes of London Bridge.

Thomas listened. His face impassive.

Edward leaned in close, and said in a whisper, despite their still being in the Thames, slowly working their way to shore, "he keeps trying to find out what happened to my cousins, the Princes."

Thomas was surprised. "Doesn't their sister, his Queen, know?" he asked.

"No," he replied quietly. "And she told me quite firmly," raising his voice to a gentle falsetto, "'it is my understanding that my Uncle, the Evil usurper King Richard, disposed of my two brothers somewhere in the tower.'" Edward paused, then continued in his normal voice, "all the while she was nodding her head at me."

Thomas let that sink in, before saying, in a whisper, "my father and I have never spoken about that day and the Princes. I tried once, after Richard died, and he simply said, 'Thomas, it's best you don't know anything.'"

"Probably true," said Edward.

"I think they must be safe," said Thomas. "and I think that your cousin, the Queen, is right. It is best for all that evil King Richard killed them." He thought for a second, and added, with a laugh, "that evil, misshapen usurper excuse for a King."

"Long live King Henry," Edward responded laughing, "savior of Britain."

"There you go," Thomas said.

Thomas Howard and Henry Percy had managed somehow to extricate themselves from the clutches of the Brothers of Saint Thomas Bridge, the traffic on the bridge, and the maze of alleys on the eastern side of Bridge Street that would let them out of the narrow spaces between buildings and onto the downstream field below the bridge. They picked the spot on the shore where it appeared More and Stafford were headed on their overturned boat.

Thomas Howard whooped, calling out, "That, gentlemen, was EXCELLENT!"

Henry Percy grunted happily and stuck his hands in his pockets.

Thomas and Edward got the boat close enough to shore that they could stand in the mud and slowly began pushing the boat the rest of the way in. Howard and Percy came out and grabbed either end and lifted the boat out of the water, flipping it upright and setting it back down.

The people on the bridge were clapping, and Thomas, now safely on land, bowed deeply to the crowd. While he was bent, the other three boys happily pushed him over back into the river. The crowd clapped harder and laughed for a moment, then began to disperse.

Howard and Percy grabbed the boat again, and brought it ashore, still smiling. Edward, smiling extended a hand to More to help him up, and quietly said to Thomas More so the other two couldn't hear, "Thomas, it is important to live."

"Edward," said More, accepting the hand, and rising from the Thames, wet and muddy, with seagrass clinging to his clothes, "my dear friend and my savior. It is unimportant if one lives or dies. It is critical, however, that one lives well."

The Archbishop, John Morton, had regular meetings with each of his pages and felt a personal responsibility as a mentor to each. He took seriously his role in guiding them and advising them. His hope, clearly was to guide them into proper priesthood and leadership of the church, of service to their King.

The day after shooting London Bridge, Thomas had one of his regular meetings with the Archbishop. For this meeting Thomas had made very sure that his livery, his blue and silver tunic and black underclothes were perfectly clean, and that he had washed, being very careful to get the Thames mud from the day before out of his hair, and out from behind his ears.

Thomas approached the Archbishop, head bowed. The Archbishop relaxed in his chair upon seeing Thomas, and suppressed a smile. His hooded eyes danced as Thomas came near. "There's a rumor you've been boating, Thomas," Morton said cheerfully.

Thomas held up his approach, abashed. What had the Archbishop heard? "The River is the life of the City, My Lord Archbishop," Thomas replied cautiously.

"Well answered, Thomas," laughed Morton, "neither a denial nor a confession. A diversion to a different truth."

Thomas studied his feet.

"Who told?" he thought.

*"Who told?"* the voice, *"Thomas, my young friend, you did it in front of the entire City of London. You announced your name to all who could hear. The Archbishop would have to be a complete moron not to have heard."*

"He is certainly not a moron. Do you think father knows?"

*"I'd be surprised if he didn't. One question, though."*

"Yes?"

*"Was it worth it?"*

"Yes. Oh my Lord, yes."

"Then it will all be right. You are an interesting fellow, Thomas More."

"Thomas," the Archbishop shifted looking at Thomas suddenly a little oddly, "you are a remarkable boy, and I believe you are marked to be a great man. I wonder at times when you stare off for a moment thinking as to what is going on in that head of yours, but I believe that is your secret." The Archbishop grinned conspiratorially and then, himself stared off for a moment as if in a reverie.

"He knows?" Thomas thought.

*"maybe he hears me too."*

The Archbishop straightened, and gave Thomas a little wink. He grunted a bit, then said in a low voice, "It is important, of course, to make sure the voice is who you think it is.."

Thomas started, not sure he had heard the Archbishop correctly. And started to ask, but the Archbishop cut him off with a hand wave, and then continued, in his normal voice, "Thomas, you can be of incredible service to God, and to your King and England. Your talents are remarkable, as is your....I think the work is *elan*." He paused at that and smiled indulgently at Thomas, who reddened.

"So my first question for you," the Archbishop continued," is, Thomas have you considered Holy Orders? With your talents you could be a great Priest, Archbishop, and Lord Chancellor."

Thomas shook his head a bit, processing, thinking, "Well, that didn't go in the direction I'd expected."

*"It is easier sometimes, Thomas, to assume that people like you and want to help you rather than the reverse."*

"yes, but do you think he knows about the bridge?"

*"Of course he knows, Thomas. Why do you think he is talking to you about your future? You proved yourself in his eyes. You took a big risk.*

Thomas lifted his eyes and studied the benignly smiling John Morton. He loved the old Archbishop. Respected him. Wanted to be like him. But his father had worried to him that this question would one day come. Had told him he would disown him if he took the position. He was locked in to the family business.

Thomas cast his eyes back downward and considered his options.

"What should I do?"

*"What do you want to do?"*

"I want to be like Archbishop Morton."

*"Be your own person. You can never be Archbishop Morton. You will always be Thomas More."*

"My father demands I be a lawyer."

*"You are not John More either."*

What should I do?"

*"Be Thomas More. Love and trust"*

"Thomas?" enquired the Archbishop pleasantly.

"My father insists that I be a lawyer," answered Thomas.

"Which father?" asked Morton, continuing in a very genial tone.

"My father here on Earth, John More," answered Thomas, now smiling. "My father in heaven has not yet indicated what He wants."

"God sent you to me," said Morton, reasonably.

"Yes, but God has not yet told me what he wants. I am waiting for a sign," replied Thomas openly.

John Morton laughed easily at that, and replied, "that, my dear, dear Thomas, is entirely untrue, and also an easy route unworthy of your gifts." He steadied his gaze directly into Thomas's eyes, put his right hand on Thomas's shoulder and asked, "but what do you want?"

"What do I want?" thought Thomas

*"Interesting question."*

"I really want more time."

"Hmmm."

Thomas's face broadened, and he returned the Lord Chancellor's gaze, and said, honestly, "More time." Only he put a slight emphasis on More.

The Archbishop broke into a hearty laugh. "Very well, my young page. Then More time you shall have. Do you think I can convince your father to allow you two more years of education under my care?"

"I don't know," stammered Thomas. "He seems pretty insistent."

"Well," replied John Morton, chuckling, "we shall see if my positions as Lord Chancellor and Archbishop of Canterbury have any sway with him."

He paused, thought for a few seconds, and then continued, "it's just that I see a lot of myself in you Thomas, and your term with me ends soon, coincidentally on St. Thomas's day, July 7. I would like more time with you as well. I would like you to consider going to Oxford."

"I would love to do that," said Thomas, immediately and enthusiastically.

"The work is hard," cautioned Morton.

"Yes," said Thomas, "but I could study languages there."

"You do have a facility for that," said the Archbishop, "at least judging by your Latin. And your French. And your Spanish. You should try Greek. Different letters. Lucian was Greek. You have, as I recall, a special affinity for him." Morton winked.

Thomas warmed rapidly to the idea. His hopes rising.

"I could go to Oxford?" he thought. "Father will be pissed."

*"He'll get over it. And he will be happy for you."*

"Oxford?!?!?!"

The Archbishop continued. "If you went to Oxford under my care, you would study at Canterbury College. They have six novices a year."

Thomas looked up, a vague panic on his face, before the Archbishop continued quickly, "Of course we wouldn't call you a novice within hearing of your father." He paused and smiled, continuing, and you are, of course, under no obligation to take orders."

Thomas considered rapidly.

*"See what I mean about not burning bridges."*

"Is it possible? I could go to Oxford?

*"Of course it is, Thomas. And the Archbishop is as good as his word on this. You don't have to make a decision. Just do what he wants. And, of course, remember to let people love you."*

"I will gladly do this, My Lord Archbishop," Thomas burst out with happiness.

The Archbishop laughed with joy, slapping his knee. "Brilliant, Thomas More of London! Canterbury is a small school. It's no Magdalen, but it is run by the monks of Christ Church, Canterbury."

"Will they accept me?" asked Thomas with a little anxiety.

"I'm the Abbot of the monks of Christ Church, Canterbury," replied John Morton with a conspiratorial grin.

Thomas stopped and studied him. "I will still need my father's permission."

"I've already spoken with him," said Morton happily. "He's not particularly happy. He thinks I'm stealing you for the church. He's suspicious of me. But that's fine. I'm the Lord Chancellor. Among other things, I collect money for the King. Everyone is suspicious of me." Morton paused happily, laughed, then continued, "your father agreed to two years, after which you will study law. Our deal. Of course a lot can happen in two years," and he winked at Thomas. "He even agreed to send you with a little bit of money."

"How did you do that?" asked Thomas, impressed.

"I am the Archbishop of Canterbury and the Lord Chancellor of England. I am King Henry's best friend. I was great friends with the late King Edward and swore to help protect his children." He paused slightly for effect, looking directly at Thomas, who gave an involuntary start. "In short, I am very persuasive. Even to a London lawyer." And he laughed his deep laugh.

Thomas looked worried.

"Don't worry about your father, Thomas," said Morton gently, reading his face. "You are a very special young man, and your father did not need any convincing in that regard. He wants what is best for you."

"Is father in trouble?" thought Thomas

*"The Archbishop said he wasn't and he isn't."*

"Father agreed to money?"

*"Oxford is a big honor, but don't expect a lot of money. The family doesn't have it."*

"No. It's not that. It's just that if he agreed to any money, then he must think it is important."

*"There you go. Let people love you, and love them in return."*

Morton waited patiently while Thomas processed his news, then added gently, "Thomas, there are two more things I want you to do for me."

"Anything, my Lord Archbishop," said Thomas enthusiastically, stars in his eyes.

The Archbishop grinned, "Thomas, regardless of how you are called, lawyer, priest, Archbishop or Lord Chancellor, you should never agree to 'anything,' before hearing what is asked, even to me." He paused before continuing, "but I still appreciate your enthusiasm." Another pause. A paternal smile. Then continued, "Since God has not yet revealed to you whether you are to be priest or lawyer, and since your term as my page ends on St. Thomas's day, and since I must be in Canterbury for the Feast, I want you to make the Pilgrimage and meet me there. Put your trust in God."

"A pilgrimage, My Lord?" asked Thomas.

"No, Thomas," corrected Morton heartily, happy with his sudden inspiration. "The Pilgrimage. Thomas Becket. Chaucer. The Knight. The Pardoner. The wife of Bath." He gave a wink at Thomas which caused the 14 year old boy to blush. "The Pilgrimage, Thomas." He continued. "And while you're on it, Thomas, I want you to pray to God for guidance on a calling." Another conspiratorial nod to Thomas.

"Thomas Becket's tomb," whispered Thomas with awe.

"I believe you've heard of him," laughed Morton. "Thomas. Of London born. There's a nice little Chapel on London Bridge dedicated to him."

Thomas ignored the thrust and said excitedly, "I hear that you can really see his body!"

"And, with that, be cured of any disease," said the Archbishop, nodding solemnly.

"I don't have a disease," replied Thomas.

"Too literal, Thomas," laughed the Archbishop. "Sometimes I forget that you are still only fourteen."

Thomas stood a little taller with pride, his page's uniform ruffling as he drew his shoulders back.

"You will leave Lambeth here on the second of July, and go to St. Thomas Acre on the Bridge," said the Archbishop, then a pause and a twinkle, "I believe you know the church. It has a door leading to the starling where the watermen land."

Thomas smiled in return to the Archbishop's amused stare. He still said nothing.

The Archbishop let the moment pass. "You will then go to the Tabard and meet up with other Pilgrims. You will make your way in prayer, making sure to arrive by the morning of the Feast on July seventh. Follow the Pilgrim's path. You are to throw your fate to God's divine mercy. And maybe, my young page, just maybe, during that time, God will tell you that he wants you to be an Archbishop."

Thomas giggled happily, then asked, "and the second thing?"

Ah, yes," said Morton. "When you get to Oxford, I want you to look up a young priest for me named Wolsey. He is thought to be a rising star there, and I want you to tell me what you think of him."

Thomas looked serious. "Me sir?" Thomas asked skeptically.

"Yes," said the Archbishop firmly. "You're young and beardless, but I have watched you and I trust your judgement of people. You appear to have an insight, the source of which you keep to yourself."

Thomas remained still.

The Archbishop laughed merrily, and waved his hand in Thomas's direction. "It's a wonderful gift, that very few of us have." He waved his hand then and said placidly, "Go away now, Thomas. I have work to do."

Thomas bowed himself out of the room, keeping an adoring eye on the smiling Archbishop.

Early in the morning on the second of July, as instructed, Thomas arrived at the Church of Saint Thomas Acre on the London Bridge. As was traditional, Thomas started his journey at this chapel on London Bridge in order to collect his Pilgrim's garments: a brown rough cloth robe, a knotted rope belt, sandals, and a small metal badge with the insignia of St. Thomas, to be worn on the robe as a pilgrim's livery badge. Thomas carried with him a small leather bag that his father had given him, grudgingly, for the journey with a few coins inside.

The chapel was part of the English military order of the Knights Hospitaliers of Saint Thomas, founded by King Richard the First on Crusade at Acre in memory of his father's Archbishop and Lord Chancellor, Thomas Becket. The monks and members of the order wore white robes emblazoned with red outlined crossed with white interiors. These monks, tending their chapel, felt strong ownership of the legacy of Thomas Becket, and because the chapel was so significant in support of the Bridge, of the Bridge itself.

In short, they were insufferable.

Thomas was certain that the monks recognized him from his run of the Bridge, but they gave no overt sign. Just looks, and head shakes. But then, as Thomas was cinching on his new knotted belt over his simple tunic, leaving his other clothes behind, and was attaching his money bag to the belt, the Prior approached Thomas with his hand out.

"Young man," he said sternly, that steel undermined with a high, reedy pinched voice with a vaguely supercilious country accent, "you are travelling as a Pilgrim. That means you put your faith in God for your subsistence." He moved his hand, palm up, towards Thomas's purse.

"I don't understand," said Thomas hesitantly.

"Yes, I do, you," thought Thomas. "Monk."

*"Think of it as a toll...Or maybe penance."*

"But it's my money."

*"You are on pilgrimage. You don't have or need money. Everything will be provided if you put your faith in God. And no more 'monk' nonsense. There are rules. Some people follow rules very loosely. Others do not."*

"It's my money."

*"A tantrum? Over a few coins? Neither auspicious nor loving Thomas. This monk of St. Thomas is sent here to ensure that the pilgrimage is of greatest effect in your heart. Accept this as love, not as theft....Though it could easily also be theft."*

Thomas laughed inwardly, and externally smiled.

"Young man," the monk repeated impatiently, hand still out, "our instructions from the Archbishop are that you are to place your fate in God's hands' you are to trust in Him completely. That you are to beg alms and be completely dependent on His divine mercy."

"Beg alms? No one said anything about that.

*"That's because you didn't consider what 'put your trust in God' really meant. If you are going to be a lawyer Thomas, you really need to be considering the meanings of words...Besides, this for your benefit."*

"This can't be happening."

"But..." tried Thomas, attempting a charming smile, before he was cut off.

"Hand over the purse," said the Prior firmly.

"But..." repeated Thomas.

"Hand over the purse," the prior repeated, now angrily.

Reluctantly, Thomas did relinquish his money, giving it to a Prior he still could only see as both smug and mean.

After Thomas relinquished the bag, only then did the Prior give Thomas his Pilgrim's badge, a small brass badge with a sharp pin consisting of a bust of Thomas in his Archepiscopal mitre, surrounded by a six pointed fleur. Thomas immediately pinned that to his brown robe front. The priest then gave Thomas a small printed map of the Pilgrim's way. He pointed out the route to Thomas in a disinterested, rote way. Thomas could see the drawings of the Bridge and the Tabard Inn, a little up Bridge Road on the left. The map followed Watling Street out of Southwarke, south through Rochester. The abbeys and way stations were marked. The same route of Chaucer a hundred years before.

As the priest was droning on, Thomas's mind wandered as he looked at the tight stones of the walls of the bridge church. He could hear the water rushing by underneath, and he felt a vague satisfaction, bordering on smugness as he remembered his river run. There was also a nervous cavern in his stomach as he contemplated the trip to Canterbury, alone, now penniless, and already hungry.

The walk to Canterbury started simply enough. Thomas headed up from the lower level of the church, and emerged into the sunlight of the London Bridge. Taking his leave of the Bridgemonks, who waved Thomas off with disinterested, but amused waves, Thomas turned right and walked south on the Bridge, past the stalls, shops and tippy houses that crowded either side of the Bridge, and which cast deep shadows across the crowds of pedestrians making their ways to and fro across the Thames.

Thomas's pilgrim attire drew some smiles from some of the shoppers. A couple of the stalls were selling roasted meats, which inflamed Thomas's youthful hunger. He was fourteen and it had been over an hour since he had last eaten. He wished desperately that someone would come up and offer him some food, what with his Pilgrim garb and all, but no one did. He couldn't yet bring himself to ask yet for either help or food.

"I'm hungry," he thought, looking longingly at a roasted beef haunch on a spit.

*"Ask for some."*

"I can't. What if they say no."

*"Then you will still have no meat. Haven't really turned yourself over yet, have you?"*

"Maybe it would be more holy to fast for the Pilgrimage."

*"So you don't have to turn yourself over for the trip? So you are willing to be both hungry and in defiance of the entire purpose of the pilgrimage? And the Archbishop's command?"*

Thomas's stomach rumbled loudly, and he flushed a bit, then picked his way slopingly through the moving crowd towards the south end of the Bridge and Southwarke. Just before the end of the Bridge was the large stone gate house with the heavy, reinforced iron gate drawn up. Remaining on the top of the gate house were the spiked poles with the boiled heads of traitors impaled at the tops. Relief. Still no one he knew. Thomas involuntarily shuddered, as he always did, at the sight of the ravens pecking residual flesh from the skulls.

After passing through the gate, Thomas headed up a little hill as Bridge became High Street for Southwarke. The crowds thinned only a little. Thomas was tempted at first to head right up Bankside, past the stews and theaters towards Lambeth Palace, his home of the past several years in his service as Page to the Archbishop. His coarse pilgrim robe chafed already on his skin in a way that his page's uniform never had.

"I will renege on the pilgrimage," Thomas thought. "Tell the Archbishop 'I have reconsidered and don't care to go to Oxford, thank you very much.'"

*"You will be fine, relax. Trust."*

"I'm alone and afraid." Words never to be uttered aloud.

*"You are never alone. I am here."*

"That's not what I meant."

*"I know, but I'm still here with you. And this congenial looking crowd of pilgrims too."*

"I don't want to do this."

*"Why?"*

"Because it's stupid."

*"You are much better than that argument. You are simply nervous. Trust. Love."*

"Easy for you to say. You're not walking to Canterbury. You also do not appear to eat."

*"Yes... Still, keep going straight."*

"Yes, what? I'm hungry."

*"yes to trust and love. And by the by, you are always hungry."*

Thomas smiled. That was true. He did seem always to be hungry. He closed his eyes and willed the gnawing in the pit of his stomach away. It eased a bit. The butterflies remained. Opening his eyes, he looked up the narrow, cobblestone street. He took in the rows of inns and taverns, the Gorge, the White Hart, the King's Head, the Queen's Head, the Bull and Bear, the Tabard. Each inn had half-timbered walls, a balcony leaning over the street, and a wide posted arched gateway in the center that led back to stables for travelers. The distinguishing feature of each inn or tavern was their sign, relating to their name, in the Tabard's case, a shirt without sleeves.

Thomas noted several members of the crowds outside each of the inns clustered in nervous little groups, dressed, like Thomas, in pilgrim attire. They too seemed unsure about beginning the adventure, trapped in small bubbles of journey-pride. Idly wondering how each had made the selection of a particular inn, what attracted a person to the Queen's Head over, say, the King's Head or the Tabard, Thomas caught several of the about to be pilgrims eyeing the tavern doors with longing. To his surprise, he even saw a few sadly pull off their pins, shake their heads sadly, and go back in. Decisions made.

Thomas made his way up the hill and in a few blocks he was out of the shadow of the big Church, St. Mary Ovarie, and the businesses and buildings thinned rapidly. The manor of the Bishop of Winchester spread with verdant green to his left. The road widened, and at some gradual transition became Watling Street, the ancient Roman road to Dover. And to Canterbury. Horses and carts tumbled past with loud clapping noises of their wheels on the tight, stable stones, still in great condition after a millennium and a half of hard use.

Very quickly, Thomas was out of Southwarke and into the country. The road turned to the left, and then became straight for as far as the eye could see. There was garbage and litter, filth of all kinds, pushed to the sides of the road, and pigs were getting fat on the refuse. Thomas smiled at the pigs, and made a little St. Anthony's oink.

Apparently, the casual parting with garbage had been going on for some time, because the ancient road was largely in its own sort of valley, with built up hills on either side - hedgerows, surmounted by copses of small, wild cherry trees. Happily for Thomas, the cherries were ripe, or appeared to be nearly so, red on top near the stem, and yellow on the bottom.

The July sun was bright and hot, and Thomas was feeling more than ordinarily hungry, so he wasted no time in leaving the road and clambering up the hill to eat his fill.

The cherries were small and more sweet than sour, and Thomas quickly adopted a rhythm of pluck, stuff, bite, tongue to push the stone, spit the stone, chew the cherry, lick the juice off lips, and pluck again. Not too long after getting his rhythm, maybe twenty or so cherries later, Thomas felt his stomach rumble. He felt faint and nauseous. Thomas quickly scampered over the hill from the road in search of a bush he could crouch behind, and barely made cover and lifted his robe before the diarrhea hit.

*"Moderation in everything, Thomas."*

"Funny."

Black flied quickly swarmed over Thomas's mess and rapidly made what appeared to be an organized, concerted attack on the source at Thomas's backside. With a high pitched yelp, Thomas ran, still trying to hold up his brown tunic, swatting his behind madly. He spotted a small creek, a small sign identifying it as "Peck stream,", and gratefully sat in the cool running water. The flies abated, seemingly disappointed by their target now and flew off. Thomas's clothes wicked water up to his chest, and scratchy or not, Thomas didn't care.

*"Feeling a mite peckish?"*

"What?"

*"Never mind. It's not worth repeating. You will eventually find it to be funny."*

"Probably not. I want to go home."

*"Give it time."*

Thomas heard giggles from behind him, and turned to see that he had, in his panic, jumped into the stream about a hundred feet

from a small stone bridge, crossing the river and supporting a small road going into the town of Peckham. Three little girls stood on the bridge, pointing and laughing at Thomas. Thomas quickly pulled down his tunic to cover himself. He gave the girls a helpless shrug and a smile, which only caused them to laugh harder. Gathering his remaining dignity, Thomas strode out of the river and, slipping and sliding with his wet sandals and robe, climbed up the bank, back up the hill, and down to the road, which still had a scattering of brown robed pilgrims, in addition to the horse, market, and other traffic.

As Thomas slowly walked to the south-east, a larger percentage of the travelers were pilgrims, on the road for the distance. Some were alone, some in little groups. Some of the other pilgrims were laughing, talking and carrying on. Some seemed dour or just miserable. A few solitary pilgrims seemed lonely and sad, lost in thought. A noisy few cried, or prayed aloud.

"If they're like that at the beginning of the pilgrimage," Thomas thought, "how are they going to be at the end?"

*"Be charitable. Love and Trust."*

The group of pilgrims continued to snake along the ancient road, passing through the picturesque village of Deptford. There was an old, arched bridge at Deptford, crossing the small Ravensbourne river. Blocking traffic at the side of the road leading onto the bridge, an old woman lay weeping hysterically, curled on her side in the fetal position, crying loudly, "Saint Thomas, pray for me! Oh, pray for me!"

Astride her, standing angrily with his hands on his hips, was a man Thomas presumed was her husband. He was alternating between looking angry at her and embarrassed by the passing crowds, as he hollered, "for God's sake, woman, get a hold of yourself!"

With an effort, Thomas moved on across the bridge beyond the couple without laughing.

Thomas wondered if he should try to join a group, or just pray silently to himself.

"How does one make a pilgrimage, anyway?" he thought.

*"It depends upon the Pilgrim."*

"No, I mean do you go it alone, or form a little group? Do I pray aloud, or silently? What's the best prayer to say on Pilgrimage?"

*Again, it depends on the Pilgrim. Listen quietly. Listen for the Holy Spirit. The Spirit will guide you to a proper Pilgrimage."*

"So you counsel relaxing?"

*"In this and in so many things, Thomas. Let the Spirit fill you. Trust. You will find your answer. That is what pilgrimage is all about."*

After a while, the sun began to bake the hot summer landscape, particularly on the ancient white road stones. Thomas pulled off the road at a small abbey, where he spied a well, and an unoccupied shade tree. He dipped some water from a bucket, and rested in the shade. He smiled for a while as the arguing couple appeared, the woman more composed, but still praying loudly for all to see, and hear, her piety. A group of four monks stopped to get a drink from the well, and eyed Thomas's shade. Reluctantly, Thomas arose, and gestured for them to take his place. The oldest nodded to Thomas gratefully and sank down next to the tree. Thomas wasn't ready to speak to other Pilgrims yet, and so he quickly set off down the road while the monks were still settling in.

Back on the road, occasionally a piper or a fiddler would emerge from a group of moving pilgrims and begin to play. The reasons for the sudden music were obscure to Thomas, but it did break the monotony of the walk, and so Thomas thought it, overall, a good thing. Some of the larger groups were also playing games, or dancing as they walked.

"They should be a little more reverential," Thomas thought sneeringly. "They're on Pilgrimage.

*"Love and trust are key here, Thomas. Those people love and trust enough that they are willing to have fun at the risk of being judged by the likes of you."*

Still Thomas kept his distance from some of the heartier folk.

Plodding along, Thomas found, was incredibly boring work. He tried valiantly to keep his mind on St. Thomas, or on God. His inner voice kept intervening.

*"Interesting clump of trees up ahead. Like some cherries?"*

"Shut up."

*"No. Have some fun. A Pilgrimage is supposed to be fun."*

"It's supposed to be uplifting."

*"And fun. Don't be such a prig. Why do it if you don't enjoy it."*

"I'm not enjoying it."

*"Then why do it?"*

"Because the Archbishop told me to do it. Because doing it gets me in his good graces. Can get me to Oxford."

*"That is a sad, sad answer. Suppose you didn't do what he asked?"*

"Then no Oxford. No advancement."

*"Are you sure? How about another scenario-the Archbishop loves and likes you and he wants what is best for you. By doing what he asks, without reservation, you demonstrate that you like and respect him, and, most important, that you trust him. Is that so bad?"*

"You're the one who told me not to burn bridges."

*You'll listen to anyone, won't you?"*

"Go away. No. Come back. I didn't mean it. I hate Pilgrimages. Boring,. Boring. Boring.

"You still there?"

*"Yes. Are you done pouting yet?"*

Thomas smiled involuntarily.

"Almost. There. I'm smiling. See?"

*"I think pouting may be the worst sin. It combines a rich variety of other sins into one ugly package.*

"I am smiling."

*"Nearly convincing. Trust. There is a plan for you. For example, look. Up ahead. This is interesting."*

Slightly ahead, the side hills of the road were smoothed down for a long distance on both the left and right. Thomas saw avenues and lanes cutting off to the left. There was a large grove of trees, walnuts, limes, hemlocks.  Nearly a forest, but not quite and far better groomed. As he approached, Thomas saw that the near-forest was adjacent to a large park that lead to a palace made of light brown stone, nearly a hundred yards long.

The palace was mostly three and four stories tall along its great length, with a pointed slate roof and brightly colored flags flying from high points. Beyond the palace, Thomas could see the Thames, with innumerable ships and boats, white sails and colored pendants against the green of the landscape and bright blue sky.

Drawn to the beautiful scene, Thomas wandered off the road.

*"Pilgrimage, Thomas!"*

"In a minute. I just want to find out what this palace is."

*"Thomas, watch out!"*

Thomas walked towards the palace in a kind of daze. Oblivious to surroundings, Thomas was nearly run down by a boy and a girl, both on large horses.

"Pay attention, boy!" cried the horsed boy, quickly reining to avoid striking Thomas.

Thomas started from his reverie over the beauty of the Palace to jump sideways away from the horses, landing in a dirty brown woolen pile next to the road. Unhurt, he stood, about to respond angrily, quickly checking himself.

"Thomas!?" said a girl with a haughty surprised voice.

"Alinor?" said Thomas, suddenly recognizing Alinor Percy, now eighteen. His heart sank. He knew who the boy was. Didn't want to be seen like this.

Alinor Percy Stafford recoiled angrily in her saddle at Thomas using his name, and hissed, "boy, I am the Duchess of Buckingham. You will address me as 'Your grace.'"

The Duke of Buckingham, Edward Stafford, had succeeded in getting his horse under control, had not heard his wife, and had now recognized Thomas. "Oh, God…Thomas," cried Edward as he scrambled off his horse to help Thomas to his feet. "I almost killed you. I'm so sorry. But…what are you doing here? And why are you dressed like that?"

Thomas flushed bright red, embarrassed in front of his oldest friend. "The, ahh, Archbishop sent me on Pilgrimage," was all he could manage to say.

"And you went?" Alinor sneered incredulously, looking at his clothes, "like that?" Her lip curled for extra emphasis.

It's how Pilgrims dress," said Thomas defensively, yet still red faced. A long pause as she stared at Thomas, before Thomas dropped his eyes and added, "your Grace."

Edward started. "Your Grace?" His wife stared at him with dagger eyes. Edward elected to let that pass, and laughed genially, saying, "The Archbishop's got his hooks in you, for sure. Or is this punishment for shooting the Bridge?"

Thomas laughed and relaxed. He decided to ignore the Duchess. "No, he wants to send me to Oxford," Thomas said, looking at his friend's genial face, before quickly adding, "he wants me to become a priest, and Archbishop, and Lord Chancellor," again a pause, "but first I have to make this stupid pilgrimage."

"That's the spirit, Thomas," laughed Edward. "Yet if you're not going to perform the Pilgrimage well, then why bother?"

Thomas couldn't answer this and was silent.

*"I've always like Edward!" came the voice.*

Alinor suddenly filled the quiet, saying, "Well, I think that it's good to have Thomas doing a pilgrimage. He might learn his place, after all."

Edward's face betrayed his anger, and he immediately replied to Alinor, "Ali, you may be my wife, and you may be a Percy, but your father paid the King 4000 pounds for you to marry me. He didn't pay me. Thomas is my oldest friend. His 'place' as you call it is at my side, or wherever he wants it to be."

Alinor glared angrily now at both Edward and Thomas. Her eyes darkened and her face became as red as her hair. She paced back and for a little, thinking, then, pulling herself together, she angrily remounted her horse and rode off in a fury back towards the splendid Palace.

"I'm sorry, Edward," said Thomas sincerely, noting the chagrin on his friend's face. He took a leap. "Trouble in paradise?" he asked, looking at Alinor riding furiously away.

"Edward looked as if he were going to cry. His big, round face was pink. "The King demanded I marry her," he said quietly and sadly. "He restored my title and lands, but kept me as his Ward so he could steal from me. Mother was happy…They married me off at twelve. I'm now fourteen. Alinor is eighteen." He sniffed. "Everyone is always leering at me. Thomas

Boleyn keeps laughing at me. Alinor's brother, Henry, laughs at me too, but in a different, angrier way. I spoke to the King. Asked him what I was to do with a wife. The King laughed at me too. Then, everyone in his court felt that they could laugh as well."

Thomas listened sympathetically, placing a hand on Edward's shoulder. He too had no earthly idea. Wasn't entirely sure he wanted to know. He thought to divert his friend's attention.

"Edward," Thomas said suddenly, looking around, "where are we anyway?"

Edward looked startled, and asked incredulously, "You really don't know, Thomas?"

Thomas shook his head, laughing ruefully, happy to have moved Edward's mind to a more comfortable area. "No," he said, "I left London Bridge this morning, walked through Southwarke. Could have sworn I saw Thomas Boleyn going into the stews again, by the way." Thomas smiled, but immediately realized that it put Edward back to his question of what you were supposed to do with a girl, then hastened. "Since then I've been walking Watling Street all day. This map," Thomas waved his little Pilgrim's map, "is just useless. No idea where I am. I can see the river, though. Is this one of your castles, Edward?"

Edward laughed. "No, Thomas," he replied, "this is Placentia Palace. The King's Palace at Greenwich." He looked impressed with Thomas. "You're making pretty good time if you've made Southwarke to here." Do you want to come in?" Edward asked kindly, "My cousins, the two princes are here."

"The Queen is here as well," Thomas asked casually.

"No Thomas," Edward laughed, "the Queen is heavily pregnant at the palace at Sheen. To be delivered any day now."

Thomas was torn. He was very hungry again. Maybe, certainly. But then he looked down at his soiled clothes. Such as they were. He was dirty. He thought of Alinor, who was probably in the Palace throwing a fit about he and Edward right now. Making a decision, Thomas said reluctantly, "No…thanks. Not like this."

A glint appeared in Edward's eye, and he leaned in, saying in a very low voice, "You know, Thomas. Prince Arthur is very sickly, and the new baby Prince Henry isn't much healthier. The Queen is weak and ill, and just about to give birth again. I am the only Duke in the Realm. I could be King someday. If I am, then you will most definitely be my Archbishop and Lord Chancellor."

Thomas was moved, but very frightened on a basic animal level by his friend's thoughts. He whispered urgently, "Edward, you must be very careful."

Edward was taken aback, "I am," he said quickly, "but not with you. You've kept with me the biggest secret of the realm for seven years now." He winked at Thomas. "You've told no one, as nearly as I can tell. I know you can be trusted."

Thomas was moved by this, but still frightened, feeling a swimming in his head. He asked, very quietly, looking around nervously, "what happened to the Princes?"

It was Edward's turn to look about nervously. "Your father got them placed under assumed names. The Queen knew that they are alive from her mother before she passed a month ago. The King doesn't want to know, so long as they stay out of the way and don't make any moves."

"Perkin Warbeck and Lambert Simnel?" Thomas asked.

Edward laughed nervously. "Not even close," he replied. "They were efforts to flush out the true Princes. Since only a few know who they are, the plotters missed their mark wildly when the real Princes didn't budge from their spot."

"Archbishop Morton?" Thomas asked.

"Don't know," Edward replied. "He's a wily one. I presume that he does know, because he was great friends with the old Queen, the Princes' mother. For all I know he was part of the planning."

"I miss King Richard sometimes," Thomas said quietly.

"Now that is dangerous, Thomas." Edward said, taking a step back. "Do not ever say that aloud again." He thought for a moment, and then added, "and remember what Richard commanded, that he be thought a child murderer. It was the Princes' best hope."

The two mulled this over a moment, then Edward asked plaintively, "So what should I do with Alinor?"

"Get Thomas Boleyn to take you to the stews," Thomas said fiercely. "Find a nice girl there who will quietly teach you what you need to know. Then do, for God's sake, what she tells you!" Thomas and Edward both laughed uproariously. And nervously.

"Go back on pilgrimage, you monk!" Edward commanded, still laughing. "I need a Saint in my corner."

Thomas and Edward clasped arms in their old way, then reluctantly, Thomas returned to the dusty road, and restarted his pilgrimage. Standing stock still, looking sad, Edward watched his friend walk slowly out of sight.

Chapter 13 - July 2, 1492

By evening, Thomas was ravenously hungry. He could think of little beyond his knotted stomach. He kept walking. He wanted to make Dartford, where there was an abbey, before nightfall. Fortunately the July nights were quite short, and he had a few hours before it became dark. He still had neither idea nor plan as to how he was going to beg for a place to sleep and something to eat.

"Maybe they're supposed to just give me food and a bed." Thomas thought. "maybe I don't have to ask."

*"Maybe you've got peacock feathers growing out of your ears. Turn yourself over to God, to the goodness of others. Trust. Love. Ask."*

It was getting dark when he finally reached the abbey doors. They were closed. Thomas's legs ached, it seemed, from his toes to his hips. He had blisters across his feet from the sandals, and a sore area on the ball of his right foot where a persistent pebble had been lodged.

Thomas stood at the door, trying to will the door open without his having to knock. After a while, his hunger and fatigue overcame him, and he stepped forward and rapped.

After a moment, the door slid open a bit and a snakelike head appeared, with a matching voice, "yesssss?" The man, Thomas could see, was thin, with a pinched nose and face, topped by a tonsured head of black hair. "What isssss it you want, little boy," the monk lisped with a sneer.

"Little boy?" Thomas thought, "how dare he?"

*"Love...no matter how tired you are"*

Thomas's mind and pride raced. "I want nothing," he said defiantly, before adding, "and I am not a little boy."

*'Oh Thomas."*

136

"Well, then," asked the monk reasonably, "why are you here knocking on our door?" Then looking at Thomas's simple costume, and the dirt caked on the hem of the robe, adding, "by the way, nisssse attitude from a Pilgrim."

"*Thomas.*"

Thomas's heart was sinking. He was too tired to think precisely, but he knew this was not going the way he wanted.

"*Love and trust.*"

"Pride is a terrible thing, young man," said the monk sadly, as he began to slowly shut the heavy wooden door in Thomas's face.

"*I will second that Thomas. Love and trust. Maybe throw in some humility.*"

"No…wait," Thomas blurted. "I am sorry, kind sir. My name is Thomas More, and I am a pilgrim to Canterbury." He settled down a bit, "and I was hoping you might have a place I could sleep tonight."

"That's more like it," the monk said genially. "And I am Brother Will. Issss there anything elsssse you would like?"

"Some food, Please," Thomas said quickly and nervously, "if it's not too much trouble, Sir."

A kind of peace fell upon Thomas and he relaxed. His shoulders sagging with fatigue.

The monk studied Thomas shrewdly. "That was hard for you, Thomas More, wasssn't it?" he asked.

Thomas murmured a soft, "yes," and looked downward – embarrassed, anxious, tired, about to cry.

"You are on a pilgrimage, Thomas More," the monk asked, curious, "yet your are very young. What are you sssseeeking?" Healing? A girl?'

"Divine guidance," said Thomas heavily.

Brother Will laughed, "well I think food and a bed sssshould be easier to come by than that," and he opened the door to admit Thomas and said kindly, "come in, Thomas More."

Thomas entered the Abbey, looking around the entry hall with its pointed gothic arches. There were a few monks he saw down a left-hand corridor, and a cacophony of noise from the right that sounded like several of the hearty pilgrims who had passed him earlier.

"Thank you for your kindness, sir," Thomas said sincerely.

"The pilgrim'ssss quartersss, Thomas More, are up this way." He led Thomas down an arched corridor. "There is a basssin for washing. I noticed that you were by yoursssself. That's unusual in one ssso young."

There was a knock at the entry door behind them. The monk excused himself. "I mussst greet the next group." Then he added kindly, "why don't you go ahead into the dining hall and get yourself ssssomething to eat?"

Thomas nearly melted with gratitude, and started off towards the hall as the monk made towards the entry door, but then lingered, liking Brother Will, and needing company. As Thomas stood uncertainly, the monk noticed, and arched an eyebrow. "One thing I might sssssuggest, Thomas," he said gently, "is that you talk to other pilgrims. Learn their sssstories, why they are on pilgrimage."

Brother Will opened the heavy door. There was a group of hearty pilgrims standing blinking at the lights of the entry. "Good evening," he said. "What can I do for you?"

A large man, his chest bursting against his too small brown robe, the leader of the group, called out in his deep booming voice, redolent with a norther accent, "we are simple pilgrims to the shrine of Saint Thomas Becket in Canterbury. Brother, we beg your kindness for a night's bed and a little food."

"You are, of coursssse, welcome here as pilgrims," said Will with a little bow. As he bowed, he turned his head a little to the left, and gave Thomas a little wink. Straightening, he said to the group, "and may I introdussse you to another pilgrim? Young Thomas More," gesturing to Thomas with a small wave of his hand.

The big man eyed Thomas appraisingly, and asked with a knowing look, "the young boy who doesn't speak too much?" Then he laughed and clapped Thomas on the back, "yet a young boy on pilgrimage by himself, and that's brave enough!" They eagerly greeted Thomas, several of them calling out, "Come Thomas, be with us!" as they led him into the common dining hall. Passing Brother Will, Thomas shot him a thankful look.

Thomas's fatigue caught up with him during the meal. The group was enthusiastic, and stories from the day, and from lives very different from his own were told, but the stories were pale imitations of Chaucer, in fact, most of the stories were lifted directly from the tales, then modified, as if passed down orally from person to person, rather than read directly. Thomas realized after a while that none of this party could read, and so their knowledge of the tales was entirely verbal. Several of the party seemed intent on reenacting a favorite character, rather than being themselves.

Even with that insight, though, Thomas was unable to bring himself to probe for the Pilgrim's real stories. His mind wandered, back to Will, to his conversations with the

Archbishop, to the Abbey, and its architecture. He fought to keep his eyes open, and his fatigue turned into anxiety. He would relax, then clutch up  He longed to speak with Brother Will.

The food had been spare- gruel, a thin broth, a little piece of coarse old bread, a little square of meat. Thomas remained extremely hungry after the meal, and the presence of the others actually made him sadder, more withdrawn and homesick.

Thomas felt even worse when the Pilgrims made their way up to the men's dormitory and he saw the bed that he was to sleep in; it was one long trestle in which approximately thirty male pilgrims. It was rougher than the common sleeping hall in the Archbishop's palace, and as pilgrims arrived, more crowded.

Lying down on the board, tired beyond caring, Thomas had immediately fallen asleep, despite the noise and motion,, but, by the middle of the night, as his extreme fatigue gave way to simple tiredness, he awoke, groggy and vaguely nauseated. He tried to get back to sleep, but the loud snoring from the large, hairy pilgrim kept him from going back to sleep. Fatigue gave way to anger. Fairly soon, his mind reeling out of control, Thomas was angry at everyone, his bedmates, who appeared to be traveling with private supplies of fleas and noxious gasses; the fleas that were causing incredible itching, the monks of this abbey; Cardinal Morton, for sending him on this trip; his father for not preventing this; God, for creating such a stupid thing as Saints and pilgrimages. You name it, and Thomas had a bone to pick.

"I hate pilgrimages," Thomas thought for the fortieth time in the past twenty minutes as he scratched a flea off his arm.

*"No, Thomas. You hate this. You're overtired and lonely."*

"I hate pilgrimages. I will always hate pilgrimages."

*"That may be true. And sometimes we discover that our way of approaching God is not the same as the rest of humanity. Sometimes, if we allow ourselves, we discover small miracles."*

The room was unbelievably hot and humid. The summer air had not cooled off a bit indoors. Lamenting his fate again, Thomas reached out to his voice, "hello?"

No response.

Thomas went to the chamberpot and urinated again. Went back to the crowded pallet, couldn't find a comfortable position. Tried the rushes on the floor, but they were filthy. The hall was dark, close, and smelly. Thomas was thoroughly miserable.

There was a carved pie a dieu in the corner. Thomas went over and knelt.

"Father, why am I here?" Thomas prayed. Tears came to his eyes.

*"Why do you think you're here?"*

"To seek guidance."

*"You know better than that."*

"To learn about cloistered life."

*"Better."*

"To see if I am fit for cloistered life."

*"Best. And?"*

"I don't think so."

*"Is this cloistered life?"*

"I'm in a cloister."

*"Are you? Then what about service? Who have you served today other than yourself?"*

"It's hard. You don't know. You can't know."

*"Really?"*

"I'm not doing this any more."

Thomas closed his eyes and prayed aloud, "Father, get me out of this. I hate it."

*"It doesn't work that way."*

"Make it Tuesday."

*"That way either. Look for lessons in your experiences. Learn to trust and love."*

The conversation calmed him, and gradually, his exhaustion won out. Despite the irritations all around him, Thomas's head began to nod, and his body relaxed as he drifted into sleep, leaning on the rail of the prie a dieu.

Thomas awoke with a start to find that it was already mid-morning and that the other pilgrims had left. They had seen Thomas asleep, still leaning on the prie-a-dieu, his back to them, and they had assumed that he was deeply in prayer. Not wanting to disturb him, they had respectfully, and quietly, left, one by one.

When Thomas finally opened his eyes, he was sore and stiff all over from the long night spent in the kneeling position. His arm, long draped over the arm rest was asleep and tingled when he finally moved. He felt sticky and thick all over. His eyes were full of crust. His bladder longed to empty.

Brother Will came in, and was surprised to see Thomas stirring. "Thomassss More," he lisped pleasantly, "you are ssstill here?" Everyone else struck out a while ago."

"I…was..asleep.." Thomas replied. He was still kneeling and trying to decide if he really wanted to try to straighten his legs.

"Did you sssleep like that, Thomassss?" Will asked, concerned.

"Yes," replied Thomas with a groan as he straightened his knees.

"That looked painful," Will said sympathetically. "Your knees must be sore."

"My whole body is sore," replied Thomas, gingerly trying to stand, and then to flex his stiffened back. "Itchy too," he added with a small grin, scratching a flea bite.

"Well," said Will, helpfully, "the room needs to be cleaned, so have at it."

"I'm sorry?" asked Thomas, not hearing.

"The chamberpot, everything needs to be turned down," explained Will patiently. "You are the lassst Pilgrim still here. Your fellow Pilgrims left. Someone's got to clean the messss. I'm not going to. That leavssss you."

Thomas cursed his fate once again, and added an additional, "I hate pilgrimages," under his breath.

"We have a cesssspit down in the basement, and the river nearby that you can ussse to clean it out," Will explained patiently, even kindly. "I suggesssst plugging your nose," he added with a smile. "The beds all need to be turned down, and the rushes on the floor sssswept into the fireplace. You don't need to put down clean rushesss." With that Will turned and left Thomas.

Thomas moved and stretched, getting the aches out.

"I am not cleaning this room."

*"Why not?"*

"Why not?!?"

*"Yes, why not? Is it beneath you?"*

"You know I don't think like that"

*"And yet. Here we are. Work is like prayer. There is no bad work."*

"I didn't mean that. It's just, why me?"

*"Because you are special."*

"How am I special?"

*"In many ways, but the discovery of how is the most important part. Think on that. In the meantime, cleaning this room is a good start."*

"Hrumph," grunted Thomas as he looked around the room.

The chamberpot smelled terrible, but, compared to the cesspit in the basement, the pot was a rosebed. Thomas gagged and wretched, felt the clear liquidy bitterness of gall in the constant stream of a pre-emesis haze. Thomas carried the pot heavily to the edge of the cesspit, dumped the contents, and backed quickly out of the room. He was sorely tempted to just throw the chamberpot in after, but thought that the monk would probably make him swim in after it, so he held on bitterly.

Thomas found the small door off to the side leading out onto a small porch over the river. He washed the pot, and his hands, then, remembering, emptied his own bladder into the river. There was a small path to the left side of the porch that led down a short ways to the riverbank, conveniently upstream. He looked quickly right and left, and seeing no one, stripped off his robe and jumped naked into the Thames. He was much cooler and felt much better. He pushed his wet hair off to the side out of his eyes.

Feeling much better, the cool water having completed his awakening, Thomas made his way back up the shore, and, remembering, grabbed the pot and cleaned it in the little eddy. Satisfied, he took the dripping pot, and, redonning his sandals, and now incredibly itchy robe, he set back up the stairs to the dormitory.

Thomas turned up the stray pallets against a wall, allowing them to air. Finally, he retrieved a broom and swept the old rushes into the fireplace where they could be burned. He looked around the cleaned room, feeling satisfied.

Brother Will suddenly returned to the room, and looked appraisingly. "Thomasss," he said, "you've done well."

Thomas beamed, immensely pleased with the praise.

Brother will softened. "Thomas, you look famished. Would you like some bread and cheese, maybe a little wine?"

Thomas nearly collapsed with gratitude. "Yes Brother, I would," he said softly.

"You are having a hard time with begging, with turning yourself over, aren't you, Thomas?" the monk asked in a concerned voice. "I suspect you aren't used to having a hard time of it."

"No Brother," Thomas admitted.

Brother Will paused in thought for a moment, then said, "Thomassss, it is very nearly mid-day. How about if we eat, and then sing our hearts out at the Sext mass? You can pray on trust and love while singing."

Thomas looked confused. "I don't understand," he said.

"Someday you will," the monk said kindly, "but for now, take this bread and cheese."

Thomas devoured the food, almost as soon as it came into his hands.

After finishing, and smiling at Brother Will, the two entered the abbey chapel. The chapel was full of the nuns of the Priory, who had already started singing the service. Sext was incredibly calming. Thomas stood in the back with a few monks, enjoying the place, the people, and the mass. The rhythms of the service were familiar and calming. Refreshing.

Thomas did notice a small, very young nun, whom he immediately recognized as the twelve-year old Princess Bridget, the youngest child of King Edward, sister to the Queen, and cousin to Edward Stafford. She had just returned from burying her mother, the late Queen Elizabeth Woodville a month before. She initially looked to Thomas to be sad and lonely, but as the chanted ancient music took hold, her face brightened and glowed. She looked happily at the nuns around her, adjusting her headpiece.

After the service, Thomas and Will walked out together, Will introducing Thomas delightedly to the community, "This is young Thomasssss More of London. The Archbishop himself ssssent him on pilgrimage at 14 by himself!" All were pleasant and kind. The young

Princess-nun happily recognized Thomas and waved, smiling merrily as Thomas gave a polite bow. Bridget expressed great joy that Thomas More of London was on pilgrimage.

As Thomas and Will finally reached the front door, they turned to look at one another. Brother Will smiled. "I will tell you what, Thomasssss," he said, looking appraisingly at Thomas, and holding forth a small, blackened badge. "Take this as a souvenir of your stay in Deptford Abbey."

Thomas took the small pin and looked at it. There was a small circle with three swords welded onto it.

"This is a medal of the Altar of the Three Swords," said Brother Will.

Thomas looked confused.

"It's the Altar in Canterbury Cathedral where Thomas Becket was murdered," Will explained, "soon you will see it for yourself. They knocked out his brains, Thomassss. On the Altar." Will looked revolted at the thought, stopped and sniffed. He then went on quietly, "I found that place to be very moving." He paused in reflection and memory, then continued with a warm smile, "This was mine, and I give it to you, another Thomasssss." He pinned it onto Thomas's chest, below his other, the six pointed figure with the bishop's mitre, thought for a second, then removed it and re-pinned it again above the mitre. He patted the medal gently, and said softly, his voice cracking, "and now it is time for you to go, Thomasssss More. But as you are leaving, Thomas, let me give you a special treat."

Thinking of more food, maybe something sweet, Thomas looked up.

"On your way out of town, go next door to the Holy Trinity Church. There is something there I would like for you to see."

Thomas slumped a bit that the treat didn't involve food. He tried not to show it. He failed.

Will appreciated the effort not to show it, and smiled at Thomas. "It may not be more food, Thomas," he said consolingly, "but I think you will like it all the same."

It was one in the afternoon, and the sun was hot. There were no other pilgrims to be seen on the road any more. Thomas blinked a few times in the sun, looked back and Brother Will, who was slowly closing the door, looking affectionately at Thomas. Thomas gave him a small wave of thanks.

As instructed, he crossed the Abbey lawn to an ancient church on the High Road, that he had missed the night before. It was a beautiful, very old building with a square central tower, stones darkened from age. Thomas gingerly climbed the old stone steps of the porch to the front door. Seeing no one, he gingerly opened the door. The church was silent. Beautiful inside, lovingly lit by the sun through the stained glass windows on both the East and West gables of the church.

Thomas noticed a small group of silently praying people ahead and to the left, on the south side of the church.. He quietly approached to see the chapel, oddly as large as the nave, nearly twenty feet, both wide and tall. There were rounded windows above, letting even more light into the chapel. There were benches in the chapel, mostly occupied by praying visitors. Thomas followed their eyes to the far wall of the chapel, which was occupied by an enormous fresco painting of St. George, slaying the dragon.

Thomas involuntarily sat down, overwhelmed by the painting, which sent his fourteen year old mind swimming into the scene, the smell of Sulphur from the dragons mouth. The sweat on George's brow. Still a little tired from the morning's exertions, Thomas let himself sit and relax at the site, studying the painting.

It appeared relatively new, judging by the whiteness of the plaster underpainting, still visible at the edges and in unpainted clouds hovering over the epic battle. Smoke had also not yet darkened the brightly colored paints. With a big smile, Thomas turned to a nearby visitor to remark upon the greatness of the art in front of them, but was pointedly ignored.

"I've no one to share this with," Thomas thought sadly.

*"You've let no one in to share with you."*

"I just tried."

*"And you expected him to reciprocate. You felt as though you deserved him to interact with you."*

"Not deserved. But it would have been nice."

*"I agree. But no groundwork was laid. Still, enjoy the painting. Enjoy the memory of the peace here. Bring that to your pilgrimage."*

Deciding to move on, Thomas silently rose, and left the church. He blinked a few times in the bright sun outdoors. Rejoining the ancient road, Thomas turned to the East. The bridge across the Darent had fallen, but there was a kind townsman who directed Thomas north a few hundred yards off the road to where there was a ford in the shallow tidal river. By this time, the tide was out, and so the river was only a few inches deep, and about 25 feet across. Picking up his pace, Thomas quickly waded to the opposite bar, pausing only a few times to kick up water, or splash, or to look at interesting rocks.

After crossing to the chalky shingle bank on the far side, Thomas saw the old road to the right. There was a small wooded hill ahead of him, with an old path leading into the scrub. Thomas heard voices from the wood, so Thomas ascended the hill, carefully watching the narrow exposed dirt of the path.

Reaching the top, there was a hovel, really a pile of old rocks that had attracted the attention of eight or ten straggler pilgrims. Coming closer, Thomas overheard that this was an abandoned Shrine to Saint Edmund.

Thomas recognized immediately the blustery, hairy man with the northern accent from the night before. That gentleman was incongruously in deep prayer at the small, abandoned open air altar, vines and weeds crowding along its sides. The man was mumbling in a guttural language that Thomas had occasionally heard Mr. Cheeseman mutter quietly, and which he recognized as the old Saxon tongue. He only caught a few words. Curious, Thomas found a preserved small house in the middle of the clearing. Closer investigation revealed a sign declaring this to be Wat Tyler's house.

"The Wat Tyler?" Thomas thought. "Cheeky bugger."

*"Then again, Thomas, he led a huge army of the people, really trusting only in the rightness of what he had to say."*

"Against the King."

*"No, against an oppressive nobility."*

"Either way."

*"You are better than that argument, Thomas. Why are you opposed to Wat Tyler?"*

"He wanted a revolution."

*"Are you sure of that?"*

"Yes…..No…never mind."

*"Remember Wat Tyler. Things aren't always as they appear. Put your faith in others. Learn their motives and history before you judge."*

Troubled, Thomas nosed around the house and grounds for a while, but found no relics. From the vantage of the hill, Thomas looked back towards the west, his past, his home.. The river he had just crossed, the Darent, flowed northward into the broadening Thames, which in turn, serpentine its way towards London. He saw the Abbey he had just left, and further on, Placentia Palace. A long ways off, he could still make out the top of the spire of St. Paul's. Not much else except a cloud of smoke hanging over the city.

Thomas looked back again at the grounds of Placentia and thought about his friend Edward. Involuntarily, Thomas shivered a bit at Edward's talk of becoming King.

"I would be his Archbishop and Lord Chancellor," Thomas thought.

*"That worked out beautifully for Thomas Becket, being the King's best friend."*

"It wouldn't have to be that way."

*"Whatever you say."*

"You don't agree?"

*"No. But you'd better get a move on. It's pretty late. The others left."*

Thomas started, took one more look to the west, and turned to the road and began walking at a good pace. The road was hillier today, and the ground had exposed fault lines of white chalk. Thomas had, happily, found a good walking rhythm, and he quickly made his way past the old chalk quarry at Bean.

From Bean, the road descended at a slow, but steady pace, continuing, however, to be unnervingly straight. Thomas would occasionally climb the low rise on either side of the road to see the countryside around. He had never imagined a world as heavily populated with fat sheep as the countryside he was now seeing. It seemed the whole world was one big sheep pasture, broken only intermittently by a wheat field or an orchard.

Eventually, the road stopped descending, and, by that point, had become raised compared to the marshy land surrounding. There was a small stream, marked "Fleet" on his map. The sun was hot, so Thomas waked into the marshy wetlands along the creek. The tide was coming back in, but the water was still low. Thomas was able to make out oysters on the bed, but having no knife, and having been warned against oysters in the summer, he let them lie. There was a lovely crop of watercress, however, growing in every eddy of the stream. He took some, and ate it. On the side of the bank, Thomas caught the red of some ripe, wild strawberries. He was leery, after the cherries of the day before, but tried a few, had no immediate problems, and was reminded of the bit of bread and cheese Brother Will had given him for the road. Thomas ate hungrily. Occasionally he would drink a little water from the stream from a cupped hand, but the rising tide made the water increasingly salty.

Thomas found himself curiously refreshed by his small ration, and happy and proud at his small display of self-sufficiency. He returned to the road and, given the time, set himself a faster pace. He gradually began to overtake stragglers, the old or lame, people who had stopped for a holiday pilgrimage picnic. He recognized some of the people from the night before in Dartford. He began to uncharitably scan the road for some of the men that had left him alone to clean up, but then decided, when he looked at his new-old badge that they had all done him a favor. When Thomas eventually saw a few of the men, he simply smiled warmly and waved, then passed them by without speaking.

"Perhaps," Thomas thought, "I am, at heart, an Anchorite, a hermit, an enclosed person."

*"Perhaps not."*

"What?"

*"Talk to people, Thomas. Love people. You are on Pilgrimage."*

"They left me to clean up."

*"And who profited from that experience, you or them?"*

"But that's not the point."

*"It is exactly the point."*

"I'm not talking with you, either, right now."

The road began to rise again, steadily, then undulated over exposed chalk beds, always straight. Eventually Thomas reached another hilltop, and down, before him, he saw a wide, winding river, the Medway. The road ahead made a series of rightward sweeps down the hill and across to a sturdy, ancient, arched stone bridge that was about a hundred fifty yards long. In the long walk the time had come in and was now in ebb, leaving small mud flats on either side of the river.

On the other side of the Medway, adjacent to the eastern bridge landing, were the castle and the Cathedral of the City of Rochester. The Cathedral had a lovely attached monastery. The castle was a square bailey, shaped a lot like the White Tower in London, rising much taller than wide or broad, with four battlements, one on each corner. Only the upper portion of the building had windows, and those were small and black. On the river side, next to the castle structure, there was a sheer stone wall, a curtain, and on the north side, took a dip and then rose to some stairs leading into the battlement. At the top, Thomas saw happily that the Archbishop's flag, its light blue and reassuring white Y with yellow trim and small black crosses, flapped in the gentle breeze, giving Thomas hope that the Archbishop was about.

"If the Archbishop is here," Thomas thought, "I could talk him into taking me off pilgrimage."

*"Do you think it likely?"*

"Are we speaking again?"

*"Yes." "*

"Do you think it likely?"

*"No. I think you have a long way to go on Pilgrimage."*

"Still….couldn't hurt to ask."

*"yes, it could…Asking the Archbishop to relieve you of a task he requested of you, and that you freely accepted means that you failed. You were not up to the task. You will not likely ever be asked anything again."*

*"Thomas?"*

*"Are we still speaking?"*

Behind, and to the left of the castle, was the cathedral. Like the castle, the cathedral was also made of the light ochre Caen stone. It rose a hundred feet into the air, the western façade, and the nave facing Thomas. It was shaped in the usual cruciform shape, with the nave to the west. The three other arms of the cross, the north and south transepts and the presbytery to the east, were all the same length. There was a tall, square central tower with a square, mitered wooden spire elaborately decorated. Thomas had heard the bells ringing from a distance on the hike in, presumably from that tower.

Thomas noticed the scaffolding and workmen in the corner between the south transept and the nave. They appeared to be finishing the construction of a small additional Lady Chapel. Their tools were spread around as were blocks of cut and uncut stone. A few of the younger appearing workers also appeared to be carving figures of stone off to the side. The chalk dust combined with the construction stone dust spread a great white haze over and around this area of the cathedral grounds.

As Thomas descended the western chalk hill on the road and approached the bridge across the Medway, he carefully studied the Cathedral. On the western main entrance there was a large, beautiful central arched stained glass window, under a somewhat flattened castellated gable. The stonework of this gable appeared much newer, fresher in design, than the surrounding stones, and the stone fretwork of the window still white and new. The window from the outside appeared to be a collection of dark blues and reds in the shape of some saint or another.

The large, tall windowed center of the façade had two flanking towers. The leftmost, northern tower was square and divided into eight arcades, about half again as tall as the rest of the façade. This tower was topped with a stubby mitered spire.

On the right, the southern tower was square only to about the height of the upper section of the central window, and then two circular arcades and an octagonal mitered wooden spire, coming to a pointy end just higher than the central gable.

The asymmetry of the two towers as Thomas made his first impressions of Rochester Cathedral were jarring, but not unpleasant. Thomas wondered idly about why the architects made different decisions on tower design rather than opting for strict gothic symmetry.

There was a large porch extending from the central door, which was made of a dark, ancient wood, and about twelve feet tall. The door was surrounded by a massive, carved stone entrance, with a very old appearing worn carving in the arched semilunar between this door and the great glassed window centered above it.

As he neared the cathedral, Thomas noticed a monk in a black cassock, with a fringe of jet black hair surrounding his bald tonsured scalp. He was thin and wiry underneath his black robe, and his face had the unpredictable look of a moderately friendly eagle. He was looking both at, and around Thomas.

With a start, Thomas realized he had been walking staring agape at the great cathedral. He looked around to notice several other pilgrims walking nearby, equally stunned at the sites. One of the pilgrims was the hearty pilgrim he had seen praying in the little glade earlier. Thomas had overheard enough snippets of conversations on the road to surmise that this man's name was Godfrey Wooler.

The monk approached what had now become a group of wide eyed pilgrims.

"Ah, Pilgrims," said the monk happily, used to, and pleased by, this common reaction to his home.

Thomas smiled at him, and stood tall. The others bowed, and answered, "yes, Father." The monk looked at Thomas expectantly.

"I bow for no one," thought Thomas, immediately embarrassed by the thought.

*"The Archbishop?"*

"Well him, yes."

*"The King?"*

"Obviously, yes, the King, too."

*"God?"*

"If he were standing in front of me, and I was sure it was him, yes."

*"When did you become like this, Thomas?"*

"I don't know. But I' unhappy with everyone right now."

*"You must stop fighting the experience and live your pilgrimage. It is normal to be frightened. Letting go is a part of trust in God. Fear is a lack of trust in God."*

The monk studied Thomas. Finally, after a small battle of wills, the monk said, "and you, young man, standing stiff and upright, are you also a pilgrim?

Thomas nodded, bending his head slightly.

The monk's face darkened a bit, "you do not speak?... Perhaps also a rude deaf mute?"

Thomas laughed, answering, "No, I am sorry Father. I was distracted by the cathedral and I forgot both my manners and my tongue."

Thomas bowed deeply, as at the Archbishop's court, and the monk, mollified, smiled thinly at Thomas.

Thomas then asked, looking up at the stonework and pointing, "Father, in the carving, why the four creatures surrounding Jesus?"

The monk, happy to have the situation defused, and the opportunity to show off his cathedral, happily answered, "these carvings are over four hundred years old. They were carved for Bishop Gundulph, himself, at the request of the Conqueror."

Oddly, the big hairy pilgrim in the group gave an unintentional snort at "Conqueror."

Thomas noticed, but the monk apparently did not, for he continued, "the four creatures are the symbols of the evangelists; the Angel for Matthew, the winged bull for Mark; the winged lion for Luke; and the eagle for John." The monk looked conspiratorially at Thomas and added in a whispered aside, "Gundulph also built the Tower of London for King William, but he did his best work here, in Rochester." He gestured expansively all around, at the square Norman keep, so much like the Tower.

Smiling to the monk, Thomas made a motion towards the door of the cathedral, a motion followed by the other pilgrims. The monk held them up, holding up his hand, palm towards them all. "No, no," he clucked. "That is not the way for pilgrims. You all go around to the side, to Saint William's shrine." And he laughed heartily. "Trust me," he added, "you will cherish the memory."

Thomas thought, "Not bloody likely."

*"Thomas."*

"Come with me," said the monk happily, "I will show you the way." He then strode quickly up around the northern corner of the church, to Thomas's left, into a passageway between the nave of the church, and the lower, longer monastery building adjacent to the church.

Thomas and the other pilgrims meekly followed, mostly looking up at the tall northern spire.

The passageway was about fifteen feet wide, and in deep shadow from the two buildings on either side. A little way down, on the right was a small entrance. Ahead was a brick archway under a passage connecting the cathedral with the cloister on the left. Through the archway, Thomas could see another large, square tower, twenty or twenty-five feet to a side, rising higher than the church to which it was attached. It had fenestrations instead of windows, and those only at the top. This tower rose like a turret, square and foreboding, in contrast to the graceful gothic church to which it was attached.

"What's that tower?" Thomas asked for the group, pointing through the archway.

"That," the monk responded proudly, "is Gundulph's Tower. It was built first, and the church came later." He paused for dramatic effect. Then added, "no one knows why it was built – and so like a castle. One rumor is that Gundulph, a Norman, was very afraid of being attacked in his Cathedral by the Saxons, and so he built this defensive position before his great cathedral, so that he would have a safe place to live."

The big hairy man spoke up. "Well isn't that something," clucked Godfrey Wooler in an odd accent. It was the first he'd spoke at all in a while. He crossed his immense arms, then looked knowingly at his companions.

"Norpmandiso hundwéalas áhellap in hiera stántorre," he said smugly. His companions laughed.

Both Thomas and the monk stared at Godfrey incredulously, the monk also combining fear and outrage into his face.

"I'm sssorry," the monk stammered, "what did you say?"

"Nichts, Vater," said Godrey, still smiling smugly. The others looked pleased, as well, though also a little more nervous.

The monk elected to disengage. "Well," he said to the group. "Go through that door, and go to the left. You will find some stairs. They lead up to the shrine of Saint William of Perth. He is our local patron. He was a baker… a pilgrim who was stabbed to death as he slept. A holy death for a pilgrim." He smiled sadly at the pilgrims, and shook his head at the theological mystery of it all.

"What!?!" thought Thomas.

*"Relax, Thomas."*

"No, wait. Let me understand this. A baker, on a pilgrimage three hundred years ago is stabbed to death near a Cathedral and becomes a saint? And his death is holy?"

*"See the shrine. You didn't think much of poor Saint Edmund either. Look and move on. He was a baker like your grandfather."*

"What did Godfrey Wooler say, anyway?"

*"Why don't you ask him? It will take your mind off of Saint William."*

The monk had moved off while Thomas was pondering, and Godfrey and the group had moved towards the door. Thomas stepped quickly to catch up. Pulling up next to Godfrey, he asked in a quiet voice, "Master Wooler, what was that you said back there?"

Godfrey stopped and studied Thomas, a big grin on his face. "Hear that?" he said to his group, "the little Frenchman wants to know what I said." The others laughed nervously, looking around the passage as the monk sped off.

Thomas reddened in confused embarrassment. "I'm not French," he said hotly, "I'm from London."

The group laughed, less nervously, all looking at Thomas.

"You act French," Godfrey said, slowly and haltingly, oddly, easily taming his previous thick northern accent. "All High and Mighty. Besides, Londoner, Frenchman, same thing – young man with soft hands. Out on pilgrimage instead of working. Not even enjoying the break. Acting like he's been sent to prison instead of vacation. Like I said. A Frenchman. No… Sorry. A Londoner." With that he bowed deeply to Thomas, aping the deep, yet surly court bow Thomas had earlier given the monk.

"You cannot insult London to me!" Thomas replied angrily. "I'm an Englishman, like you. But better yet, I am a Londoner, through and through."

"Ach, ein Londoner," Godfrey said cheerily, though with an angry tone in his voice which thickened his accent again. "Worse dan ein Frenchman. Ein geld trader," he spat. "Suck de geld out of the people and into deinem own pocket. Das ist how die family sent a suckling child on pilgrimage."

"No," Thomas objected immediately, cutting him off, "My father is not a moneychanger. He's a lawyer. And I am on pilgrimage because my Master sent me."

"Ach," said Godfrey happily, again controlling his accent, "a lawyer. Well, that is better than a thief. Though not much." He paused, thinking significantly, daring Thomas to interrupt, before adding, "Though not much. Well, no. Really no difference when you come down to it."

He laughed heartily at Thomas's expense, then looked at Thomas thoughtfully, his accent gone again as he added, "so, what is a lawyer's son doing on pilgrimage? Studying to be a Norman monk?"

"I told you," Thomas repeated, starting to break, "I'm English. And you're stupid, and I don't want to be here." He sank to the ground, hugging his knees, and began crying.

Godfrey moved to him, concerned. "Now then, boyo. I didn't mean to make you cry." He moved to put his big arms around Thomas. "Just having a little fun at your expense."

Thomas pushed him back. "I didn't want to do this," Thomas said, looking up at the bearded face. "I was perfectly happy where I was. But no! 'go out and throw your trust to God…Let God provide…Go to Canterbury….I will meet you there…'" All of the past day's frustrations came welling out. "The priests took my money. And I'm supposed to be enjoying myself? How? I'm hungry. I'm tired. My feet hurt. I'm lonely."

It turned out Thomas was no match for Godfrey when the big hairy man wanted to give a bear hug. He was enveloped. The big man smelled of the wild. "There, there," Godfrey said soothingly, "be with us. Then you'll not be lonely. Food, I can't do anything about."

Thomas was confused.

*"He's throwing you a rope, Thomas. Take it."*

"I can't trust him."

*"You can and you will. You are on Pilgrimage. God sends messages, and hope, and help to His Pilgrims."*

"Like Saint William of Perth?"

*"He was called home. He's a Saint. He sits with God."*

"He was brutally murdered."

*"An eyeblink in time. A moment's suffering. And for God's love."*

Thomas stepped back, out of Godfrey's arms, and looked him intently in the eyes. He decided to trust.

"Thank you Master Wooler. I accept your kindness on one condition," Thomas said firmly, looking directly into the big man's eyes.

"Godfrey eyed him, and asked, "what condition?"

"That you tell me what is was you said about Gundulf's tower," Thomas said earnestly.

Godfrey laughed uproariously. "Done, Thomas More," he said, extending his hand in the deal. One they had shaken, Godfrey said, smiling, "I said in the old language, 'Chickenshit Norman dogs hiding in their stone towers.'"

Thomas laughed uncontrollably, the tension draining out of him.

The rest of the pilgrimage to Canterbury would be spent in the good company of Master Wooler and his family. The Wooler clan turned out to be very generous and friendly, sharing their food and their stories with Thomas. They were, as it happened of an old Saxon line, from the far north, near Carlisle, on the marches with Scotland.

The group made their way into the crypt of Rochester Cathedral, down stone stairs that were so enormously worn that it was nearly a slide to the basement. The Shrine of Saint William was interesting, but not particularly captivating to Thomas, until Godfrey became eloquent that Saint Williams martyrdom was a glaring testimony to the outrageous dog-like behavior of the Normans in their treatment of the Saxons.

Thomas helpfully pointed out that Saint William was a Scot, and therefore a Celt.

Godfrey pointed out in a friendly way that since the Saxons had long ago conquered the island, that all true people of the island, even Scots, were really Saxons.

Thomas bit back a question about how since the Normans had then conquered the Saxons how that the right of civilization didn't pass, then, to them. Instead, Thomas decided, wisely, to remain quiet, and to learn about the northmen.

The people of the north really had no truck with any of the rulers or leaders of England over the past five hundred or so years. They thought that Harold Godwinson, the last Saxon King, should have been canonized instead of Edward the Confessor, whose weakness ("nearly French," in Godfrey's opinion) had led directly to the Norman Conquest.

There was one exception in that line, however. They did like Richard, the late King. Godfrey was delighted to hear that he and Thomas had something in common – they had met the late King.

"Tell me, young Thomas," Godfrey asked at dinner, smiling broadly, his voice booming, "What d'ye think of King Richard, bless his name, the only true English King?"

Thomas instinctively shrank, and looked around nervously

"Treason! Danger!" thought Thomas.

*"What are you afraid of, Thomas?"*

"That King Henry's men will overhear us."

*"First, why would they be listening? And second, do you disagree with what he said?"*

"First, I work for Archbishop Morton. I am a page for the Lord Chancellor."

*"You take yourself way too seriously, Thomas. Absolutely no one for a great distance cares about you. You are a lonely pilgrim. You are not wearing the Archbishops livery or badge any more. In fact, you turned it in. Your time of service is over. You are a free boy."*

"Man."

*"Boy."*

"Still, if someone did overhear, then we could all be arrested."

*"You think that in this England it takes a crime to be arrested. Mere Existence is enough to be arrested. The charge can be found later. If you are this afraid, then you need desperately not to circle the crown. Otherwise…trust in God is your only hope. Trust in God, and chance the rest."*

Thomas continued to look nervously around the room. Reading his thoughts, Godfrey added kindly, "Good King Richard was never afraid."

Distracted suddenly from his thoughts, Thomas blurted out, "Yes he was. He was afraid for his life, for his crown, for his family, and for his Kingdom. I met him and he was afraid for all these things, but that does not in any way diminish him as a King. It's the Kings who are afraid of nothing that I would worry about, because they are simply daft."

Thomas stopped abruptly, noticing the sudden small motions in response to "for his family," looked one more time nervously, then giggled. The giggling turned quickly into unrestrained, unrestrainable laughter. Infectious laughter. Soon the entire table was laughing, and Godfrey clapped Thomas hard on the shoulder.

"Interestingly and passionately said, Thomas," Godfrey choked out between gasps. "I didn't think you possessed that much passion." The big northerner calmed and regained himself, looking steadily at Thomas. "You are, of course, correct Thomas. King Richard wasn't great for happiness, always so sad and stern. I don't think it was fear, though. More concern. I worried that the world was always only a series of grim possibilities and options for him. I believe that he saw a better way, but got cut down for it. The cowardly French bastard that done it, and who is now the King, was about to run away when his mercenaries, French mercenaries, managed to knock Richard off his horse. They swarmed him, they did. The King was shouting 'Treason! Treason!' as they hacked at him until his armor broke, his crown cut off his head and rolling into a hawthorn bush." Godfrey's voice broke, his eyes welled with tears as his voice lowered.

"John Howard was already dead in the vanguard," Godfrey continued softly, clearly fighting back tears. "no leaders….men scattered. Percy refused to budge. The Stanley's turned coats and attacked Richard's men. There was no quarter….None expected, I guess." Godfrey paused, having said the last as a strangled whisper that Thomas had to lean in to hear. He distractedly pushed a spilled bean on the table with his finger, his eyes, his mind far away.

After a moment he continued, his voice still choked with emotion, "the King…He died bloody, a mess of wounds, the crown in a bush. The bastard Stanley grabbed the crown to give to Henry. Then he paused…hesitated like….I suspect he considered putting it on himself. Really, almost anyone on the field had earned the crown as much as Henry that day."

The distant, haunted look in Godfrey's eyes persisted, as tears welled.

Thomas gently placed a hand on Godfrey's shoulder, which slumped. His wife moved in. The children and the clan looked surprised, as if their father and leader had never told the story before.

"You were at Bosworth?" Thomas said quietly, more a statement than question.

"I was," Godfrey answered quietly, his voice nearly a sob.

"You were with King Richard?" Thomas asked, pulling gently at a loose thread on the big man's sleeve.

Godfrey looked up, his face startled, then, reddening, angry. With the transformation in his face, Godfrey pushed back a little from the table, from Thomas, from his family, and hissed, "No. I was with that fucking asshole French traitor, Percy. I was kept from helping the King. From doing my duty. As a soldier. As a Saxon. As a man."

After this explosion, Godfrey slumped, spend. His family looked stricken. As if they had never heard this central story. Except for his wife, who looked sorrowfully, compassionately at her husband, as if feeling his guilt, his pain, as her own.

Thomas had imagined the battle in his mind's eye. The glory surrounding King Henry. The crown by right of conquest. He remembered the parade. Also Thomas Howard's reaction to the new King. He remembered the scene in the guildhall half his life ago. He remembered black mustachioed John Howard, his friend's grandfather, killed with King Richard.

And what of Edward Stafford, his friend, and Edward's wife Alinor Percy? Alinor and her brother Henry Percy's father? Godfrey's general who had stood by. Betrayed King Richard. And now, only seven years later, Godfrey racked by guilt, Alinor married to Edward, Henry Percy at Court, Thomas Howard working his way back up slowly with his father.

*"Your Father was right."*

"How do you mean?" Thomas thought.

*"The nobility watches after itself, but mostly each noble watches out for himself."*

"Why did Percy stand by?"

*Watching out for himself. Afraid of being on the wrong side of history. Listened to the wrong voices. He couldn't believe that anything was more valuable to him than his position. He wanted to be on the winning side. So he sat and waited with his men to see who was going to win."*

"But suppose that Richard had succeeded? He would have known what Percy had done."

*"Yes, but he would have overlooked it. Percy would have congratulated him effusively on his bravery and incredible military prowess. Richard would have accepted his praise. Percy would have lived, and returned to his lands in the north. To be a kind of King there."*

"Which is what happened when Henry won."

*"Yes. Except for the people of the North. Percy forgot about them. He always did. People like your friend Godfrey."*

"What?!?"

*"Ask him."*

"Godfrey," Thomas hesitated briefly, then asked gently, "what happened to Percy? After the battle?"

Godfrey looked askance, then furtively glanced at his wife before saying, "that fucking French traitor got what he deserved."

"Which was?" Thomas pressed, though quietly and uncomfortably.

"Well…" Godfrey smirked a bit. "I can't rightly say, you see, as I wasn't there, but I hear tale that he came back to the North and tried to make himself out a hero. But the people knew what he had done. He tried to order, to bully the people like he had before, but his authority was gone. I'm told that he came upon a village outside Carlisle, in the Marches, where some of his old soldiers lived." Godfrey's voice was uncharacteristically flat.

"He didn't recognize the old soldiers, of course, 'cause they were common, always beneath his notice. Percy was on his horse, and nearly ran a woman down. Knocked her into a ditch. He reined his horse and circled around the woman as she was getting up, yelling at her for being in his way. He took out his whip. His men had reeled around as well, laughing. The men of the town had heard the noise and come outside. The woman's husband saw the whip and rushed forward to take the blow for his wife. One of the Earl's knights drew a sword. The husband drew a knife, knowing it was death to do so. He didn't care. Seeing Percy, knowing what he had done at Bosworth, all he saw was the dead King, and his endangered wife."

"The husband charged the Earl, screaming 'fucking traitor. I was at Bosworth!'" Anger rose in Godfrey's tight voice before he paused a moment, regaining control, the group silent, some looking away, some eyes wide, looking at Godfrey.

"Seeing the husband with the knife, the Earl's man laughed, well laughed that is until an arrow from the door of another house hit him in the throat. He stopped laughing then. So did the rest of Percy's dogs after a hail of arrows came at them from every corner of the village. Percy was suddenly alone, facing an angry town, an old soldier with a knife, with only a whip in his hand. There was a noisy stampede of horses, some with slumped riders still stuck in their stirrups, some now riderless. The Earl screamed, 'Traitors!', but it didn't sound like King Richard at the end, there was no valor in the voice or the man. 'I surrender,' he tried.

"The husband with the knife had reached him. Percy had soiled himself, but while doing that, he had unsheathed his sword and was fumbling it. He tried a feeble swing, but the husband ducked, then came up behind the sword, jumped and grabbed the Earl's arm. He pulled, but slipped in his grasp. The Earl wheeled the horse, trying to stomp him. The man came up with his knife, missed the Earl, but stabbed the horse. The horse reared and bucked, screaming. The Earl fell off backwards to the ground, his sword clattering away.

"The other men from the village had run up, seven or eight of them anyway, all at Bosworth, and a couple of the husband's sons. They took the Earl apart with their knives. Piece at a time. Percy screamed like a baby until the very end."

The table was quiet. Thomas realized he hadn't breathed in a while and took a shallow breath. His heart raced, a flop sweat on his face. Godfrey's wife looked down, tears rimming her eyes. Godfrey stared straight into Thomas's eyes. Trust….and maybe a challenge in his expression. Thomas met his eyes without breaking.

"What happened to the villagers?" Thomas asked quietly.

Godfrey hesitated. "I don't rightly know," he answered, looking away. "As I said, I wasn't there. But I heard the villagers sent the Earl's body along to Carlisle in baskets. That was stupid. The Frenchmen in London lost their minds. 'There's an uprising in the North,' they screamed, and Henry's army came along quickly to put it down. It was hard for the Northmen. The King leveled the village, but the villagers had all scattered. None was ever found." Godfrey returned his gaze to Thomas.

"And what happened to them?" Thomas asked again.

Godfrey blinked, then smiled, "as I said, I don't know, but there are a lot of reasons to go on pilgrimage, Thomas. Vacation and kissing the Lord Chancellor's arse are simply two of them."

Without smiling, Godfrey looked down at his food, and he and his family ate quietly for the rest of the meal, leaving Thomas feeling cold and empty, alone in the Great Hall surrounded by people.

*"People are complicated, Thomas. You mustn't judge."*

"That's why he was at Wat Tyler's house," Thomas thought.

*"That too is complicated."*

"But he killed the Earl. He should be punished."

*"What kind of punishment?"*

"Traitor's punishment."

*"Really!?"*

"No, not really. I..I don't know."

*"Better answer. Who are you to judge? And do you know for sure that he is guilty of anything?"*

"But he said…"

*"He said that he 'had heard."*

"I've used that too."

*"But he doesn't answer to you, Thomas. He answers to God, and he maybe answers to the King. Do you not think he had cause?"*

"Yes, but my father says that if an Earl is unjust, they can be tried by the King."

*"Did you every ask your father how many Dukes and Earls have been indicted for being mean to a villager? Or even killing a villager? Look at Wat Tyler."*

"Probably not many."

*"Remember too, the Archbishop told you that the Earl had been killed during a rebellion against taxes in Yorkshire."*

"Yes, but Godfrey…"

*"People often come up with a story that fits the narrative they have already planned in their heads. It is much more comforting to the nobility that it was a tax rebellion than it was an act of rebellion against them. This was small. An Earl and a couple of his henchmen were killed. Wat Tyler is known because the story, the rebellion, was simply too massive to be covered up, or explained away as not wanting to pay taxes."*

"But Godfrey…"

*"Let the nobility have their story this time. They will be angrier at the messenger, and infinitely more frightened, if that messenger upsets their comforting narrative with a truth, than they would be with Godfrey for his minor rebellion. Remember too what Godfrey had experienced. Is murder ever justified?"*

"No."

*"In war?"*

"Well, obviously war is an exception."

*"How about in self-defense?"*

"Yes, that too."

*"So, exceptions exist?"*

"Yes"

*"Then, dear Thomas, one word answers won't suffice. Remember too that Godfrey trusted you with his story. Why do you think that was?"*

"I don't know."

*"Remember, Thomas, Godfrey has absolutely no reason to trust you. He barely knows you. Either he sees something in you, or he doesn't care."*

"He sees something in me?"

*"Maybe. Maybe not. But Godfrey has great trust in God that everything will happen the way it is supposed to. He trusts in God that in telling you his story that you will do the right thing with the information."*

"What is the right thing?"

*"You don't get to know yet. That is to be discerned and lived."*

"But Henry Percy's father…"

*"Henry is now the Earl. Life goes on. It is now Henry's choice how he leads his life, how he treats others. Remember what your father said, for, let's say some of, the nobility, personal survival is paramount. That means, for them, they cannot truly trust anyone but themselves. That is the difference between, say, the old Earl and Godfrey Wooler."*

"But someone should know. Henry should know."

*"Two questions. Is it your news? And will it bring his father back?"*

"No."

*"Will that knowledge change Henry's behavior, or Alinor's?"*

"Probably not."

*"And who are you to decide what's best for everyone?"*

"Henry's friend."

*Ultimately, you are probably nothing to either Henry or Alinor."*

"That's not true!"

*"Well, I will concede that you are, or could be, useful to them. But so is an ox. A piece of advice. Love them instead of trying to impress them. Love them and you are doing God's will. Then trust that everything else will work out the way it's supposed to. You are in no position, Thomas, to judge the late Earl, young Henry Percy, or Godfrey Wooler. Love them all instead of judging. And smile, Thomas. I'm tired of your frowning face, all pinched up like a persimmon."*

"How much longer to Canterbury?"

*"Relax and enjoy the trip. Time will pass more quickly."*

"I want to go home."

*"Then continue on your pilgrimage. And love, Thomas. And smile every once in a while, just to show people you can."*

Eventually Thomas noticed that he was alone in the Great Hall. The rest of the pilgrims had skittered off to the edges, next to the cool stone walls of the abbey. The fire in the center of the room had burned down to embers which occasionally hissed from some long covered pocket of sap. Godfrey Wooler slept fitfully in the darkest corner of the hall, his breathing irregular, punctuated by gasps, leg kickings, then the appearance of struggling for air against some unseen pillow held onto his face. As he became louder, his wife would kick him and say, "Left side, Geoff," and he would roll back over onto his left side, and his breathing would ease for a while.

Thomas felt a little guilty about watching, but was fascinated none the less. Every so often, Godfrey would sit up and blink his eyes, muttering something unintelligible. There was fear in his eyes, though, sometimes terror. Then it would pass, and he would lie back into his snoring, fitful rest. Always, though, his wife was there reflexively holding his hand, comforting him through the long night.

Thomas felt a sudden, uncontrollable surge of affection for the Woolers. And for Henry Percy, Edward Stafford, his father, the Archbishop. Everyone really. In a flash, Thomas recognized humanity, his own, in others. The drives and the impulses that led to action or inaction, to passion or passivity, to love and to hate. Thomas suddenly saw his place in the world; not the details, just the location, a glimpse into the cosmos, into God's mind, illuminated like the flash of a lightning bold, searingly clear, then quickly fading, but leaving the image, a shadow with attached sensations, smells, tastes, emotions, an outline forever etched into memory.

*"This is what I mean, Thomas. I'm proud of you."*

And with that entire revelation, and the peace that followed it, Thomas fell asleep. A smile on his face.

What seemed an instant later, Thomas was awakened by the massive, gentle hand of Godfrey Wooler.

"Thomas," Godfrey said, quietly, lovingly.

It took a few seconds for Thomas's brain to process that it was Godfrey calling him from sleep, and not his dream of a big breakfast in his home on Milk Street. Suddenly, though, as if being jerked upwards, his dreamscape shattered, light filling all of his senses, and he was awake. Thomas opened his eyes, and looked into the smiling, laughing face of Godfrey.

"Gut morgen to ye, Thomas," Godfrey said, cheerfully. "Another big day of Pilgrimage? And what's this? Yer smilin'?"

Thomas realized he was smiling, and made no effort to hide it, then he tried to move. Every sinew hurt. He had fallen asleep in a chair. A second night sleeping in some odd position or another had left him stiff and sore. His brown robes were itchy and felt impossibly dirty again. Still, he smiled, and, instead of moving right away, he nodded cheerfully at the big Northman.

"Help ye up?" Godfrey asked pleasantly, extending his hand.

"Thank you," Thomas said gratefully, accepting the hand and being mostly pulled upright. With too much creaking for a fourteen year old, Thomas managed to walk awkwardly and stiffly around the room, testing his knees and back.

The entire Wooler family, and a few smaller groups of Pilgrims, laughed involuntarily at Thomas's plight.

"Do you ever sleep lying down, Thomas?" Mrs. Wooler asked pleasantly.

Thomas grinned ruefully. "I used to, ma'am," he replied, then added volubly, "but then I came on pilgrimage and it somehow seems more appropriate to sleep like a German pretzel to anticipate the joys of the day to come." Thomas then laughed, slowly at first, but then in waves as he discovered that his tension, his anxiety about his place in the world was gone. He was free, truly free.

The Woolers, led by husband and wife, slowly approached laughing Thomas and embraced him warmly.

"Thank you," Thomas both thought and said.

*"That's what pilgrimage is all about, Thomas."*

"What's next?"

*"You enjoy your lovely walk to Canterbury and you meet the Archbishop there. But happily."*

The morning was a blur for Thomas, ensconced as he was with his new friends, and with his new found inner light. After cleaning up their area in the monastery, the group of Pilgrims left and continued on their path to Canterbury. Thomas, now released, chatted volubly and amiably with the Woolers, as well as the rest of a now enlarging group of Pilgrims, some coming into Watling Street from different paths, different roads, different origins. The road actually widened a bit, as rivers inevitably widen from feeder streams.

The Thames itself, never far off to the left, had widened considerably since the span of the London Bridge, miles, epochs, ago. The hills had become chalkier, and occasionally Thomas would get a glimpse of the Swale, a side channel of the Thames that had cut off the Island of Sheppey from their side of the Thames shore.

Godfrey seemed invigorated, and really seemed to swell as they walked further into the countryside. The group passed through ancient towns with what sounded to Thomas to be odd sounding names. When he mentioned this to Godfrey, the big Saxon laughed, snorting, "That's because you're a wee French lad, Thomas. These are good Saxon names, with great history! Soak it in. Maybe you will find your true people and fill out a bit." They both laughed.

The Wooler family was kind and fun. Since leaving their northern village outside Carlisle, the family had really been wandering for three years before starting the pilgrimage in Southwarke. They had little money, and mostly subsisted on the kindness of strangers, the network of abbeys and monasteries across England that took in wandering strangers.

The pilgrims had fallen into a gentle pace through the Kentish countryside. Conversations among the walkers were generally of the two or three person variety, and the composition of these small groups shifted constantly as individuals sped up or slowed down, joining and leaving as each pleased.

Being a big man, Godfrey seemed content to remain in the lead, but would join interesting conversations in Pilgrim groups that he overtook. Thomas preferred eventually to lag back a bit, getting to know, not only members of the Wooler clan, but also pilgrims on the edges.

Thomas was delighted to discover that Chaucer had not exaggerated the diversity of the Pilgrims; from poor wanderers to minor nobles the road contained all walks of English life. The Pilgrims did entertain on the road with songs and some stories. Thomas was, in fact, young for a solitary pilgrim, but there were, he found, a fair number of children on the road with families.

As the Pilgrims moved to the southeast the fields and orchards would occasionally give way to a village or town. After a few hours of walking, Thomas entered the village of Rainham.

Godfrey's eyes lit up at the site of the very old town with its central ancient oaks in the yard of the church, Saint Margret's, on the right side of the road. He had arrived in the town ahead of the little group, and, atop the small hill that crested the town, pointed gleefully at the church, and to the small group of tables along the side of the western yard.

"Proper Saxons here!" Godfrey exclaimed gleefully at the smell of the soup that that church had made ready for pilgrims, the money for which came from ancient bequest, the original donor's name long forgotten. Thomas smiled, noticing that even Godfrey's family rolled their eyes at his enthusiasm.

The churchyard had a small well, and the water was cool and fresh. Thomas drank a healthy dose, then retrieved some of the pottage from the ancient cauldron, placing it in an old wooden cup, lying on a nearby table.

The food was simple and filling. Made of village leftovers and water, a clear act of generosity from the town and its church, which over countless generations had become used to the steady stream of pilgrims to Canterbury.

Thomas settled under a shade tree to quietly eat, and to get out of the hot midafternoon sun. He looked at Godfrey admiring the church, gesticulating at the tall tower, and, smiling, decided to sit next to a pale young man, about 5 years older than Thomas, who was sitting by himself, quietly studying the group.

"This is a beautiful place!" Thomas observed happily as he approached. Settling into the shade, he asked, "Mind if I sit down?"

The other boy smiled and shrugged, gesturing with a shrugged shoulder and a turn of his head towards his left.

Thomas said confidently, "My name is Thomas More."

The boy smiled, and replied quietly, "I had heard that. I am Cuthbert Tunstall."

Happy that Cuthbert had spoken, Thomas said, "pleased to meet you, Cuthbert!" Then asked, "Where are you from?"

Cuthbert relaxed a bit, his posture opening as he took some soup. "Mostly the north, but for the last year I've been studying at Oxford."

Thomas practically leapt up. "Oxford!!," he cried, "I'll be going there soon! Is it fantastic!"

Cuthbert's face fell a little, as he stiffened. "It was until the plague hit this spring." Thomas started. He hadn't heard about that. "I was at Balliol, and, well…plagues are bad. I got sick, but didn't die."

Thomas nodded his head sympathetically. He added in a quiet voice, "I thought people went to Oxford to avoid the plagues in the larger cities?"

Cuthbert nodded, "makes sense and usually works. But not this year." He paused, his eyes dreamy, "the sickness hit in April, just as spring hit. That too was unusual. When I got sick, I was sent out into the countryside where I had relatives. They were kind."

Thomas shifted his position a bit, a chill coming over him. Cuthbert noticed, and stiffened as he expected Thomas to withdraw out of fear of obtaining the plague from someone who had once suffered from it.

"He had the plague," Thomas thought.

*"And he was at Oxford," replied his inner voice.*

"Plague"

*"Oxford"*

"Mother also died from a fever."

*"But you didn't. And he didn't either."*

Thomas eyed Cuthbert and noticed that he still had some swollen nodules in his neck, presumably from the disease."

Thomas made a decision, and moved over to Cuthbert, sitting down next to him.

"You sure you want to do that?" Cuthbert asked, concerned.

"Yep," replied Thomas. "You seem nice, and I want to know you better. And besides," Thomas added with a mischievous smile, "besides…We're on Pilgrimage to Canterbury. If I get sick, we just lug me to the shrine and I will be cured!"

Cuthbert looked askance, asking, "what possible flaw could there be in that plan?"

"None that I can think of," replied Thomas confidently. He gestured to the soup, "I've been wondering," he asked seriously, "how's the food at Oxford?"

Cuthbert laughed uproariously, drawing the attention of several nearby Pilgrims. He finally managed to ask, "what College are you attending?"

Thomas smiled and replied, "Canterbury."

Cuthbert stopped laughing. "The Archbishop's school?" he asked with a raised eyebrow.

"Yes," replied Thomas hesitantly.

Cuthbert smiled kindly and looked at his soup, raising the cup a bit. "This will seem like manna from heaven," he replied.

Thomas inhaled a bit, and looked nervously at the older boy. "Seriously?" he asked.

"Mostly," Cuthbert replied. "I've not heard of any Canterbury students eating shoe leather, but the rations are pretty meagre."

"Perhaps they've gotten better since you left?" Thomas asked hopefully.

"In three months?" Tunstall replied, "I think not."

Thomas was uncomfortable, but still quite intrigued by his new acquaintance. He decided to shift tacks. "Will you be going back to Oxford?" he asked.

Tunstall coughed then said with a mixture of sadness and pride, "No. I don't think so. There is a scholar at Cambridge named Erasmus, who invited me there when he heard I had been with plague. Besides, Oxford doesn't want plague survivors back. We're bad luck. Kind of like lepers." Then he smiled and used his thumb and forefinger to make it look like he had lost his nose like he was a leper.

Thomas laughed, then looked around a bit at the now descending sun. The Woolers had stood and were gesturing to Thomas to come along with them. He looked at Cuthbert, and said, "We should get along. Our goal was to make Milton Regis tonight. Godfrey thinks there is a Saxon Saint there that he can pray to."

"The big man?" Cuthbert asked, also rising. "What is his story?"

"Great fellow from the North. Very proud not to be a Frenchman like you or me." Thomas replied smiling broadly.

The two took their empty cups over to a tub of water and rinsed them out, leaving them to dry on a nearby table.

"A Frenchman?" asked Cuthbert, confused.

"He doesn't like Normans very much," Thomas replied still beaming. "It seems they have ruined England." He laughed involuntarily, but with great affection for Godfrey and his family.

"But its been over four hundred years!?" Cuthbert exclaimed.

"Long memories, the Saxons," Thomas replied with a smile and a shrug. He turned and started to jog a bit towards the Woolers waving.

Tunstall caught up, though easily winded from his illness.

"Woolers! Woolers!" Thomas called. " I have a new Frenchman for our band."

Godfrey stopped as Thomas approached, smiled very broadly, arms outstretched which even made the smile seem larger, and called back, "well, Thomas, what is one more worthless Frenchman to me?" He then eyed Tunstall, particularly his neck, and his smile faded just a shade, and said, "a Frenchman who had the plague? Well I guess its good we're on our way to Canterbury."

The big man paused and stole a glance at his wife who gave a little nod of her head. Godfrey's smile regained its radiance. "Well come on then, new Frenchman! Yer welcome to march with us!"

And the group of brown rough clad Pilgrims set forth again down Watling street. As they left the lovely churchyard in Rainham, there was a peal from the eight beautiful bells in the church tower.

## Chapter 18 - July 4, 1492, evening.

The rest of the afternoon walk from Rainham to Milton Regis took about three hours. It was only about six miles, but there were so many interesting things to see and to talk about on the way that the group wandered mostly aimlessly.

The first village after Rainham was called Newington, which had a few interesting diversions for the travelers. First, at the corner of Watling Street and the Church lane there was a cross, made of simple stones that all pilgrims stopped at, for it was the location of several miracles attributed to St. Thomas Becket, largely because he had apparently stopped here and blessed some children on his way to martyrdom. The group was interested, but lackadaisical at this site. Less interested because of the Friars hawking junk from the cross at the corner, collecting "contributions" from Pilgrims in exchange for some cheap tin pilgrims' badges from Newington. Thomas examined the badge, and felt his own from Brother Will, and moved on.

Infinitely more interesting, however were the two stones standing erect by the side of the Church lane, a few hundred feet north of Watling. These two large boulders served as kind of side markers to a slight bend in the road, and each had the clear raised imprint of what appeared to be a man's shoe. These were the famous "Devil's Stones." There was a little stream nearby, the Libbett stream, and a churning of the water created a mist in the afternoon heat that made the water appear to be boiling. A local priest from the nearby church explained that Satan had stolen the church-bells and had taken them down underground leaving only two marks, the boiling water where he had descended, and his footprints on the stones of the road.

Thomas thought the water boiling was a little vague for his taste, but did think the marks on the stones looked like shoeprints. At the priest's encouragement, Thomas and the others each took turns placing an index finger atop the stone while circling slowly three times around the stone.

This was supposed to bring good luck. Thomas felt unchanged, but excited to see what the day would bring.

Godfrey circled last, and uttered some unintelligible chant under his breath as he circled. Thomas could not make it out, but thought he heard the words "Nisse" and "Seaxburh" or something like that.

The afternoon was beginning to lengthen, and so the group decided…well really Godfrey decided, to move on to Milton Regis.

It was late, then, as they arrived at the abbey in Milton Regis. Godfrey was waxing very enthusiastically about somebody named St. Seaxburh, who Thomas took to be an old Saxon Queen who had become a nun and had created miracles of one sort or another. There was a field just east of the town, and Godfrey relayed with great indignity how Edward the Confessor, the earliest French King, the one who traitorously gave England to the Norman William, had destroyed an army led by one of his lords, Godwin, who, of course, was the father to the last true Saxon King, Harold Godwinson.

Godfrey's beard shook with emotion as he relayed this damning history to Thomas and Cuthbert, and the small knot of other Pilgrims, some rapt, some milling about smartly, half listening.

Godfrey was a good storyteller, and acted out for the crowd some of his gorier fantasies of the final battle scenes, the Saxon soldiers bravely falling were they stood with their battle axes, the victorious French mercenaries of the King ransacking the bodies of the Saxon dead.

The story was, Thomas admitted privately, thrilling. Mostly Thomas like the way his new friend told stories – with complete abandon, with the wildness of his north-country, yes Saxon, blood in full fire and fury.

Thomas noticed again that as Godfrey's accent became thicker as he grew passionate, as if he was retreating into some primal existence that had been only hinted at before. As he regaled the group, he seemed, as well, to grow taller, his hair bushier, his eyes wilder, more feral and predatory.

Thomas had known that Godfrey was a soldier with some burdensome secrets, but before this moment he had not seen his new friend's soul. His life played out in a kind of pantomime dance in front of an audience.

Thomas shifted uncomfortably.

"Now," Godfrey intoned, "it's a good weapon, but there is nothing like its grandfather, the Saxon battle axe. Now that's a real tool of war….A stone's weight and an 8 foot reach. Not anyone can even pick it up, much less swing it. A housecarl's job, if ever there was one."

Cuthbert interrupted, "Sir, what's a housecarl?"

Godfrey stopped and smiled. Some of his family shook their heads, almost imperceptibly.

Too late. Godfrey was off to the races.

"The Housecarl," Godfrey started rapidly, "was the Saxon King's personal guard. The inner circle in a very real sense. In battle, the King would be surrounded by a fearsome circle of these men, all with their axes swinging.

"At Hastings, King Harold was at the top of the hill, surrounded first by the Housecarls, 30 in number, and then by his large army of a few thousand. The French Bastard, Guillame. Ha!....William….and I mean that literally, was in the shallow valley below.

"All day the French troops, including three divisions of horse tried to dislodge the stout Saxon army. They failed each time. French archers tried to break up the Saxons and they failed. The Saxon troops were proud and brave. Only three weeks before they had destroyed a Viking army in the north, in Yorkshire, at Stamford Bridge. They had marched without rest down to Hastings.

"The French, being a tricky lot, tried a ruse. This was a last effort, the sun was lengthening. The day was ending. Harold could win by not losing.

"Onc French division attacked the front of the great Saxon army, but at a glancing blow. Then the scheming Frenchmen taunted the Saxon soldiers most grievously, and turned tail and ran off to the woods.

"The noble Saxons were outraged. The French cowards! In fits of passion a significant portion of the Saxon army ran off to the woods after the retreating French, leaving King Harold and his Housecarls exposed. King Harold called vainly after his men. With that opportunity, Guillame...I won't use his English name...loosed his arrows and quickly sent his two remaining divisions into an all out assault on the now depleted Saxon line."

Godfrey stopped to take a breath. He was red and shaking. His wife handed him a bottle and he took a generous swig of ale. He crouched a bit, his right hand on his knee. He brought his voice in low, so the listeners had to lean in to hear.

"One of the French arrows," Godfrey said, genuine sorrow lacing his voice, "had found a lucky mark and had killed King Harold on the top of the hill. It pierced his eye, passing, as if the Good Lord himself had guided it with His very hand." Godfrey held up his hand sadly.

"The arrow passed through the eyeslit in his helmet, drove through his eye and into his brain. The King died instantly, falling into the center of his Housecarls. And yet the Housecarls fought on. For England…For Saxons. " His voice trailed off.

"Guillame's army eventually killed every one of the Saxon Housecarl's. All who stayed at their posts. All fighting to the death. Still surrounding, defending King Harold. None ran."

Thomas noticed that a small crowd had gathered, listening intently to the Wooler's tale. Thomas realized that his own breathing had become shallow. He had stopped fidgeting.

Godfrey looked out at his listeners and wiped a little spittle from the side of his mouth. Thomas noticed that he allowed himself a little smile.

A blond youth of about 10, the child of some affluent appearing parents who stood off to the side, blurted out, "Well, then what happened to them?"

Godfrey now smiled openly, and asked, "to whom?"

The child was both confused and impatient, "The housecarls, of course."

Godfrey played with him a bit longer, "to honor that kind of bravery, son, you must speak their names correctly, it's house – carrrrrls. An a like in Adam and roll the R until it feels grrrrreat on the tongue."

The crowd laughed.

The boy tried a few times, and Godfrey worked with him until he could speak it "like a Northern Laird."

The boy then tried again, this time elaborately pronouncing the word.

Godfrey grew solemn. "They were Northmen all." He said slowly. "They held their circle, gradually pulling back, more tightly around King Harold's body, until the last four had linked arms. Then they too were cut down. Arrows, swords…you name it, all poured in. No

quarter asked, none given."

The group was silent. Thomas broke the silence by asking gently, "Godfrey, it was four

hundred years ago, but you talk about it like it was yesterday. Why?"

Godfrey looked up, smiled gently at Thomas. "Because, Thomas," he said, "because my

people were the Housecarls, my family. My King. Sworn to defend the King, even the King's

body, to the death."

Thomas nodded, and said, "Bosworth?"

Godfrey nodded, and said, "Bosworth, aye. Hastings, Agincourt, Crecy, the Holy Land.

It's all the same to us. We defend the King."

His sons nodded vigorously.

Thomas repeated, "and Bosworth?"

Godfrey grew solemn. "History isn't really ever truly history, Thomas, since it keeps

coming around. At Bosworth, King Richard was the attacker, the aggressor. Henry Tudor was

surrounded by men….French men….And Richard attacked their circle. Them all around Tudor,

some new lance held out we'd never seen before. Richard attacked almost by himself. Chopped

and sliced his way through. The very picture of a king in battle. His horse rose up and took a

lance in the side. Richard tossed off the back. Beautiful horse. Red on its breast.

Richard….Richards helmet with the crown on top got knocked off, rolled off the hill into a

bush…King Richard rose up. John Cheney, the biggest man near Tudor approached. Richard cut

him in half with one swing of his sword. Never seen the like. Richard moved on up. His men

struggled to catch up, but Richard had the war fever in his brain…he pushed forward…Henry's

Housecarl's held…..the French bastards held….Henry seemed to shrink in the center, or his men got larger….King Richard moved on in but one of the bastards got in a lucky shot to his head…The King went down….The French swarmed over him and killed him….Killed the…my…King."

Godfrey stopped, overcome. He slumped and began to cry. The group was silent. His children looked at him with a speechless awe. He had clearly never spoken to them of Bosworth, now twice in two days. Of what he had seen. Godfrey's wife moved quickly to him and placed her arms in a tender embrace.

Thomas rose and walked over to Godfrey, bent over and quietly hugged him. Overcome, Thomas whispered into the big man's ear, "King Richard saved the Princes."

Godfrey looked up quickly, uncomprehending, then processing. He opened his mouth to speak, struggling to find words, but Thomas shook him off.

"Later, Godfrey, Later. It's not safe," Thomas whispered urgently.

Godfrey closed his mouth. His eyes now comprehending.

Thomas stepped back, and stood, looking at the still quiet group. Thinking to alter the subject, Thomas said to Godfrey in a loud voice, "Godfrey. I honor you and your family." With that, Thomas bowed and went off to the door of the church.

Cuthbert Tunstall followed Thomas and as soon as the pair was out of earshot, tugged at Thomas's elbow.

"That was amazing!" Cuthbert said quietly but enthusiastically. "Do you think it's true?"

"I do," replied Thomas. " In fact, I am completely convinced that it is true."

Cuthbert paused for a second, and added, "Its almost like he was at both Hastings and Bosworth."

"For him," Thomas replied, "they are the same. His family, his ancestors, and now on down to him. We've asked families to bear these burdens all through time."

"What burdens" Cuthbert asked.

"Of being a soldier," Thomas replied, "not of being a knight or an officer, but that of being a soldier. Of fighting someone else's war, and dying but not having anyone remember your name. I think Godfrey takes the weight of the past on himself. That is his burden. I love him for it."

Thomas looked up at the lovely stained glass of the square Norman tower that had been added onto the old Saxon church. He pointed up at the church tower. Cuthbert followed his finger.

"Odd, isn't it," Thomas asked, "that all of the Norman church additions I've seen here in the country look like castle keeps?"

"Not odd, at all, Thomas," Cuthbert replied. "Think about it, think about Godfrey. The Normans were an occupying force. Kind of still are. They needed places to sleep secure from the masses."

"The bishops and priests?" asked Thomas.

"Especially them," Cuthbert responded emphatically. "Think about it. Who's in charge? The nobles and the clergy. The nobles move around and don't really have to interact with the people. But the churchmen? They are the ones that interact. And the churchpeople administer the government. They actually have to interact with the people. Your father is a lawyer, Thomas. What language do they speak in Court?"

"Norman French," Thomas replied, realization downing.

"Exactly," Cuthbert responded. "So four hundred years after the Conquest, the Courts, the Law, is still conducted in a language that most people do not understand."

Thomas paused, pondering that, and Cuthbert continued, "and in what language is the mass?"

"Latin," replied Thomas.

"you are going to Oxford, Thomas," Cuthbert went on. "In what language must you study?"

"Latin," replied Thomas.

"So, as a nation we conduct all significant business in languages that the majority of the people do not speak?" Cuthbert concluded.

"Yes," Thomas replied quietly.

"So ask me again why the priests built fortresses attached to their churches," Cuthbert said.

"Because they needed to," Thomas said almost inaudibly. Thinking a bit, he asked Cuthbert, "are you studying to be a priest, Cuthbert?"

"Yes," said Cuthbert. "I am. I want to help the church help the people." He paused, "Thomas," he asked, "what do you know of humanism?"

"I've heard the word," Thomas replied. "Is it big at Oxford?"

Cuthbert laughed sadly, "We will talk, Thomas, but it's about valuing humans, about valuing life and allowing everyone access to contact with the divine. But think about it, Thomas, think about how a Saxon would see life in England four hundred years after the conquest. And then understand your friend Godfrey."

"Our friend Godfrey," came the voice of the big man behind them. He had improbably approached the pair very quietly from behind. "That was nice, Cuthbert. Ye might not be such a Frenchman after all." He smiled broadly and clapped the young, thin man on the back.

Cuthbert looked pleased at the attention. With a gentle pull on the young man's shoulder, Godfrey gently moved him a little sideways and said, kindly and with a smile on his face, "go away now. I need to speak with Thomas."

Thomas shuddered a bit, regretting his impulse to have revealed to Godfrey what should never have been revealed.

Cuthbert looked confusedly at Godfrey and Thomas and, despite the pleading look in Thomas's eyes, he turned and left.

As soon as the room had cleared, Godfrey approached Thomas in a stern, fatherly way, gesturing Thomas to a nearby stool, and then kneeling beside him." Situated thus, so that Thomas was in a corner of the stone vault, and the rest of his field of vision occupied by the bulk of the Northman, Godfrey whispered to Thomas, "tell me what you mean, 'the princes live?'"

Thomas shuddered and looked pleadingly at Godfrey, gulping, "I'm sorry Godfrey, I shouldn't have said anything. It was just…."

Godfrey cut him off, sternly, "Son, I am King Richard's sworn defender. I failed at Bosworth because I didn't stand up to Percy. My family has defended the King for hundreds of years. My ancestors died doing their duty. I lived not doing mine. And now I am useless. What do you know?"

Thomas had looked into Godfrey's eyes as he was saying this. There was nothing but sincerity there. He decided to take another tack, asking "what do you know of King Edward's Princes Edward and Richard?"

Godfrey considered this for a moment, unsure how to answer. He stumbled a bit. Finally, he replied, still in a whisper, "I was with King Edward when he died. That rotten family of his all around, dividing up the realm. The King was calling for his brothers, Edmund, George, and Richard in his delirium. The family ignored him. Then he cleared and called for Lord Hastings, his greatest friend. Hastings came forward, and the King told him that Richard was Lord Protector, and that Richard knew what to do. That seemed to concern the Queen. Her hands started twitching. She went to the King and knelt beside him. He smiled at her and said, 'Richard knows what to do, my Queen.'"

Godfrey paused, overcome. Thomas had looked down during this, imagining the scene, the death of the King.

Thomas's returned gaze seemed to give him strength, for he continued, "my group of guards was dispatched to retrieve Prince…no… King Edward who was in Wales with the Queen's brother Lord Rivers. We were to get them and bring them back to London. The new King was only 12, but I was now his sworn protector.

"We retrieved the new King, and we were met halfway to London by Richard, with Buckingham and a large contingent. Richard was the Lord Protector, so naturally we gave way. Was never sure how or why, but Rivers was arrested and executed right there. The group came on to London, and King Edward… Well, we placed him in the Tower for safekeeping. Added his brother Richard soon after.

"Never really sure how it happened, but things seemed to go out of control, and then one day Richard is King. We was happy about that. He was quiet and somber, not cheerful and full of life like his brother, but he seemed a good man. We never knew what to make of the young King

Edward in the tower. Now just Edward. He and his brother seemed like nice boys. But that was all they were to us was boys. Princes, sure. But boys."

"French?" Thomas asked with a little smile.

Godfrey's turn to look down. "Well, yes," he said, "maybe a little French." Then he chuckled a bit.

"I'm sorry," said Thomas.

Godfrey looked grateful, then continued in a quiet, determined voice, "the other guards and me, we were happy with King Richard. He was a good man. His wife and son were also very quiet. No airs. All acted like Saxons and Northmen." He puffed his chest, and looked dreamily away for a moment, imagining a family he loved, and loved serving.

Thomas kindly allowed Godfrey's reverie to play itself out naturally. The smile on the big man's face reward enough. After a bit, he returned to the conversation and asked Thomas, "so what about the Princes, then?"

Thomas steeled himself, and looked Godfrey in the eyes, and replied, "I was seven when my father and I met King Richard." He stopped and looked around the room to ensure that they were alone. He then lowered his voice enough so that no outside listeners could hear, moving in close to his friend's ear, breaking eye contact, but generating a closer, still more intimate connection.

"I am sworn by King Richard, himself," Thomas continued, "a solemn promise I made to him. I am certain that you understand the kind of promise that I made." He moved back a bit again to look Godfrey in the eyes. Godfrey nodded assent. He did understand very well.

With that Thomas moved back in again, and said, quietly. "King Richard told me that he had sworn an oath to his brother, King Edward, that he would protect Edward's children. No matter what. He had decided that the best way to protect the boys was to make everyone believe that they were dead. That he had killed them."

Thomas moved back. Godfrey's faced was a mask as he processed this. Thomas saw bits of hope, resentment, compassion, understanding and admiration pass through those dark, Saxon eyes. Finally he spoke, hesitantly, "ye men?.....ye mean?....."

Cutting him off, Thomas went back in, "Shhhh… We can't be heard by anyone. I have told no one."

Godfrey just moved his lips, then whispered, "Lambert Simnel??....Perkin Warbeck?..."

Thomas soothed, "both fakes. I wouldn't be surprised if they were supported by people who wanted to flush out the real Princes, figuring the real Princes would step forward at some point."

"Where are they?" Godfrey asked.

"I have no idea," answered Thomas honestly. "It seemed to be a very small group, but King Richard told me that they would be best served by people thinking he was a monster capable of killing his nephews."

"Did you see them then?" Godfrey asked.

"Yes," replied Thomas.

"Have ye seen them since?" continued Godfrey

"No," replied Thomas.

Godfrey thought for a few minutes, looking around the room, taking in enormous drags of air as he pondered.

"We must do nothing, then," the Saxon said, determinedly. "The King's plan is working."

Thomas agreed, then added, "and Godfrey, you must never tell anyone, and we must never speak of it again. I swore an oath to the King."

Godfrey nodded assent. His eyes glistened with tears and his hands moved aimlessly. He looked at Thomas and nodded, but then added very sincerely, "Thomas, thank you for telling me."

"We should get back," Thomas said, looking at the door to his left. "People will be wondering what we're up to." He giggled a bit, and surprisingly, so Did Godfrey in a little high pitched noise that came incongruously out both his mouth and nose.

They walked back slowly, Thomas looking anxiously at Godfrey hoping that he had just done the right thing, and Godfrey, in a reverie, still laughing occasionally, a happy look on his face.

"I hope I've done the right thing," Thomas thought anxiously.

*"We will see, Thomas."*

"That's it?"

*"You made a decision for all the right reasons, Thomas. You made a decision to include Godfrey out of love and compassion."*

"Yes, but."

*"But there are consequences to every decision, no matter how correctly decided."*

"I was kind of hoping for 'That was good.'"

*"It was good. I'm proud of you for it. Whether it works out well remains to be seen."*

"Thanks again."

Godfrey and Thomas rejoined the group as they were heading into a small hall attached to the church that had been built to house and feed pilgrims. There was a good porridge, weak ale, and some coarse bread. Thomas sat with Cuthbert Tunstall and a younger Wooler son at a side bench in the corner. Godfrey seemed a bit like a man freed, as he sat at a larger table with his older children and wife. A few other Pilgrims mixed in with these groups and at other tables.

The room was lively on this, the third night, the midpoint of the pilgrimage. People were getting to know one another, their shared experiences of the past few days lubricating the acquaintance as much as the ale. The religious of the small abbey were quite attentive and kind. The abbey had long been supported by the generosity of affectionate alumni of the pilgrimage, and their kindness engendered fond memories of the journey, enhancing that natural generosity.

Thomas marveled at the transformations that had occurred in the pilgrims over the past few days. He had started to know names, and since his experience the day before, had been feeling very generous and loving to everyone. He found himself wanting, even craving to know more about each of the people he travelled with.

After all of the Pilgrims had finished eating and had cleared their rough bowls and cups to the side, Thomas, on an inspiration, climbed and stood on his table.

Raising his arms to get attention, Thomas cried out, "Friends!"

His voice was a little high for his own taste, but after a few more call outs, the Pilgrims at the tables stopped their talking to turn their heads towards the skinny fourteen year old who was standing on a table in their midst.

Godfrey called out genially, "Thomas, our young Frenchman, wants to tell us something!" He then winked broadly at Thomas.

Thomas waited for silence, then smiled, patting his hands on his sides looking for pockets. Finding none, he placed his hands up towards the crowd.

"Friends," Thomas said again, louder and, thankfully a little lower this time. "We are now together here in Milton Regis as, I hope you will all agree, friends and fellow pilgrims. We come together in peace and in love as we work our way to the shrine of Thomas Becket in Canterbury."

There were some cheers from the friendly group. Thomas waited them out.

"In honor," he continued, "of this momentous feat that we are accomplishing together…" more huzzahs…"I hope I would not be out of order in asking that we spend some time telling each other tales, such as our learned ancestor Geoffrey Chaucer suggested."

Some laughs in the group. A few more cheers, and two or three laughing Pilgrims, led by Godfrey, calling out "You first, Frenchman!"

Thomas smiled broadly, and bowed a bit.

"As it happens, I do have a story for you all…" More laughed. There were, a few claps on the back.

"I would like to tell the tale of Zaccheus the tax collector," Thomas said seriously.

The crowd paused. "God! Some cried." "Boring," cried others.

Thomas waved his hands up and down. "My friends," he cried with a smile. "I beg patience, for you have never heard me tell the story of Zaccheaus."

"Fair enough," yelled Godfrey, "But ye better make it short, Thomas." He gestured to the group. "They seem a little impatient tonight." He laughed with the crowd.

"A short story then," Thomas cried to the crowd, holding his hand about three feet from the ground. Several in the crowd, laughed, Cuthbert included, Thomas was happy to note.

"My good friends," Thomas said, still smiling broadly, "Jesus comes into Jericho. A large crowd surrounds him, listening to him, cheering him. The richest man in town, despised for being a tax collector, hears the commotion, but is pointedly ignored. He's trying to see Jesus, but because he is very short, cannot see over the crowd. He tries to penetrate the crowd, bobbing and weaving, standing on tiptoe, jumping. He still can't see anything, but he sees a tree up ahead. He scurries around to the tree and climbs it, getting above the crowd, hanging from a branch, his toga flailing, his dignity completely and comically gone.

"So Jesus approaches and looks up and sees the rich, short tax collector hanging from a branch. I do not believe that underclothing was worn under robes in those times." Thomas stops and, to general laughs pulls on the rough brown pilgrim's robe he is wearing, looks down at his own groin and shrugs. The crowd roars, and after a beat, Thomas continues, "So Jesus says Zacchaeus, hurry down, clearly the party is with you tonight!"

The crowd cheers, and when they quieted a bit, Thomas says in a low, and gentle voice, "my friends, think about this scene and where we all are together tonight. In my eyes, I see the look on Zacchaeus's face. He is now the center of Jesus and the crowd's attention. I cannot for a moment imagine him climbing down from his tree. I think he was so surprised that he lost his grip and did in fact hurry down, well really fell, landing right at Jesus's feet. Upright, and unhurt, but now in the crowd, part of Jesus's crowd, part of us, without his prior dignity, but still marked by his great enthusiasm

"And in my vision of this wonderful scene. With kindness, with joy, and with love, Jesus laughs."

Thomas laughs happily at the vision, the story, and with his love for his fellow pilgrims. The group applauds, as Thomas bows. Even the few remaining monks on the side acknowledge Thomas as he climbs down from his perch.

Cuthbert Tunstall clapped Thomas on the back as he helped him , and says "well done, Thomas."

Godfrey looked around the room, calling out, "Thank you, Thomas… So who wants to follow that?"

The rest of the evening was spent in happy story telling. Godfrey's teenage sons came out of their shells to sing old Saxon songs in beautiful voices. Thomas replied with a sweet rendition of a Robert Fayrfax song musing on life, which caused the crowd to challenge him.

"Thomas," Godfrey's eldest son, Robert, called out, "how about something of yours?"

There were cries of agreement from others and Thomas blushed a bit and looked down.

Finally Thomas replied, looking up, "well, I have written some poetry…"

"Yes," cried the group. "Let us hear it!"

Thomas smiled. Truth be told, he enjoyed the attention. He began, "My poem is called 'A Pageant of Verses.'"

The crowd quieted in dramatic anticipation.

Thomas began, quietly, doing a pantomime with each verse.

Thomas pulled up his robe to his knees, and then made a show of mussing his hair into an unruly mane, and then folding his arms as if he were rocking a baby.

"Childhood," Thomas said in what he thought was the high, squeaky voice of a child.

> "I am called Childhood, in play is all my mind,
> To cast a quoit, a cokstele and a ball,

A top can I set and drive it in his kind;

But would to God these hateful books all

Were in a fire burnt to powder small;

Then might I lead my life always in play,

Which life God send me to mine ending day!"

Thomas stopped and took a little bow at the smiles of the appreciative audience. He then dropped his robe, and smoothed his hair. Striking a confident pose, hands now on hips, Thomas continued in an unnaturally deep voice, "Manhood-

"Manhood I am, therefore I me delight

To hunt and hawk, to nourish-up and feed,

The greyhound to the course, the hawk to the flight,

And to bestride a good and lusty steed-

These things become a very man indeed.

Yet thinketh this boy his peevish game sweeter,

But what, no force, his reason is no better."

Thomas then mussed his hair again, and playing both sides of besotted lovers, swinging back and forth, hands in a little heart shape clasped to his breast, Thomas sang in his natural fourteen year old high voice, "Venus and Cupid-

"Whoso na knoweth the strength, power, and might,

Of Venus and me her little son Cupid;

Thou Manhood shalt a mirror been aright,

By us subdued for all thy great pride,

My fiery dart pierceth thy tender side.

Now thou who erst dispisedst children small

Shall wax a child again and be my thrall."

Thomas dropped his hands and stood still, before spying a waking stick, which he took then seemed to visibly age as he slumped into a crooked back slouch, his voice breaking and sad as he continued, "Age-

"Old age am I, with lockes thin and hoar,

Of our short life the last and best part,

Wise and discreet; the public weal therefore

I help to rule, to my labour and smart

Therefore Cupid withdraw thy fiery dart.

Chargeable matters shall of love oppress

Thy childish game and idle business."

Thomas dropped his stick, clutching his chest dramatically, falling back onto a table,

crying out in an sonorous, deep monotone, "Death-

"Though I be foul, ugly, lean, and misshape,

Yet there is none in all this world wide,

That may my power withstand or escape;

Therefore sage father, greatly magnified,

Descend from your chair, set apart your pride,

Vouchsafe to lend, tho' it be to your pain,

To me, a fool, some of your wise brain."

The group of Pilgrims was silent, enraptured. Some shivered a bit at the invocation of

Death. Godfrey simply looked pleased as Thomas suddenly stood up lifted his arms with a huge

smile on his face, continuing in a bright, cheerful, clear voice, "Fame-

"Fame I am called, marvel you nothing,

Though with tongues am compassed all round,

For in voice of people is my chief living,

O cruel Death, thy power I confound.

When thou a noble man hast brought to ground,

"Maugre thy teeth, to live cause him shall I

Of people in perpetual memory."

Thomas dropped his arms, and adopted a serious mien, saying "Time-

"I whom thou sees with horologe in hand,

Am named Time, the lord of every hour,

I shall in space destroy both sea and land.

O simple Fame, how darest thou man honour,

Promising of his name and endless flower;

Who may in the world have a name eternal

When I shall in process destroy the world and all."

Thomas wondered at the silence of the crowd, so he paused again, looked out at what he decided were very interested faces, then squared himself to the Pilgrims. He raised his arms a bit from his sides, and looked upwards, his eyes closed and he went on, "Eternity-

"He needeth not to boast, I am Eternity,

The very name signifieth well,

And mine empire infinite shall be.

Thou, mortal Time, every man can tell,

Art nothing else but the mobility

Of sun and moon, changing in every degree;

When they shall leave their course, thou shalt be brought,

For all thy pride and boasting into nought."

Thomas looked straight ahead now and smiled. His voice was happy and clear as he concluded, "The Poet-

"These figures are all false, no matter how applied,

But what a wonderful skill,

For the person, able to feed, so tried,

A wandering Pilgrim, a picture still,

Of life, of love, of the goods of the world,

Traversing joy and praise, with flags unfurled

The Poet arises to o'ersee the light, the plot, the fall

And give God's gift of life to all.

There was applause, and smiles. Thomas bowed deeply to the group. The religious on the sides smiled widely.

Theo arose with Cuthbert Tunstall, both saying, "That's better, Thomas. Much, Much better."

Godfrey cleared his throat amidst the din, and the room silenced a bit. "That was a Saxon poem, Thomas! I knew ye had it in ya." Then he looked around the room, smiling, and, noticing the darkness outside, said, "and perhaps, we should all catch a few winks before tomorrows adventure."

It took a bit, but the crowd eventually wandered off to different areas of the, now, sleeping room. A few went over near the fading cooking fire, hoping for the comfort of the dry heat against the summer humidity. Others went to sheltered tables or corners. Godfrey moved off with his wife to the dark far corner of the room, and Cuthbert and Thomas, sat quietly at a remaining table in the center.

They spoke quietly, comparing notes on Oxford, life, the plague, and families. Cuthbert was anxious to learn of London, and about the Archbishop of Canterbury, John Morton. For his part, Thomas wanted to know about Oxford, Oxford, and, really, Oxford. They spoke well into the night until Thomas, fourteen year old Thomas, exhausted at the long day, fell asleep in mid sentence, his head drooping, his eyes falling closed, and finally leaning forward, he was asleep on the table.

Cuthbert Tunstall found this very amusing, and he moved off a bit, stretched out on the floor, and quickly fell off for the night, a happy smile on his face.

Thomas awoke with a start while the dawn was still a dreamy possibility. He was awakened by the gentle, very English plainsong from the Milton Regis church next door. He hadn't remembered falling asleep, and was confused as to both his whereabouts, and the explaining why's of his surrounding. Seeing his new friend Cuthbert Tunstall to the side, snoring quietly, made the events, the happy events, of the previous day come back to him.

*"Well, it's morning."* his voice greeted him.

"Almost," thought Thomas, still a little wooly around the edges. Then, after a pause and a little shake of his head, "Milton Regis?"

*"Yes…Great job on your poem last evening."*

"Thank you. What's in store for today?"

*"We will have to see. You should go to Lauds."*

"Lauds"

*"Lauds…the early morning service at a monastery you have slept through the past several days.*

"Do you think they will let me in?"

*No harm in trying."*

Thomas rose gingerly, careful not to awaken or disturb any of the Pilgims, and made his way to the doors of the church. He found a small outhouse to the side, and was able to relieve himself, happily, of the previous evenings liquids. He made his way to the main porch on the west side of the old gothic church, increasing rose colored light starting to stream over the hills to the east.

Peeking in through the large, heavy wooden church door, which he was able to pull ajar with modest difficulty, Thomas saw a few sputtering candles, and about a dozen religious, in their black Benedictine robes, in a heavenward cast, finishing a joyous, to Thomas's ear anyway, hymn.

An older monk rose to the front of the little group, and turned to face them. He spotted Thomas in the back, and smiled broadly, motioning to his right, welcoming Thomas to join the group.

When Thomas skirted lightfootedly to his left, to the side of the group, the older monk proceeded in Latin, chanting, "Oh God, come to my assistance!" The group responded in Latin, chant-singing the "Glory Be!," chanting, Thomas included, "Gloria Patri, et Filio, et Spiritui Sancto, Sicut erat in principio, et nunc, et semper, et in saecula saeculorum. Amen"

This chant, 'glory be to the father, the son, and the Holy Spirit, as it was in the beginning is now and ever shall be world without end, Amen" had an immediately calming and centering effect on Thomas. His body lost tension as his mind entered the ancient monastic service celebrating the rise, the resurrection of the sun. Thomas crossed himself for the father and the son and the Holy spirit as an involuntary reflex.

The service proceeded through some readings and some more songs, some call and response. On one level, Thomas listened to the readings, but at another, he was awash in the service, dreamily, as if the whole, gentle, comforting litany was awash around him, bathing him.

Thomas's reverie turned his eyes up into the enclosed central tower of the ancient church. The light of the day was starting to whiten a bit, and the bright colors of the stained glass up high on the eastern side of the church began to swim to life for the day.

The readings were finishing, as the older monk came forward again, this time with the "Book of Benedict," the ancient guide to monastic life and the life and liturgy guided by the hours.

The ancient and gilded book fell open naturally to the Canticle of Zachary. Without needing to consult his open reference, the older monk sang in a clear tenor,

> *"Blessed be the Lord, The God of Israel.*
> *He has come to His people and set them free.*
> *He has raised up for us a mighty Saviour,*
> *Born of the house of His servant David.*
> *Through His holy prophets He promised of old*
> *That He would save us from our enemies,*
> *From the hands of all who hate us.*
> *He Promised to show mercy to our fathers*
> *And to remember His holy Covenant.*
> *This was the oath He swore to our Father Abraham:*
> *To set us free from the hands of our enemies*
> *Free to worship Him without fear*
> *Holy and righteous in His sight*
> *All the days of our life.*
> *You, My child shall be called*
> *The prophet of the Most High,*
> *For you will go before the Lord to prepare His way,*
> *To give his people knowledge of salvation*
> *By the forgiveness of their sins.*
> *In the tender compassion of our Lord*
> *The dawn from on high shall break upon us,*
> *To shine on those who dwell in darkness*
> *And the shadow of death,*
> *And to guide our feet into the way of peace."*

And then they finished this with another call of Glory Be.

Thomas had been made to attend the occasional Lauds while the Archbishop was in a monastery in the morning. Most of the time, though, the pages had been excused, having been up late the previous night with the various social functions of the travelling Lord and Head of the Church in England.

Now, alone, but surrounded by the simple monks of this lovely little church along the old Roman Watling Street, Thomas felt….complete….made whole by the morning service celebrating the return of the sun and the resurrection of the Son.

To finish off Lauds, the older monk began to speak in a low gravelly voice, which matched his thin frame, and tonsured head in an oddly fitting manner,

"My brothers and sisters," the older monk began with an uplift of both hands to his gathering. He smiled, then looked at Thomas, continuing, "it seems we have a young visitor today." A gesture to Thomas. "A young pilgrim, it would appear." He nodded to Thomas. "You are welcome here, my son." He paused as the religious around him turned and smiled cordially before returning their collective gaze to the senior monk.

"Today, my brothers and sisters, we have heard from Isaiah that the Lord's throne is here on heaven and in Earth. We are the keepers of the throne. We make it beautiful and ready for the Lord's New Day. Let us therefore, go into our day with the joy and happiness of our sure knowledge of the value of what we do today and every day for our great God above. Amen and Thank you."

After that, there was another hymn, a lovely chant about Mary that Thomas had never heard before, and then all rose, singing a *Te Deum* as they filed from the church into the yard.

Thomas stood shyly off to the side, feeling a little shy, until a young bright-faced monk approached him, saying "Welcome young Pilgrim! I am Brother James." Brother James then held up his right hand, palm towards Thomas, in open greeting. The Brother smiled.

Thomas returned the smile at the monk, who appeared to be only a few years older than himself. Thomas said, "Thank you! I am Thomas More. From London, but now from this road. Thank you all for your hospitality here, and for allowing me in to that beautiful service."

Brother James was radiant, an emotion that passed easily into Thomas. He suddenly recognized Thomas from the prior evening, and gushed enthusiastically, "Thomas, I loved your poem last night, and your stories as well. Did you really write the poem yourself?"

Thomas stood a little taller, pleased with the praise, and replied, "I did. I had a lot of fun writing it."

James studied him, impressed. "You have a definite gift," he said warmly. "It was a pleasure to have experienced it."

Refreshed after some sleep, some praise, and the dawn service, Thomas looked enthusiastically, and hungrily, at his new friend. "Thank you very kindly," Thomas replied warmly, "Now that everyone's awake, can I be of service here… help in any way?" He looked towards the kitchen.

James laughed. "You clearly also have the gift of tact as well!" He looked kindly at Thomas, thinking, then he said, "We're Benedictine's here. We laugh and pray, and work together. We follow the Rules of Saint Benedict pretty closely. Benedict calls us to eat after *Sext*, the sixth hour, when the sun hits its peak for the day. We have some bread and ale for the Pilgrims in the morning so they may depart after Prime, but we work and clean and tend to our lands through *Prime* and *Terce*. One of the ways we honor God, Thomas, is through the regular cycles of the day."

Thomas nodded, thinking. After a moment, he asked, "If I were to work with you through Sext, might I then leave after dinner?"

James smiled broadly and happily, "That would be wonderful, Thomas! Of course you could. For this glorious morning you are one of us!"

Thomas beamed, happy to be included. "What shall we do together, then?" he asked.

"As it happens, Thomas," James said proudly, "I am an assistant to the Scribner. We shall go and copy this morning." He paused, winking, "how fair is your hand?"

It was Thomas's turn to puff a bit. "I was taught at Saint Anthony's in London," Thomas said. "The master there, Nicholas Holt said my hand was 'as fair as any monk's'."

James laughed. "Then lets go down to see what Ludolph the Carthusian has for us today."

Thomas asked, "Ludolph?"

James turned and gushed to Thomas, "You don't know Ludolph? He's fantastic! An old French Carthusian. He wrote the *vita Christae*. It's a series of meditations on the life of Christ, Tells the stories, like you did last night with Zaccaeus. You will just love him. I've been working to make a copy of him for a year now. It's hard work, but the act of copying, you really get to learn a book."

"How far are you?" Thomas asked politely.

"I have completed nearly 20 pages," James said proudly.

"Twenty pages," said Thomas, mentally doing math, "how long is the book?"

"just over 300," James said, noticing Thomas trying to do figures in his head, "so, to answer your next question, about 15 years, if I get a little faster as I go on."

Thomas sputtered a bit, surprised. "Fifteen years?" he asked, "for the one book?"

"It will be a wonderful book!" James replied, a little defensively, "and I will know it, and Ludolph completely."

"That is true," Thomas said thoughtfully, before asking, "has Caxton thought about printing the book?"

"Caxton?!" James scoffed. "I doubt there is enough money in Christendom to drag Caxton away from his high paying pamphlets."

Thomas looked a little crestfallen and James immediately noticed. Curious at the reaction, James quickly asked, "that's right, you're a Londoner. Do you know Caxton?

Thomas brightened. "I do," he said. "My father takes me to his shop in Westminster sometimes. He's very nice. He once gave me some scrap printing. I've kept it."

James grinned at Thomas, saying, "you keep surprising me, Thomas. Let's go down and work on a book together properly, in our own hand"

James took Thomas by the elbow and guided him out a side door of the church, through a narrow alley into the now brightened early morning. The sun was still low, and the shadows long, but the light was clear and crisp.

There was a small stone building that James ushered Thomas into, explaining that this was the *Scriptorium* for their little outpost. There were several tall desks, and deconstructed books, copies in production of the large tome that occupied the central table. There were paint and ink pots neatly along a side set of shelves, and sheets of vellum in a tray. There was a monk carefully cutting hides, off in the opposite corner, trying to maximize the usable pages of hide for the careful calligraphy of others.

Thomas had seen this process from a distance before, at Westminster, for example, and had also seen Caxton at work with his printing press, but nothing prepared Thomas for the details of even this very small operation.

Brother James took Thomas to his table and showed him the page that he was working on, one of Ludolph's meditations on Jesus and his parents escaping to Egypt. A small inset painting had been done in the right upper corner that included a Capital "A" carefully inserted around the Holy Family. James explained that this had been done by Brother Michael, an older monk who was currently at work on another copy of his small painting on a similar page at the next desk.

The page, a light vellum, had been carefully, and very lightly, lined with a sharpened pencil. Brother James then was taking the same pencil and doing a very light first draft, copying from the page of the original Ludolph, which had been disassembled very gently.

James explained that they were making ten copies of Ludolph for various patrons, including one for their own library, and one as an eventual gift to the King.

Thomas took a stool and watched James light and gentle writing then, with the page full, watched him go back with a sharp feather pen and a jar of ink go back and ink in the letters, carefully sanding on each line before going on.

Thomas was fascinated for the first hour of watching this, and wanted to try his own hand, but James said, "wait until after Prime, but look around the room for a bit."

Thomas enjoyed inspecting the ink and paints, and spoke happily with the other monks in the room, learning what each did in this book construction. They each spoke quite warmly about how their particular task celebrated God on this wonderful day. Thomas exulted in the Joy that each brought to this room.

The bell rang for Prime, the next service of the day, right at, Thomas learned, six in the morning. The monks all came together and filed again into the church.

The service of Prime was a neat, symmetric, and very old liturgy composed to three Psalms. The monks, standing, were greeted by the thin older monk, who, upon seeing Thomas, smiled happily at him and gave a small wave then sang the first line alone in a booming deep voice, *"In finem Canticum Psalmi resurrectionis Iubilate Deo omnis terra."*

Thomas's Latin was very fluent, and he knew this, this sixty sixth Psalm by heart to know this as a cry to the whole Earth to "shout with joy to the Lord!" Thomas sang along for the rest of the Psalm with the Brothers in their black robes.

After Psalm sixty-six, the brothers immediately proceeded to recite Psalm fifty, then sing a little antiphon, then Psalms 87 and 89. There was another glory be, a lesson from the Gospel was recited by one of the monks who had prepared for this, and then the service closed with Saint Ambrose's very old hymn, *Te Deum Laudamus,* Glory to God.

All of the monks were smiling as they reordered themselves to leave the church and go back to their workspaces. Thomas and Brother James clustered with the three other monks from the *Scriptorum.* Thomas was deeply affected by how happy each of the monks seemed to be, how they seeped joy and happiness at simply being alive.

As they moved out of the church into the little yard, Thomas saw, some of his fellow Pilgrims rising for the day, and stretching a bit. Cuthbert Tunstall was standing at the door, having seen Thomas walking with the monks. Cuthbert smiled broadly and gave Thomas a little wave.

Returning to the small *Scriptorum*, Thomas briefly pondered the small ache in his stomach but let it pass when Brother James approached him with a smile, and a piece of clean vellum. Thomas noticed that the surface had already been lightly lined.

James said, "Thomas, we were wondering if, rather than you simply watching us, whether you could do us a favor?"

Thomas straightened a bit, allowing a little pride to seep in but returned his smile, saying, "Surely. Anything, Brother James."

Brother James replied, "Thank you!" then paused, moving a little closer. "We were talking, and we all just loved your poem last evening. We wondered if you could write it down for us?"

Thomas beamed. "I would love that," he replied. "Could we do little drawings with each section?"

"Well of course!" interjected Brother Michael, the painter. "We wouldn't have it any other way."

Thomas thought for a second, then shyly asked, "Might we be able to make two copies?"

The monks laughed, saying collectively, "we thought that we would make five copies, one each by each of us, do a little competition."

They seemed very enthusiastic about the prospect, but Thomas eyed Ludolph, asking, "what about Ludolph?"

The monks laughed heartily, "Ludolph is definitely not going anywhere," they replied, "this will be a fun break today."

"How do I start, then?" Thomas cried.

The monks all came in close, as Brother James smoothed the vellum on a cleared workspace for Thomas. He seated Thomas on a high stool, next to him.

"Thomas," Brother James said kindly, "the most important part is the first copy. You need to dictate to me your poem, each of the, I counted nine stanzas you had written."

Thomas mentally ran through the poem, counting the stanzas on his fingers, before agreeing, in a serious voice, "Yes. There were nine."

"Excellent!" said Brother James, taking up a pencil. "So you will dictate to me and I will write. Each stanza was seven lines in an ABABBCC scheme, a Royal Rhyme?"

"You were paying attention," Thomas smiled.

"It is a lovely bit of work," Brother James replied, "you should think about your gifts as a writer."

Thomas bowed his head in gratitude, then looked up at Brother James and smiled. "Shall we start?" Thomas asked.

"Yes, let's," replied James. He then lightly blocked out eight blocks side to side, a few inches down from the top of the page. For the bottom few inches, James blocked out the Ninth block centered, allowing room on either side. At the top of the page, James placed the title, "Pageant Verses," in pencil in a lovely script, and just below, "by Thomas More, of London." In a smaller cursive.

Thomas beamed.

In each of the eight blocks, James made a little square in the upper left corner, "For Brother Michael," James said with a wink, Then little subtitle lines followed with seven neat lines in each box for the first eight stanzas.

In the bottom section, James made two larger illustration boxes on either side of the stanza section, which he sized to match the paired boxes above.

With that completed, James then settled the paper on the desk, and looked expectantly at Thomas, saying, "so as I recall, the first stanza was entitled 'Childhood'?"

Thomas nodded, a little overwhelmed at James's skill so far.

James accepted the nod, saying, "Brilliant," and he penciled that in the title line of that box. "Now go ahead with your poem, Thomas," he said gently.

Thomas closed his eyes, reliving the night before a little, and feeling the affection of these monks, his new friends. He repeated his performance of the previous evening, reciting his poem again, though more slowly.

When he had finished, he opened his eyes to see James smiling at him, the poem neatly transcribed in pencil, stanza for stanza in each respective box. The faint pencil handwriting was beautiful. Thomas gasped involuntarily. Regrouping, he asked involuntarily, "What do we do next?"

The monks all looked very pleased at Thomas's reaction, at the pleasure he took in their work.

Brother Michael, the painter, stepped forward, saying, "now that this rough is done, we each get a sheet, and copy it, you included, while Brother James is inking his in."

With that, another monk swept in placing individual sheets and pencil nubs before each monk in the room, six in all, including Thomas. With varying degrees of speed, each scribe made copies of the blocking, then copying the text. Thomas copied Brother James's script, which was mostly inked in by that point. The other monks appeared quite free to use any script of their preference. Brother Michael, finishing first, had used a very lovely old script that was almost a gothic cursive. He looked quite pleased with this, and, before inking in his script began to pencil in his drawings in each corner box.

Thomas was very slow and careful in his lettering and finished last, just as a bell announced *Terce,* the next service of the morning. "How can it be nine o'clock already?" thought Thomas.

The monks, along with Thomas, quickly straightened their desks and sheets of paper, stood, smoothed their robes, and walked back through the yard and into the church for the service.

*Terce* had a different feel and rhythm from the two earlier services. First, the villagers and Pilgrims were awake. Many of the Pilgrims had already eaten a spare breakfast and were attending the service prior to departure for the day's walk.

Thomas's little group, the Wooler's, Cuthbert Tunstall, and a few others were standing in the back of the church as Thomas arrived through the side door with the Scribners. There were shy waves, but Thomas was swept up into the service too quickly for any more contact than that. The older leading monk, Thomas had discovered his name was Brother Mark, stood and faced the enlarging crowd, smiled warmly at the visitors, cleared his throat and intoned "Incline unto my aid, O God!" and then he and the other monks began singing a hymn, with which Thomas was unfamiliar. Brother Mark then read aloud three Psalms from the large, very ornate lectionary on the simple wooden pulpit at the front.

Thomas supposed that the monks, his new friends, had created that very book with their own hands, and, in his mind's eye, as Mark was reading, Thomas saw Brother Matthew's beautiful script flowing by with the reading.

Brother Mark then read a very short lesson from the gospel, a nice part about Jesus curing the ill from a boat. Thomas imagined the scene, but found his mind wandering back to the Scriptorum, wanting to get back to their project, now getting very hungry, but still having three hours and another service to go before lunch.

Thomas snapped back, as Brother Mark made some short remarks about their work glorifying God, then the monks all cried, "Lord have mercy on us," and the service ended.

James turned to leave, but Thomas said, "could we wait a moment? I need to go speak with my fellows in the back."

James smiled, and replied, "by now Thomas you know how to get back to us," and he turned to leave with his fellow monks.

Thomas ambled back to the group in the back, wishing he had pockets to hold stuffed hands. He smiled broadly, as did the entire group as Thomas approached.

"Becoming a monk, Thomas?" Cuthbert enquired archly.

Thomas laughed, saying "It is so very interesting here!" The words and the thoughts just gushed out of him. "I heard a noise and it turned out to be Lauds. I came in, and, well it was just so lovely. I met Brother James, and we have been working in the Scriptorum. We've been writing my poem!"

Godfrey stopped him kindly. "Thomas," he asked, "have ye eaten?"

Thomas held up, suddenly reminded of his hunger. Then a steely determination arose, "I decided to work with the monks until *Sext*, which is the next service in three hours. After that the monks all eat their daily meal."

Godfrey looked confused and a little concerned, "Are ye staying here, Thomas? Givin' up the Pilgrimage?"

Thomas returned the confused look, then, in a flash, saw how this would appear to Godfrey. He smiled to the big man, he hoped reassuringly, "No. No. No, Godfrey. I'm sorry. I woke up this morning hearing the monks doing *Lauds,* and I was intrigued, then joined them."

Godfrey relaxed a bit as Thomas went on, "at first, it sounded like there was more food if I waited until midday, than if I ate a bit and left."

Thomas stopped and smiled broadly, tapping his stomach, then continued, "then I met Brother James, and saw the *Scriptorum...."* Thomas paused at the confused look on Godfrey's face, "at the place where they copy books. They are really nice, and we thought we would spend the morning copying my poem from last evening." Thomas stood up very proudly. "They really liked it," he added.

Godfrey laughed, "some teenagers get themselves lost chasing girls, Thomas, you get lost copying books! I love it!" He clapped Thomas on the shoulder strongly enough that Thomas staggered a bit. "Tell you what, Thomas. If ye don't mind, we like you in our group, and we will go help in the fields or something until after supper. Pay our keep, like. And we can all set out together this afternoon. Would that be alright with you?"

Godfrey asked with such genuine humility and affection for Thomas, that Thomas was overcome with emotion. They both teared a bit at the corners of their eyes. Thomas answered after a bit, "Of course....Godfrey....Thank you," and he went forward and hugged the large, hairy northerner.

Godfrey, looking over Thomas's shoulder noticed that Brother James had returned to check on Thomas. Godfrey saw him smile at the hug. Gently tearing Thomas away, Godfrey said, "Thomas, if we're going to get a good start this afternoon, you better get a move on back to your project." He thought for a second, then reached a meaty hand into a pocket, withdrew a piece of bread, and said, "before ye go, Brother Thomas," he winked, "can I tempt ye?"

Thomas looked at the bread, and looked at Godfrey. With resolution, Thomas tamped down his suddenly screaming hunger, and said, seriously, "No.. Thank you Godfrey, but my meal is on a schedule here with the Brothers."

Godfrey laughed, and pointed to the shrine of the dead Saxon Queen and Saint on the left wall and roared, "That's a Saxon answer my young friend!" He then gently turned Thomas to Brother James, and gave him a little shove in that direction.

Thomas laughed, and strode quickly to Brother James, looking quickly over to Godfrey in a grateful gaze, and said, brightly, "see you in a bit."

Rejoining James, the two walked quickly back to the *Scriptorum*. The room was quietly bustling with activity among the three monks as Thomas and James rejoined them.

Brother Michael excitedly showed Thomas the sheet that Thomas had been working on before *Terce*, saying, "Thomas, I took the liberty of working a bit on your sheet." Thomas saw that the older monk had penciled in quick cartoons in each of the picture boxes. Michael proudly showed Thomas his visions for each of the Stanzas.

"Thank you, Brother Michael," Thomas said, moved.

The other monks applauded, happily, until Brother James said, "we all need to get back to work, Thomas is on a schedule here today – *Sext*, food, and back to the trail for him." Hearing himself, James involuntarily blushed.

The monks laughed, and straightened their own sheets. A few still needed to finish lettering, Thomas included. Thomas forgot the bread, his hunger, and even the outside world as he buried himself in the work of producing, of publishing! his poem.

"This is so fantastic!" thought Thomas, as he lettered his stanza on old age.

*"I'm glad. Why do you think it is happening?"*

"I am reasonably certain you think it is because I opened myself up to God."

*"Yes, and..."*

"Because I am learning to trust and to love."

*"Well done, Thomas. I am proud of you."*

"I am pretty hungry though."

*"Not in the important ways."*

Thomas's contemplation was interrupted when he noticed Brother Michael, and the older monk who had been leading the services, Brother Mark, standing beside his desk, quietly observing him, small smiles on their faces. The Scribner, Brother Michael, was holding his sheet of Thomas's poem.

Thomas started, "excuse me," he said, pulling himself together. Brother James suppressed a smile off to the side, and continued working.

Thomas wondered if he had fallen asleep, but, looking down, he realized that he had, in fact finished his inking in of the lettering rapidly and well.

Brother Mark leaned over and looked at Thomas's sheet. "Very impressive, young man," he said kindly, nodding his head in appreciation. "And you wrote the poem?"

"Yes, sir," said Thomas, coming forward off of his high stool to a fully erect position. "Everyone here is so very nice." He gestured broadly around the room.

"And I've heard that you are 14 and on Pilgrimage to Canterbury by yourself?" Brother Mark asked.

Thinking about it, Thomas answered sincerely, "Well, Brother Mark, I started off by myself." He paused, then added, "Now I have lots of new friends." He laughed happily, thinking about his initial misery.

"You seem to have a capacity for friendship that is unusually broad," commented Brother Mark, almost absently.

"I don't know about that," said Thomas, adding, "but I do like other people…most of the time."

This time everyone laughed.

"I don't suppose I could convince you to stay here and be one of us?" asked Brother Mark. "I think you would make a wonderful follower of Benedict."

Thomas looked serious. "Thank you Father," he replied. "Maybe someday, but this afternoon I must set off again with my friends. I'm to meet people in Canterbury for St. Thomas's Day."

"Anyone I know?" asked Brother Mark, curious.

Thomas smiled, and paused before answering. He did not want to reveal a confidence, or have anyone treat him differently by mentioning the Archbishop. Still, he wanted to be honest with these kind monks.

"How do I answer this?" Thomas thought.

*"What are you afraid of?"*

"That if I answer the Archbishop, that they either won't believe me or will treat me differently."

*"And yet the honest answer is…"*

"The Archbishop. But…"

*"No buts. Trust in God. This entire experience should have taught you this by now. Trust and Love."*

"Suppose they laugh at me?"

*"Suppose they do?"*

"I want them to like me."

*"They clearly already do. Do you think they print poems for everyone?"*

Thomas cleared his throat, and felt his courage building. He looked directly into Brother Mark's eyes, and in a calm voice said, "My name is Thomas More. I am from London where my father is a lawyer. I have been a page for the past two years to John Morton, the Archbishop. He sent me on Pilgrimage to see if I was 'Oxford material."

Thomas paused and caught his breath.

Brother Mark's face didn't change at first, then he broke into a smile. He looked appraisingly at Thomas, then asked, "and how is the pilgrimage going? How do you feel about Oxford now?"

Relieved that there was no laughing, Thomas adopted a serious expression as he considered the Monk's question. Finally, he answered, "It's hard, the pilgrimage, but I have learned a lot in three days. And yes, I am more committed to attending Oxford than ever. And Canterbury College is Benedictine, and I am loving the hours…."

Fearing he was running on, Thomas stopped talking, and looked at Brother Mark.

After a moment, Brother Mark spoke, quietly and kindly. "Thomas," he said, "I think that you will be a capital addition to Canterbury College. If you decide to be a Benedictine monk after, I think you will be wonderful at that, as well. Remember Benedict's motto…"

Thomas cut him off, looking at the writing at on the wall near the ceiling on the far wall,
*"ora et laboris?"*

Brother Mark laughed, "yes, Thomas, *'work and prayer'*" he said. "You will have an
excellent time of it at Canterbury College. When you are there, please give my regards to Brother
Thomas Humphrey. He is the Warden, the Prior there, and he taught me. But now I see that I
have kept you and all of my skilled *Scriptors* from both their work and their prayers. Thank you
Thomas."

And without allowing any further questions or conversations, but still with a warm smile
on his face, Brother Mark turned on his heel and left.

The other monks, led by Brother James moved in to ask Thomas questions, but the
*Scriptor,* Brother Michael, cut them off. "Brothers, you heard Mark," he said gruffly but
genially, "work and prayer. We have a task to finish, and only an hour or so to do it before *Sext.*"
He paused, "though, as I think of it we really only need to finish two, one for Thomas and one
for him to give to the Archbishop."

The monks quickly picked two sheets, Thomas's and Brother Michael's and cleared off
two tables. They were able then two work in from each corner of the table on each sheet. Brother
Michael moved like the wind penciling in drawings in each box, and Thomas and the remaining
monks took little pots of paint and simply filled in Michael's drawings. James kept up with
inking in script, or adding little flourishes around the now drying boxes.

Surprisingly in a little over an hour of frenzied, but careful work, the group had finished
both of the sheets and were hanging them up to dry. Before doing that, however, Brother James
cried, "Wait!."

All eyes turned to James, as he took his quill and ink, and, in careful letters wrote *"oro et laboris"* at the bottom of the sheet, then under that, *"Milton Regis, 1492."*

Thomas asked if the Monks could each sign their work, but they each demurred, replying that monks work for the greater glory of God, not their own glorification. They thought, however, that Thomas should sign each of the sheets, and, after thinking it over, Thomas thought their answer should apply to him as well.

There were congratulations all around, then Brother Michael cleared his throat and, when the group had quieted, said, "I think a little prayer would be in order."

The monks clasped their hands together, and bowed their heads, as Michael went on, in a joyful voice, "Our Dear God, thank you for bringing young Thomas into our midst today, and for the great gift of his poetry. Please protect him on his journey, and…"

The church bell rang for *Sext*.

"..and," Michael continued with a grin and a wink towards Thomas, "as we head to *Sext*, and to our meal, please keep young Thomas fed."

There were quick cries of "Amen" and "Hurrah," then the entire group, Thomas included, lined up and returned to the church for *Sext*.

The noon, or *Sext*, service, so named because it was at the sixth hour since to *Prime*, or first service of the morning, was very similar to the *Terce* service. The group cried again, "Incline unto my aid, O' God." Then to celebrate all of the theological marvels of noon, including that Christ himself was nailed to the cross at noon, the group sang a lovely old hymn that Thomas knew from St. Lawrence Jewry with the noontime services, *Rector Potens*. There were three psalm readings, all kept short.

Thomas noticed the increasing heat in what had been the cool stone church. The noon sun came strongly through the main church stained glass, and cast colored light all around the interior of the church.

Thomas looked towards the back, and did not see the Woolers or his friend Cuthbert. He wondered idly where they had gone, but the combination of the heat, and his hunger, and, now the smells from outside, had made him a little tired and sleepy.

Thomas's head bobbed once, but an elbow from Brother James caught him back. He blinked his eyes a few times. They were scratchy and dry. Thomas rubbed them involuntarily then, remembering himself, sat up straighter.

Fortunately, the *Sext* service was shorter than the others, and the psalms shorter. After reciting the *Kyria,* and finishing with a call for the Lord to have mercy on us, the service finished, and Thomas was able to move more easily. The monks gathered and readied themselves to eat.

Since it was a warm day, Brother Mark announced, the meal would be outdoors. Mark looked happily at his brother monks, and pointed at Thomas, happily saying, "and we have a special guest, here with us, today. Young Thomas More of London, only age 14, and on pilgrimage by himself, yet, he tells me, not by himself. He has trusted God, and made friends, including, I believe, several here. And…he is a poet! Thank you for sharing yourself with us Thomas."

Brother Mark stepped forward and warmly clapped Thomas on the shoulder, and many of the monks did the same. Brother James hugged him, whispering, "he doesn't do that every day."

Thomas smiled, then smiled even more broadly, after Mark said, "and now let us sup."

The monks all made for the door and out towards the smells coming from an outdoor kitchen that had been set up. All smiling broadly, the entire Wooler clan was acting as servers and helpers for the meal. A thin, elderly monk who had excused himself quietly right at the end of *Sext* and gone outside, Thomas now realized was the *cellarer,* the monk in charge of provisioning this small wayside priory.

It turned out that after their brief conversation several hours before, the Woolers had gone and found the cellarer and both described their abilities, and their willingness to work, and had prepared a great meal. The *Cellerer* had made sure that the Rules of Benedict were applied soundly, as there were two cooked dishes, as well as fresh fruits and vegetables from the garden. Thomas was a little disheartened to see strawberries, but chose neither to comment nor to partake. Each person had a loaf of bread of their own and butter and honey. There was ale and sweet well water available.

Thomas ate happily with the monks, but was delighted when, after every monk had been served that Brother Mark, stood and insisted that all of the servers must also take their portions of food and bread, and sit with the monks. The Woolers, Cuthbert Tunstall, all happily took their food and joined what turned out to be a very nice party on the church lawn.

The conversation was happy and meaningful at the same time. Thomas learned that most of the monks were from the area, a few, including Brother Michael and Brother Mark, were from well off families, and had studied at University, Mark at Oxford, and Brother Michael in Cambridge.

Both were interested to meet Cuthbert, who had gone to Oxford, and who was going Cambridge. Michael asked Cuthbert if he had met Erasmus yet. Cuthbert replied that he had not yet and Michael smiled broadly.

The monks asked all of the pilgrims if they had heard anything about a possible war between England and France. Godfrey's ears had perked up. The monks said they had heard of great Naval preparations being made in the small harbor at Sittingbourne, the next town over.

Brother Mark graciously diverted the conversation to the upcoming Feast of the Translation of St. Thomas Becket, and asked if the pilgrims were planning on being there in time.

Hails of "yes" came in return, and Brother Mark loudly replied, "then you should probably get moving. We monks will clean up. *Ora et Labore!*"

The monks looked a little confused, but then, led by Brother James, they cheered, and began clearing.

The Woolers also looked confused, and tried to help with clearing, but were firmly rebuffed by the now cheerful monks, who alternated between, "Thank you, kind sir, you have done enough," and *"Ora et labore"*

Thomas and Cuthbert Tunstall simply stood off to the side shaking their heads happily and in wonder.

Godfrey came over to them, shaking his head with a big smile on his face, saying, "Well then, lads, I guess we should get a move on. I'd like to stroll through Sittingbourne before we get back on the road, if that's all right with you all."

Cuthbert and Thomas replied, "Fine with us," in unison.

While Thomas had been working in the Scriptorum the other had already cleaned the rough Pilgrim's dwelling, piling their meager belongings, including Thomas's small, bag and stick by the entrance. Since the priests at the Chapel of Saint Thomas on London Bridge had emptied Thomas's bag of coins, Thomas had filled it a little with small or interesting stones he had found along the way, as well as bits of food, and, of course the map. Thomas carefully removed the small map and placed some leftover bread and cheese into the sack. Before replacing the map, he looked at his course, allowing himself to chuckle about the places he had been, and to wonder about the places to come.

Replacing the map, he tied the bag to his belt, rechecked his first pilgrim badges, and joined his group on the small road heading west out of Milton Regis towards Sittingbourne.

As they were leaving the churchyard, Brother James came out of the church, calling after the group, waving two rolls of vellum, neatly tied with twine. "Brother Thomas," he cried, "Don't forget your Poem!"

James came up to the now halted group and placed the rolls into Thomas's hands. "They are dry now, Thomas," James said, panting a bit. "Brother Mark asked me to be sure to remind you that one is for you, and one for the Archbishop."

With thanks, Thomas borrowed a small sheet of oilcloth and some string from the group and made a type of case for the rolls, with a sling. Content that these precious scrolls were protected, he slung the rope over his shoulder and hugged Brother James farewell, saying, "Thank you for everything, James."

With tears burning in his eyes, Thomas and the group set off on the afternoon journey.

Thomas and the group walked the very short distance to Sittingbourne along a very narrow, ancient country road, lined with old chestnut trees, the large branches forming a canopy over the road. Occasionally not quite ripe fruits would fall from a branch making a little pop as it hit the dirt road.

The road to Sittingbourne was only about a half mile, and the trees lasted for about half, before giving way to fields with grazing sheep on either side of the road, and then a sudden widening of the road as they entered the larger, more industrial village.

Sittingbourne was located on a fortunate tongue of the Swale that had been laboriously dredged deep enough to allow for a protected harbor for ships. The Milton Regis road opened onto that harbor and shipyard. There was loud, not frantic, but nearly so, work being conducted as ships were being constructed.

The group of pilgrims bobbed a bit to dodge carried beams and supply baskets as they worked their way around the yard towards the High Street. Godfrey seemed distracted, and Thomas asked him why.

"See the troops in the green and white striped doublets over there," Godfrey said, gesturing towards the yard entrance, but clearly not wanting to point. The yard bustled around them, but Godfrey was taking no chances. He pointed to a brown haired, arrogant looking gentleman on a white horse. This man was wearing the green and white livery. Godfrey and Thomas noted the man on the horse to have a great deal more gold on his uniform.

Godfrey had leaned in to whisper something to Thomas while pointing surreptitiously, but he saw something on the man's uniform and turned white, gripping Thomas's arm tightly enough to bruise.

"What's wrong?" Thomas asked, concerned and in pain.

"D'ye see the symbol on his chest?" Godfrey hissed. "A red rose on a Hawthorne tree with a crown on top."

"So," asked Thomas.

"Those are Henry's men….The King's guard," Godfrey said. "We need to get moving."

"And why would that be, Godfrey Wooler? You old dog!" boomed a voice from behind them.

Godfrey turned more quickly than Thomas imagined anyone could, and somehow produced a small knife which he wielded defiantly.

Thomas turned to see the source of the booming voice, concerned. He saw a big man, Wooler sized, also in the green and white uniform. Laughingly the giant pulled a sword quickly, and still chuckling at the confusion on Godfrey's face, bellowed, "that's a pretty puny little French sword, you worthless git."

Godfrey simply stared, his muscles going limp with surprise. "R.R.Robert Eglisfield?" Godfrey stammered.

"Never could get anythin' by you," exclaimed Eglisfield. "Look at ye.. On pilgrimage?" he enquired. Then thinking for a second, and taking pity on the horribly surprised Godfrey, he added, "ye want to put down that toothpick and come here to give your old brother a hug?"

Godfrey, still stunned, did as he was told, re-sheathing his apparently small knife, and with eagerness the two big bears hugged.

Thomas studied the scene with mild concern. They were now in on the edge of the shipyard. An obvious officer had now noticed them. Tunstall, the Wooler family, and the few new straggler Pilgrims attached to their group had shrunk off to the side, except for Woolers eldest son, Robert, a young man of 18, who was now advancing on his father with the look of a man seeing a ghost. Thomas studied Godfrey's friend's face, thinking it looked familiar…

Suddenly a clap on the shoulder from behind, and a hearty, "Thomas More…What are you doing here in Sittingbourne?"

Thomas wheeled to that voice, to see his friend Thomas Howard standing there beaming, red hair aflame. Howard too was wearing the King's white and green, hawthorn, crown and rose on his breast.

Thomas's head was spinning.

"Too much," Thomas thought desperately.

*"Calm,"* came his voice. *"Everything is in its place."*

Calming a bit, Thomas thought, "how is it?"

*"You don't get to know that. Remember to trust and love."*

"Where do I know Godfrey's friend from?"

*"Trust and love, Thomas."*

Better composed, Thomas grinned happily at Thomas Howard. "Howard," More said cheerfully, "I should ask you the same thing! For myself, I am on Pilgrimage."

Thomas Howard eyed his friends simple brown robes and laughed, saying, "Clearly!" After studying some more, Howard looked at More, noticing a change in his friend. Not sure what it was, he explained his own presence, "the King has decided to invade France. I am here in Sittingbourne assisting with the preparations. I've been given a position as an assistant to the Lord Herbert, over there." Howard pointed towards the man on the horse, who had now started moving towards this oddness in his ranks.

Thomas More shook his head, "Charles Somerset is now Lord Herbert? Since when?"

"Since he married Lizzie Herbert…sorry 'Baroness Herbert' a month ago," Howard replied.

"Missed that," Thomas More replied ruefully.

"Even you can't keep up with everything, Thomas," Howard said with both kindness and with happiness at knowing something had eluded his friend.

Somerset approached the group, calling out, "Howard! What is going on in my staging area?"

The five standing there, Howard, More, Godfrey, Godfrey's son Robert, and Robert Eglison turned abruptly towards Somerset. Robert Wooler and Robert Eglison, More noted, had been suddenly, inexplicably hugging. All five bowed a bit, and instinctively placed knuckle to forelock.

Thomas Howard stood up straight, looking upwards at the man on the horse. "My Lord," Howard began in a voice that Thomas noted was both respectful and even, a command voice. Howard, too, had changed. "Several wandering Pilgrims to Canterbury have, it appears, crossed into our lines."

"And what explains the obvious familiarity with my men?" Somerset asked gesturing at the Woolers and Eglison. No one could be sure if there was a little sneer on his face.

"I can't explain these people and Yeoman Eglison," Howard replied, "but for myself, this is my old friend from London, Thomas More, until recently a page to Archbishop Morton."

"John More's son?" Somerset replied.

"One and the same, my Lord," Howard replied with a gesture towards Thomas.

Charles Somerset, intrigued, climbed down from his horse. As he alit, he called out, "the one that ran London Bridge a month ago in one of Morton's boats?"

"One and the same, my Lord" Thomas More repeated with a little bow and a shy smile.

From the corner of his eye, Thomas saw Godfrey start at this information.

"That was fantastic!" Somerset said happily, approaching Thomas, as if to examine him more closely.

Godfrey, son, and Eglison came closer as well.

Looking at More's pilgrim's robes, and the attendant road dirt, Somerset asked, "so Morton sent you on pilgrimage as your punishment?"

Thinking for a moment, looking around with love at his friends, his badges – feeling the slung poems at his back, Thomas grinned, bowed his head respectfully, saying "My Lord, I cannot, of course, speak for my Lord, the Archbishop. I am grateful to him for this experience no matter his intent."

Somerset laughed. "Well said, Thomas!" he exclaimed, clapping him on the back. He turned his attention to Eglison, enquiring, "Yeoman Eglison, and who are these pilgrims standing here with you?"

Eglison put a knuckle to his forehead and nodded his head at Somerset and to Howard, "My Lords," he replied in his gruff voice, "I am blessed to have met my old friend Godfrey Wooler from the North."

The burly Yeoman gestured to Godfrey, who, Thomas realized quickly, was mostly succeeding making a mostly successful effort to appear calm. He had a slight fidgeting of his feet that Somerset, thankfully either didn't notice or took as unease at addressing a Lord.

Yeoman Eglison didn't miss it however, and he quickly moved on, saying hurriedly, "and this is my friend's eldest son Robert." Thinking quickly, he smiled winningly at Somerset, who was won.

"Very well," said Somerset, having lost interest, and returning to his horse, now ignored the Woolers and Eglison. Before alighting, he turned to Howard, saying, "Thomas Howard, don't spend too much time on reunions. We have a war and a King's arrival to prepare for. I'm thinking you will see them in Canterbury in two days anyway?"

"My Lord?" enquired Howard hesitantly, not wanting to appear ignorant of some basic information.

"Howard," Somerset replied with exasperation, as if to a child, "we are ten miles away from Canterbury. The King, the Queen, and the Archbishop will all be in Canterbury in two days for the Feast of Thomas Becket. The King will be here in Sittingbourne in one month to personally oversee our preparations to invade France. We are charged here with the advance party of the Kings own Yeomen of the Guard. They will be attending the King in Canterbury. Their Captain," he paused and placed a hand on his breast before continuing, "and his oh so naïve Lieutenant," he made a hand sweep at Howard, "will be in attendance to the King then." He stopped and looked at the gangly seventeen year old Lieutenant, who now knew he was about to wait on the King.

Somerset allowed himself a small smile, as he placed a handsomely booted foot into his stirrup and swung into his saddle. Looking at Howard, he grinned, "better clean up, son."

Somerset laughed, actually not unkindly, and cantered over to a group of drilling yeomen in their green and white and began issuing orders on a close order drill they were conducting with their Halberds.

Thomas noticed their weapons for the first time.

"Halberds!" he thought excitedly.

"*Steady, Thomas,*" thought the voice.

Reluctantly returning his eyes from the big axes to Thomas Howard, Thomas had a thought and exclaimed, "Thomas Howard…you are his Lieutenant!?"

Howard's face became as red as his hair before he replied, studiously looking down, "yes… turns out I'm good with soldiers. I was going to Scotland with my father. But the French have been acting up and the King wants to invade. They needed men, so I was detached down here to help Somerset….Sorry… Lord Herbert." He shot an admiring glance at Somerset, before adding, "he's really a good egg."

Thomas wasn't so sure, but decided to accept his friend's judgement.

The Woolers and Eglison had pulled closer. Godfrey Wooler had an urgent look on his face, as he leaned in and asked in a whisper, "My Lord, I heard them call you Thomas Howard, and you've bright red hair. Are ye by any chance related to John Howard, the Duke of Norfolk?"

Howard started, then looked around furtively, a mixture of pride and concern on his face. "He was my grandfather who died at Bosworth, I am still attainted because of it, but the Howards return, good sir. My Commander and King were on the other side, so I will thank you not to remind everyone." He gestured around the shipyard, and particularly at Yeoman Eglison.

Yeoman Eglison smiled sympathetically at Thomas Howard, saying, "not to worry, My Lord, so was I, and so was Wooler here."

Thomas Howard started. "You two were at Bosworth?" he asked incredulously.

Thomas More looked down, not wanting his eyes to give away any confidences to his friend, remembering that Howard, while a very good fellow, was also of the nobility and deeply affected by the politics of the age.

Wooler and Eglison each nodded. Thomas Howard pointed his hand at Eglison, asking, "then how is it you are one of the King's Yeoman? Does Somerset know? Does the King know?"

Eglison stood taller, and grew a little angry at the young Lord, then suppressed it, saying calmly, "Of course they do, Lord Howard. They brought me on anyway. My family has been protecting Kings for hundreds of years. I served the King at Bosworth. I serve and protect the King now."

Howard's jaw worked furiously. Thinking further, he spat out, "yes, but King Henry dated his reign to the day before Bosworth, making everyone who fought for Richard a traitor at Bosworth."

Eglison leaned in, saying intensely, "and it is the King's prerogative to forgive whomever he chooses." He paused, then softened a bit, adding kindly, "which is why, Lord Howard, you are now a Lieutenant here, and your father a re-ascending soldier in the King's service."

There was a pause. Godfrey Wooler looked at both his friend, Eglison, and his own son and to the two Thomas's. He paused, searching for words before quietly saying, "Lord Howard, please forgive me. I did not mean to cause you distress, or problems for my friend Robert here." He patted Eglison on the shoulder with affection, before adding, *sotto voce*, "I merely wanted to tell you, my Lord, that your Grandfather, the Duke of Norfolk, was one of the greatest, best men I ever served." He stopped.

Thomas More noted that Godfrey had tears in his eyes as he spoke. Moved, he stepped between his friends Howard and Wooler, clasping both on the forearm, as he spoke, with quiet intensity, "Thomas Howard, I've known you forever, and I've known Godfrey only a short while. But my knowledge of Godfrey, my friend, is that he is a giant, noble man of honor. I am certain that he did not intend you distress and that his admiration for your grandfather is both pure and honorable."

Thomas Howard looked around, distressed that he was about to cry. With effort, the young Lord pulled himself into a soldierly, ramrod posture, his face, save his eyes, a mask. In a voice of admirable control, Howard said, "thank you Godfrey Wooler. I appreciate your thoughts….and your courage in expressing them." He then extended his hand to Wooler in gratitude.

This discipline, this new…soldier in Thomas Howard impressed his old friend More, who still gripping forearms, guided his two friends' hands together.

Howard then shifted his gaze to Eglison. "You served my grandfather as well?" he asked very quietly.

"I was at his side when he died," Eglison replied, hesitantly, mournfully. "It was the worst moment of my life, and since then I have wished most intently that I had died in his stead."

Thomas Howard said, almost to himself, "you never told me."

"Yes, my Lord," Eglison replied, slightly emphasizing the Lord, "I didn't want to cause you distress or worry. And besides…It wasn't my place."

"I see," said Howard, reflexively straightening his green and white doublet. "Thank you," he added sincerely. He looked affectionately at his old friend Thomas More, and said again, "Thank you, my friend."

Somerset, still over at the halberd wielders, suddenly barked, "Howard, enough standing around! I need you over here."

"Coming, my Lord," Howard cried reflexively, as he turned quickly. As he ran off, his red hair bouncing, he cried excitedly over his shoulder, "see you in two days. In Canterbury, Thomas!"

Smiling, and turning back to the Wooler father and son, and Yeoman Egliston, Thomas was surprised to find them in deep conversation. Their voices were very low, and Thomas saw Godfrey periodically shaking his head. When he caught a glimpse of Thomas, he turned a bit so Thomas couldn't see his face, which was now red.

Mrs. Wooler had seen it too, from afar. She had been watching, shyly, Thomas thought, the exchange with the two Lords, but on seeing them take their leaves, she had moved closer, more rapidly as she saw her husband's face redden.

She suddenly put on a huge smile, and came up directly between Robert Egliston and her husband, crying "Robert Egliston, I do believe it's been years!"

This stopped both men in their tracks, and Yeoman Egliston, looking mildly stunned, shook his head then took in Mrs. Wooler. A happy smile replaced his purse lipped look of concern as he cried, "Mary Wooler! I can't believe it!" He turned to her and put both hands on her forearms in greeting. "Let me look at you, my dear! It has been far, far too long that you have been hanging with this stubborn ass of a husband of yours."

Mary laughed, a little too loudly, "Aye, Robert," she replied with more sass than Thomas had ever imagined from her, "he may be stubborn, but he's my ass."

Without any real choice, the Yeoman, Mary and Godfrey all laughed. It was perhaps a bit forced, but as the three reflected, each laugh became warmer, especially when the Woolers saw the confusion on their son's face.

Godfrey turned to his son, and said, "Don't ye worry, sonny. Egliston's a good egg. Ye haven't seen him in about ten years so ye don't remember. He and I were in the King's service together, both Edward and Richard. We got separated at Bosworth. This man apparently decided to go with Henry, and I came home." He jerked his thumb at Egliston.

Egliston bowed to Robert Wooler, "at your service son. I am most happy to meet you." He then turned to Godfrey and said, emphatically, "please, my old friend, think about what I said. I mean really think about it. For yourself and your family, and for all your kin before ye."

Mary looked curiously at her husband.

Godfrey, stood up to his full impressive height, which actually was about the same as Egliston's, so not as intimidating as he might have wished. He was about to reply, but Mary cut him off, asking, "what did Robert say, Godfrey?"

Godfrey deflated a bit, and Yeoman Egliston failed to suppress a small smile. Godfrey said to his wife, "we will discuss it later, Mary. Right now we need to get back on the trail, it's late afternoon, and I suspect that 'Yeoman' Egliston," he paused for emphasis and practically spat the word "Yeoman," "has important work to be doing right now." Godfrey gestured at the shipyard. He gently grasped his wife's elbow with his left hand to move around the big yeoman, but then stopped, and placed his right index finger on Egliston's chest, "but Robert," he said, when we meet at Canterbury in two days and I answer you, I would like to know how ye can live wearing a hawthorn bush topped by a crown on yer breast."

Egliston reddened a bit, but checked it with a stern look from Mary as the Woolers walked off.

Thomas was curious, and so he held back a bit as the Woolers left, just off behind a saddened Yeoman Egliston. When his friends were out of earshot, Thomas quietly asked the

Yeoman, "Good sir, what did you and my friend Godfrey speak of that you will hear an answer in two days?"

With a little start, and a harrumph, the Yeoman turned to Thomas and studied him for a moment, before answering, "that is between he and I."

Thomas tried another tack, "why was Godfrey so upset about the hawthorn and the crown on the King's men's doublets?" Thomas pointed, like Godfrey had a moment before at the Yeoman's uniform.

Egliston looked at Thomas, and answered stiffly, "because at Bosworth, the fatal blow to King Richard was a strike to the head that knocked his crown from his head. As Richard died, his crown rolled from his head into a hawthorn bush. Lord Stanley, fresh from standing by the battle and not committing to either side, picked up the crown from the bush and placed the bloody crown, still with bits of Richard on it, onto Henry's head. This made Henry King by right of conquest, so Henry placed it on his soldiers uniforms."

Thomas was silent for a moment, then contemplating, "but if you were at Bosworth with Thomas Howard's grandfather, then you were right there. How can you wear it?"

"You are too young to understand," the Yeoman replied defiantly.

"Try me," challenged Thomas.

Egliston continued to ponder, then replied simply, "I serve the King… No matter who the King is. When Henry became King, I was Henry's servant. I wear the badge to remind me of that fact." Egliston paused for a moment, before adding, "I serve the King, as my fathers before me."

With that the Yeoman turned and started to walk off sadly towards the shipyard.

Rushing to one final thought, Thomas called out, "Wait, sir!"

Egliston stopped and turned to Thomas, and Thomas said, 'Thank you, sir."

Egliston smiled a bit, shrugged, and turned again to the shipyard.

Thomas stood and thought a moment.

"They were at Bosworth," thought Thomas.

*"I think we established that, Thomas"*

*"*On Richard's side."

*"Now one is Henry's guard, and the other is lost and unsure."*

"What do I do for Godfrey?"

*"Love and trust."*

Thomas broke his reverie, noticing how far ahead the Woolers had trudged into Sittingbourne, both mother and father appearing to have weights on their shoulders.

"Wait up," Thomas called.

The Woolers stopped in front of the Red Lion Inn, a famous old tavern along the high street.

Seeing that they were waiting, Thomas ran, holding the sides of his gown to keep from tripping. Godfrey, cheered at the site, smiled a bit, and stood a little, his weight lifted a bit. "C'mon Thomas," he called. "It's getting late in the afternoon, and we need to get to Faversham this afternoon."

The bell in the Sittingbourne church nearby tolled for Nones…three o'clock. Thomas looked around for Tunstall, and didn't see him. He turned to one of the smaller, younger Wooler boys, Edward, and asked if he had seen him. He pointed into the Red Lion, saying that Tunstall had apparently seen a friend in the courtyard, and had headed in, a few minutes before.

The "Lyon" was an old, famous inn right near where Sittingbourne's High Street met with Watling Street. It had started as a simple roadside stop on the way back and forth on the old

Roman road between the ports at Dover and the Channel, the seat of the church in Canterbury, and the capital in London. Its location, and its growth and luxury had led to increasing luxury and cachet, such that it had become the resting place for Kings and Queens returning from France to London. It was widely reported that King Henry the Fifth had rested a day or two on his return from Agincourt in 1415.

The front gatehouse had a red brick two story home with four paned leaded windows facing the street on the second floor. The first floor had a small shop selling meat pies, the smell of which immediately attracted Thomas's attention. There was a green façade above the shop opening, and on the left side of the first floor was a gated opening going through the building into the Inn courtyard. There was a flag hanging above the gateway with a bright painting of a red, upright pawing lion.

There were quite a few people going through the gate, to and fro, street to courtyard and back. There were King's soldiers in the green and white, and clerics, young women and old men. It wasn't London, thought Thomas, but it was certainly busy.

Thomas went through to the courtyard. Once inside, there was a brick courtyard, and long two story buildings on either side. On the right, the second floor of the inn building had walls that leaned about thirty degrees, creating an oddly unsteady appearance to the building, that was reinforced by the fact that the windows on the second floor were small and high, and the walls brick, instead of exposed timber with wattle and daub.

The afternoon sun also created shadows from these buildings, and the shadows cast on that wall made to concavity, the tilt, seem deeper.

There were some long tables with benches that had been moved closer to the tilting

building, and Thomas quickly say the brown Pilgrim's robe and happy face of Cuthbert Tunstall

speaking animatedly with another young man, also of about fourteen, though very well dressed

and by all appearances, well-fed.

Thomas vaguely recognized the fellow as William Blount, also known as Lord Mountjoy.

He was spectacularly clad in a black and gold doublet, black hose, and golden slippers. He had

long blond hair, with oddly colored bits of string gently plaited through some of the bunchings

on the way back to a tie at the back acting to hold the hair together.

Thomas watched the two, Tunstall and Mountjoy, greet each other. Mountjoy was only

fourteen, like himself, and Tunstall only eighteen, but both seemed to Thomas to be much older,

more experienced and worldly. He felt an outsider, and poor, acutely aware of his empty pockets,

and his Pilgrim's robe, particularly in comparison to the splendid attire of Mountjoy.

Thomas blushed involuntarily, remembering the rich young man from his time serving

the Archbishop, when Mountjoy served the King. They hadn't really interacted, though

occasionally Edward Stafford, also born in 1478 would push them together in close.

"He never liked me," Thomas thought despairingly.

*"On what do you base that?"*

"We never connected. I think he may be a toff."

*"He seems perfectly fine with Cuthbert."*

"Cuthbert is different. Already been to Oxford..Going to Cambridge."

*"And yet the Lord and the Cleric seem to be just fine together."*

"He's rich. Look at him."

*"He's smart too. He's even smiled shyly twice at you already."*

"Really? I hadn't noticed."

*"To busy feeling insecure? There! He looked at you again."*

"I saw that one."

*"Then smile back. See how that works out for you."*

Thomas smiled and gave a little wave. Cuthbert and William waved Thomas over, smiling.

Cuthbert called out, "Thomas, come on over. Meet my friend Mountjoy."

"Will, to my friends," Mountjoy said, standing and offering a hand to Thomas. "Thomas and I have met a few times, but never had the time to really connect."

*"Ha!"*

"Quiet."

*"Trust and Love."*

Thomas put on his best smile, and approached the pair, saying, "Yes, we have, my Lord."

"Stop that Thomas," Mountjoy said genially, but very firmly, "I am sure that it will always be Will for you."

Thomas laughed and took the extended hands, saying warmly, "all right, then, Will it is. It is my pleasure."

Cuthbert looked at his two friends, and said, "much better Thomas! I've been telling Will all about our Pilgrimage."

"You shouldn't bore the fellow, Cuthbert," Thomas replied.

"Are you kidding, Thomas!" Will replied earnestly. "It sounds fantastic!"

Thomas blushed, pleased. Then composed himself, reminded about pride being a sin. Still, that was nice.

Will went on, "You've had quite a summer, Thomas. Shooting the bridge…

Pilgrimage…." He paused, looked at Thomas and smiled, asking, "What's next? Holy Orders?"

Cuthbert stepped back. "Shot the bridge? That was you?" he asked incredulously.

"In a boat boosted from Lambeth Palace!" Will gushed. "Edward Stafford fished him out

after Thomas fell in. It was brilliant! A blow for pages everywhere!"

Thomas had not looked at it that way, and reddened further.

Cuthbert whistled. "So is the Archbishop punishing you?" he asked, emphasizing "is."

"He may have, at first," Thomas replied, "but he said he wanted to see if I was material

for Oxford."

"Well I would say you are!" Will said admiringly. "I'm to go to Cambridge next month."

"I'd heard that," Thomas replied. "What will you be studying?"

"Anything but Scholastics," Will replied. "I will leave that to my priest friend, here. I

don't care about the number of angels on a pin."

The boys all laughed. After a pause of a beat, Will asked seriously, "So fellows, how are

you doing getting to Canterbury? Will you make it by the Feast?"

"Not at this pace," came a grumbled Northern voice from behind them.

Thomas brightened further, crying, "Godfrey!" He turned to his big friend, and said gaily,

"My friend Godfrey, please meet our friend Will Blunt, the L…"

Will cut him off abruptly, "Godfrey," he called, pushing out his hand in greeting, "I'm

Will Blount. Cuthbert has been telling me about you.

Thomas started to finish, but realized his error and bit his lip. He looked at Godfrey, and

Will, who didn't appear to have much to say to each other after the greeting. Thomas laughed,

and said, "Will, Godfrey is our leader. They waited around today for me while I was playing at being a monk." Thomas winked at Godfrey, then continued, "then we keep running into friends, old and new, and so now we've made all of a half mile today and its later afternoon."

Thomas made a show of looking up at the sun in the sky significantly. Then he laughed, asking, "what are you doing here, Will? Are you here for the invasion?"

"Ah...," Will said. "You must have run into Thomas Howard." He laughed joyously, adding, "and Somerset. The two of them, I declare, are desperate to win their spurs."

Tunstall clucked a little bit, gently correcting, saying, "Will, judge not. There is disgrace in both families. There is none in yours. Your father died in the King's good graces. Thomas Howard's grandfather and father were with King Richard at Bosworth, and Somerset's a bastard. You lead, perhaps, more of a charmed life than you know."

Will smiled genially, replying, "that I know, my good and honest friend," nodding in agreement.

Thomas broke in, asking, "So Will, what are you doing here? Are you going to the war?"

Mountjoy shifted uncomfortably. "Not really, no," Will replied hesitantly. He leaned forward and lowered his voice to a whisper. "The King is planning on leaving for France from here."

"Sittingbourne?" Thomas and Cuthbert asked simultaneously.

"Well, yes and no," Will replied. "Here, I mean. The Red Lyon. This Inn." He gestured plaintively with his hands at the inn surrounding them and the Courtyard.

Thomas asked, a little too incredulously, "Why?" Even Godfrey was interested in this, and he too leaned in.

Will looked around furtively, responding, "Because Henry the Fifth stayed here returning from Agincourt! The King, now the Seventh Henry feels that it would complete a circle to leave in triumph for France from the return site of the victor of our Greatest Battle ever."

"That makes good sense," Thomas replied thoughtfully, then he repeated, "so Will, why are you here?" With the emphasis on "you."

"My uncle and master, James Blount, is King Henry's right good servant," Will replied. "He has been with them since before Bosworth. The King asked me to come down here and see if I thought there was any way that he could be accommodated here."

"And what do you think?" Cuthbert asked, very curiously looking around the tilting buildings.

"I think for the small party he would have around him as a matter of war, that 'The Lyon" would be fine. His troops can sleep in barracks or on ships. The twenty or so close servants would sleep around town. The Chamberlain and others would be fine either here or a couple steps down the road."

"And then?" Godfrey asked, surprising everyone.

They small group started and then laughed.

Will continued, "I'm to meet the King and report to him in Canterbury on the Feast Day, Thursday."

Cuthbert asked, "Why there?"

Will looked incredulous, replying "You two are really disconnected, aren't you? The Queen had a baby girl, also named Elizabeth on the second, at Sheen."

Thomas worried quietly for the Queen, made a little prayer that she not die in childbirth. Thomas still adored her, and wanted her to be well. He asked gingerly, "how is the Queen."

Will looked genially at Thomas, whose courtly love for the Queen, well really his crush, the bond between them, was well known among all the pages. "The Queen is faring well, Thomas," he said with a smile. "But not taking any chances, the King will be at Canterbury for the feast to pray to St. Thomas for his wife, the Queen's and the Princess Elizabeth's health."

Godfrey leaned in again, asking, "Does your Lordship mean that the King will be in Canterbury in two days with the Archbishop?" He seemed to want to stomp his foot with impatience.

The young men, looking at this moment much younger that before, all nodded their heads in dumb agreement with Godfrey.

"Then," Godfrey intoned in what must have been his battlefield leader voice, "we must get moving now. In order to not arrive late for the King and the Archbishop." Godfrey said this in an odd voice, as he straightened his brown robe. "C'mon," he intoned, "ye can talk on the road. My Lord," he added, making a little bow to William, "ye are welcome to accompany us, or to go on ahead with your horse."

In agreement, Will moved first, and paid the serving girl. The boys clustered a bit, pushing through the crowd in the courtyard towards the gat onto the High Street. Will paused, and looked up at the rooms, saying, "go ahead to Ospring, go the the *"Maison Dieu,"* and I will catch up. I need to get my things, and my horse."

Godfrey acknowledged Will's plan with a grunt and a little head nod in his direction, and he went off to get his family up and moving again, finding them resting in the little churchyard of St. Michaels, a hundred or so feet up Watling Street.

Godfrey, Cuthbert and Thomas found rest sitting under an enormously old oak tree, the shade of which was cool and refreshing. The church was lovely and old. Thomas was immediately attracted to the small addition on the side of the church, a fifteen foot by fifteen foot lean to addition off the side of the nave. There were high small windows, that Thomas, who had been drawn like a fly, could just see into.

Thomas's hopes were realized in that there was, in fact, an Anchoress, a strictly cloistered woman who had been bricked into the little annex some time before. The Anchoress, who Thomas learned was named Anna, communicated with the outside world through people coming to her window, and talking or asking for advice, and who used the small window inside facing the altar to watch mass. Food and drink were also passed in through the little window, gifts of supportive parishioners, and waste passed out to the sainted caretakers.

The Anchoress was quite nice, though quiet. She seemed of indeterminate age, and was neatly, but inexpensively dressed. Thomas saw through the window that she appeared to have a bed, a desk with a simple chair, a prayer kneeler, and a few books. The windows were opened in the summer heat, and when Thomas first stole a glance inside he saw her kneeling silently at her *prie a deux*, motionless, barely breathing. Thomas would have thought her ill, except that her eyes were open, and she had a dreamy, far off gaze in her eyes.

Thomas had, of course seen, even spoken to Anchorites and hermits before. Many churches had, over the years built the small annexes, or anchorholds, to house them. After the Anchorite died, the church would either open the room as a side chapel, or another would volunteer.

There was even a church rite for sealing the Anchorite in their cell, nearly a funeral when the about to be anchorite took vows of hermiticism and stability of place – they could not leave their cell for the remainder of their lives.

This was the first time, though, that Thomas had ever been alone with an Anchorite. Before stealing a second glance into the cell, he looked around furtively. His walking party had decided, apparently against Godfrey's wishes based upon his posture and voice, to rest in the shade "a bit longer." Cuthbert wasn't participating in this discussion, but was clearly enjoying the show.

Satisfied that he had a few minutes to himself, Thomas turned back to the window to look inside. Anna had, by this point, turned to the window, quietly awaiting Thomas's renewed gaze. She was smiling, and as soon as Thomas had looked in at her, she waved, and said, "Thomas More…So good to meet you!"

Thomas shrank down below the window with surprise.

"How did she know my name?" he thought wildly.

*"How do you think?"*

"No idea."

*"Perhaps she heard Godfrey or someone else in your party."*

"They aren't that loud."

*"Really?"*

*"No idea. Just a thought. But when she was praying, where have you seen that look before?"*

"I haven't"

*"Really?*

"I don't think so."

*"the Archbishop?"*

"That's true."

*I suspect that she has moved closer to the window. Perhaps it would be less rude to stand and talk to her. Maybe start by asking how she knows your name."*

"Good idea," Thomas thought, his anxiety lessening.

Thomas stood, and was, in fact unsurprised to find the Anchoress standing quietly at the window, awaiting his return. She smiled warmly, and in a lovely lilting, dreamy voice, said, "Ah, Thomas, there you are."

Thomas, feeling more confident, smiled in return and said, "yes, Lady Anchoress, I have returned. I was anxious as to how you knew my name."

The dreamy look returned to her eyes as she appeared to be having an internal conversation.

"I think I know that look."

*"Well done, Thomas."*

They both returned to the conversation at the same moment. The Anchoress smiled warmly, and offered, "I was hoping you would stop by my cell. My name is Anna."

"Thomas, as you well know," replied Thomas. He placed his hand through the window to touch her hand in greeting, but she stepped back, the smile never leaving her lips.

"That is not allowed, Thomas." She replied, gaily. "The rules of the Anchoress."

Thomas, nod offended, returned his hand limply to his side, and Anna stepped forward again quickly.

Anna gestured with her head towards Thomas's travelling companions. "You haven't much time, you need to ask me your question."

A little flustered, Thomas regrouped, saying "All right, then. How long have you been in that cell?"

"Three years, but that is not your question," replied Anna.

Mind racing, Thomas asked, "Why did you agree to the cell?"

"You are getting closer, Thomas," she replied. "My family all died in the fever of 1485. I survived, but barely. This church meant everything to me, and I thought that devoting my life in this way was my best approach to truly serve God, and these, all my friends. Still not your question."

"Are you happy in there?" asked Thomas.

"The first few months were hard," Anna replied, slowly and thoughtfully, "but routine set in. And except for the occasional visitor," she paused and smiled at Thomas with a little head nod, "I am alone to pray with my voice."

Thomas started. "Your v.v.v.voice," he stammered.

"You know that perfectly well, Thomas More," she said kindly. "Now you are getting to your question."

"Did your voice tell you my name?" asked Thomas.

"Yes," she replied.

"Does my voice mean I am to be an Anchorite?" Thomas asked, dreading the answer.

"No, Thomas, it does not," she replied.

"*Absolutely not,*" came the voice, "*you take the path that you discern to be the correct one.*"

Anna smiled. "Exactly," she said. "It is your gift, Thomas, to have an interior voice to discuss concerns with. This was my choice. Yours will be yours. The important thing is to partner with the voice, not be subservient to the voice. It is there to advise, not to command."

*"There!"*

"And the very nice thing, Thomas," Anna continued, her voice soft and dreamy, "is that you are never truly alone. You will always have company because of your voice. Ask your next question."

"My next question?" Thomas thought.

*"Go ahead and ask, you already know the answer."*

"Is it God?" Thomas asked in a whisper.

Anna smiled gently, and answered, "I suppose it depends. You must be open to listening, and listening to the right voice, I suppose. Others may come, and the trick is to know it is the right voice...that one is listening to the right voice."

Thomas murmured, "Speak Lord, for your servant heareth."

"Samuel," Anna said, "yes, Thomas, exactly. Your next question, and you must hurry, for your friend comes."

"Why me?" asked Thomas.

"It is a gift from the Lord, Thomas," Anna said gently, "the proper response is 'thank you,' and then to treasure the gift."

Thomas paused for a moment, not really thinking, just absorbing.

"Thomas," Cuthbert called as he approached. "Who is your friend?"

Thomas started, and looked back and forth between Anna and Cuthbert, struggling to make a sound.

Anna laughed merrily, "I'm afraid that Thomas here has lost his tongue for a moment. I am Anna the Anchoress here at Saint Michaels."

Cuthbert smiled broadly, and bowed to her, his hands at his sides. "It is a pleasure to meet you my Lady Anna." As he stood, erect, he added, apologetically, "I am sorry that I must steal my friend Thomas, but it is really quite late, and we must head on before nightfall.

Anna laughed again, "such is the way of the Pilgrim! Off you all go! I must return to my prayers." With that Anna gave Thomas a little wink so only he would see it, then backed up two steps, before turning and returning to her *prie a dieu*, folding her hands, and returning, now with a smile on her lips, to her dreamy state.

Cuthbert gently took Thomas by the elbow, and maneuvered him into a slow walk away from the window of the Anchorhold.

"I don't know what to say," Thomas thought.

*"You don't need to say anything, Thomas.*

"What should I do?"

*"Trust and Love. Realize your gifts."*

"Such as this?"

*"This gift and many others."*

"Can everyone hear you?"

*"Very few listen hard enough to hear."*

"Should I call you Father?"

*"We are together inside of you, Thomas. You may call me whatever you like. Or, as before, you may not call me anything. You always knew it was me."*

"This changes everything."

*"You will find that it changes nothing. You are now facing what you already knew but wouldn't face. Trust and Love."*

"Anna mentioned 'my gifts.' What are they"

*"That is for you to discern, my friend."*

"We are friends?"

*"Of course we are. We always have been. Since you first awoke that morning and heard me."*

"So what do I do now?"

*"Well, I would normally say 'trust and love,' but since everyone is now staring at you, and since Cuthbert has been leading you by the arm for a few hundred yards, I would say 'trust and love and pay attention.'"*

Thomas snapped back to the world, and found that he had indeed walked a good ways down Watling Street blindly, guided gently by Cuthbert. Godfrey had taken a protective position to his left and was walking, but rapidly scanning Thomas for evidence of a problem.

Thomas's focus returned quickly on the faces of Cuthbert and Godfrey, and he smiled at the two of them, he hoped reassuringly. At Thomas's return to his senses, their faces melted with relief.

"Thank God! Where've ye been, Thomas?" Godfrey asked, in a rush. "Ye were talking to the Anchoress, then ye went blank."

Thomas searched for the words; considered retreating interiorly again for advice, and decided that would raise more concern. He smiled and cleared his throat, electing on a version of the truth. "I had a lot to think about from this Pilgrimage," he said hesitantly. "I don't know what happened. Maybe I just fell asleep and have been walking in it." Warming to the idea, he yawned, adding, "it has been a very long day." He patted his printed roll, still slung over his shoulder.

There were some startled looks on faces, then, wanting to accept that, they all laughed with relief. Godfrey most reluctantly, keeping a little corner of a wary eye on Thomas's face.

Thomas changed the subject, asking, "It is getting late, how much further to Faversham?"

Godfrey clucked reassuringly, "only another hour or so of walking." He paused, "that is, if we all manage to hold it together for that time."

Thomas smiled nervously, and looked for his walking stick, remembering he hadn't seen it for a while. Godfrey's son, Robert slid over and handed Thomas the staff he had been carefully guarding for the day. "You'll be wanting this, Thomas." He smiled warmly. "Long day."

Thomas thanked him. And leaned a little tiredly on the staff as they tramped on.

## Chapter 22 - July 5, 1492, evening

After about an hour of steady walking, the small group approached the village of Ospring, just east of the somewhat larger village of Faversham. As they approached, the traffic on the road thickened up again, as they caught up with other pilgrims who had, in many cases arrived at the famous pilgrimage rest stop far earlier.

The *Maison Dieu* had grown over the years into a fairly large complex of buildings, all exposed timber and wattle, surrounding several courtyards. At three storys, the combination of inn and *hospitail*, for three centuries had already catered to the Canterbury Pilgrims.

Thomas was a little anxious as they approached the building that there would not be any room, or food, for them; that they had arrived too late in the day. He was pleasantly surprised to be warmly welcomed by a priest, a small, gregariously friendly man of about thirty in a white tunic with a black sash and a black cape, emblazoned on his chest with a red circle with a large cross. The priest had dark, longish somewhat unkempt hair sticking out from a small black cap, brown eyes, and an open mouthed smile framed by thickened red lips.

"Late Travellers!" the priest cried. "I love late travelers!" With that he threw up his arms again in welcome.

Thomas, Cuthbert, and the Woolers were all quite fatigued but delighted at the welcome. Godfrey, of course, pulled himself together first from some bottomless well of reserve energy he possessed.

"Father," he cried, also raising his arms in greeting, standing tall, "we are overjoyed to see you. We are but humble pilgrims to Canterbury," he turned a bit, gesturing with a wave to the group. "And, though the hour is late, we beg your kindness and charity on our poor souls." He bowed.

"Faithful Pilgrims we cherish and protect," the priest responded with a bow, then a wave of welcome. "I am Father Theo, one of the Brethren of the Holy Cross here at our humble house of God."

Father Theo came up and hugged each of the pilgrims in their group in turn, welcoming them into the fellowship of the *Maison.* With that greeting, he asked, "follow me, my great new friends!" and he turned and led them through a little gateway, giving a tour of the place and talking about their Order.

Thomas found that he was both fascinated, by the place and the history, but also really flagging in energy. He heard snatches of the tour, including "founded 1234," "Chaucer stayed here," and a bit about the Holy Cross priests being Augustinian followers. He heard Godfrey snort, very quietly, as the priest spoke of the order being originally French.

After entering the first floor hall, which was stone walled, the group passed to the back to a set of stone stairs. These were quite well worn from time, and led up to the white plastered walls of the upstairs, and a large, rectangular chamber. The fading light of the day came through the glassed, slit windows along each wall. There was an open beamed support for a leaded roof, and the brightness of the room was enhanced by the walls and ceilings being whitewashed. There was an open fireplace with a chimney on the far wall, with a large cauldron bubbling with a fire kept low in the summer heat.

Even still, the room was quite warm, the windows didn't open, and there were quite a multitude of earlier arriving Pilgrims in the room, in various states of eating, soup and bread, of sitting and talking, and of, lying straw pallets on the floor or already sleeping.

Thomas had perked up quite a bit as they entered this room, the *camera regis,* or King's Chamber. He liked the thought of the various King's Henry, or Edward, or Richard, staying in this very room with retainers. He was also perked up by the smell of the porridge and rough bread by the fireplace, and by the thought of lying down. The moments of enthusiasm were dampened fairly quickly by the heat and the smell in the room, and his eyes began to flag again. A consuming weariness overtook him again and he stumbled a bit and turned ashen.

Cuthbert and Godfrey both noticed, and moved immediately by the elbows to help support him. Father Theo noticed Thomas's little stumble as well, out of his peripheral vision. And he instinctively turned towards Thomas. The look of concern on his face effectively ended the tour, as he asked, "is the boy alright?"

Mrs. Wooler stepped up, "he will be Father. He's overdone today, awoke for Lauds in Milton Regis, worked through the day, and walked here. I think he is spent for the day, but also famished.

Thomas murmured an, "I'm fine, really," that was mostly neither heard nor believed.

"Since Lauds, but didn't ever go back to bed or rest?" asked the Father, both impressed and concerned. "One may overdo exertion to the Lord, my son."

Thomas smiled weakly, agreeing quietly, "apparently."

Theo turned to Godfrey and Cuthbert, asking, "does he have a fever."

"No father," they replied in unison. We would not have brought him in here with all these people if he did. We think that he is just spent." They paused, and both looked significantly over at the kettle.

Father Theo got the hint. "Let's get some food and drink in him first. You lot do that, and let me get a chair." He ran off through a small door on the side to another room.

The Woolers and Tunstall, now all working as a group, gently herded the unstable Thomas over to the fireplace. It was hotter there, but there was nothing to do about that. Mrs.

Wooler grabbed some bread off the table, and Godfrey grabbed a simple wooden bowl and, instead of using the ladle, he simply scooped the broth into the bowl.

"Lean on the table here Thomas," Robert Wooler gently insisted. Cuthbert had found a flagon, Thomas liked that word, of cider and the group began systematically trying to cram food and drink into Thomas's mouth, like he was a tired baby bird. In fact, Thomas found quickly, that the best way to endure all of these very good intentions, was to tilt his head back and open his mouth, accepting whatever was put into it.

This system worked well for longer than one might have expected, but after a few minutes, Thomas choked, ending the accelerated feeding as he slowly revived. With the choking, on bread actually, Mrs. Wooler retreated a few steps in horror that she might have hurt him, Thomas turned his head and coughed a few times. Then extricated himself gently from his caregivers, and said, "Thank you. All of you. I am better now."

An audible sigh of relief, not only from the friends, but also from a small knot of other concerned pilgrims who had gathered around the scene. Then there was laughter from all, as Father Theo emerged from his door accompanied by two other enthusiastic priests pushing a large wooden chair, gilt on the back and legs. "The only chair we could find, No windows in the storage room, and it was dark" Theo rasped as he gulped for air. "It hasn't been used in quite a while. It is a little dusty." He coughed from a little cloud of dust that erupted from the upholstered seat and back of the chair.

The laughter stopped as the assembled realized that the priest had, in his hurry, taken the throne out of long storage and brought it into the King's chamber. There was an awkward silence, and all eyes were on Theo, who, at that moment, was comprehending what had just happened.

"Oh my," said Theo as his face reddened. The other priests stepped off to the side, and began to look left and right, as if they had nothing to do with the chair.

The room began to laugh, more comfortably as Father Theo put his hands up on either side of him and shrugged his shoulders, as if to say, "I have no idea how that happened." He too began to giggle.

Thomas, taking advantage of the attention being turned away from him, had worked in some bread and cider, and found that he could stand unassisted. He was still profoundly tired, but he slowly stood and walked erect over to Father Theo and his fellow priests.

The crowd hushed again, seeing Thomas moving forward. Godfrey and Cuthbert, suddenly aware that Thomas was out of their grasp, lunged forward, but were belayed by Mrs. Wooler, in a soft, understated order saying, "Leave him be."

Thomas went forward, still a little unsteady, some sweat on his face, and approached the three priests, Father Theo closest, a gilt throne in between them. Thomas smiled broadly, stopped and bowed to Theo.

Theo exhaled with relief upon seeing Thomas, saying "I'm glad you are better, lad."

Thomas started to sweat a bit, and felt a little woozy, but he suppressed these feelings through will, so as not to re-alarm everyone. "I am much better, Father," Thomas said in a low even voice that Thomas hoped sounded convincing from a wan, ill, fourteen year old boy.

The priest looked relieved, but suspicious. "I wonder if a little lie down might be best at this point?" Thomas asked, helpfully.

Godfrey, Father Theo, and Cuthbert all looked momentarily startled, but then in a "why didn't I think of that?" explosion, a straw bed was created in the corner of the room furthest from the fire and close to a high oriel window which, combined with the door, created a little air movement in the large room.

Solicitously, Godfrey gently guided Thomas to the straw, and Mrs. Wooler instructed him to lie down. Cuthbert took the precious roll of the printed manuscripts off Thomas's shoulder and promised to guard them while he slept.

The sun was finally set, and the last, red rays of dusk were slipping into the westerly windows of the chamber. After he was recumbent, Mrs. Wooler made Thomas sit back up a little, and she forced him to eat a little more soup and bread, and drink the lasts of the cider in the flagon.

Recumbent again, Thomas began thinking about how much he liked the word flagon, rhymes with dragon....I'd like to see a dragon…St. George………………….

Thomas's sleep was initially dreamless and deep. The restorative he so badly needed after the long, interesting day.

Thomas heard a knock at a door. Not sure where he was, he opened his eyes to find himself back at his house on Milk Street in London. He cautiously tried a breath, but no air moved. The room around him was as he remembered it. The light came through the window. It was morning.

There was another knock on the door, more insistent. Thomas swung his long legs around, and stood. He was in a court doublet of red, with red hose. The King's livery. Thomas thought, "well, what is going on?"

No response.

A third knock at the door, rattling the still room. Thomas decided he'd better answer it.

Thomas opened the door, to find a man standing in the doorway, smiling pleasantly. He was wearing an white surplice and archbishop mitre. He was holding a simple wooden crozier. Thomas knew instantly that this was Thomas Becket, though he didn't look like the statue in the chapel on the bridge.

"Hello, Thomas!" Becket called cheerfully. "Mind if I come in?"

Without waiting for an answer, the Archbishop and his robes flowed into Thomas's little room and, went over to try to see out the little window.

"Ah, right," he said, "There's Wood street over there. I loved living there."

Thomas was too startled to really speak.

"Mind if I sit down?" Becket asked kindly.

"Dream?" Thomas More asked after a second.

"Of course!" laughed Becket. "Different centuries and all!"

"Why are you here?" Thomas asked with a little hesitation.

"Well," the Archbishop responded, thoughtfully. "You're making all this effort to come visit me, I thought it polite, I suppose, for me to come visit you."

"That was kind of you, sir," Thomas replied with a little bow.

"I've been watching you, Thomas," Becket continued. "I thought you a little headstrong on the strawberries, but I believe you've regrouped nicely." He smiled warmly at the much younger Thomas.

"Thank you," replied Thomas not knowing really what else to say. Then he heard a noise from the window, a soft song. He knew immediately who it was. He moved quickly around the long dead Archbishop, who remained smiling, and, climbing on his bed as he used to, he was able to look through the small window, down into the garden, to see his mother working on the little mulberry tree, now ripe with summer fruit. His heart leapt.

"My mother's working in the garden," Thomas said in little gasps to Becket.

"Yes," the Archbishop replied warmly. "She is always there. That's her place."

Accepting that, Thomas eyed the Archbishop, and asked, "and where is yours, my Lord?"

"Perceptive question, Thomas," the Archbishop replied proudly, "that's why I follow you around. It's in Canterbury, where I made my stand."

"And where is mine?" Thomas asked, simply. His eyes returned to the happy vision of his mother.

"Ah," said the Archbishop. "That is not yet determined."

"What do you mean?" replied Thomas, curious.

"You are not defined yet, you are too young to know where your place is," Becket said kindly. He thought for a second. "But then I suspect you already knew that. Your mind is like that. Ahead. Yet still curious about where others are."

Thomas thought to protest, but held back, changed tack, instead asking, "why did you do what you did?"

Becket smiled, saying, "I did a lot of things, Thomas. Be more specific."

Thomas nodded his head, clarifying, "resist the King."

"Even at your young age, Thomas," Becket replied, "you also know the answer to that. There is a line one may not cross, else one loses one's self."

"I don't know what you mean," Thomas exclaimed.

"You will," Becket replied blandly. "and now it is time to awaken."

## Chapter 23 - July 6, 1492 The Eve of the Feast of the Translation of Saint Thomas Becket.

Thomas cried out, "but wait!" as his old room dissolved, and the morning sun on Milk Street became sunlight filtering through the high oriel window in the Royal Chamber in Ospringe.

As Thomas stirred and cried out, Godfrey turned around from the guard position he had assumed in front of Thomas for the evening.

"Thomas," he cried out, "you're alright!" The big man bent over and pulled Thomas up from the straw pallet, embracing him in a great bear hug.

Thomas coughed a little bit, smothered in the beard, straw, clothes and smell of the consuming joyous embrace. He managed to whisper into Godfrey's ear in a choked little voice, "Thank you Godfrey….." Then a little pause before adding, "could you put me down, though?"

Godfrey seemed to realize the size discrepancy, mumbled an apology, and gently set Thomas into a standing position, a little to the side of the used straw.

The sun felt nice on his face, but Thomas was still a bit fuzzy from the night before. He also had a dreadful knotting hunger pain in his stomach. His group was fussing around him like flies, but he also noticed that there were more people in the chamber than he had expected. He also suddenly noticed the smell of cooking meat, which just made him hungrier.

"What time is it?" Thomas asked with a yawn, scratching his side, still trying to process the room.

"Nearly mid day, dear," Mrs. Wooler cut in gently, pressing a cup of cool water into his hands. "How are you feeling?"

"Mid day?!" Thomas thought with a start. "How long was I out?"

Cuthbert replied, "at least half a day. We were worried about you, Thomas."

A dashing figure in gold and black swooped up suddenly, some dripping beef on a big fork. Lord Mountjoy cried out, "Thomas! So good of you to finally awaken! Eat this. It's been all I could do to save you some."

Thomas grinned as Mountjoy pressed the dripping fork into Thomas's hand. "Thank you William," Thomas said happily. "When did you get here?"

"Middle of the night," Mountjoy replied with a smile. "Came with that lot over there," he added, jerking a finger to a group of uniformed men standing by the fire, cutting meat off with their knives.

Emerging from that group, Thomas saw Thomas Howard in his uniform, hawthorn bush, crown and all emblazoned on his chest. Their eyes met, and Howard's face and very red hair all lit up with pleasure, and he started to make his way over.

Eating his meat, and talking with his mouth full, Thomas More asked, "How was I able to sleep through your arrival?"

Mountjoy laughed, and pointed at the Woolers and Tunstall, "'The More guard!'" he exclaimed. "Your friend Godfrey, here, told me that he would personally emasculate me if I woke you."

Godfrey reddened, but didn't deny it, as Mountjoy continued, "and, well…looking at him," and he waved up and down to emphasize Godfrey's size, "I was in no position to disagree with him." We went back downstairs and camped for the rest of the night outside the Maison. And yes Godfrey, we were on the lookout for anyone who might make noise outside that could awaken our gentle lad."

By this point, Thomas Howard had arrived to the group, and with a very concerned voice, said, "Thomas. Thank God you're awake. We heard all about last evening. Are you alright?"

Thomas More reddened, and said, "I am, Thomas. Thank you. I overexerted yesterday and it caught up with me!"

Father Theo unexpectedly popped up, no one was clear from what corner. "Thank God, Thomas More! You're alright!" The small priest was bobbing up and down with excitement, his happiness at Thomas's restored condition bubbling over onto the rest of the group.

Spirits rising further the boys - the two Thomases, More and Howard, Mountjoy, and Tunstall embraced, and burbled explanations of their current presence in Sittingbourne. Thomas More repeatedly eyed the meat in the fireplace. Eventually, Godfrey, standing off to the side, said "any chance you boys could babble closer to the meat so Thomas More can catch up to what you lot have already eaten?"

The group all started, then laughed, mumbled some apologies, and moved over to the meat on a spit. Howard took a knife and ut off a piece, handing it to More, who immediately devoured it, casting a grateful look at Godfrey.

"This beef is fantastic!" Thomas More exclaimed between chews. "Where did it come from?"

Thomas Howard beamed proudly, and struck Mountjoy on the shoulder, saying, "Mountjoy here is a resourceful and well funded traveler."

Mountjoy blushed, rubbing his shoulder and mumbling, "it was nothing."

"Nothing!?" exclaimed Godfrey, unable to stay out of it, much to the boys amusement. "It was fantastic. They brought it in at about during Lauds at the Abbey. Started cooking it. They were right about my punishment for waking you. Never seen anyone cook a beef so quietly.

Watched him until it was cooked. Ate some too." He thought for a second, before adding proudly, "and ye never stirred."

Tunstall added immediately, "Thomas, ask Godfrey how he knows all that?"

Godfrey shook his head imploringly.

Thomas More didn't see Godfrey or Cuthbert as he was cutting off another piece of meat at that moment, so he obliged Cuthbert while chewing happily as he turned back, "How do you know all that Godfrey."

Godfrey turned red and mumbled embarresedly, "it was nothing."

Thomas looked confused, and Cuthbert happily clarified, "when you collapsed last night Godfrey was so worried about you that he set up a guard perimeter all around you, guarding you against everyone all night. You were not to be disturbed."

Godfrey looked down, red-faced. The others looked at More happily. Thomas looked at his big friend, his heart full. He ran forward, and hugged Godfrey, exclaiming, "Trust and love, my friend," and "Thank you."

The boys clapped each other on the shoulders, and the rest of the Wooler clan, and even Father Theo came forward in a great group hug. The hug lasted a moment, then the group looked at each other with wry "what's next" looks.

Thomas Howard voiced it before the others, his eyes moist, "So what do we do now?" he asked.

Everyone looked at that point at Thomas More, and Howard added, "Thomas, this is your pilgrimage. Woolers and Tunstall, yours as well. What would you like to do?"

The group looked at each other, and Thomas More, pulling himself erect and smoothing his dirty brown robe, spoke, "today is the Eve of the Feast of the Translation of Thomas Becket.

I am to meet the Archbishop of Canterbury at the Cathedral tomorrow. I need to make it to St. Dunstan's by tonight."

"Aye," said Godfrey, "and we are your fellow pilgrims my friend."

"Thank you," Thomas More said simply, before looking at Howard and Mountjoy, as well as the uniformed soldiers off to the side and that he could see out the window in the courtyard. Noticing them, More turned to the young soldiers and asked, "and what of you soldiers? Will you be going back to Sittingbourne?"

Thomas Howard and William Blount looked at each other and laughed, "Well, Thomas…If you must know, we are also en-route to Canterbury. Since the King will be there to celebrate the birth of a daughter, and to pray for the safe recovery of his beloved wife, the Queen, we decided that we should be there, available to guard His Highness."

"Somerset, too?" Cuthbert asked innocently.

Howard face reddened a bit, with a little darkness in his eyes, before answering, "My Captain did not want to leave Sittingbourne and the preparations for war for so long a time as four days. He instructed me to get the troop to Canterbury by tomorrow. He will be riding down tonight to Canterbury."

Godfrey leaned in with a smile, "then you are in Command, good sir?"

Mountjoy laughed, but stifled with a look from Godfrey. Howard turned this over in his mind before replying, "Why yes, Master Wooler, I believe that I must be."

"Is Robert Egliston with you?" Godfrey asked insistently. "I haven't seen him so far."

"No," Thomas Howard replied with hesitation, "the Captain said he was needed in Sittingbourne."

"Who is helping you to lead this rabble, then?" Godfrey asked with a little alarm in his voice.

Thomas Howard reddened a bit more, then stammered, "well, I have Mountjoy here."

"That conniving bastard," Godfrey exclaimed hotly.

"Who?" they all asked, amazed at Godfrey's response.

"Robert Egliston, of course," Godfrey said. "That dirty conniving bastard."

"I don't understand," said Thomas Howard, genuinely confused.

"How many men did you come with," Godfrey asked, looking out the window and through the door down the steps into the entry hall. "How many started yesterday?"

Thomas Howard replied quickly, "I had thirty."

"And at muster this morning?" Godfrey asked patiently, bringing himself under control very rapidly, but with an icy precision that only Mrs. Wooler had seen before. Thomas More, out of the corner of her eye noticed that she was smiling.

"Well," Howard replied, stammering a bit, "Since it was only a two day journey, and since Thomas More here was ill, and I didn't want to wake him… I mean you had warned us about noise... And since Mountjoy was here with me… I didn't.."

Godfrey cut him off kindly, and with a smile "Sir, you didn't see the need for a morning muster? Thank you sir for respecting my wishes about protecting young Master More, here."

Howard lowered his voice to a whisper, "Did I err, sir?"

Godfrey also leaned in, and asked in a whisper, "how old are you sir, if I may ask?"

"Seventeen," Howard replied nervously.

"A solo command at seventeen?" Godfrey said, "of the King's personal troops?"

Howard turned bright red and stammered a bit. His mumbled answer was unintelligible.

Godfrey persisted, "I'm sorry, my Lord. I was not able to catch your answer. The men I see are in King's Guard uniforms. Although on a closer look, I don't see the hawthorn on their breasts."

Howard looked up, his face bright red. "Actually, Godfrey. They are not exactly the King's Yeomen of the Guard…" His voice trailed off, and he looked to Mountjoy, who shrugged.

"What exactly are they, then, my Lord?" Godfrey persisted, adding, "if you don't mind my asking."

It came out in a rush, as Howard blurted out, "Captain Somerset, and Yeoman Sergeant Egliston felt that they couldn't spare any of the real yeomen to go attend the King at Canterbury, busy as they were with preparations for war with France… But they still felt it important to make an appearance. So they picked some of the non yeomen soldiers that were around, and put them in uniforms that without looking too closely might look like the King's yeoman guard. They told me to take the men down to Canterbury, and from a distance…They were careful to tell me that I should be at a distance only, make sure the King saw us."

As he spoke the plan, Thomas Howard's face went white as it dawned on him how he had been set up by Somerset.

Godfrey's face, in contrast went red, as he slowly, and methodically asked, "and…did…Yeoman…Egliston….have….any…words…of….advice…for…you…as…you… were…leaving?"

Thomas Howard's face, now sunken and pale, looking as if he were going to cry, looked up at Godfrey. "Why yes," Howard replied in a low voice, "he said I should find you and talk to you."

Godfrey's face softened, and he shook his head a bit. "That Egliston," he muttered softly. Then, making up his mind, he looked squarely at Thomas Howard. "My Lord," he said in a kind voice, "how old are ye again?"

Thomas Howard, quietly replied, "seventeen."

Thomas More was about to cut in for his friend, but received a warning glare from Godfrey.

Godfrey continued, "and am I to understand that your Grandfather was John Howard, the Duke of Norfolk, killed at Bosworth?"

"Yes sir," replied Howard.

Godfrey raised his hand, "No my Lord, you are a leader of soldiers. You must never call me, a common man, 'sir.' Godfrey or Wooler will do nicely."

Thomas Howard nodded. Lord Mountjoy looked on with a small smile.

Godfrey continued, "and my Lord, is it true that Thomas More of London here is a friend of yours?"

Both Thomases, More and Howard, nodded assent, but with a look from Godfrey, Howard voiced, "yes, Godfrey, it is true."

Godfrey stroked his bushy beard, thinking, then said gravely, "My Lord, your Captain has done you no favors, but I suspect that may be because he fears you. I believe that he is correct in that assessment. In one day, you, alone except for your cub friend Mountjoy here," he jerked a thumb in Mountjoy's general direction, "moved thirty men overland, victualed and rested them, and they, or at least by appearance before we count, most of them, followed you."

Mountjoy started to object to the term cub, but at a look from, well, everyone, he stood down, realizing that at fourteen, the word "cub" was probably reasonable.

Godfrey thought a bit more. "Not thinking to have muster would not be an error on your part, my Lord, since neither your Captain nor your Yeoman Sergeant thought to send you with a Sergeant to handle the men. Soldiers are men of discipline. They need a regular order. If they are deprived of a regular order, things get mixed up. It's like young Thomas More's monk friends, every three hours they require a mass to keep their days orderly. Deprive them of that order and, well…same thing."

Howard nodded his head, looking in a new way at his men, saying, "I should have done muster this morning…"

Godfrey cut him off. "No my Lord," he said kindly, "I did not mean that. Officers and Lords and such do not muster men. They have other things to think about – when to attack, when to stand down, where to march. It's the Sergeant at arms job to muster the men, keep them in line and sober, ready for the Lord's call."

"But I haven't got one," Howard said, confused. "You said so yourself."

"Begging your pardon, sir," Godfrey said quietly. "You have one at the asking. Me. That is what that no good schemer Egliston was telling you. It was his way of drawing me back in."

"You?" Howard asked. "How would that work? I have no money to pay you."

"Egliston told me," Godfrey explained patiently, "that if I would return to the service, he would make sure that I received the six pence a day, from whatever day I agreed to serve." He looked at his wife, who was smiling, and shook his head ruefully, adding, "and that if my son Robert Wooler joined me, that he would receive three. He also told me that I could have my pick of captains to serve." He looked significantly at Thomas Howard, and added, "if you will have me, my Lord, I choose you."

Thomas Howard stammered, "W-W-W-Why?"

Godfrey stood tall and proud, flexing his muscles, his chest swelling as he returned to something from before, something noble and feral, a proud soldier and warrior. In a booming command voice, Godfrey replied with pride, "Because, My Lord. I am a soldier. My family going back to the Saxons are warriors, protectors of the King. I look at you and I know that you are as well. You may be young, but your eyes are old. I was with your Grandfather and Father at Bosworth and at many other battles before. I choose you, because you and I are meant to be together."

Thomas Howard's posture stiffened into a lance, and he wiped a tear from his eye, before asking quietly, "Thank you, Godfrey. What do I need to do?"

Godfrey stroked his beard some more and gave thoughtful looks at the men he could see from where he was standing. "My Lord," he said finally, "any great commander needs a Sergeant at arms to deal with the common soldiers. If you will, sir, make me your Sergeant, and call the men together and tell them that I am to be Sergeant. Let me take it from there with them. We will need a plan for how to advance the King at Canterbury if he arrives."

Thomas More, amused and curious at Godfrey's transformation, asked quietly, "Advance this King, Godfrey?"

Godfrey looked sternly at More, and growled, "The King, Thomas, and be careful. He is the only one we have. My duty is to serve the King, to be the King's good servant" He emphasized the word "the."

More shrank back into the crowd. He had developed a crick in his neck overnight, presumably from his odd sleeping positions over the previous nights, and he massaged it gingerly.

Howard, growing in this moment, his voice dropping, extended his hand to Godfrey, and said in a measured, serious voice, loud enough for the room to hear, "Godfrey Wooler. I have on this mission no secretary to record my agreement with you, but," and he raised his voice, "so that all may hear…" Howard raised his right arm and waved it to all corners of the room, continuing then, "Because of my special faith in Master Wooler for his military and personal qualities, I hereby declare him to be my Sergeant at Arms." He paused and turned to Godfrey, saying, "Serjeant Wooler, are you willing to swear an oath of service?"

Godfrey solemnly nodded, and loudly replied, "I am, my Lord."

Howard grinned, and looked around the room, and said, "I am told, that there is a wonderful priest here….a Father Theo?...."

A little squeak came from the back of the group, and the diminutive priest scurried forward, saying, "yes, my Lord."

"Father," Howard said with a little straight backed formal bow to the priest, "You have been kind and holy in your treatment of my soldiers and my pilgrim friends. I was hoping that I could beg another favor of you."

Father Theo replied happily, "I am at your, and of course the Lord's service, sir."

"Thank you Father," Howard replied. " realize that it is an off hour, and the morning is escaping us, but I am wondering if you could celebrate a short mass for us here, at Maison Dieu, that will consecrate the oath of service my Sergeant is taking in front of my men, and for us all to celebrate our respective pilgrimages in this world and the great gifts God?"

Deeply moved, Father Theo agreed. Mountjoy suggested that the service be performed in the yard across the street from the *Maison*. While that was being arranged, Godfrey and Howard continued speaking, with Godfrey asking about what weapons they had with them and so forth.

Thomas More drifted off first, and began packing and cleaning. Mountjoy left that conversation next and approached More.

"Thomas," he whispered so as to not disturb Howard and Godfrey, "did you imagine Howard could have that much steel?"

Thomas stood and smiled. "Actually," he replied, "yes. I knew him before Bosworth. His grandfather a Duke and a friend of the King. Back then, we would play in St. Paul's. He is very much tougher than people give him credit for."

"I felt a little ignored, there," Mountjoy confessed.

"William," Thomas More replied kindly, "Howard is older, has more to prove, and is clearly already a soldier. That's what Godfrey saw. You're like me. 'Unformed clay,' as my old headmaster would say."

Mountjoy replied immediately, "Thomas, I don't think that's true for either one of us. And I suspect that neither do you." He paused, thinking, "No. I think it is for us to determine what we are. Look at you. Four days on pilgrimage and vastly different from the boy who shot the bridge not so very long ago."

Thomas conceded the truth in that with a nod of his head and a shrug of his shoulders before Mountjoy continued, "So if neither of us is soldiers. Then what are we?"

"Well," Thomas replied hesitantly, "we are different. Take Cuthbert Tunstall, for instance. Survived the plague at Oxford, switching to Cambridge, wants to be a philosopher priest. I think he is one already. And you, a nobleman to study at Cambridge. I'm going to Oxford and I don't know what I will be, but we should be together, evaluate our gifts, work together to make England a better place."

Tunstall approached, and Mountjoy's eyes brightened. "I've an idea," he said with happiness. "Let's the three of us finish the Pilgrimage together. It won't count for me because I'm joining so late, and because I don't look good in brown homespun, but still, the three of us together joining in would be, I think, a lot of fun."

Tunstall spoke first. "I agree, William," he said. "but we need to work out with the Woolers how we proceed."

Thomas More looked back over at the Woolers, standing in a little knot to the side of where Thomas Howard and Godfrey were making plans, with young Robert Wooler, the same age as Howard, trying anxiously to be both noticed and unobtrusive at the same time. Mrs. Wooler looked pleased for her husband, but also mildly irritated at having been forgotten. The other Wooler children simply looked confused and nervous. One of the younger girls, Mary, who was very bright and about 10, looked over at Thomas More hopefully.

"C'mon, fellows," Thomas More said abruptly, "time to lead." With that he picked up the last and most precious of his belongings, his roll of his poems, slung it over his shoulder, and walked back over to Godfrey, Thomas Howard, and the Wooler clan. Without pause or pardon, Thomas More entered Howard's and Godfrey's conversation, saying, "Excuse me gentlemen," with a smile.

They stopped short, looking at Thomas blankly, so engrossed in planning were they. Thomas took their surprise and blank looks as an opening, jumping in with, "you both, and the soldiers clearly have a great deal to do today, and I fear that we will all be in the way and a burden to these duties." He paused and looked at them kindly, catching Godfrey give a small apologetic look to his wife.

Thomas More went on in the silence, "I am wondering if, perhaps after Father Theo finishes his brief commissioning mass, whether, my friend Godfrey, you would allow Cuthbert, Mountjoy and myself to escort your beautiful family safely to Canterbury where we could meet, either tonight at St. Dunstan's or tomorrow morning at the Cathedral?"

Godfrey worked his mouth, and Mrs. Wooler shot Thomas a grateful look. Thomas added, "Your son Robert Wooler is, of course welcome to join us, but my suspicion is that you have plans to use him with the troops?"

It was Robert's turn to shoot Thomas a grateful look.

Godfrey stopped working his jaws, and opened a big smile. "Thomas More," he cried, slapping Thomas on the shoulder, "Thank you for bringing me to my senses." He stopped and looked at Thomas Howard, after casting a brief glance at his wife, who nodded. "My Lord," he asked Thomas Howard, "would Thomas More's suggestion be acceptable to you?"

Thomas Howard smiled. More noted a glint in amusement in his friend's eyes. "My Sergeant, I think those both excellent suggestions, if your kind wife is willing to loan you and your son to me for at least a few days." He bowed at Mrs. Wooler.

Mrs. Wooler made a curtsey smiling broadly, saying, "quite fine, my Lord."

Howard looked gratefully at More, smiled and said, "settled then." He reached out to shake More's hand.

Mountjoy looked pleased, and looking out the window, coughed and said, "Well, then. It looks like Father Theo is ready. We should head out."

The group laughed a bit. Howard took a moment to introduce Godfrey to the knot of his troops that was in the *camera* by near what remained of the meat haunch provided by Mountjoy that morning. Howard was vague with these men on why Godfrey was being introduced, and Thomas More noticed the faint shadow pass over their eyes.

"That was interesting," thought Thomas.

*"They know something is up, and the sooner Howard gets Godfrey properly announced the better it will be for all sides. Too much time wasted talking already."*

Thomas More examined the room, and decided to intervene after a plaintive look from Mountjoy. "I think now is a great time to head downstairs," Thomas said, "Don't want to keep Father or the men waiting." He paused a moment and looked at his friends Thomas Howard and Godfrey, "and I think, my friends, that your men can barely wait to meet you."

The group laughed, including the soldiers in the room, although they laughed nervously. Howard took the lead at that point, saying, "exactly right, Thomas, my friend. Let us go downstairs. I think civilians and Mountjoy first, then these good men here, including you, Robert Wooler." He gestured to his soldiers, adding, "and finally Godfrey and I. Let us proceed."

The group left the room, descending the stairs in good order. Thomas More paused as he left the *camera regis*, to cast a look around the room, and one last thoughtful look at the leftover meat. He received a playful nudge from behind from Tunstall.

Exiting the *maison* through the atrium, which Thomas barely remembered from the trauma of the night before, Thomas blinked as they entered the bright sunshine outside. It was nearly midday. It was hot out in the sun, and the old roman stones of the road shimmered with the heat.

Thomas was immediately struck by the heat, and he felt a little woozy, still not recovered from the day before. The strap of his rolled up parchments immediately chafed a bit at his neck, and his brown robes, now truly filthy, itched quite a lot.

Looking around, Thomas saw that Father Theo had thankfully set up under a large, old, oak across the street and down a bit. He had made a small altar. The others had passed him while he adjusted, though most slowed and asked Thomas if he was well. To each, Thomas simply said "yes, thank you, fine," or "I'm just getting my bearings back." None believed him, but elected to give him some time.

Thomas slowly made his way to the shade, which also had a small well nearby with a ladle. He got himself a drink of the cold spring water and felt much better. Taking a chance, he took another ladleful and poured it on his head.

While the water ran to his shoulders, soaking, and cooling the upper part of his clothes, Thomas simply thought that pleasant, and, looking around, took one more ladle and again doused his head. Only then did he notice a few of the soldiers watching him, laughing.

Thomas smile agreeably and shrugged his shoulders helplessly. The soldiers laughed again and moved towards Thomas Howard and Godfrey. Thomas More noticed then that the soldiers, there did seem to be about thirty, had grouped into five or six groups, each group displaying a range of interest and affection towards Thomas Howard, or curiosity towards Godfrey. More noticed the differences in posture and attitude, not to mention distance, that each group affected as the group gathered for the service. Some of the further away groups muttered amongst themselves, pointing at Godfrey. Several of the soldiers, though, just seemed, Thomas struggled for the right adjective…rudderless and lost: not sure what to do.

Howard and Godfrey seemed to notice the same thing, and Godfrey leaned over and spoke a few words quietly to Howard, deferentially, his eyes cast downward. Howard nodded, and cleared his throat, the called out in what Thomas More recognized as his friend's new "command voice," steady, with a measured lower octave range that both carried and tended to cause the listener to lean in a little, pay attention so that nothing was missed.

"Soldiers," Howard's voice rang out, "and friends. Father Theo of this great and famous establishment, *Maison Dieu,* 'The Mansion of God,' will be kindly favoring us with a Sext service in a moment to send us on way in service to God and to Our King. We should be well remembering that today is the Eve of the Feast of the Translation of Saint Thomas Becket, once Lord Chancellor and Archbishop of Canterbury. Tomorrow marks the day that his preserved, saintly remains were placed into his proper memorial and tomb in the Cathedral.

"It is said that there is a hole in the tomb, and that a proper pilgrim may look to Saint Thomas and be cured, to have suffering or doubt relieved.

"My friends here," and he paused, gesturing and making a small bow in the direction of Thomas More, Mountjoy, Tunstall, the Woolers, "are pilgrims, making their way on a holy journey to be of one spirit, one body with Saint Thomas. They are the King's good servants, of course, but God's first.

"My soldiers," he bowed to his men, "we are, of course, the same. We each have our roles to play. This is a time where the King needs the service of his soldiers, not just in France, but here, in England. It is the King's divine right that we should serve him with our mortal bodies. It is the King's need, that brings us, his soldiers here today."

Thomas More noticed the soldiers listening, some of the further out groups subtly moving in, if for no other reason than to better hear Howard speaking. Their faces had become masks of intensity. Some nodded. No one shook their heads.

Howard continued after a brief pause, "My soldiers, my men, we are all King's men with our roles to play. You are all, I know brave and true. I am as well, though, as you may have noticed, I am also young." He paused and smiled. There was some relieved laughter among the men.

"Many, if not all of you," Howard continued, "have more experience of soldiering than I do. I confess it, and as we all must, when we make confession, we must learn, we must advance, we must progress, because to fail to do so compounds the sin."

Everyone under the old oak and on the edges was now listening intently.

"I failed to conduct a muster this morning, leaving you all leaderless, unguided about the day," Howard continued then pausing at a low murmur among the men. "I am sorry for that. There were many explanations, including a sick friend, but there are no excuses. There can be no excuses with men as fine as yourselves."

Howard paused to let that sink in, then in a voice of humility, a little softer so the men would have to lean in a bit closer. The outer groups shuffled in a bit more closely.

"I confess to you my error. I apologize to you, and I want to make amends," and then Howard paused. Godfrey looked on impassively his head moving from the men, soon to be his men, and to Howard, his commander.

The men looked a little askance at each other, all with a single, worrying thought, "a Lord apologizing?"

Thomas Howard had let this unusual step sink in a bit before, his voice rose in volume but not in tone, "My men, we are together here in the service of our great King Henry. Anointed by God, but wearing a crown won in battle. A victor, a champion. Our King... and serve him ably and well we will. But for us to do this, for me to lead this, we need a Sergeant at Arms of tested experience and valor. Generations of experience soldiering for England... God be praised, yesterday just such a man was provided to us by the Lord, on this sacred and holy route this Pilgrim's way....This man here, Godfrey Wooler."

Howard paused again and gestured with his right hand towards Godfrey, who continued to look impassive, but now just at the men. A couple of the men muttered and looked down, but most looked curiously at Godfrey.

"As a sign of God's love for us, Godfrey a proven soldier, and lifelong friend of our Sergeant Robert Egliston, happened by us yesterday at Sittingbourne. He is on pilgrimage with his family, including his son Robert, who is named after his Godfather Robert Egliston." That surprised the men and Thomas More, who looked at Godfrey, and noticed that he was beaming at his son.

"Godfrey and Robert Wooler will be joining us. Here. In Ospringe. In the sight of God. Godfrey is our Sergeant. We will be celebrating a mass of Thanksgiving here. Now. And then our band will be proceeding on the Canterbury to be of what service we can to our King as he also goes to Canterbury for the Feast day day tomorrow."

Interestingly, without waiting for questions, and ignoring the questioning looks on his men's faces, Thomas Howard, an impervious look on his face, turned to Father Theo, and saying, "My good priest. With that, and in God's good time, I would ask our mass of Thanksgiving to commence."

Thomas More, standing off to the side observing, felt a twitch, a pang, as if he was watching his old friend grow into manhood in that instant in front of him. Howard cast a glance at More. The corners of both's lips curled up a bit, but it was noticeable only to the two that it passed between, a secret code. Thomas More nodded slightly, to acknowledge and say "well done."

All in the area instinctively turned to Father Theo, who quickly applied his alb and vestments, looked at all gathered and called out, "Since we are all here, gathered under this old English Oak, we shall dispense with the processionals. We shall use the Sarum rite, of course, though Thomas More, I'm told that you've become something of a Benedictine in the past few days." Father Theo smiled happily at Thomas, who grinned back, patting his manuscript roll for safety. There was some laughter from the Wooler family, but the soldiers either looked confused or stood stone faced. Howard looked at the priest a little impatiently, worried about losing his audience.

"Thank you Father, " Howard said gently, " I am wondering if with the heat, and the press of time today, we might also just pass on the hymns, and consecrate our host?" He smiled at his little pun, which confused many in the group, including Father Theo.

"Certainly, Sir," Father Theo replied, a little quickly, "this may be done. Looking at the sky, it also appears likely to rain. Perhaps that will cool things off a bit."

Defused, the mass began with the usual prayers, a *Kyrie*, the *Pater Noster*. After that introduction, looking around happily, Father Theo said, looking shyly at the group., "I have a few psalms for our service today that represent a translation from the Greek into English that I would like to share with you all." Theo removed an old tattered book from a side pocket nervously. There were some shocked, and some happy looks from the group. The soldiers murmured uncomfortably a bit.

Before anyone could say anything, Father Theo said quickly, "I should like to begin, in honor of the soldiers here, and to commission good Godfrey Wooler here, the ninety first psalm, the Warrior's psalm:

> *"He that dwelleth in the help of the highest God;*
> *shall dwell in the protection of God of heaven.*

*He shall say to the Lord, Thou art mine up-taker, and my refuge;*

*My God, I shall hope in him.*

*For he delivered me from the snare of hunters;*

*And from a sharp word.*

*With his shoulders he shall make shadow to thee;*

*And thou shalt have hope under his feathers.*

*His truth shall compass thee with a shield;*

*Thou shalt not dread of the night's dread;*

*Of an arrow flying in the day.*

*Of a goblin going in darknesses;*

*Of assailing, and of a midday fiend.*

*A thousand shall fall down from thy side, and ten thousand from thy right side;*

*Forsooth it shall not nigh to thee.*

*Nevertheless thou shalt behold with thine eyes;*

*And thou shalt see the yielding of sinners.*

*For thou, Lord, art mine hope;*

*Thou has set thine help alder-Highest.*

*Evil shall not come to thee;*

*And a scourge shall not nigh to thy tabernacle.*

*For God hath commanded to his angels of thee;*

*That they keep thee in all thy ways.*

*They shall bear thee in the hands;*

*Lest peradventure thou hurt thy foot at a stone.*

*Thou shalt go upon a snake, and a cockatrice;*

*And thou shalt defoul a lion, and a dragon*

*For he hoped in me, I shall deliver him*

*He cried to me, and I shall hear him;*

*I am with him in tribulation;*

*I shall deliver him, and I shall glorify him*

*I shall fill him with the length of days;*

*And I shall show mine health to him."*

Father Theo stopped for a minute and looked at the rapt group in front of him. He smiled a bit and turned the page to a marked spot a little further on in his tattered book.

Thomas More looked around the group. Most seemed happy to have finally understood the priest in English. Alone in the group, Tunstall had turned white, clasping and unclasping his fists at his sides. Thomas touched Tunstall, who turned abruptly to look at him, startled. More mouthed, "what?" to his friend. Tunstall leaned in and whispered, frightened, "he's reading Wycliffe! Lollardy! It's death to have that book."

Thomas More looked about confused. He had heard of Lollardy before of course, but before he could ponder Tunstall, Father Theo had found his page and continued.

"The next Psalm, my friends," Father Theo continued, "is a Psalm for Pilgrims, number one hundred thirty two:

> *"Lord, have thou mind on David;*
> *and of all his mildness.*
> *As he swore to the Lord;*
> *He made a vow to God of Jacob.*
> *I shall not enter into the tabernacle of mine house;*
> *I shall not ascend into the bed of my resting.*
> *I shall not give sleep to mine eyes;*
> *And napping to mine eyelids.*
> *And rest to my temples, till I find a place to the Lord;*
> *A tabernacle to God of Jacob*
> *Lo! We heard that ark of testament in Ephratah*
> *We shall enter into the tabernacle of Him*
> *We shall worship in the place where his feet stood.*
> *Lord, rise thou into thy rest;*
> *Thou, and the ark of thine hallowing.*

*Thy priests be clothed with rightfulness;*

*And thy saints make full out joy*

*For David, thy servant;*

*Turn thou not away the face of thy Christ.*

*The Lord swore truth to David, and he shall not make him vain;*

*Of the fruit of thy womb I shall set on thy seat.*

*If thy sons shall keep my testament;*

*And my witnessings, these which I shall teach them.*

*And the sons of them till into the world;*

*They shall set on thy seat.*

*For the Lord chose Zion;*

*He chose it into dwelling to himself.*

*This is my rest into the world of world;*

*I shall dwell here, for I chose it.*

*I blessing shall bless the widow of it;*

*I shall fill with loaves the poor men of it.*

*I shall clothe with health the priests thereof;*

*And the holy men thereof shall make full out joy in full out joying*

*Thither I shall bring forth the horn of David*

*I made ready a lantern to my Christ*

*I shall clothe his enemies with shame;*

*But mine hallowing shall flower out on him."*

Father Theo, excited, the group hanging on his words, quickly turned to a page marked

with a faded ribbon, saying, "my friends, my favorite, from Jeremiah.

*"For I know the thoughts which I think on you, saith the Lord, the*

*thoughts of peace, and not of torment,*

*that I give to you and end and patience.*

*And ye shall call me to help,*

*And ye shall go, and shall worship me, and I shall hear you;*

*Ye shall seek me, and ye shall find,*

*When ye seek me in all your heart.*

*And I shall be found of you, saith the Lord, and I shall bring again your captivity;*

*And I shall gather you from all folks and from all places, to which I asked out you,*

*Saith the Lord; and I shall make you to turn again from the place, to which I made you to pass over."*

As if in a hurry, fearing interruption or arrest, Theo took a last deep breath saying, "Our gospel today commissions the apostles, as I do you all, my friends, pilgrims and soldiers. From the tenth Chapter of Matthew.

*"And go ye, and preach ye, and say that the kingdom of heavens shall approach;*

*heal ye sick men, raise ye dead men, cleanse ye mesels, cast ye out devils; freely ye have taken, freely give ye.*

*Do not ye wield gold, nor silver, nor money in your girdles.*

*Not a scrip in the way, neither two coats, neither shoes, nor a staff;*

*For a workman is worthy his meat*

*Into whatever city or castle ye shall enter, ask ye who therein is worthy, and there dwell ye, till ye go out.*

*And when ye go into an house, greet ye it, and say 'Peace to this house.'*

*And if that house be worthy, your peace shall come on it;*

*But if that house be not worthy, your peace shall turn again to you.*

*And whoever receiveth not you, nor heareth your words, go ye forth from that house or city, and sprinkle off the dust of your feet.*

*Truly I say to you, it shall be more sufferable to the land of men of Sodom and of Gomorrha in the day of judgment, than to that city.*

*Lo! I send you as sheep in the middle of wolves; therefore be ye sly as serpents, and simple as doves.*

*But be ye ware of men, for they shall take you in councils, and they shall beat you in their synagogues;*

*And to mayors or presidents, and to kings, ye shall be led for me, in witnessing to them and to heathen men.*

*But when they take you, do not ye think, how or what thing ye shall speak, for it shall be given to you in that hour, what ye shall speak;*

*For it be not ye that speak, but the Spirit of your Father, that speaketh in you."*

The group was silent as Father Theo finished reading from the old book. No one stirred for a few moments, absorbing the reading, and that they had heard the Gospel in English.

Thomas was confused, both liking it but also feeling unsettled.

The Wooler's and the soldiers looked enraptured. They all had beatific looks on their faces. Mouths moving as if trying to determine if somehow God moved with their jaws.

Cuthbert Tunstall remained white faced – anger and fear both in uncharacteristic display on his face. He turned away from the altar to Thomas More, touching his elbow and motioning him quietly to the periphery of the service.

The priest quietly closed his book and replaced it in the large hidden pocket inside his black robe. He turned to a breviary that had been placed near him, intending to resume the mass.

Reaching the outer edge of the group under the old oak, Cuthbert hissed into Thomas's ear, "Wycliffe….How dare he bring Wycliffe to our group…Dangerous…No permission…"

Cuthbert was quickly dissolving away from sense, and Thomas also noticed his voice becoming slightly louder – his fury making him forget that he was whispering.

"Wycliffe?" Thomas enquired. "Are you sure?"

"Entirely," replied Tunstall, "Wycliffe was from Oxford, a hundred years ago. We studied him, but always under the table because it is death to have a copy of his English bible. They even dug up Wycliffe's body and burned it. The Nobility view the people hearing the word of God in English as a great threat. To their lives."

Thomas was about to ask why, when he and Cuthbert noticed that the Mass had ceased and that everyone, including Father Theo was looking at them. Both of the boys turned red, and stammered about looking for somewhere to hide.

Father Theo looked amused though still quite kind. "Yes," Theo said gently to Cuthbert, "it is Wycliffe. It is much more common out in the provinces than you would imagine."

Cuthbert moved his mouth to speak, but Theo went on, "turns out that people enjoy understanding the word of God in their own tongue. That, as it were, Babel was the curse God intended it to be, but, with Grace and wisdom it could be overcome." The priest then turned to the rest gathered. "And so," he said, "where were we?"

Godfrey, smiling at Thomas, said, "we were about to ask for the intercessions of the Saints, Father."

Theo smiled broadly. "Ah yes," he said. "Excellent. I love that part!" He looked at Godfrey, sill bursting at the seams of his brown Pilgrim's robe. "I'm guessing St. Thomas?" he asked.

"Well, Father," Godfrey replied a little hesitantly, "Sure. Of course. But I am becoming a Sergeant of my Lord Thomas Howard, here." He paused and gestured respectfully towards a beaming Thomas Howard. The soldiers shuffled a bit, unsure. "So we must include St. George, and, if you don't mind, me patron is St. Edmund."

Father Theo nodded happily, "Excellent!" he responded, and then continued the mass, now back in Latin, calling for the intercessions of the three Saints.

Thomas More looked about the gathering under the old oak. At the still white face of Cuthbert, at the Woolers, at Howard and Mountjoy, at the soldiers. The heat of the day was still a bit oppressive, but it seemed to be cooling off some as Thomas could se clouds through the tree canopy beginning to darken.

"This is perfect," thought Thomas.

*"Trust and love, Thomas. It's what I've been telling you."*

"I see that now."

*"I know that you do. I'm proud of you."*

"Thank you. Cuthbert still looks upset."

*"He is. Do you know why?"*

"He spoke of Wycliffe. I know of him and the sin of Lollardy."

*"What was the sin?"*

"I wondered about that. I'm guessing pride. The idea that one could translate the word of God themselves into a native language."

*"What did Jerome do?"*

"Translated the word of God into Latin from Hebrew and Greek."

*"So how was Jerome not a heretic if Wycliffe is?"*

"Jerome is a Saint, called by God to translate his word"

*"Thomas, you're better than that. First Jerome wasn't a Saint when he translated. Second you can really have no idea who is called and who not."*

"That's a fair point. Jerome's translation was sanctioned, Wycliffe's not."

*"By whom?"*

"I guess by the government."

*"By Caesar."*

"Well yes."

"Avoiding an argument about rendering, let's look at why Jerome would be sanctioned, and Wycliffe not."

"Latin was the universal language of the time, as Greek was before it."

"In Roman territory. The world was much larger than that. Greek was the old language of power, as Latin is now. At the time of Jerome, though, Latin was the language of the people, as English is here, now, in England."

"How can you be sure it's not a bad translation?"

"Fair enough, but Jerome was translating as well. How can you be sure that Jerome was translating well?"

"You can't, except with divine guidance."

"And the Greeks translated the word from Hebrew and Aramaic, and many other languages?"

"Yes, but…"

"And those stories, the Word of God, were written down versions of old oral traditions?"

"Yes, but…."

"You don't yet read Greek. Or Hebrew."

"You know the answer to that. No, I don't."

"Did Wycliffe?"

"I've no idea, but presume not."

"Correct. The Wycliffe bible is his translation of the Word from Jerome's Latin, not from the earlier versions."

"So that the Wycliffe bible not only contains his own errors of translation, but also Jerome's and even earlier, the Greeks errors in translating the older languages?"

"Yes, precisely."

"And that's why Cuthbert is so upset?"

"That has nothing to do with why Cuthbert is upset."

"Seriously?!"

"Yes. It has long been thought that religion is the best way to control the people. That access to God, that access to a better afterlife could be tools towards getting people to follow meekly."

"Rulers don't want the Word of God in English to better control people?"

"Of course not. How better to control people than by making them believe that the King, or the Lord controls even access to heaven? To make them believe that unless they obey the ruler here on earth they will be condemned to eternal damnation?"

"And Cuthbert?"

"Why do you think he was so frightened? They dug up Wycliffes body years after he died and burned it so that he could not be found on Judgement Day."

"But heresy…"

"What is heresy, Thomas? Defiling the Word of God? Denying God? How does rendering God's word in English defile God? It honors God!"

Thomas shifted uncomfortably, no longer hearing the mass, as the voice continued.

"Thomas, you had the advantage of Saint Anthony's school where you learned to read Latin."

"Yes, of course."

"And Robert Wooler did not?"

"I suppose…"

*"And so you, because of your advantages, may read the word of God yourself, at least as far as Jerome was accurate, in a language you understand?"*

"Yes."

*"And Robert Wooler may not."*

"I see where you are going with this, but.."

*"Does that seem like an arrangement a loving God would design? Or does it seem more of an arrangement designed by men for their own power?"*

"By man."

*"Then, my friend, to whom much has been given, what do you propose to do about it?"*

A loud clap of thunder startled Thomas out of this reverie. The sky had turned dark, and the weather cooled. Thomas brought himself to his surroundings. The congregation around him had been startled by the thunder and was hurrying through communion.

Theo held the Host aloft, reciting "Hail forevermore, Thou most holy Flesh of Christ; sweet to me before and beyond all things beside. To me a sinner may the Body of our Lord Jesus Christ be the Way and the Life."

The rain began to fall, but the group remained rapt as Theo had communion. They moved forward with a little more urgency as the rain began to fall, though the leaves of the oak shielded them from much of the rain. Thomas kind of shuttled forward, adjusting his clothes and his mind to the world around him. As he reached Father Theo, a gust of wind tried to rip his carefully wrapped manuscript from its shoulder perch. Thomas steadied his package, then coming up to Theo, bent forward at the waist saying, "I am God's servant, Thomas."

Theo placed a host on Thomas's tongue, all while looking at him curiously. He made a blessing and Thomas moved off, just again as the wind picked up, blowing rain through the tree branches, making a fine mist around the group. Outside the protection of the trees, the rain fell

hard for a few minutes, water collecting in shallows alongside the road. Thomas saw happily that

the rain just skirted off the ancient stone road into side ditches, just as it had done for a

millennium or more.

With the completion of communion, the rain began to slacken, and it had stopped entirely

as Father Theo made the sign of the cross, and bade the congregants to "Go in Peace." Thomas

noticed that after dismissal, Theo quietly said a short prayer to himself. As Theo finished that

prayer, Thomas approached respectfully. Tunstall trailing off to the side.

"Father Theo," More asked quietly as Theo appeared to finish. Theo finished his prayer

with his eyes closed, then opened his eyes to smile benignly at the two boys. "Thomas!

Cuthbert!," Theo called happily, "how did you like the mass? For a bit you seemed...distracted."

The rest of the congregants were dispersing, starting to attend to their days. Howard,

Godfrey and Robert Wooler were gathering with the soldiers, Mountjoy stood somewhat

anxiously off to the side of that group, not sure of where he belonged.

Both Thomas and Theo flushed a bit with embarrassment, but Thomas persisted, "Father,

we apologize about that.. Truly we do. But Cuthbert studied at Oxford and is moving to

Cambridge, and he was concerned that you read from a Wycliffe Bible."

Theo smiled more broadly, and gently removed the old volume from the pocket, saying

"Wycliffe?" He paused, continuing to smile, "Cuthbert...Right...you're an Oxford man...I can

see how one might think that..but that would be forbidden....and as you can see here on my

treasure here.."

Theo gently placed the book in Cuthbert's hands, who initially reacted as if the book

were very hot. Tunstall gingerly passed the old book back and forth, hand to hand. It had a white soft calfskin cover, was about three inches thick, and about five inches by 8 inches in size. The paper was a very old parchment, and had been printed…printed! Inside. The plain cover bore no markings.

Theo reached over proudly, and opened the soft cover to reveal the stained inside front sheet, and pointed to the title, saying fondly, "this is my only possession of any value. It is a copy of Ludolph of Saxony's Life of Christ. It's in English! It was printed in 1460 by John Carolus himself in Argentum, Strasbourg. Carolus trained Caxton! My father gave this to me before he died."

Thomas marveled at the print, and the soft paper. A small deep part of him wanted the book and envied Theo. Cuthbert stepped in, asking quietly, "but Father, Ludolph told stories of Christ, didn't translate, where did the translations come from?"

Theo reached over again and pulled on a small ribbon place marker, moving the book to about the half way point, pointing, saying, "right there in the middle of the book are psalms and new testament in English, just the way the great Monk, Ludolph placed it!"

"But Father.." began Thomas before Cuthbert cut him off, closing the book gently, and slowly and reluctantly passing it back reverently to the ever so proud Theo.

"Father Theo," Cuthbert said with great warmth and respect, "that is a truly remarkable volume. I give you great joy of it, and I apologize for my confusion and concern. Ludolph was a remarkable scholar, and you are blessed to have hold of him, and we are blessed that you shared him with us here today. Thank you."

Theo looked as if he were about to burst, and, after carefully replacing the book in his hidden pocket, leaned forward to hug the boys. "It is I," Theo said, tears creeping into his voice, "who have been blessed to have met the two of you."

During the hug, and the nice thing about three people hugging is that the two outside people would look at each other, Thomas gave a questioning look at Cuthbert, who shook his head in a very firm "Later" gesture. Thomas relaxed, smiled, and murmured, "Thank you Father for everything, including your great and loving care of me in my extremity last night."

"My son," said Theo, pulling back and looking seriously at Thomas, "It was my honor. I see great things about you. A solo pilgrim at fourteen! Remarkable!"

Thomas looked seriously at Cuthbert, replying, "you see, Father, that's the thing. I started out a solo pilgrim, but haven't been for a long time. That may be the thing about pilgrimages. With trust and love, one is never alone."

"Nicely said, Thomas," said Cuthbert, Theo, and Thomas's voice in unison.

Cuthbert coughed and looked over to the Wooler family who had been making preparations to leave, saying, "I think that we should probably start getting moving to Canterbury, Thomas. It's afternoon, we have a few hours walk, and it looks like the Woolers may be ready."

Theo looked over, and became a little flustered, "Oh, my yes. I'd forgotten about the time. You all must get a move on."

The three strode over to the Woolers. Mrs. Wooler had taken charge of the group with her husband and son over with the soldiers. Thomas asked, "Mrs. Wooler, what should we do about Godfrey and Robert?"

Mrs. Wooler laughed a deep and happy laugh. "Look at my two boys over their with their soldiers. I'm not even sure they remember us. As far as I am concerned, all is right with the world. No worries, my Thomas, we shall meet them again tomorrow in Canterbury."

"They aren't coming with us?" Cuthbert asked.

"Heavens no, dear," Mrs. Wooler clucked. "They have soldierly things to do together. Pull together as a unit."

As if on cue, Godfrey had placed Robert in the center of the men, lining them up in front of the *Maison*, on the ancient road as a muster. The Wooler family watched silently as Godfrey, in his element, and also still in his too small brown pilgrim's robe, went down the line with a serious look on his face, speaking with each of his new soldiers, Thomas Howard at his side.

Sensing his dismissal, Mountjoy walked over to the little group of Woolers, More, and Tunstall. He had a wry smile on his face and was shaking his head with amusement.

"Is everything all right?" Tunstall called out, a little concern in his voice.

Mountjoy looked up, and replied as he got nearer, "right as rain, my friend. God's love connected us with Godfrey Wooler here. He is what we were missing. The unit is improved a hundred fold in a moment." He stopped and gestured back at the troops with his right hand, adding, "see how quickly they've come to resemble a military unit."

"Thank you, my Lord," said Mrs. Wooler to Mountjoy with a little curtsey.

"Thomas," Mountjoy asked seriously, "how did you find these people?"

Thomas replied with a smile, "you said it yourself, Mountjoy, 'God's love.'"

Tunstall still looked a little confused, asking, "so are we taking our leave of Howard's army?"

They all laughed, and Mountjoy said, "yes, I think. For a day. Godfrey and our friend Thomas Howard…I guess we should call him 'Captain Howard' now, need to do some arrangements today. They are cooking something up between themselves to make a good impression tomorrow."

Thomas More asked, "did they say what."

'Yes," Mountjoy replied with a wink, "and they added that it was a 'military secret.'"

"Boys," laughed Mrs. Wooler, "with that we should get a move on, then."

## Chapter 24 - July 6, 1492 – The eve of the Feast of the Translation of Saint Thomas Becket

The group of pilgrims – the Wooler family minus Robert and Godfrey, Thomas More, Cuthbert Tunstall, and young William Blount - the Lord Mountjoy set forth again down the Roman road to Canterbury. At the outset, the group stepped quietly behind the thirty or so soldiers lined up along the side of the road being inspected by their new Sergeant-at-arms, Godfrey Wooler and their young Captain, Thomas Howard. As they passed, Thomas More caught Godfrey's eye and gave a little wave. Godfrey didn't smile, but acknowledged Thomas with a small nod of his head and the barest smile.

Thomas More thought he heard something about poles, but couldn't make out any more to give him a clue. He looked back and saw, at the door of the *Maison,* Father Theo waving farewell, a wistful look on his face. Thomas waved back, then, gently nudged Cuthbert's elbow, which caused Cuthbert to stop, look back, and wave enthusiastically at the little priest.

The brief pause in their walking allowed the Woolers to go on ahead, with Mountjoy in the lead talking quietly with Mrs. Wooler. The small separation allowed Thomas and Cuthbert to speak quietly.

"Cuthbert, my friend," Thomas asked in a low voice, as the two turned back to the road and began again to walk slowly East. "What happened back there? First you are white, muttering about Wycliffe, and then when you see the book, you cut me off from asking about it."

Cuthbert walked on a few steps, contemplating his answer, then replied, also in a low voice, "the readings were Wycliffe, Thomas. Forbidden translations. I know. I studied them, memorized sections from an old book I found hidden in the Balliol College library at Oxford. How it survived there I do not know. Balliol got hit pretty hard when the King banned Lollardy,

They even blamed Wat Tyler and the Peasants on Wycliffe, though I heard that Wycliffe and old John of Gaunt were actually pretty close. Anyway, I found an old hidden copy of Wycliffe in the library and I decided to protect it."

"What does that mean? 'Protect it?'" Thomas asked, having stopped his walk again. "I moved it to another library at Oxford, hid it again figuring that if I could find it, others might as well."

"In which College did you hide the Wycliffe," Thomas asked.

Cuthbert furrowed his brow in contemplation, replying after a moment, "Let me think about that, Thomas. It's death for me to have the book. Not sure I want to share that information, just yet."

Thomas accepted that, imagining the book, then thinking about Theo's book. He paused, then asked, "so you were so sure, but looking at Father Theo's book you seemed to stop. You kept me from asking about the book. I can't imagine that Ludolph has a Bible inserted in the middle. That's why Ludolph is allowed and even popular, it tells stories about Christ but isn't a translation of the Word."

"Yes, Thomas," Cuthbert replied, "that is true. I've read it."

"So why didn't you let me ask him about that?" Thomas asked insistently.

Cuthbert stopped and looked kindly at Thomas, replying with patience and kindness, "Thomas, what did Father Theo say about the book?"

Thomas stopped, "…that it was his greatest possession. Really his only possession. But.."

Cuthbert drew Thomas up short, "and who gave him the book?"

Thomas replied, "his father before he died. But…"

"No buts, Thomas," Cuthbert said insistently, "the only thing that your line of questioning would have uncovered is that Father Theo's greatest possession, a gift from his own dying father, had somehow had banned text inserted into it. What would have been the point of spoiling that book for Theo?"

"But the truth must be known!" Thomas replied hotly.

"It is known, Thomas," Cuthbert replied gently. "It is known by us."

"But Theo…" Thomas interjected.

"If he doesn't know, Thomas," Cuthbert said sadly, "why does he need to learn that from us? It is likely that we will never see him or his book again. What is gained?"

"The truth is inviolable.." Thomas began, but he was cut off by Cuthbert with a little impatience.

"So is kindness, Thomas," Cuthbert responded, "So is trust in God that everything is right. Who made you the Grand Inquisitor of England."

"We don't have Inquisitors in England," Thomas replied, missing the point.

"Exactly," Cuthbert replied, "we kept them out for a reason. The Sarum liturgy is English, not Roman. We are ruled by King, not Pope here."

Thomas drew up, aghast, "Cuthbert, stop. You are going to be a priest, you will serve the Pope."

"True," Cuthbert replied, "but I also am an Englishman and serve my King. And what I am saying, Thomas, is that despite all those lofty thoughts, as a practical matter, Father Theo showered us with kindness. We had a duty to respond in kindness to him, as loving fellow Christians. And, as for truth…Well…as I said, my friend, we know the truth."

Cuthbert then ended the conversation with a kind tap on Thomas's shoulder and a point forward indicating that the two had lagged considerably behind the leaders of their group. He then turned and picked up his pace in an effort to rejoin them on the road.

Thomas, a little stung by Cuthbert, held back, continuing at his same pace, though now clasping his hands behind his back as he walked.

"The nerve of Cuthbert there," thought Thomas.

*"What do you mean? That sounded about right."*

"What? The truth was right there in front of all of us."

*"And you feel an obligation to point out every truth to everyone?"*

"Well yes. That's what I always do."

*"To what end?"*

"Everyone should have the truth in front of them."

*"Really? Why?"*

"Because its important!"

*"Why is it important?"*

"It just is. I can't explain it any more completely than that. I feel that the truth is what is important more than people's feelings."

*"Perhaps when it is convenient or advantageous to you."*

"What do you mean by that?"

*"I can't help but notice that you don't do share every thought with people you perceive as superior to yourself, or when it puts you in a bad light."*

"Such as?"

*"Well…let's get to Archbishop Morton. Did you give him the 'complete truth,' as you so describe it?"*

"Weeeellll…"

*"So you see, Father Theo does not impact your future. So you felt you could make yourself look smart at his expense. Cuthbert, who by the way is a true friend, recognized that urge, and stopped you."*

"I didn't mean…"

*"Of course you didn't mean to Thomas, it is intrinsic in you, and you need to be aware of that tendency and control it. Have insight into yourself… I should add that to 'love and trust.' He… three things, love, trust, and self-awareness. I like it when things come in three."*

"Since I've made you so happy, anything else?"

*"Now that you mention it, go thank Cuthbert Tunstall."*

Disturbed, Thomas turned his attention back to the road to discover that he was now a few hundred yards behind his group, as he caught a view of a few familiar heads, and the yellow and black of Mountjoy's doublet ahead on the undulating hills of eastern Kent.

Thomas quickened his pace, and in a few hills had caught up to the group. He first approached Tunstall, who was walking quietly near the back edge of the group, not really interacting with anyone. His breathing had become strained in the chalk hills, his face, always pale, now matching the chalk. Thomas touched him on the elbow, and quietly asked, "Cuthbert, may I speak with you a moment?"

Tunstall stopped, and turned to Thomas, his face impassive, and his breathing still a little rough.

Thomas waited in vain for Cuthbert to open the conversation, but he just stood there, looking at him.

Thomas finally cleared his throat, a little color rising in his face, saying, "Cuthbert. I am very sorry. You were entirely correct back there. I would have hurt Father Theo terribly, and for no reason. Thank you for protecting me from myself." Thomas nodded his head in respect to his friend.

Cuthbert's face softened, but still no smile. "Thomas," he said, "I appreciate your saying that. We have only known each other a few days, but what a few days! I consider you to be a friend for a lifetime. And we must watch out for each other. I was upset at hearing Wycliffe. You saw that. I'm sorry to have put you in that position."

Thomas started a bit, then disagreed, "No Cuthbert, I must be honest, your being upset had little to do with it. I saw an opportunity to look smart to you, and didn't care about Father Theo. I was wrong, and you were a true friend both to me and to Father Theo."

Tunstall considered this for a moment, then smiled warmly, "so it seems we are both kind of rotten, Thomas, because part of my anger was to show you how smart I was about Wycliffe."

Thomas laughed, saying, "Well, I will insist, my friend, that we watch out for each other, and will reiterate my thank you."

Cuthbert nodded and laughed, crying, "Agreed!" He then looked up ahead on the road and said, and I think that we should probably catch up, and maybe see what we can do for Mountjoy."

Thomas raised his eyebrows and smiled, asking, "you were looking a little pale, a moment ago, you okay with a quick pace?"

In answer, Cuthbert turned and began a fast walk, looking over his shoulder at Thomas mouthing, "that was a guilty conscience."

Thomas gave a short guffaw and quickly caught up, and the two see-sawed back and forth in the lead until they had caught up and rejoined their group. Reaching Mountjoy, Thomas and Cuthbert, laughing, each tapped Mountjoy on either shoulder, saying "William!"

Without turning in either direction, William Blount, the fourteen year old Lord Mountjoy, simply said, "I was wondering when you two would be joining us."

"A little grumpy there, William," said Tunstall.

"I left my horse with Howard," William replied, "I don't much like walking, especially by myself."

Mrs. Wooler looked amused, but gave Thomas a slight downward nod of his head to imply that he should not press the issue.

"I'm sorry, William," Thomas said, "please forgive us. On the brighter side, we're here now!" He then gave a very winning smile to William which caused general laughter, including Mrs. Wooler.

With that tension released, the group set forth on the last part of the road to Canterbury, all speaking congenially about everything and nothing. The road actually widened a bit, as rivers inevitably widen from feeder streams. More and more pilgrims seemed to congeal into the stream of the road as well – brown robed objects bobbing slowly in their stream. The Thames itself, never far off to the left, had widened considerably since the span of the London Bride, miles, epochs ago. The hills progressively became chalkier, and undulated with more vigor as they entered the downs.

In fact, as the group approached Canterbury, it also seemed to Thomas that as he had gotten further from London, everyone in the group had begun to display more of their true selves than had seemed possible to possess before. Mr. Wooler, before leaving them a few hours before, seemed hairier and more feral, but also more martial than before. Mrs. Wooler had become much wiser and loving at the same time. Even the little shrines they kept passing set up along the side of the road – a lost shoe of St. Thomas – an alleged shard of skull, still splattered with his holy blood – all of these relics seemed to glow with virtue for Thomas.

The group crested a hill and saw the road curving in a leftward slope down into Canterbury in the valley. The first view of Canterbury from this hill was a long known inspiration to pilgrims for centuries. Rising up out of the valley was the town, with its walls, and enormous cathedral in the center. The two gothic towers rose up higher than anything else visible. The central tower of the cathedral was under construction, had been for years, and was only about half rebuilt, scaffolding and workmen set up around that from the distance looked like busy ants working on their colony. The hammering of the stone masons could be faintly heard off in the distance. To the right and behind the cathedral, Thomas could see the abbey building and its huge surrounding fields, extending out to a ragged treeline on an opposite hill. A haze of smoke added an otherworldliness to the scene, the green valley, the stone cathedral, the narrow streets, the low city wall, all given a hint of haze, a little bit of grey. The sun sun then came out from behind a cloud, illuminating the towers in a halo of spectral haze.

As they had been walking, the July heat had returned and the larger knot of pilgrims present were perspiring despite the pleasant breeze at the brow of the hill, Church Hill in Harbleton, they were on. On the right side of the road, there was a yard, with a small stand, behind which there was, up a little hill a red roofed old church with a single tower, and to the right, a long building, a hospital.

Thomas ignored the priest, basically a barker, at the stand, who was loudly announcing to the passing pilgrims that this was St. Nicholas's church and hospital, and that for a donation, the pilgrims could see a slipper worn by St. Thomas himself. Instead, Thomas focused on the people sitting in rags in the warm summer air just outside the whitewashed hospital building.

On the narrow side of the hospital building that was closest to the road, about thirty feet off, there was a clump of about ten people varyingly ravished by leprosy. They were of all ages, and mostly men with a few women scattered in. Thomas's eyes were drawn to, and then met by a boy of about Thomas's age. The boy was thin, and wearing rags. His face was marked by the lumps and bumps of the disease. He was using a cane to support himself, and Thomas noticed that several fingers had succumbed to the disease. The boy waved to Thomas, who, riveted to his spot, could only wave.

Cuthbert and William suddenly called to Thomas, which ended the moment when Thomas turned his head in response to their call. After an "I'm coming" wave to his two friends, Thomas turned back to the boy, who was shuffling off with his cane towards an entrance to the hospital.

Thomas thought for a moment about going up to the hospital, but the group was moving on, he had neither money nor interest in the slipper, and, deep down, he knew his courage was failing, so he turned and continued along the road, now gently downward from the top of the hill into the valley that led to the ever nearing Canterbury.

When he had re-caught the group, the heat seemed to be getting the better of several of the children. They walked on a little further down the hill past a few older road houses, until, on the right, they caught sight of a very old church, with a large tree and a well in the yard. Mountjoy nodded at the church and said simply, "Saint Dunstan's."

"Boys," Mrs. Wooler said, concerned for her tired younger children, "Perhaps we should rest here?"

The church was on a corner of the road that made a gentle right turn. The single towered, very old ragstone church was on the right and ahead was a red brick wall enclosing a farm estate. As the group made the corner, and went into the churchyard, Thomas could see ahead about a hundred feet that there was a red brick arched gateway. Down the road a few hundred yards, Thomas could make out the imposing grey stone double towers and arch of the gate in the wall to the city of Canterbury.

There Wooler children and a few other souls that were now with their group had settled happily in the shade near the well and were drawing water. Some bread had also been miraculously produced from some bags and was being happily shared amongst the pilgrims.

After helping her children achieve a rough state of rest, Mrs. Wooler stood a little off to the side, looking at her children and gnawing absently on a fingernail. She was composed, but had a thin bead of sweat on her forehead that Thomas hadn't ever noticed before. She had taken a rough cloth from a bag and wiped her brow. Seeming to make a decision, she approached Thomas shyly.

"So Thomas," Mrs. Wooler asked quietly, her eyes cast down, "will ye be meetin' the Archbishop in Canterbury?"

"Yes," replied Thomas simply, and with a generous smile.

She cleared her throat nervously, and said, "my husband might have had ein bisschen too much ale the other nacht for his own good."

Thomas stopped her, and pulled her a little off to the side, gently touching her shoulder with deep affection. "Mrs. Wooler," Thomas said quietly, but with deep feeling, "your husband, you, your family, are just wonderful people. Full and generous spirits. You have been my guides in more ways than I can tell you. The Archbishop once told me that the Earl Percy was killed by landowners in Yorkshire during a riot over taxes. The leader of the riots, Sir Reginald de Sey has already been punished. And, anyway, as Godfrey said, there are many reasons for going on pilgrimage. Who can truly know another man's mind?"

From the corner of his eye, Thomas saw Cuthbert relax his posture and smile.

"Would you all like to meet the Archbishop?" Thomas asked earnestly.

Mrs. Wooler boomed a laugh, "That Frenchman!? I'm sure he would be delighted to meet us! Nein. I have met my purpose here and am content."

"Mrs. Wooler," Thomas asked, "did you like the service Father Theo gave?"

"Aye, I did, Thomas," she replied fondly.

"What did you like about it?" Thomas asked.

"I liked being able to understand the readings, Thomas," she replied simply. "I don't know Latin and the priests always make me feel stupid when they go on in Latin."

Thomas caught Cuthbert out of the corner of his eye, who smiled.

"Thank you," Thomas said simply. "What will you do when we get to Canterbury?"

"That depends upon my husband and son, I suppose," she said a little wistfully. "I'm so grateful that he had a chance with your friend, Captain Howard. We'll see how it goes."

"Would you be alright if he goes back into the military?" Thomas asked.

"Its what my husband is," she replied, "a soldier. Part of him died at Bosworth. This is a blessing." She paused, then laughed a beautiful happy laugh, "and if it works out the six pence a day won't be unwelcome either. Wandering is a stress. Feeding the children is a challenge."

Thomas pondered that and said simply, "I'm glad for your Godfrey and your family. You're sure about the Archbishop?"

"Very," she laughed.

There was a clatter of horses hooves on the stone road behind them as a group of men on horseback, led by a man of about twenty slowed to make the corner in the road. The noise attracted his attention from Mrs. Wooler, and he smiled broadly at the sight of the men, who continued to slow after their right turn as they approached the red gate up the road on the left.

Thomas moved quickly, and grabbed William and Cuthbert by the arms calling, "come with me quickly," before he ran off after the men.

The hem of Thomas's robes nearly tripped him, until he gathered them in his left hand and pulled up to knee level. The group of men had stopped at the Roper gate, waiting for the gate to be opened from the inside. The lead, a young man in his early twenties had called in over the gate and rung a bell.

Thomas neared, with William and Cuthbert in hot pursuit. Thomas skirted around the backs of the men, who were dismounting their horses. There were six, all dressed in riding black, with black felt berets. They seemed quite jovial, and were laughing at something an older man, on Thomas's left in the group, had said.

Thinking quickly, Thomas pulled the previously unused cowl of his pilgrim robe up over his head, and came up behind the right shoulder of the genial looking man on the far side of the group. Thomas took a deep breath, and reached out and pulled the elbow of the gentleman, scrinched his voice up high, and said, "Please sir, some bread for a poor pilgrim?"

All the men heard the high voice, and turned to it. The tagged gentleman turned with surprise, saying, "Eh?"

Thomas repeated his plea, "Please sir.." But only got that far before Cuthbert and William came huffing up behind, calling, "Thomas! What is happening.?

The gentleman, light dawning in his eyes, exclaimed, "Thomas!?" and reached out to gently pull back the cowl to reveal Thomas's smiling, and very dirty, face.

"Hello Father," Thomas cried. "Surprise!"

John More's round face went quickly from confusion to joy as he took in his son. His knees buckled a bit, and with both arms clasped Thomas by the shoulders, exclaiming with a shocked exhale of breath, "Thomas?!"

Thomas nodded happily, and John More brought him into a full bear hugged embrace, crying, "Thomas! I had so hoped we would see you on the road!"

The other men had now figured out who the ragged pilgrim was, and the older gentleman, his grey beard shaking, came forward, saying in a low, rough voice, "I take it, John, that we've found Thomas at last." The gentleman paused, and took in Thomas's two friends, who's breathing was slowing, "and I see he has found some interesting friends." He paused, and nodded at William before adding, "including, I see, my Lord Mountjoy." He bowed his head towards William.

William nodded seriously saying, "Sergeant Fineaux."

The King's Sergeant-at-Law, the leading lawyer of the realm, John Fineaux, turned to Cuthbert and said, "and if I'm not mistaken, you are Thomas Tunstall's son?"

Cuthbert bowed nervously.

"Well, John More," said Sergeant Fineaux, "this is very interesting…Delightful really." He laughed, his beard shaking.

Thomas looked confused, and asked, "have you been looking for me Father?"

John More replied, "for the past two days, Thomas! You've left quite a wake along the Way of the Pilgrims. I am so proud of you!" He re-embraced his son.

Thomas laughed happily, and returned the embrace. After a moment he pulled back a bit, aware of the other older gentlemen and his two friends looking at him, and asked, "why, Father?"

John More looked down a little, saying, "perhaps in more closeted circumstances, Thomas, but, in brief and in public, the King is coming to Canterbury to pray for the Queen, and the Archbishop has asked that several of us attend him in that aim."

"Several of us?" asked Thomas.

"Well…," John hesitated, then diverted with a wave of his hand to the group around him, "I think introductions are in order. Gentlemen," John nodded to the older group of men, "this is my son, Thomas More, and his two surprising new friends, Cuthbert Tunstall and William Blount, the Lord Mountjoy, who's father John was well known to us."

Thomas and his friends bowed.

John then continued, turning a bit to Thomas, "and Lords and Lads," he paused to chuckle, "these are my friends and colleagues, some of whom you already know, Thomas." There were some chuckles from the men, who nodded and smiled to Thomas. "But for your friends, first," he paused and gestured towards the Sergeant, "this is the King's Sergeant-at-Law, John Fineaux." A pause as Thomas and the boys nodded. "And over by the gate is his son-in-law, and the owner of this estate, John Roper." John More waved to the 22 year old beardless gentleman who had finally gotten the gate to open, showing a verdant estate behind.

"Thomas," John continued waving to familiar faces of a father and son, "of course you remember the former Lord Mayor Henry Colet, and his son, Father John." John paused and gave a little snort at "his son, Father John."

Thomas and friends bowed again.

"Finally, Thomas and friends," John said after clearing his throat, "I'd like to introduce two young friends of our group…" He gestured with a little bow to two younger men, both blond and both in their late teens, adding, "Sir Edward Guildford, from Broadwater, and young Doctor John Clement from Yorkshire."

Thomas nodded at the to young men. They seemed a little familiar. He looked at both William and Cuthbert who also acknowledged the teens.

John took a deep breath and said, "well, with the introductions done, we have a lot to talk about. Let's head into Roper's house and catch up."

The group of men started to turn to head into the estate, but Thomas, William and Cuthbert hesitated. Thomas cast a look over his shoulder at the Wooler family under the tree at St. Dunstan's, Mrs. Wooler standing watching Thomas and the group.

Thomas said haltingly, "Father a moment please, may I speak with you?"

Sergeant Fineaux looked askance, and a little annoyed, and began to mutter, "there really isn't time…," but John More held up his hand and said, "Certainly Thomas, but not too long."

John then turned to his group and said, "give me a moment gents. Why don't you all just go on in, and we will follow in a moment."

John Roper, taking a cue called out, "come on in gentlemen, we can get situated at the house, I'm sure the Mores will be on in a moment."

With a little grumbling the black clad group walked their horses through the gate of the Roper estate, eventually leaving the two Mores alone with William and Cuthbert a little off to the side.

"What's up, Thomas?" asked John More in a friendly voice, looking clear eyed at his son.

"Father," Thomas began hesitantly, "I want to finish my pilgrimage. I know it's only been a few days, but…. Well I can't really express it. I'm different. I've changed."

John More smiled happily, replying, "a good pilgrimage will do that to a person, Thomas. But the King and the Archbishop have called and need our help. We need," he stopped and looked at William and Cuthbert, "you and I need to meet with the King and the Archbishop tomorrow after the mass…"

Thomas gently interrupted, "but Father, that is tomorrow, after the mass that completes my journey…"

John, mildly annoyed at the interruption, but still kind, completed, "Thomas, one does not meet with the King and the Archbishop without preparation. We need to decide what we are going to say and do when we meet them." He stopped to let Thomas mull that over.

After a moment, Thomas said, "Father, I understand that, but I don't know the question that needs preparing. Or how long is really needed to prepare. And I wonder, how would you have handled this if we hadn't just found each other."

John More laughed a bit, saying, "Thomas, you need to be a lawyer! England needs you to be a lawyer. Our plan was to pull you aside as you entered the cathedral."

Thomas smiled, "well, I wouldn't have liked that either." He paused, and looked back over to the church. "Father," Thomas began, "I have a compromise to offer." He paused and smiled broadly, turning to William and Cuthbert.

John smiled at his son in return, eyes arched in both amusement and surprise, and said, "go on.."

Thomas proceeded, trying his most compelling adult voice, "Sir, I propose the following, I've made a number of friends on this journey that have become very important to me." He gestured broadly at both his two friends standing there and to the grey edifice of St. Dunstan's back up the road. "The nice lady standing by the tree up there is Mrs. Mary Wooler from the north with her children."

John cut him off with a grumble of, "I don't see how…"

Thomas paused out of respect for his father, and when he had trailed off, he said, "The King is preparing an army at Sittingbourne to invade France this Autumn." He paused. His father simply looked at him.

"The army is being led by Charles Somerset," Thomas continued, "and until recently Thomas Howard and the Lord Mountjoy, here, were Officers in that service."

The elder More's jaw worked a little as he looked at William, still in his black and gold doublet, though considerably dirtier. John said, "We saw Somerset in Sittingbourne. He didn't say anything about…"

"A few days ago, Thomas explained, "Somerset detached Thomas Howard and William to take a body of men to attend to the King in Canterbury."

"He didn't do it himself?" John asked.

"That is another long story, Father," Thomas said gently, "best left to soldiers to explain amongst themselves."

"All right," John said with a tilt of his head, conceding the point.

Thomas cleared his throat, "Well, it turns out that Mary Wooler's husband, Godfrey Wooler, whom I met on the path, and who has become quite dear to me, is an accomplished soldier, a member of King Edward's private guards…."

Thomas paused for a moment, trying to decide how much more to reveal, looked at Cuthbert and William, both of whose eyes were a widened a bit, and both of whom made nearly imperceptible shakes of their heads.

Both Thomas and John caught the looks, but John smiled, and said, "you met Godfrey Wooler on pilgrimage?"

Thomas reeled back in surprise, "you know him?"

John smiled, "very big guy, hairy, Saxon, doesn't like 'Frenchmen'?"

Thomas laughed, "yes, that's him. How do you know him?"

John smiled broadly, and replied with a wink, "that is another long story Thomas, best left to Mores to explain amongst themselves. Suffice to say that if Godfrey Wooler has become a friend of you three, then I am very pleased and proud. It also means, Thomas, that you have learned to see everyone in a room, not just nobility, and I am very pleased at that."

The younger More bobbed proudly at that. Thomas suddenly realized that he and his father were now the same height, and that instead of his own usual subservience, he was now, for the very first time, looking his father in the eye, not as an equal, perhaps, but at least as a person in his own right.

Thomas looked at his father's round rubbery face as if through eyeglasses. It was genial face, a little florid at the cheeks. His father's mouth and chin seemed, suddenly, a little weak, but his eyes were remarkable, sharp and incisive and sad all at once.

"My father needs to take me seriously here," Thomas thought.

*"What makes you think he isn't?"*

"His face. His answers. He has already decided what I am doing."

*"You are doing a decent job of explaining your reasoning to him."*

"And he doesn't care."

*"Look at him more closely, Thomas, I think he does. Very much. But your relationship just changed. He needs time to adapt."*

"I don't have time about tonight!"

*"Then start with tonight. Make it about tonight, not whether you will continue to son child-like obedience, or be your own person for the rest of your lives together."*

"What do you mean?"

*"You two just started, this minute, renegotiating your relationship. Start small."*

Thomas realized that he was staring, and blinked. John More smiled, happily, knowing from fourteen years of loving his son what had just happened.

"Thomas?" John asked his son gently.

"Father," Thomas began seriously, still working the words out in his head. "First, let me just say how incredibly happy I am to have met you here so far from home. And I want you to know that I understand how important the matter must be for you and your friends to have travelled so far, both searching for me and to meet the Archbishop and the King here tomorrow for the Feast of St. Thomas."

Thomas paused, and searched his father's listening face. Interestingly, his father showed no adverse reaction to that. John More was simply listening to John's argument.

Thomas continued, "I have heard that the Queen has been ill since delivering at Richmond four days ago. Word travels fast in the Pilgrim's trail." He stopped and smiled, adding, "and I truly love the Queen." Another pause.

"Father continues to listen."

*"That's because you are speaking like an adult. Pray continue."*

"I am not sure," Thomas went on with a little more confidence, "what my role in the Queen's recovery may be, but please know that I would always do what I could within the law, for our monarchs."

John More smiled a bit at Thomas's reference to the law, then nodded, saying quietly, "well said."

Thomas then came to the thrust of his argument, "Father you have said many times within my hearing that under the common law, oral contracts are binding, more so when witnessed." Another pause.

"Yes," John replied gravely, "they are indeed."

"Well, sir," Thomas replied, "I am currently engaged in several oral contracts, all of which are witnessed."

Father More arched his eyebrows, took brief glances at William and Cuthbert behind Thomas, then returned his gaze to his son, who was standing surprisingly firm. John, after a pause, said, Is there any proof of such contracts having been made? Any documents under seal?"

"No, sir," Thomas replied, "but *compurgation* would suffice to achieve enforcement of each of the three oral contracts I have in mind."

"You are willing," John replied slowly, enunciating each word, now not sure if he was angry, amused, or impressed, "to make a '*wager of law,*' offer sworn statements of observation of existing contracts that you say would prevent you from coming with us right now, and would delay our reunion until after the Mass tomorrow?"

"Yes, Sir," Thomas replied without hesitation.

John tossed this over in his mind, before asking, "and I presume that these two here are your witnesses for these contracts?" He made a vague gesture with his hand towards Cuthbert and William, who were now looking anxious, not sure what they were being drawn into.

"Only to the third and final contract, Sir," Thomas replied. He continued to look directly into his father's eyes, not daring to shift, lest he appear insecure.

"And the nature of the this third contract, Master More?" John asked.

"I promised Godfrey Wooler that I would see his wife and children safely to Canterbury, and keep them safe until Godfrey and his son Robert Wooler, now Sergeant and soldier with Thomas Howard and thirty of the King's men were reunited in Canterbury after the Feast Mass of St. Thomas Becket at the Cathedral." Thomas gestured to Mrs. Wooler and the children up outside St. Dunstan's.

John turned to the two friends, "and you two are prepared to swear that you witnessed this contract between Thomas and Godfrey Wooler?"

"We are, Sir," both replied in unison.

"Well then, Thomas," John replied, "you would seem to have met the terms of that contract. You have safely seen the Wooler family to Canterbury, and your friends here may honorably act as your agents for the second part."

"With Respect, Sir," Thomas replied, "I have met neither of the terms of the contract, and no provision for agency was made in the contract with Godfrey."

John was intrigued, but a little frustrated as he replied, "you have seen them to Canterbury."

Thomas, sensing his father's frustration simply pointed, "the gates to the City of Canterbury are over there. We are at St. Dunstan's *outside* of Canterbury. We've stopped short."

John laughed. "My son! I love it!" I will accept that as a prior contract, but I cannot accept that agency cannot be created when both the King's and Archbishop's needs are in consideration."

"Very well," father, Thomas replied respectfully, "then I must come to my second contractual obligation."

"Which is?" asked John, curious.

"I promised the Archbishop," Thomas replied carefully, "that in return for completing the Canterbury Pilgrimage by the Feast of the Translation on July 7, and meeting him in Canterbury on that date, that he would, in return, send me to Oxford to study at Canterbury College."

"I see," said John thoughtfully, "and I presume that your witness for this is the Archbishop himself?"

"Yes, sir," Thomas replied. "But I would respectfully offer that you were aware of the agreement as well."

"Indeed I was, Thomas." John replied kindly, "indeed I was. So, I will accept that your prior contract with the Archbishop should outweigh the Archbishop's current needs. But that does not abrogate the needs of the King."

Thomas looked uncomfortable. John misunderstood this to mean that he was about to concede. John looked at his son, and asked, "well?" and he crossed his arms.

Thomas was unfazed, and said, "Sir, for the hearing of the third contracts, I would ask that the witnesses to the first be excused."

William and Cuthbert, stood up, surprised and hurt, saying together, "What?!? Thomas! We are on your side!"

Thomas turned to his friends, saying, "I realize that, my friends, but the third contract may only be discussed More to More. Also, we've left the poor Woolers alone up there at St. Dunstan's for quite a while. Might I beg you two to go tend to them and make sure the children have eaten?"

"Thomas…," John asked, concerned "those children haven't eaten?"

"None of us have since this morning," Thomas replied simply, "it is the way of the pilgrim to love and trust the Lord on the trail for provenance."

"What of the money I gave you in London?" John asked.

"The Brothers of St. Thomas Acre robbed me on London Bridge at the beginning of my journey," Thomas replied simply.

"You've made it from London to Canterbury with no money? At all?" John asked, incredulous.

"It was hard at first," Thomas answered, "still is, I suppose. But I worry about the children."

John rocked back a bit, then looked at Cuthbert and William, saying, "My Lord Mountjoy, and my son's friend Tunstall…Would you two be so kind as to go to John Roper in there and ask him to kindly come out here?"

"Certainly, Master More," William replied, "and when the others ask what has become of you and Thomas?"

John smiled, "you are a quick study, Lord Mountjoy. I am glad of your acquaintance with my son. If they ask, would you please offer my respects, and tell Sergeant Fineaux that there are issues of prior contract that are being very ably argued, and, since he is Judge of the Assize, it might be helpful for him, if convenient, to attend."

William and Cuthbert nodded gravely and sprinted into the estate.

When they had gone, John turned to Thomas and said, "Thomas, I am so very proud of you. You have clearly done things profound and holy. And I admire your devotion to your fellow pilgrims. Moreover, I understand the source of your devotion."

Thomas nodded, blinking back tears from his eyes.

"But Thomas," John continued, moved to tears of his own with the sight of his dirty, thin, and now…adult…son standing before him, "surely you understand why I must insist that you come with us, the first two contracts notwithstanding…."

"But Sir," Thomas gently interrupted, "there is a third contract."

"What do you mean?" John said, exasperated, "more pressing than the one with the Archbishop?"

"yes, sir," Thomas replied. And he stopped. "And you and the Lord Mayor, Henry Colet, and…what did you call them? Edward Guildford and John Clement?"

John recoiled, "you recognized them?"

Thomas looked around furtively, to make sure no one had come near. He nodded, saying, "not at first, Father, but the context…I just realized a moment ago who they were."

John More rocked, stunned, looked at Thomas, his eyes wide, saying, "the Queen is dying. It's the only way we can think of to help her. To bring her brothers to her. To let her know for sure that they are alive."

"I know you see it that way, Father," Thomas replied, "but my third contract, of which you were both witness and cosignatory, was with the King. King Richard. I swore a solemn oath to King Richard that I would never reveal his secret.." Thomas stopped, his eyes welling with the memory. He took a deep breath and exhaled, composing himself before continuing, "I swore a solemn oath to the King that I would never reveal his secret that 'the King of England protects children….'"

John looked at his son, tears in his eyes. "I couldn't hear what he asked you that day," John said, "I would have protested. He shouldn't have asked that."

"But he did," Thomas replied. "I swore an oath to the King of England. I may have been a child, and it may have been coerced, But I swore the oath knowingly and willingly. Before Bosworth. I cannot betray that oath."

John paused for a moment, trying to look at his son, but his vision obscured by tears. "No," he said finally, "you are correct. You may not be part of the reveal here. I didn't know until now, Thomas, that we swore different oaths to the King that day. Henry Colet's and my oaths were to protect and serve King Edward's children. All of them including our current Queen Elizabeth, now ill."

John paused, looking at his son as a genially curious John Roper, and his angry father-in-law, Sergeant-of-Law John Fineaux appeared through the gate led by a flushed appearing fourteen year old William Blount, Lord Mountjoy, and his friend, an amused appearing seventeen year old pilgrim and scholar Cuthbert Tunstall.

"John More," stamped the Sergeant impatiently, "what is the meaning of this?" Interestingly, Thomas noticed, he shrank a bit, a tiny bit, when Mountjoy shot him a glance.

John More, now again a prominent London lawyer, turned composedly to the Sergeant-at-Law and pacifically said, "Your honor, my son has three relevant and superseding contracts that prevent him from accompanying us until the afternoon tomorrow…."

Fineaux angrily cut him off, "What nonsense contracts has this boy that supersedes the needs of the Archbishop, the King, and the Queen?"

"Sir," John More replied calmly, placing his face directly into the Sergeant's line of sight, eyes meeting eyes. "Sir," he repeated, "the contracts are valid, are sworn by witnesses, though are without seal, and are presented *en compurgation* by my son. I am witness to two of these contracts. The Lord Mountjoy and his friend are witnesses to a third."

This did not, of course, calm Fineaux all that much, and he angrily rose, "I will hear the cases then…I am the King's judge here."

John More gently pulled John Roper and Roper's father-in law to the side and said in a low voice, "sirs…the three of us here are the lawyers present for the group. In effect, in this matter, we three are the law. My son has made compelling cases for preexisting oral contracts.

"The first is an arrangement he made with Godfrey Wooler, now again in the King's service and on his way here with Lord Thomas Howard and thirty of the King's men at arms with the purpose of serving the King here tomorrow." The elder More paused, and noticed Fineaux's eyes arch quizzically.

"Yes, John," More continued, "that very same Godfrey Wooler."

"How did?..." Fineaux began, before saying, "never mind. The Lord works in his own ways."

"My son," John More continued, "has been entrusted by Godfrey with the safe transport of the Wooler family to Canterbury."

"Well, they're in Canterbury," Fineaux grumbled.

More answered patiently, looking at the young John Roper, "as my son, whom I am confident will one day be quite the lawyer, maintains, since the family is situated up that hill at Saint Dunstan's outside the gate of the city, they are assuredly not yet safely delivered to Canterbury."

The young John Roper looked up the hill at the Wooler family. He looked back at John More. "Have they eaten recently, John?" Roper asked. Concerned.

"Thank you for asking that Master Roper," John More said smiling kindly. "I gather from Thomas that the custom on Pilgrimage is to beg food, a custom rigorously enforced by the Brothers of St. Thomas Acre on London Bridge who assiduously stole from my son the money I gave him for his adventure. I am sure that a skinny fourteen year old may fend for himself, but providing for a poor family on the road as well might prove a challenge too far."

Roper nodded, saying, "John," and he paused and nodded to Thomas and his two friends, "if these three would come with me, let my estate care for feeding their pilgrim group."

"That would be extraordinarily generous of you sir," More replied with feeling. "and not to put to much of a burden on your house, I suspect that another thirty or so of the King's men may be coming down the road this evening."

Roper nodded and gestured for Thomas, Cuthbert and William to join him, "come, friends, let us collect the Woolers and get everyone fed." Those four left, ambling up the hill to St. Dunstan's, leaving John More and John Fineaux alone for a moment.

"Just a moment, John Roper," the elder More said suddenly, "It might be best for Thomas to remain with us."

"Certainly," said Roper, who nodded for Thomas to rejoin Fineaux and the elder More.

Thomas detached himself from the group and returned reluctantly to his father, looking over his shoulder at St. Dunstan's church.

"Well, John," Fineaux asked impatiently, looking at the two Mores before him, "what are contracts two and three?"

Thomas began to speak, but as cut off by his father.

"Those are trickier," John More replied hesitantly, "but the second is a promise to complete the pilgrimage that Thomas made at the order of the Archbishop in return for a position at Canterbury College, Oxford…"

Fineaux cut him off. "John," Fineaux said holding back his frustration. He had not known why Thomas was on pilgrimage, nor why this particular group had been sent. He stumbled a bit in producing speech as he was thinking furiously. "John," he continued, "the Archbishop is the one who ordered us to find Thomas and bring him with this particular group to meet with the King and he at the Feast in Canterbury."

"Well…." John More said patiently, but then noticed over his shoulder the dispatched group, including the Wooler family coming down the road towards them. "Well, John," More regrouped, "I think we should wait just a moment before continuing."

Fineaux turned, then broke into a smile, calling out, "Mary Wooler, as I live and breath, you haven't changed in the ten years since I last saw you!"

John More's head turned abruptly, "You knew Godfrey Wooler's wife?"

"I've got to keep you on your toes, old friend," Fineaux said happily as he went forward to hug Mrs. Wooler in welcome.

John Roper and Thomas's friends had approached by now. At the sight of Sergeant Fineaux and Mary Wooler embracing as old friends, Thomas shot his father a questioning look. John More, a smile fixed on his face, briefly gave his son a shake of the head.

Fineaux and Mary Wooler stepped back from each other and smiled shyly. Sergeant-at-Law Fineaux harrumphed a bit at his son-in-law's open-mouthed expression, and finally said, "I should make some introductions.."

Mary Wooler nodded shyly.

Fineaux continued, "Mary Wooler, I believe you've just met my son-in-law John Roper. This here is John More of London."

Mary leapt forward, calling, "Thomas's father!?! Of course, sir. It is a great honor to meet you! Thomas is a most remarkable young man."

She took John More's hands in hers and gave them a forceful shake, then came forward and embraced him, softly saying, "Thomas's father… I can't believe it."

John More stepped back a bit embarrassed and overwhelmed, but proud. His face was red, but he placed his hands on Mary's shoulders and looked at her simple smiling face. "My son in a very brief time has shared with me his fondness for you and your husband and family, as well, Mrs. Wooler," John said warmly. "I shall be delighted to make your better acquaintance, even if for no other reason than to hear about how you also know my friend here, John Fineaux."

John More laughed a deep hearty and warm laugh that quickly spread among the whole group. With the group now introduced and congenial, John More turned to John Roper and asked, "Master Roper, might I impose upon you to take this group inside for food and rest, and let me finish a few things up out here with your father-in-law?"

Thomas interrupted, "I thought we would stay at St. Dunstan's tonight, to await Mr...Sergeant Wooler and the others when they arrive?"

John Roper replied soothingly, "Thomas, we will keep a lookout for the soldiers, they will also stay at the estate tonight. Outside if anyone desires to be close to the pilgrims road. St. Dunstan's is not a fit place to rest your head." He laughed at his obscure joke.

Thomas looked at John More for support, saying, "this is fine, Thomas. We are not interrupting or prematurely ending your pilgrimage or taking you captive. We accept your contractual agreements. We simply feel a duty of care to you all, particularly, as it turns out..." He stopped and winked at Fineaux, "for Mrs. Wooler here, and her fine children."

Tunstall and Mountjoy both tugged at Thomas's sleeve, saying, "This is all right Thomas. I think that you've said often enough that we should all 'trust and love.'"

Thomas hung his head, shrugged his shoulders, and said, "well put.. You all go on in." Then he got excited, saying, "and I saw John Colet there with his father." I know him a little. You two would really like him."

As the group turned to leave John More and John Fineaux again, the elder More tugged at Roper's sleeve and asked, "John, if I could impose for one more thing, could I ask you to send Henry Colet out here?"

Roper nodded as he left, herding his charges through the gate onto his estate.

After the group was safely out of earshot, John More and Fineaux studied each other, smiles fading. Thomas stood quietly by the arched gate watching.

"John," said Sergeant-at-Law Fineaux finally, "I am here on this errand for the Archbishop and the King because as the Sergeant-at-Law, I am the civil attorney for the King. Everyone on this errand was named by the Archbishop for reasons that he wouldn't share with me. I've done what I was asked, and like a good attorney I haven't pressed beyond what the client would willingly offer…"

"You have, old friend," John More agreed.

"I brought my son-in-law, John Roper, along," Fineaux continued, "with the agreement of the Archbishop, because of his estate here, but also because he is a young attorney who can serve as my assistant and may serve as notary."

"Yes, that was smart," John More agreed.

Fineaux then looked at John More with his intelligent eyes, his mouth moving involuntarily as he thought things through. Finally, he said, "John More you are an excellent lawyer, and I know that you were close to King Edward, but I've not seen that closeness with Henry or the Archbishop. Perhaps I am mistaken, and I would never presume to believe that I had complete knowledge of the affairs of Archbishops or Kings. Therefore, while I do not understand, your presence makes sense to me."

"Thank you," said John More simply, a wry smile on his face.

"But," Fineaux continued, in an earnest, intense hiss "as much as I admire Henry Colet and his son, I have no idea why they are here, and I am at a loss to explain the presence of the two beardless boys from the country on this trip. But most importantly, I have no earthly idea why we needed to find your son, Thomas, and deliver him to the Cathedral, and still more curiously why a fourteen year old boy would have "preexisting contracts" that would prevent me from fulfilling a specific request from the Archbishop."

As he finished, Henry Colet strode up, the former Lord Mayor of London wearing a care-free smile on his face, and said, "Hello friends named John! I believe I heard my name called."

John More turned to Henry Colet, and said warmly, "Henry, thank you for coming out. Our friend John Fineaux, here has been a good soldier, but I do not believe that he can reasonably fulfill the duties requested of him by the Archbishop in his position as Sergeant-at-Law without a deeper explanation of why we are dispatched to Canterbury in an, admittedly odd, group."

Henry Colet's smile faded and he looked concerned and thoughtful, asking, "what do you think the Archbishop knows?"

"About what?" asked Fineaux, angrily.

More and Colet ignored him for the moment, John replying to Henry, "he named the group accurately, except for your son, and Edward Stafford."

"The young Duke of Buckingham?" Fineaux nearly expelled.

"What I didn't know," John More said, continuing to ignore Fineaux, "was that my son also entered into a separate contract with the King when he whispered to him. Thomas feels, and I agree, that the promise is binding to him."

"What was the promise?" asked Henry Colet, turning slightly towards Thomas.

"I may not say," John replied, "it was private between Thomas and the King, never to be revealed."

"How did a common boy make a promise to King Henry?" Fineaux asked disbelievingly, angrily and loudly.

"Not King Henry," More corrected, "King Richard. In my presence, and that of Henry Colet and of the two princes."

Fineaux gasped disbelievingly, jaw now working furiously, but all he managed to emit was a "Whaaaa…." He then stood gaping for a moment, finally demanding, "The… story… now... as…. if…. you…. were…. under…. oath…. which… given… my… position… you… are… "

John More and Henry Colet looked at each other and both shrugged. Finally, John More cleared his throat and began, slowly at first, "John Fineaux we owe you an apology. We should have explained this to you when you became Sergeant… "

Fineaux crossed his arms, and gave an "I'm waiting" look at the two men before him.

"Just before Bosworth," Henry began, "Richard was looking for money and men from London. He summoned John and I and a few others to meet him secretly at the Guildhall. That was the stated purpose of the meeting."

"I'd heard about that," said Fineaux.

"Well," said John More, "it turns out that London support wasn't on the King's mind. It was the safety of the two sons of his brother, Edward and Richard."

"The Princes?" Fineaux exclaimed with a loud outbreath of air, "I'm sorry, King Edward the Fifth and his brother, Richard, the Duke of York!?!"

"Yes," Henry answered calmly, "them."

"They had disappeared well before that," exclaimed Fineaux. "The rumor was that either King Richard or the Duke of Buckingham had killed them in the tower."

"That explained our surprise at seeing them in this meeting," said More with a little smile.

"W.h.h.h.y…y…y…y?" asked Fineaux.

"We wondered that as well," replied More. "Apparently, King Richard felt that he had made an indissolvable contract with his brother, King Edward, to protect and care for his children. All of his children."

"That certainly goes along with his taking the crown from young Edward and placing it on his own head," Fineaux said sarcastically.

"If you think about it," John More replied mildly, "it does…If you are willing to believe that King Richard valued his promise to Edward more than even his own life or crown."

Fineaux let that sink in, then said, "so at this meeting you all had with King Richard where the Princes were displayed, what was asked of you two by the King?"

Henry and John More looked at each other and shrugged. Henry volunteered, "the King asked us to make his nephews disappear."

Thomas stared intently at the three older men as Fineaux involuntarily took a step back. "How?" he was able to gasp after a few seconds.

"Well," John More said, "he left the details to us. Didn't want to know them. Just that the boys were safe."

"How?" Fineaux repeated. "False identity is a crime, and a crime for the lawyer who arranges it."

"Turns out there is a loophole to that if the change is declared, so therefore not false, but the paperwork is buried."

Fineaux smiled, "that is correct. It wouldn't be a false identity. So the King needed a lawyer.. A very good one with loyalty to his brother." He nodded respect at More.

"But why involve the Lord Mayor of London?" Fineaux asked. "Not bound by the attorney relationship, and independent, as one can be of the King?"

"King Richard thought that one through," Henry Colet replied with a sad smile. "I had lost twenty two of my twenty-three children to the various plagues. Leaving me only my dear son, John, a deacon, now priest, at Oxford and at St. Paul's. The King knew that I would do literally anything to protect the life of a child, of two boys, and that my son, John, could ease the way with the church, any necessary documents, and so on. Also, I have money which greases a lot of skids."

"Brilliant," admitted Fineaux. "But I don't understand why Thomas More was needed?"

Thomas leaned in to listen more closely.

"Two fold, I think," replied John More. "First, it made me more reliable. I think that, whether he would do anything or not, Thomas was a hostage for my good behavior." His eyes welled, and he looked at his son, saying, "I'm sorry that I put you in that position, Thomas. Ever so sorry." The elder More paused for a second to collect himself, "the other reason was Edward Stafford, who had been Thomas's very close friend for a number of years." A pause. "Again I am sorry Thomas."

"King Richard was using me as a hostage?" Thomas thought.

*"Does that seem likely?"*

"I thought him nice. He seemed to like me."

*"That means literally nothing Thomas. What matters was what he said and how he said it."*

"He was kind when he said 'the King of England protects children.'"

*"Correct, but his actions, protecting Edward and the Princes made that not much of a secret."*

"An open secret."

*"Yes. And your father knew of, actually engineered the protections for the princes, with Henry Colet suggesting it."*

"Yes. In fact father suggested that I was a hostage at the time."

*"Yes. Your father and Henry Colet seem to have forgotten that. Are telling themselves stories now out of fear. Not knowing what the Archbishop knows, or, for that matter, what John Fineaux knows."*

"He doesn't appear to know anything."

*"Appearances are sometimes deceiving. At the very least he is figuring it out. He has also travelled with the two princes now, and didn't recognize them."*

Thinking quickly, Thomas quickly interjected, "no apology needed, Father. Besides, I liked King Richard."

Two of the older men tensed and looked furtively around. John More immediately hushed Thomas, saying, "that is dangerous for all of us, Thomas." John Fineaux remained impassive, staring at Thomas with a small arch of an eyebrow indicating curiosity.

Thomas looked at his father, saying softly, "King Richard's actions indicated the secret that he shared with me that day."

Fineaux spurted, "the King made a contract with a boy that was conditional?!"

"John," John More said gently, remembering the conversation with King Richard a little more clearly after the prod from Thomas, "not conditional, his actions, I believe, belied his confidence with my son."

"No," Fineaux said abruptly, "this is nonsense, John More. How old was Thomas then?"

"Seven," said Thomas abruptly and firmly. "And quite clear on my conversation with the King. It was….memorable."

"And with his father present," Colet said, "and myself...As witnesses." Understanding was starting to show on Colet's face, as well.

"Thomas," his father said, "would you be violating the King's confidence to state that the King's actions in protecting the Princes demonstrated in deed the secret that he shared with you?"

"If you add my friend Edward Stafford, the Duke of Buckingham, as also protected, yes," said Thomas happily, adding, "also me."

"You?" John asked quietly.

"I have been protected as well, Father," Thomas replied. "Love and Trust. That is what I have learned on this pilgrimage. I trust you. I trust the Archbishop. I trust the King. And I trust God."

The three older men looked a little dumbfounded at Thomas, and Fineaux rolled his eyes a bit, which drew a sharp look from John More, who then kindly asked Thomas, "Completely, without reservation?"

"Yes, Father," Thomas replied patiently, "at least until someone proves themselves unworthy of that trust. Then, of course, it must be earned back."

"Er...Well then," John Fineaux said with a little impatience, his beard bobbing up and down, and his intense eyes looking not at Thomas any longer, but at John More and Henry Colet. He continued, "Back in the real world, where people, as we have all seen, can be real swine...."

John More cut him off, "John, with all respect, I'd like to stay on this for a moment. You and I are lawyers, and the law exists as the rules of how we behave. If we break the law, then we are punished, and assumed to be untrustworthy until we make amends. I do not see how that is any different from what Thomas just said. Except of course for the assumptions made about the innocent." He then flagged his eyes a bit to Fineaux.

"The Mores stick together then?" Fineaux replied.

"When we are right," John More replied, to Thomas's great satisfaction, though both More's then consciously willed themselves not to smile.

Fineaux responded exasperated with, "Bah!"

Henry Colet did allow himself a smile before asking, "given all that, Sergeant Fineaux, what is our plan?"

"I think," Fineaux replied slowly, "given all we have learned here today, and based upon my understanding of what the King and Archbishop want…that it would be fine if Thomas simply met us after the mass tomorrow and finished his Pilgrimage." He nodded to Thomas who appeared delighted.

John More interrupted, asking "why?"

"My impression now," Fineaux explained, "is that Thomas was meant to ensure your conduct, John, though perhaps not in the way you intended. I think the King wanted to see what kind of father you were before asking this for the Princes, ostensibly his wards. When Richard saw that you were a good father, and that you would watch out for your son, he trusted you with his nephews."

He let that sink in for a moment before continuing, "and I can also say, having ridden with Masters "Guildford" and "Clement" that his faith in you was merited." He bowed.

Thomas asked meekly, "If I may, sir, what will happen to the Princes when you tell the Archbishop and the King about them?"

Fineaux smiled, "maybe not so trusting of the King, Thomas?..." He allowed Thomas to redden a bit, "I think the Archbishop already has most, if not all of this figured out. He's wily, with some of the best sources of information I've ever seen. It's interesting that Edward Stafford was not invited along…." Again he looked significantly at Thomas who had a blank look on his face.

"As for the King," Fineaux continued, "the two Princes have been admirably quiet through the entire Perkin Warbeck imposture. I suspect that will be noted, and the King will take no action against his Queen's brothers…" He paused before continuing, "provided they remain, what did you call them, "open secrets" … no threat to the crown or the heir, Prince Arthur."

Henry Colet said, "I think it significant that they've not said a word publicly in seven years, and remain unknown."

Fineaux smiled, "So Thomas would counsel 'trust' in them, I presume?"

Thomas nodded.

"Then Thomas," John More said warmly, "I think there is nothing further for you here than to go into the Roper estate, find your friends, eat something, please, clean up a bit, and then finish your pilgrimage. Be sure to mark us during the nones mass tomorrow at the high altar of the cathedral. As we are set to process out, make your way to me and, I suppose, come with me to meet the King and the Archbishop."

Thomas nodded, and bowed nervously at the three elders. When none objected, in fact had gone back to conversing as if Thomas had already left, he shot off through the Roper gate in search of his friends.

# Chapter 25 - July 6, 1492, evening.

Thomas ran up the path in the lawn of the estate the fifty or so feet to the house, holding the bunched lower portion of his robe in his right hand to avoid tripping in front of his father. He wasn't sure which way to go, to the house or to a side, when he heard laughing, heard Mountjoy's happy voice off to the left and behind the house to the left.

Thomas arced to the left, around the red brick house and found that a table had been set up, and a hasty, but voluminous meal created on some table brought outside. There was also fruit juice, ale, and fresh water in decanters. And strawberries!

Thomas gulped at the strawberries, but, on closer inspection also saw a bowl of white mulberries. He looked up at the lawn and saw a small grove of mulberry trees in a beautiful garden behind the house.

The Wooler children were still devouring food as if they had never eaten. Mary Wooler was standing behind the table shyly, helping make sure that her children ate. Cuthbert, Mountjoy, and John Colet were in an animated conversation. John Roper, "Edward Guildford," and "John Clement" were not present, and presumably in the house.

Thomas approached Mary Wooler first, as she was closest to the food, and despite a vigorous hailing from Colet, Mountjoy, and Tunstall.

Mary Wooler smiled broadly at Thomas, saying, "emerged from the lion's den, I see, Thomas?"

Thomas smiled back, saying "Thorn from the paw, madam, Thorn from the paw," He paused, then added, "no sign of Godfrey out there yet."

Thomas took some food, some ham and some boiled turnips, and avoided the strawberries but took a handful of mulberries.

"Mores Morae Morus," he thought, giving a wink to his mother.

*"You did well back there, Thomas. I am proud of you."*

"Love and trust."

Balancing his wooden plate, Thomas made his way to his friends, happily tossing a white mulberry into his mouth every few steps. He relished the acidy, slightly bitter juice as the ripe fruit exploded in his mouth. Upon reaching Mountjoy and Tunstall, Thomas took a step back, turned his head, casting a little sideways glance at the two, and then gave a little wink.

Mountjoy and Tunstall rose up excitedly at that, saying simultaneously, "tell us!"

"I can't really," replied Thomas evenly, "the important thing is that I can finish the pilgrimage."

"That's the important thing?" Tunstall asked sarcastically. "Your father, the former Lord Mayor, the Sergeant at Law, and two people I've never seen before come racing down from London to find you at the direction of the Archbishop of Canterbury, and the *important* item in all that is that you can walk a mile to Canterbury Cathedral like you planned."

"You forgot the King," said Thomas with a smile.

"Oh yes, the King," said Mountjoy. "How very silly of us."

Mountjoy and Tunstall crossed their arms and looked at Thomas expectantly.

"Really, fellows," said Thomas a little pleadingly, "I can't tell you. It's a promise I once made to a nice man."

"Who?" demanded Mountjoy.

"I can't tell you that either," said Thomas. "Now, may I eat?"

Tunstall and Mountjoy looked at each other with exasperation, finally shrugged, and said, "sure, Thomas. We will give you some peace as well." The two walked off leaving Thomas alone with his thoughts.

"That didn't go very well," thought Thomas as he sat down under an old ropey oak, setting down his plate and cup.

*"that's because it was neither trust nor love."*

"But I had promised not to tell the third part, and telling them is a remarkably bad idea for them."

*"But still, they have been with you on this journey. You could have explained better."*

"I don't know how." Thomas began to eat, slowly chewing the salty ham.

*"Yes you do. You have gifts with people. And you tell the truth."*

"Tell them why I can't tell them?"

*"To the degree you can."*

Thomas noticed the two standing sulkily off a ways, close together but with backs turned to Thomas. Every once in a while one or the other would look over at Thomas, then quickly turn away if they thought Thomas was looking.

Thomas continued to eat and drink in silence, steadily looking at his friends. After a few glances, Thomas started smiling or waving each time they looked, which caused a more rapid head snap away.

Finally finishing his meal, Thomas thought, "Enough. This is stupid."

*"There you go."*

Thomas stood, picking up his plate and cup, and walked over to Tunstall and Mountjoy.

"Brothers," Thomas said with empathy, "I apologize for earlier. I was a bit of a prat there."

"A bit?" both declared.

"A complete arsehole?" Thomas offered helpfully.

"Closer," Mountjoy replied, breaking a smile.

"I apologize for that," Thomas said, also smiling now hopefully at Tunstall.

After a moment, Tunstall, still serious, said, Thomas you have no idea how badly off you were last night. We were really worried about you. And now you are feeling better, but won't tell us what we need to know…"

Thomas cut him off gently, saying, "that is where I apologize. I presumed to know best what you needed to know." He paused.

The other two waited for him to continue.

After a moment, Thomas said, "let me try again. If I were to go get more food and cider, and then came back to the tree where I met you, could you be there and let me start over?"

Mountjoy and Tunstall looked at each other and nodded, Cuthbert saying, "that sounds fine to us."

Thomas sloped off to the table, waved at the Woolers, still grazing the table. There was still no sign of the older party from inside the house. Thomas loaded his plate again and filled his cup. With a final smile at Mary Wooler, Thomas ambled back to his friends and the oak tree.

All three sat in the shade as Thomas took a biscuit, put some huckleberry jam and butter on it and took a bite. His friends waited expectantly.

Gathering his thoughts, Thomas began slowly, "when I was seven I used to go on errands with my father in London..." Thomas paused. His friends studied him.

"One day," Thomas continued, "we went to the Guildhall and met the King."

Cuthbert and William looked at each other, doing math in their heads, finally asking, "which King?"

"Richard," Thomas replied quietly. "The King told me a secret, and made me swear never to tell anyone…"

"But you just told the adults," Mountjoy exclaimed.

"I didn't," Thomas explained patiently. "I swore to the King never to reveal his secret."

"Why did he put this expectation on a seven year old?" asked Cuthbert suddenly.

"No idea," replied Thomas. "But he did, and said it quietly enough that my father couldn't hear it."

"Do King Henry or the Archbishop know?" asked William.

"I don't think so," Thomas replied, "which is why, I think, my father and the others were sent. To see if King Richard's secrets might help the Queen."

"Is the Queen badly off?" Mountjoy asked, concerned.

"It sounds like it," Thomas replied. "The King is coming here for St. Thomas's to pray for an intercession for the Queen."

Mountjoy whistled softly, thinking, then said, "Thomas, does the Queen know your secret?"

"I don't believe so," Thomas replied, adding humbly, "if she did, then I suspect that I would be less interesting."

"Fair point," laughed Tunstall and Mountjoy together.

Mountjoy looked around, and at the Roper house. He caught a glimpse of John Fineaux through a window. Suddenly inspired, Mountjoy whispered, "fellows, when Thomas is done stuffing his face, we should get out of here."

His mouth full, Thomas sputtered, "Why?"

"Because those are powerful men in there," Mountjoy explained. "They are likely merely regrouping. Can change their minds with regards to you and your pilgrimage any time they want."

Thomas retorted, "..but my father would never…"

Mountjoy responded, "Thomas, we may be the same age, but I live in Court. I know how they work. We made a little headway together, in part, because of my position in court. The others weren't sure how to respond to me."

All stopped, as Thomas also noticed Fineaux, and now Roper, looking out the window at them. Mountjoy waved to them happily, a smile frozen on his face. When the two had returned their gazes back into whatever conversation was going on in the house, Mountjoy turned to the others and asked, "Thomas, what did you promise your father?"

"I promised to meet him at the Cathedral after the Nones mass," Thomas replied.

"Did you make any other promises?" Cuthbert asked anxiously.

"No," replied Thomas.

"Then your father was giving you a message," Mountjoy replied. "Let's get out of here. You will keep the letter of your promise, and forestall any attempts at additional demands from the others."

Thomas was incredulous, and said, "you don't really think?...."

"We think that exactly," Cuthbert said, as Fineaux looked out the window at the boys yet again. "So let's get going."

"We need the Woolers," Thomas said resolutely, "I promised Godfrey."

"They may help," Tunstall replied. "For now, Thomas, take your plate and cup and let's wander back to the table like we're still hungry."

The boys did a fairly careful job of acting nonchalant as they made their way to the table. Upon reaching the table, they spoke quietly with Mary Wooler, informing her of they need for the group to leave. While she was gathering the children, quietly, Thomas noticed, looking back down the path, that the main gate to the road had been closed, with two guards standing on either side.

"The gate is closed," Thomas said, concerned.

"That sounds about right," replied Mountjoy, his jaw tense. He scanned from the corner of the house, following the wall from the gate to the left. About fifty feet from the gate, the wall made a right angle to the left, and about fifty feet from that was a small door opening through a side street. There was only one guard there, in Roper livery. That guard appeared quite relaxed.

"If we go around the front of the house to the left, there is a little gate with one guard," Mountjoy said. "He does not appear to be as….uh…attentive as the two at the main gate. I think I can bluff my way through, hoping he won't know what to do with a Lord of the Realm." He smiled wickedly, pulling himself to full height, and straightening his black and gold doublet, before adding, "we need to stay out of window view and move quickly just after Sergeant Fineaux pokes his head out and back in again."

The Woolers had arrived and the group was miming an animated happy conversation just as Fineaux's head poked out, and then back in.

"Let's go," said Mountjoy, and the group quickly grabbed their small possessions and quietly and quickly went around the house to the left, the building immediately screening the group from the room Fineaux was in.

After clearing the house, the smallest Woolers were hoisted by older Pilgrims, and the group made an orderly dash to the side gate. They covered the hundred feet or so, quickly, arriving to the guard only slightly winded.

Mountjoy approached, chest puffed and an arrogant leer on his face, saying "open the gate!"

The guard appeared confused, and mumbled, "can't…orders." Without looking up.

Mountjoy moved directly into his vision, pulling his sword. He kicked the guard's foot, as said, quite forcefully, "You oaf. I am the Baron Mountjoy. You will open this gate for us immediately or face my and your Lord's wrath."

Thomas felt for the guard, his hesitancy and confusion.

"I am waiting!" hissed Mountjoy.

The guard shrugged his shoulders and touched his forelock at the young Lord. He turned and took out a large key, which which he unlocked the gate. The group hurried through onto the small lane, the main road being off to the right.

Thomas, bringing up the rear, looked back to thank the guard, but noticed Fineaux and several others tumbling out of the house.

Thomas nodded pleasantly to the guard, said, "Nobility," and shrugged his shoulders, then added, "you will want to remember to lock this gate securely, sir."

Thomas left and was at the main road with the group before hearing the angry shouts back at the small gate.

Smiling broadly, Tunstall said, now we need to get lost in Canterbury. Herding the now dismounted Wooler children, Tunstall loped happily down the road, mixing in with the increasing traffic and other pilgrims in brown towards the West gate of the City of Canterbury less than a quarter mile down the road.

Mary Wooler looked at Thomas as they tried to keep up, asking, "any sign of my husband?"

Thomas smiled kindly, answering, "none yet, but, not to worry, we will find him. I am gathering that everyone is going to the same place at the same time." He paused and winked, "and Godfrey is kind of hard to miss in a crowd."

Mary laughed.

Thomas looked ahead at the gold and black accented figure of Mountjoy bobbing ahead of everyone in the crowd. Moving far ahead of their group of pilgrims into a small crowd of brown robed pilgrims slowly amassing on the road.

"He will be hard to miss," thought Thomas.

*"He knows that."*

Thomas looked back up towards St. Dunstan's and saw Fineaux and several of the other men coming out of the Roper's gate. He looked down at the other pilgrims, many of whom had removed their shoes to make the final walk from St. Dunstan's to the Canterbury Cathedral on foot, as Henry the Second had walked that route in atonement for his "Will no one rid me of this troublesome priest," comment that had led directly to Becket's death.

The twilight was also starting to rise, and, looking ahead, Thomas saw the watch starting to make their way to closing the town gate for the night. Thomas decided to keep his sandals on and hurry Mary Wooler the last hundred yards to the gate, to get into the city before dusk and the slam of the gate.

Thomas nudged Mary Wooler's arm, and pointed to Tunstall and the group of skipping Wooler children ahead, nearing the gate and said, "they're going to close the gate, we need to catch up."

Thomas noticed suddenly how tired Mary Wooler looked and asked her, "Mrs. Wooler, did you eat back at the Roper's Hall?"

Mary shyly shook her head no.

Thomas asked, "and have you slept at all in the past few nights, what with everything going on?"

Again she shook her head, and gestured weakly towards the children, her steps lagging.

The city guards had reached the house controlling the gate.

*"Love and trust, Thomas."*

Thinking quickly, Thomas saw two stout looking pilgrims hurrying past. He grabbed one by the elbow, saying, please sirs, will you help me hurry my friend through the gate in time? The day is late, and she is quite gone."

One of the men, the taller of the two hurried past, having not appeared to have heard, but the shorter stopped and looked at the two, saying "we'd better hurry then. Each of us an arm."

Together, Thomas and the stranger placed hands under Mary's shoulders and mostly lifted her off the ground and ran the last hundred feet through the gate, just as the gate started to come down. Mary's feet barely touched the ground until they were through.

The kind stranger then gently let his side of Mary down, and smiled at both Thomas and Mary, saying, "that cut it a little close. But we made it."

Thomas and Mary replied, "Thank you, kind sir. And they bowed."

The stranger bowed back, saying, "anything for a fellow pilgrim! Welcome to Canterbury! If you get to the cathedral before dark, I'm told, they will let you sleep there." He gestured with his hand to Mary, "and, dear, you look like you could use some rest. I need to catch up with my friends ahead. We've been together since just after London. Wanted to finish together." He nodded and touched his knuckle to his forehead and went off.

The crowd around the gate was starting to dissipate and Thomas noticed that Fineaux had stopped short of the gate and had turned back, looking into the crowds and the inn doors for any sign of Thomas's group.

Figuring that he needed to get out of the open, Thomas took Mary off to the side. Tunstall and the children had heard the clang of the gate, remembered Thomas and Mary in a panic and had turned around, relieved but worried to see Thomas and Mary, clearly exhausted, speaking warmly with a stout pilgrim. They set back to gather around Thomas and Mary.

The noise of the gate closing also caused Mountjoy to turn, and start back to his friends.

Once the little group was together, Thomas looked at Mountjoy and said, "William, I hate to ask, but Mrs. Wooler was feeding her children and had not eaten really today, and hasn't really slept in a few days either.

Mary flushed, saying, "No, Thomas, it's not that bad.." but her voice trailed off and she paled, having to bend over to avoid fainting.

Thomas looked at Cuthbert and William, and at the concerned Wooler children who were moving forward to help their mother.

Mountjoy stepped forward, crying, "Mrs. Wooler! I am so very sorry that I was so preoccupied with our escape that I failed to notice your condition." He reached into a small purse tucked inside his shirt and took out a few coins. With a big, satisfied smile he added, "I have some money. Let us get you taken care of."

Thomas nodded gratefully. The group turned to the narrowing street ahead. It was a busy road, not unlike Milk Street in London with white washed timber framed buildings jutting out into the ancient street, though not, Thomas noted, blocking out the sun like in London. The space also seemed to allow for a generally cleaner feel than his home City, the buildings much less soot stained.

The group moved slowly down the street. After a few blocks, the right side gave way to open gardens of two old abbey churches, first the Greyfriars, an order of Franciscan monks, then a few buildings, then the gardens of the Whitefriars, or Carmelites.

Mountjoy was happily leading the way, clucking as he looked up and down streets. No one was all that sure of what he was looking for. Despite the rapidly dimming light, the streets still relatively busy. Stalls were being constructed and provisioned on either side of the road. A stall-keeper called out to the group to be sure to come back to his stall tomorrow for the fair.

Thomas approached the man, asking, "the fair?"

"Yes, lad," the man replied, "we always have a great fair here at Canterbury for St. Thomas's day! Come back to my stall, and I'll get you a great deal on some wool." He eyed Thomas's pilgrim's robe, now stained, and torn, and winked, adding, "ye look like you could use some new clothes."

Thomas was swept along with the group, and Mountjoy quickly found what he was looking for. "I've read about this!" he cried out happily, pointing to the left side of a lane.

Thomas looked up the dark lane and there were shops lining both sides of the street on the ground floor and progressively jutting second and third floors with small windows. The ground floor had stone walls with arched openings for the shops. The upper floors were half timbered and very old.

The largest opening on the ground floor, at the corner of the little lane and the main street was of a brownish stone with a pointed arch and smooth facing stones. At the top of the arch the keystone had a carved lion's face on its surface. A sign hanging to the right said, "the Chequer of the Hope."

"Chaucer stayed here," Mountjoy cried happily, "and so shall we. Come along my friends."

The young Lord waked confidently up to the entrance to the inn, but stopped a moment as he noticed a small stand to the right selling meat pies. He casually tossed a penny to the stall keeper and took two steaming pies, and turned and handed them kindly to the surprised Mrs. Wooler, saying, "please eat these Madam, and forgive my earlier lack of awareness."

Mary took a bite of the still warm pie, and smiled gratefully at Mountjoy.

William returned her smile, then motioned all into the door of the inn and up some stairs to the second floor. Thomas followed, bringing up the rear still gently holding Mary's elbow to help her up the stairs. It was getting dark, and the hallway was dimming. Mountjoy spoke pleasantly with the keeper, gestured to the group, and paid a few coins.

Mountjoy then turned to the group of Cuthbert, Thomas and the Woolers, and said, Very well, Pilgrims…the dormitory is upstairs, and the privies are to the sides. There is still some soup and cider left here in the dining area off to the left."

He then looked at Mrs. Wooler, and his face reddened as he asked, "Mrs. Wooler, do you have any….ah…needs that must be attended to before we help you upstairs to sleep?"

Mary blushed as well, and nodded to the privy room, handing Thomas her pies for safe-keeping.

By the time she had returned, Cuthbert had fetched her a cup of cider, which she drank gratefully, and claimed the pies back from Thomas, which she then ate. With that, the group went up the stairs to a large open room on the third floor.

The light had faded, but tallow lamps had been light around the edges which were giving off a smoky flickering yellow light. The rafters were open, and Thomas could see the thatched roof above. Rushes had been spread on the floor, and clean looking straw mattresses were stacked against the far wall.

There were a number of people already settling in around the room, but a far corner of the room appeared empty enough. Several in the masses, mostly pilgrims in brown, sat up to look at Mountjoy in his expensive doublet. Some friendly gibes were tossed from darker recesses of the room. William replied with friendly smiles, nods of his head, and occasionally laughs.

William led the group to the emptier area and nodded for Thomas and Cuthbert to grab some mattresses, with William calling out to them, "check for lice," in a soft voice.

Retrieving the mattresses they set them down in their little corner. Thomas spotted that there was a little alcove in the wall that he had not noticed before. Mountjoy had already seen it, and had maneuvered the one straw mattress that would fit into the alcove. Turning, he gently said, "Mrs. Wooler, I hope that you will find this private enough. Climb in there and sleep. We three will watch your children tonight." He cast a significant look at the children who laughed.

The youngest of the clan, a little girl cried out, "sleep mommy."

Mary looked uncertainly at Thomas, then Cuthbert and William.

Thomas said, in what he hoped was a paternal voice, "Mrs. Wooler, you've no worries. You are nearly dead from fatigue, We will watch the children."

Thomas finished his little speech and noticed that Mary had already climbed into the alcove and was asleep.

Cuthbert laughed, saying, "impressive, Thomas."

William then laughed, and looked at the children, who looked confused. "Kiddies," he said cheerily, "your mum needs to sleep and the three of us are to watch you. How about we quietly go downstairs to see about some food before bed?'

The children clapped their hands, and William said, in a whisper, "quietly my friends." He looked at Thomas and Cuthbert, adding, "how about you two take watch here while we go downstairs?"

Thomas and Cuthbert nodded, and William and the children slid off noiselessly.

Cuthbert looked at Thomas, then at the sleeping form of Mary Wooler, and asked in a whisper, "where can we talk quietly without bothering her."

Thomas looked around the crowded, moderately noisy room and replied, "I think Mrs. Wooler is pretty soundly sleeping in this noise. Here is probably fine. You see any stools or chairs?"

Cuthbert pointed to a near corner and said, "two unowned stools over there it would seem."

Thomas quickly sloped off and returned with two stools which he placed against the wall to the left of the alcove. Seated next to each other, backs to the wall, legs stretched out in the gangly way of all teenage boys, they sat silently for a moment, then cast shy looks that quickly turned into broad grins.

"We made it to Canterbury!" Cuthbert exclaimed finally.

Thomas nodded, looking at his friend, then around the dormitory room, and at the sleeping form of Mary Wooler, finally adding, "who would have believed it?" He paused for a moment before adding wistfully, "how long do you think before Mountjoy returns? I'm hungry again and that food looked good."

Cuthbert looked slyly at Thomas and reached into a small bag he had recently acquired, producing a small loaf of bread, handing it over.

Thomas looked at his friend, questioningly. Cuthbert smiled and said, "Thomas, food is scarce for poor students at Oxford. You will find this to be true, and you will never be hungrier than when on 'student's rations.' One learns never to pass an offered table of food without nicking a little for later."

Thomas took the bread gratefully, making a mental note for later. Chewing happily on the coarse loaf, Thomas asked, "why are you switching to Cambridge?"

Cuthbert hesitated a moment before replying, "The plague at Oxford was bad, Thomas…" His voice trailed off. He sat for a moment, collecting his thoughts, "plague survivors have a mixed lot, especially when their line is….tainted." He involuntarily palpated his still somewhat swollen glands in his neck."

He continued, "my father is a good and generous man… but he has a legitimate son to think of. He simply felt that given the plague, and all, that a change of scenery would be good." He paused for a second, then added in a low, excited voice, "…and they're teaching humanism in Cambridge."

Thomas looked mystified.

"Humanism, Thomas. A new learning," Cuthbert added for explanation.

Thomas's eyes widened, and he softly said, "Wycliff?"

"No, Thomas," Cuthbert replied gently, "Not..." and his voice dropped to a whisper, "Wycliff." He paused and smiled, "but in a way yes. Oxford is still very devoted to scholasticism...How many angels can dance on the head of a pin, and so forth...Progressively more arcane debates that are eventually meaningless. All of it, I think, because in fifteen hundred years we had kind of run out of new things to talk about. And then there is Aquinas.... Reading Aquinas is a slog for me."

Thomas nodded, "The Archbishop talks of Aquinas and the *Summa* as the very peak of Christianity. I tried it. I kept falling asleep." He hesitated before adding sheepishly, "but I really wanted to like it."

Cuthbert laughed. "that's the thing about the scholastics...they have a language, a central dogma, and they are all so deeply invested in it that they lose their own agency to think in any different way."

Thomas asked, "and at Cambridge?"

"Oxford," Cuthbert replied, "is deeply invested, for an exceedingly long time, it the old way of thinking. In the old learning. And because of that devotion, there is little room for any new way of thinking. It's petty disputations about Aquinas forever there." He paused to catch his breath, then continued, "but at Cambridge, I am told, they are looking to a new way of thinking about man's relationship to the world, to a humanistic approach whereby agency and free will play a role in faith as opposed to determinism – the idea that our fates are pre-determined."

Thomas recoiled a bit, but not very much, and he said, "I had heard that, but the Archbishop..."

"Don't ape the Archbishop, Thomas," Cuthbert said, firmly, "think for yourself. Use your eyes and ears and nose. Observe the world around you. Petrarch said,..."

Thomas cut him off, "He found the Cicero manuscripts."

Cuthbert nodded, "Yes, precisely. And since we have been discovering new old works from Rome and from the Holy Land... learning from the time of Christ, from Augustine, from the Romans, that new...I should say rediscovered...learning represents a fundamental change in the source material that, Aquinas for example, had to work with. Aquinas was limited to trying to reconcile Aristotle with Jesus Christ. Feel sympathy for him, Thomas. Aristotle was four hundred years before the Lord. He was, is, fundamental to...well really everything. But he is not, in and of himself, everything."

Thomas nodded.

"The thing about Oxford," Cuthbert continued, "or, I suppose Cambridge or any college really, is that there are only a few reasons for going- to meet and join the next ruling class, or to really learn something in great detail."

"Which are you?" asked Thomas.

"I'm the bastard son of a pretty good fellow," Cuthbert answered with a sad smile. "My father wanted me to go to Oxford to meet 'the right sort of people,' who can help me overcome the circumstances of my birth, and become, hopefully, a priest with a nice parish, maybe a bishop. Oxford would help with that."

"And?" asked Thomas, who had decided to wait quietly for the answer.

After a few moments of contemplation, Cuthbert replied quietly, "Well, I liked it at first. But then the plague came and father got me out, but was too late. I got sick, but miraculously survived."

Thomas waited patiently, letting his friend talk.

"While I was ill, I had a terrible fever, and Thomas Becket came to me, at least I think it was him. He stayed with me the whole time, never left my side, even if the doctors wouldn't come anywhere near me. St. Thomas told me that when I was better, I should go on pilgrimage to Canterbury, meet people, and that after, I should go to Cambridge." A pause. "That it was important that I go to Cambridge after."

"Really!?" exclaimed Thomas More excitedly, "St. Thomas came to you? He came to me the other night at the Maison when I….uh…overextended."

Cuthbert smiled broadly at that, saying excitedly, "was he kind with you as well?"

"Yes," replied Thomas, happy to be able to speak about at least his vision. "He was quite kind."

The two boys stopped and looked at each other and laughed. Mary Wooler stirred. They dropped their voices to continue.

Thomas asked, "what do you think about me and Oxford, then?"

"Did St. Thomas have an opinion the other night?" Cuthbert asked.

"No," Thomas replied, "not on that."

"Well," Cuthbert replied slowly, thinking his answer through. "The Archbishop of Canterbury is sending you to the school he leads?"

"Yes," agreed Thomas.

"And you have already been his page in his court?" Cuthbert asked.

"Yes," Thomas said again.

"And you already appear to know an enormous number of important people, including having a Sergeant at Law, a former Lord Mayor of London, and your father travelling about Kent looking for you?" Cuthbert continued with a smile.

Thomas's face reddened. "Y-y-yes," he stammered.

"I would say," Cuthbert responded happily, noting Thomas's blushing, "that meeting important people is really not a problem for you Thomas." He paused and nodded, adding, "one might say you were built for friendship."

"Then perhaps I should be looking for specialized knowledge?" Thomas asked, wondering if he had made a mistake in Oxford, whether he should be going to Cambridge.

"You seem interested in all things, Thomas," Cuthbert replied. "Some of us are specialists and some are generalists. I am a specialist. My happiest day at Oxford was finding the Wycliffe bible. I spent days holed up in a room studying it, learning it. That is how I was able to recognize it earlier. I know as much about a pretty obscure topic as almost anyone."

Thomas nodded.

"And you, Thomas More," Cuthbert continued, " seem to know a good deal about a great many things. I don't know that you would be content in being the most knowledgeable person in the world on only one subject, You, my new friend, want to know the whole world…everything."

Thomas smiled and looked down, acknowledging the truth in that.

Cuthbert paused and looked at Thomas, "my suspicion, Thomas, is that the primary value of either Oxford or Cambridge for you will be meeting people. You will find your own bright path to knowledge without the Dons. And so…In answer to your question, I think it makes little difference in the world which University you attend. And since the Lord Chancellor and

Archbishop of Canterbury of all of England is interested in sending you to Oxford, I think that Oxford is the perfect place for you to attend." He paused for a second and crossed his arms, concluding "Quod Erat Demonstratum."

Thomas laughed quietly, remembering Mary Wooler. The boys turned back to the large dormitory room and the shifting mass of pilgrims. Thomas scratched a bit on his neck, and they sat silently, happily for a few minutes.

Eventually, the peace was broken by the return of Mountjoy and the Wooler children. They were trying very hard to be quiet, and failing. Stern looks from both Cuthbert and Thomas held them up though. Mountjoy shushed the children sternly, as if he had nothing to do with their high spirits, then shrugged innocently at his two friends. He then gently tapped the shoulder of the youngest, a girl named Mary after her mother, who shyly came up, curtseyed and presented bread and some sliced ham to Thomas and Cuthbert.

After the two boys had received their share, little Mary held forth one more portion, and whispered, "this is for mama." And she smiled with the proud radiance of a small child giving a present to a parent.

The group then retrieved some additional straw beds and lay them quietly around and outside the little alcove in which Mary Wooler still slept. The children lay down quietly in a little semicircle around their mother, with Thomas, Cuthbert, and Mountjoy forming a perimeter.

Mountjoy whispered, "one to keep watch? Two hour intervals?" Cuthbert and Thomas nodded yes, gratefully finishing their food. "Brilliant," Mountjoy added to their nods, I'll take the first watch then. You lot sleep."

Thomas and Cuthbert both nodded tiredly, and lay down on the straw. Cuthbert looked up at Mountjoy and asked, "two hour shifts?"

"Two hour shifts it is," Thomas vaguely heard Mountjoy reply.

# Chapter 26 - Daybreak, July 7, 1492 – The Feast Day of the Translation of Saint Thomas Becket.

Thomas More awoke with the early morning sun shining forth on his face from the small windows of the dormitory. He was confused as to time and place. He was foggy from sleep, and, lying there for a moment seeing the reddish light on the far wall, recollecting the previous evening, he sat up with a start to see Mountjoy seated at the stool he had been at hours before.

Mountjoy, upon seeing Thomas stir, turned happily to his friend and said, "Oh good, you're awake."

Thomas felt mild twangs of indignity rising mostly out of embarrassment, saying sleepily "You said 'two hour shifts."

Cuthbert was also stiffing at the sounds of voices. He too, apparently, had slept all night. "What's going on?" he murmured.

"Look fellows," said Mountjoy quickly, a tinge of red on his face, his eyes bleary, "before you are both fully awake and mad at me." He paused, looking back and forth at the still semi-recumbent figures of his friends before continuing, "you two weren't much less exhausted than Mary Wooler, and Thomas, you had completely crashed the night before. You two have been on pilgrimage, and I've been wandering around with Somerset and Howard looking for something meaningful to do. The you both show up, and I found my purpose, which is in helping you all finish this pilgrimage, hale and healthy. Before last evening I'd been sleeping. You two had not. So let me give you all this small gift. I let you sleep and rest up for a big day. Alright?"

There was a brief stunned silence. Mary Wooler had awakened and emerged from her alcove, treading carefully not to step on a still sleeping child. "Lord Mountjoy," she said with true affection in her voice.

Mountjoy cut her off, saying, "For you, Dear Madam Wooler on this auspicious day, I would love for you to call me by my given name, William...William Blount."

"William it is, then, dear friend," Mary said, and she leaned forward to give him a modest hug.

William turned beet red at this, but managed to ask, "how are you today?"

Mary give a little curtsey, with downcast eyes, saying, "thanks to you all, I am wonderful. I haven't slept that well in a very long time. I am so grateful. And thank you for taking such good care of my children while I...recovered."

Thomas and Cuthbert had joined William in blushing deeply. They had stood when Mary emerged, and were now fidgeting nervously.

Mary looked around the large dormitory of the inn, now light, then down at the children, before asking, "if I might beg one more favor from you three." She paused before asking in an embarrassed voice, "might you remember where the privy is? It was a long night."

The boys all laughed, and Mountjoy, the only one able to speak, said, "Ma'am, it is downstairs one flight, and thataway," he pointed to the back of the building.

Mary laughed and gathered her brown, dirty pilgrim robe's hem and made her way down the nearby stairs in the direction of the toilet.

Thomas, William, and Cuthbert looked at each other then watched Mary go down the stairs. The morning light from the far window seemed to catch her tousled hair, making it seem to shimmer. Looking back, they each reddened, then looked down at then now rousing children.

William quickly said, "I've heard a lot of activity in the street below, it's a famous Fair day in Canterbury, in addition to, you know, St. Thomas and all. I heard the monks chanting terce as they went into the cathedral a bit ago, so it must be about 6 in the morning." He stopped and looked around the dormitory again, stopping just for a moment at the stairs Mary had just gone down, adding with a wave of his hand around the room, "this lot will be up soon and will eat all the food if we don't get moving."

With his foot, he nudged the oldest remaining Wooler child, an eleven year old boy named John. He was a quiet, serious boy, who took after his mother much more than his father. John roused and opened his eyes immediately. After blinking a few times, he recognized William and smiled broadly. He popped up immediately into a kind of attention, his arms at his eyes, saying, "yes, sir."

Thomas and Cuthbert laughed together. William smiled, and clapped his hands happily, saying, "thank you John. We should be getting going. Big day today! Would you be so kind as to awaken your siblings and start stacking the mats in the corner over there?"

John Wooler, a big smile on his face saluted William and started rousing his siblings, and struggled manfully to start moving straw mats to a corner. In his efforts, he kept a careful and adoring eye on William. Thomas smiled at this. Cuthbert looked confused.

Out of the corner of his eye, Thomas caught sight of Mary Wooler re=ascending the stairs.

"She is beautiful," Thomas thought.

*"And married to Godfrey."*

"But still…"

*"Natural enough, Thomas. But still no buts. And she is your friend. You don't want to embarrass her or make her feel uncomfortable."*

"That is true."

*"Besides…Big day today! Don't spoil it mooning."*

"Fair enough. What's first?"

*"Love and trust, Thomas, as always"*

Mary approached Thomas as he snapped out of his reverie. Thomas tried to compose his face, and Mary smiled at him gently.

"Well, Thomas," Mary said kindly, "almost there. I'm anxious to see if Godfrey and Robert made it in time."

"Knowing Godfrey," Thomas said with a laugh as his spell was broken, "I'm certain that he made it both on time and in style."

The two shared a laugh and Cuthbert and William approached with the children not far behind.

"Good morning, Mother," said John Wooler with a polite bow in unconscious mimicry of William.

"Good morning to you, too, Master John," replied Mary Wooler with a smile and a curtsey, before adding, "it would seem that travelling with Lord Mountjoy has improved our manners considerably."

John nodded agreement seriously.

William, Lord Mountjoy, suppressed a smile and bowed courteously to Mary, then said, "Its still early, and the crowds won't be so thick, what with the fair and the feast day, and all. I suggest that we grab some food, and head on up to the cathedral. You Pilgrims have a lot of praying to do today." Then he let his smile loose and laughed.

Mary laughed as well, saying, "that sounds wonderful Lord...William... An excellent plan. Children, are we ready?"

Thomas and Cuthbert nodded in agreement, but said, "Er..um..maybe a brief stop at the privy for us as well on the way out?"

"Of course," exclaimed William. "I imagine children as well."

The group finished neatly stacking the straw mats and sweeping a bit, then went to the second floor, thanked the proprietor, used the toilets, then made their way down to the Chequers' entryway leading out onto the corner of Mercer and St. Dunstan's streets. The crowds were already thickening on the streets, and had since very first light. Carts and stalls lined St. Dunstan's, the main road, and up the little alley way of Mercer street, the shops were all open, and vendors were stuffed into every nook and cranny of the ancient street, selling cloth, and toys, and food.

Thomas hesitated and looked nervously up the street towards the Roper estate and St. Dunstan's church. Thankfully he saw no horses or signs of his father or the others in the crowds now streaming through the open city gate.

Thomas turned back and up the narrow Mercery, where, if he positioned himself just right to peer between the many story overhangs of the lining buildings, he could just make out the stone corner of the cathedral itself. His pulse quickened. He realized that in the two years as a page for the Archbishop he had been to the Cathedral many times, but that he had never appreciated, never even thought to appreciate, the building, the grounds, the history, in any meaningful way. Usually the Archbishop had stayed at the Old Palace, about two miles outside of Canterbury, and the pages generally stayed there while the Archbishop had gone into town to conduct church business.

Now, Thomas realized with his heart leaping, he was going to see, really see, the Cathedral. Experience it as a Pilgrim for St. Thomas. He felt a little faint, but realized that he was hungry when William handed him some bread and cheese, and a glass of cider as breakfast.

"Eat up, Thomas," William said in a friendly voice, "you never know where your next meal is coming from."

Thomas smiled and bowed in thanks to his friend. With everyone eating contentedly, the group made its way up the Mercery towards the Cathedral grounds. There was a little crossing alley, then a few open beamed houses. The houses suddenly parted, and rising up into the sky from the beautiful manicured lawns of the cathedral lawn was the Cathedral itself.

Crowds streamed past and around them, as the entire group took in a collective breath, gazing up at the two towers on their left for the church, and the larger central tower, surrounded by scaffolding, and under reconstruction, it looked like about three quarters built. Once they had passed the din of the fair in the close quarters of the market street, Thomas noticed the change in sound, quieter, more peaceful, with the chanting of the monks inside finishing *terce*, accompanied by a slow rhythmic hammering of stone masons getting an early start making block and brick into useful shapes.

The sun had risen a bit and was now over the houses, filling the yard with light, and casting a yellow aura over the entire cathedral. The gothic spires of the leftward towers seemed to rise into heaven, and the decorations rising sets of paired windows one each of the four sides of the paired north and south towers, the castellated tops with spires rising ever heavenward.

Thomas inhaled again, forgetting to exhale as his eyes scanned lovingly up and down, right and left, taking in the buttresses, the stained glass. The large western porch on their left, on their far right the rounded apse and chapel.

"Well…that's really something," whispered Cuthbert involuntarily.

Thomas asked him, "have you ever been here before?"

"No," Cuthbert replied, "you?"

"A few times," Thomas replied, "but I've never seen it like….this."

William chimed it, "you've made it, fellows. You're here! And look," he added, directing their attention earthward towards a clump of men on the lawn, "unless I miss my guess, that's Thomas Howard, the famous young soldier, and his trusty Sergeant…"

"Godfrey!" completed Mary, starting to rush forward towards her husband.

Godfrey looked up suddenly at Mary's voice and seeing her, stood up to his full, hairy height, happily yelling, "Mary!"

Leaving his slack-jawed and tired looking soldiers behind, he ran to Mary, embracing her in, predictably thought Thomas, a great bear hug, lifting her off the ground. Thomas noticed then that, though the soldiers were wearing their green livery, including Robert, who was standing uncertainly off to the side, Godfrey was still wearing his plain brown pilgrim's robe and sandals.

Thomas Howard saw Mountjoy, then Thomas and Cuthbert, and, with a broad smile on his red topped face, the boys all moved together. Thomas Howard abruptly stopped and turned to his men, and called out in a loud parade ground voice, "Company…Form Up At Attention"

The men heard this call and reflexively came together into ranks, arranged by height.

Godfrey heard the command as well and immediately, and with a sheepish look on his face, quickly returned his wife to the ground and broke with a sprint to Howard's side. As he approached, he could be heard saying in a loud, clear, audible voice, "begging your pardon, sir. I've no excuse."

Howard looked at him with a stern visage, but a little glint in his eye, saying, "Forgiven this once, Sergeant. But we haven't yet mustered. Please see to it."

"Aye, Sir," replied Godfrey. He then took out a scrap of paper and began reading names, each answered quickly, and loudly, with an "Aye."

At completion of the list, Godfrey turned to Howard, saying, "All's present and sober sir."

"Thank you, Sergeant," Howard replied, shaking Wooler's hand.

Howard turned to his men, and, again in his loudest, deepest voice, audible all over the lawn, cried out, "Men! We have arrived! We are here at Canterbury Cathedral, and we are ready to serve and protect the King. We have trained for this, and you all know your roles. Let's see the poles!"

The men shuffled about smartly a bit, and each retried from what Thomas More had assumed was a large pile of timber, poles of wood, really tree trunks, each about 4 inches in diameter and about 14 feet long. Each also grabbed a shield off another nearby pile. As they re-assembled into formation, More noticed that each pole had been rounded, removing the bark but exposing the white wood underneath. Each pole had been rather fiercely sharpened at the tip. After reformation each man stood, holding the pole upright with their right hand, a shield in their left.

There was a small crowd of onlookers now watching the soldiers with their poles standing at attention. The pilgrims coming in behind the boys and the Woolers had now pushed around their group in order to get a better look at the King's soldiers on the lawn of the cathedral.

This push forced Thomas More and the others to move closer as well. One nearby pilgrim, a man in his twenties with dark, oily hair and a several day growth of a scraggly beard, called out, My Lord….What's with the poles? Can't afford swords?"

To Thomas More's amazement, Thomas Howard turned to the man and smiled. He called back to him, in an easy voice, "That is an excellent question, Pilgrim." Howard turned to Godfrey, and bellowed, "Sergeant."

Godfrey approached, also bellowing, "Yes, My Lord."

"Pray explain to these good Englishmen why we have these poles." Howard asked.

"Yes, my Lord..." Godfrey replied, turning to face the still growing crowd. "We have these poles because we are soldiers and servants of His Royal Majesty King Henry! Our Lord and Commander here, Thomas Howard, Grandson of the late Duke of Norfolk, knew from bitter experience at Bosworth, that these very poles, used wisely by true soldiers helped King Henry achieve his rightful throne. These poles, with these warriors, make English arms unbeatable in battle. Care to see why?"

The crowd, now firmly in Godfrey's hand roared an assent.

Godfrey smiled broadly and turned to his men, crying, "King Henry's soldiers form up for battle around your Captain!"

With Thomas Howard in the middle, the soldiers quickly formed a circle around their Captain, crouched, with each holding their pole, the end planted in the ground and extended at a forty five degree angle outward. Each shield was held up with the left hand, creating an impenetrable wall with thick, long spikes.

The crowd oohed. Thomas noticed on his right that a small crowd of monks had emerged from the cathedral at the transept door, and were standing, watching from the small porch there as well.

Another male pilgrim to Thomas's left called out, "but that's only defense!"

Without turning to the voice, Godfrey, smiling now, called out, "Attack formation, on me!"

The soldiers, in unison, stood and in smooth motions pushed arms through the slings on their shields, grabbing their poles with both hands, and came to a straight line facing the crowd, snarling and waving the tips of the poles menacingly. Several in the crowd screamed, and the mass pulled back, away from the soldiers.

Thomas Howard called out, "Company… Order Arms!" and the men returned to a position of attention, poles headed straight up. The crowd clapped.

An older monk had come off the porch of the transept door, clad in a white Friar's Habit, hood up, gold cross on chest came forward and started walking quickly towards the group. He was followed by several of the other monks, clad in either black or white Benedictine habits, much smaller than the lead monk's.

Thomas More motioned with his head to Godfrey and Thomas Howard, too late noticing the gold crozier that the oncoming monk was carrying, using as a walking stick. He covered the ground quickly, pushing back his hood revealing his ruddy face and bald head with wispy hair.

"Captain, a word," the monk called out.

Thomas Howard turned, as did the soldiers, and Godfrey. The crowd turned to the voice to look.

"Greetings my Lord Archbishop!" Thomas More called and he bowed deeply and with great respect.

The crowd gasped. Several quickly also bowed or curtseyed. A few fell to their knees. The soldiers came to attention. Thomas Howard repeated, "My Lord Archbishop," and bowed deeply. Godfrey seemed a little frozen, but came to attention.

The Archbishop and Lord Chancellor of England, John Morton, approached the group with a large smile on his face, nodding to acknowledge the bows. "Well. What have we going on here? In my Cathedral?" He asked pleasantly.

Thomas Howard stood, saying hurriedly "Sir. I am.."

"Please stop, Thomas Howard," the Archbishop cut him off pleasantly. "I know exactly who you are. And this is now your company of men?"

"Yes sir." Howard replied, returning to standing at attention, "I…we… were sent here by Somerset as we were told the King was to be here today and we were to attend to him."

"And somehow," the Archbishop said clucking his tongue as if thinking, "you managed to pick up Godfrey Wooler as your Sergeant?"

"Sir?" Howard replied, incredulous.

"Oh, young Howard," the Archbishop laughed, "Godfrey Wooler is well known to me from his service to King Edward. He even tried to arrest me once. Well he and a group of King Richard's men."

"But ye got away," Godfrey said regretfully. "Never figured out how…Good morning my Lord Archbishop."

Looking around the crowd, John Morton suddenly said happily, "Mary Wooler, it is so very nice to see you!"

Thomas More looked at Mary again, surprised again at the depth of connection the Woolers possessed. He looked at Thomas Howard and mouthed, "how?" and Howard smiled and shrugged his shoulders.

The Archbishop walked around the soldiers, and approaching the crowd opposite, nodded to William, saying "My Lord Mountjoy."

William returned the nod with, "My Lord Archbishop."

The Archbishop nodded to Cuthbert, and then stood directly in front of Thomas More with a grand smile on his face, exclaiming happily, "If it isn't my young page, Thomas More, Thomas More, as I recall, of London and the Thames."

Thomas Howard burst out laughing.

Everyone else just smiled blandly, nodding to the Archbishop.

The Archbishop suddenly stepped forward and embraced Thomas More, saying, "you did it Thomas! Completed the pilgrimage! I am so very proud of you!"

Thomas beamed, whispering into the Archbishop's ear, "It was extraordinary, sir. Thank you. But I…we…haven't finished yet. We are still outside the Cathedral."

The Archbishop stepped back, a little question on his smile, "Certainly, Thomas, but you said 'we'?"

More smiled broadly and laughed, saying, "Yes, sir. I started, as you know, by myself on London Bridge, but the Pilgrim's Way is a place, I found, of friendship… of Pilgrims helping each other on the road. I've met people…friends for life, I hope. And we weathered the journey together, helping each other find…Well find either what they needed or were looking for."

The Archbishop smiled, asking, "Tell me about your friends, Thomas. Where are they?"

"Right here!" exclaimed Thomas happily. "They are right here!" Thomas turned excitedly and grasped Cuthbert, saying, "My Lord Archbishop this is my friend Cuthbert Tunstall, who I am certain will be a scholarly priest in your service."

The Archbishop nodded and smiled, and Thomas went on, "you appear to know William..Lord Mountjoy. He is brilliant and kind."

Thomas gestured in the direction of the soldiers, and politely said, "and the Woolers, and Thomas Howard, and, of course my friends the soldiers. It was a great walk."

The Archbishop's smile broadened, "I am taking it that your father and his associates did not find you along the road then?"

"Oh yes sir," Thomas replied earnestly, "they did yesterday at the Roper estate by St. Dunstan's."

"And where are they and why are you not with them?" the Archbishop asked.

"Well…" Thomas reddened a bit and stammered at first, "they were quite keen on my staying with them, but I explained to them that I had prior contractual obligations, including having promised you that I would finish this pilgrimage."

"And that swayed them?" the Archbishop asked.

"Well.." Thomas wheedled, "at first."

"But?" enquired the Archbishop.

"Then we escaped, My Lord Archbishop," interjected Lord Mountjoy. "They were 'thinking' about it all while waiting for the town gate to close for the night."

"The three of you escaped from the Roper place?" the Archbishop gasped, stepping back a bit.

"Actually, my Lord Archbishop," Cuthbert exclaimed with a wicked grin, "it was the three of us plus Mrs. Wooler and the younger children. We got out a side gate and just made it through the town gate leaving us in town and our pursuers out." He laughed quite cheerily at the memory of it.

The Archbishop took a side look at Mary Wooler who had moved closer. Mary nodded in confirmation.

Thomas More stepped up to say, "My Lord, my Father did agree that if we were to somehow be…uh…separated…that I should meet him after the *nones* mass at the Cathedral today so that he and his…travelling companions and I should be able to speak with your Lordship and with His Majesty, the King."

The Archbishop's eyes lit up "Your father appears to know you, Thomas More of London," he said with a laugh, leaning in to the three boys in a conspiratorial way. "Very well, then, we have a few hours. The King will be here after *sext* at nine. He spent the night at the Old Palace, about two miles east. The City gates will be opening very soon, and, unless I miss my guess, there will be some unhappy gentlemen, including a Sergeant-at-Law and a Lord Mayor of your London, among the first to come through the west gate in search of you all."

Thomas, William and Cuthbert also leaned in with happy conspiracy, saying in a low voice, "yes, my Lord?"

"Well, then," the Archbishop continued, "I think that several courses of action need to commence." He raised his right hand and said, "Brother John Dunster?" He turned to look, but a middle aged monk, portly and happy, in a clean white habit, adorned with a gold pectoral cross nearly as large as the Archbishop's, appeared quickly in his vision."

"Yes my Lord Archbishop," Brother John replied happily.

Morton smiled happily at seeing him, saying, "Prior John, our morning became a wee bit more complicated." He gestured towards the soldiers. "With the King arriving this morning to pray to St. Thomas for his wife, the Queen's, health, a group of his soldiers has appeared to help us serve the King. I believe that we should feed these men, their Sergeant and Captain, and then show them around the Cathedral before the King arrives."

"Yes, My Lord, Archbishop," the Prior replied happily. "That is certainly no problem at all. Anything else?"

"Well, Prior John," the Archbishop wheedled, "now that you mention it, I'm certain all of these early rising pilgrims must be hungry as well. Could we feed them?"

The crowd of arriving Pilgrims around the Archbishop had swollen to nearly 50 by now, with stragglers still coming in. The Prior scanned the group, did the arithmetic in his head, looked over at his cellerer who had appeared on the Priors right, and had been quietly listening. The cellerer smiled and shrugged his shoulders.

The Prior returned his look to the Archbishop, saying, "My Lord, as it happens we were preparing a great feast in honor of the King. That food is ready, of course, and it will be straightforward to cook more. So yes, my Lord." He turned and nodded to his Cellerer, saying, in a loud voice, "My Lord the Archbishop has had a wonderful idea! Brothers let us set up a morning feast this very moment for these Pilgrims and these soldiers as a start to our celebration of the Feast of the Translation of Saint Thomas Becket." He paused and made a nod to John Morton, adding, "who as we all know was Archbishop of Canterbury, Lord Chancellor…"

The Archbishop interrupted, smiled at Thomas More, and cried out, "and a Londoner through and through." He paused at the laughter, then added seriously, "I know that we typically fast before mass on a Feast Day, but I see that all present have travelled far, enduring great privation out of faith in our Lord, faith in St. Thomas, and Faith in our King. Therefore, as Archbishop, I declare the fasting vigil to have ended." He mumbled "*in nomine, patriae, et filia, et Spiritus Sanctus,*" making the sign of the cross with his right hand.

There was a happy cheer from the entire gathered mass of people, a few calling, "A cheer for the Archbishop!" The Archbishop smiled beneficently, nodding thanks.

The monks that had accumulated near the transept door had been dispersed quickly by the cellerer. Thomas Howard, taking a cue from Godfrey, also dispersed his soldiers in pursuit of assisting the monks with the Feast. As they ran off, they each set their poles and shields in neat piles where they had been.

Fairly quickly they began to reappear from around corners of the cathedral carrying trestle tables and food. A haunch of meat on a spit was brought out, still steaming and was set up on two support rods. Buckets of ale and cider were brought fort, as well as some fruit and vegetables. Many large loaves of bread also appeared, still hot and wrapped in cloths to avoid burning fingers.

While this was unfolding, the Archbishop took Thomas, Cuthbert, and William to the side, and said, "Boys, while this is unfolding, let me ask you some questions.

They nodded gravely, nodding their heads with respect.

"Thomas," the Archbishop asked gravely once they crowd had moved away from them, "who was in your father's party yesterday at the Ropers?"

Thomas stole a glance at his friends, then answered truthfully, "my father, Henry and John Colet, Sergeant John Fineaux, John Roper, and a Sir Edward Guildford and a Doctor John Clement."

Thomas gave his answer, and the Archbishop continued to stare thoughtfully at him. Thomas waited him out, until finally the Archbishop asked, "and no one else?"

Thomas added, "No one, sir, except of course for our little party."

"Which was you three?" the Archbishop asked.

"Any Mary Wooler and her younger children." Thomas replied.

"And who spoke with your father's party," the Archbishop asked. "All of you?"

Thinking, Thomas replied, "no sir, just the three of us."

"and did you and your father speak of anything outside of the earshot of Tunstall and Lord Mountjoy?"

"Yes, sir," Thomas replied, staring evenly into the Archbishop's face. "My father, Sergeant Fineaux, the Lord Mayor and I spoke privately about your thoughts, and my role here today."

"And?" asked the Archbishop with a raised eyebrow.

Thomas bowed with a sweep of the right hand, as if he were back as a page in the Archbishop's Court, saying, "I am always at the service of the Archbishop."

The Archbishop laughed with Cuthbert and Mountjoy at the theatricality of Thomas's gesture. The Archbishop said happily, "I see Thomas that your love of the theater survived the pilgrimage."

"I wouldn't be able to say, Sir," said Thomas with a small wink, "as I have not yet finished the Pilgrimage. I haven't yet visited Saint Thomas.

"Right you are, Thomas!" the Archbishop replied, "and I've not forgotten that you agreed to complete a pilgrimage by the Feast of the Translation. And yet here we are…outside the Cathedral."

"yes sir?" Thomas said, looking up hopefully.

"Have ye three eaten this morning?" the Archbishop asked.

"Yes, My Lord Archbishop," Tunstall replied. "Lord Mountjoy has been exceedingly kind and generous to us."

The Archbishop smiled at Mountjoy, saying, "My Lord Mountjoy, thank you. We will, of course be having to review your generosity and ability with taxes sometime soon."

Mountjoy blanched, but recovered color when Morton winked at him.

"I will tell you what, young gentlemen," the Archbishop said kindly, "I am not so hungry, and I am an old man. I would very much like to see the Cathedral through your younger, more innocent eyes. Would you grant me the honor of taking you myself on a tour of the cathedral and my predecessor's sites? That way you would complete your pilgrimage with the heir of Saint Thomas, and I with young friends and successors. Keeping the line intact, like Steven Langton."

Thomas nodded seriously, "Sir, we would be honored and thrilled." He sank to his knees in front of the Archbishop head bent in supplication. The other two followed quickly.

The Archbishop laughed happily, placing his hands on each boy's head, saying a blessing at each. Smiling, and wiping his hands on his habit, the Archbishop said, "I see I am going to need to get you three bathed at some point." He laughed, then looked around the yard, adding, "and before we go, I need to instill a little order."

The peasants were milling about, and one of the monks took charge, gently arranging them into an orderly group on the lawn near where the serving tables were being set up. Pilgrims volunteered to help with the serving, so many, in fact, that the line of servers was longer than the line to be served.

The Archbishop intervened, saying reasonably, "since the soldiers have duties very shortly for the King, and since I want them to be able to visit St. Thomas before the King arrives, let us feed the soldiers first."

All present agreed happily, and in no time, all of the soldiers, their Sergeant and Captain at the end of the line, were served and were happily sitting on the lawn.

A younger monk, in a black habit, his shaved tonsure showing some stubble, was moving past the the Archbishop, trying hard not to be noticed, to no avail. "Brother Thomas Hampton, if you've a moment," the Archbishop called out kindly.

Brother Thomas stopped in his tracks. He was only a little older than Cuthbert and smiled when he saw him, first saying, "Yes, my Lord Archbishop?" then "Cuthbert, from Oxford? I'd heard you'd died of the plague?"

The Archbishop eyed Cuthbert questioningly, then shook it off, turning to the young monk, asking, "Brother, I know how busy I've made you all, but could you please indulge me in a favor?"

Brother Thomas stood tall and proud at being asked a favor by the Archbishop, replying, "Yes, my Lord. Anything!"

"See those soldiers over there?" the Archbishop asked, gesturing over to Howard's men. "And the woman and family who have just joined them?"

"Yes, my Lord. The King's men." Brother Thomas replied.

"I should very much like for them to have a private tour of the cathedral before the King arrives," the Archbishop said, asking, "could you please do me the kindness of, when they have finished eating, conducting them yourself? Prior John tells me that you have remarkable knowledge of St. Thomas and of our beautiful cathedral."

"I would be honored, Sir!" Brother Thomas replied standing proud, his face reddening. "Thank you, My Lord!"

Brother Thomas ran off, and the Archbishop turned to the three boys, saying, "well, I think my work here is done, and that I won't be missed. Shall we?" He made a turn to the left and a sweep with his left arm towards the Cathedral. "Let me introduce you to MY Cathedral!"

After he had taken a few steps, the boys in tow, he stopped and pointed up to the under construction central tower. "I started this reconstruction of the tower because the old tower was falling down, and because, well… it wasn't tall enough to glorify God in the way that the premier Cathedral of England ought to."

He pointed to the top, saying "Bell Harry will be back up there soon. It's a lovely bell, takes two men to ring, and can be heard for miles."

He paused and pointed up, "you can see we are using a lot of Caen stone on the tower. Had to to make it match the rest of the cathedral."

He leaned in conspiratorially to Thomas, pointing about a half way up the tower, saying, "Thomas, you can see that I've left my mark, just like the arch at Lambeth, J M O R and a tun of beer." He giggled happily, adding, "I love building. Politics is about today, the law is about a decade, and a building, like faith, can go on forever."

The boys smiled.

The Archbishop continued his tour, "Our Cathedral here is nine hundred years old! Think about that. The Romans had just left, Saint Augustine brought Christianity to England, well, Kent at the time, and founded this church. It was rebuilt four hundred years ago by the Normans, who brought in the Caen stone which glows so brilliantly in the morning with the sun's first light. We, faithful Englishmen, have been building and rebuilding ever since."

He paused and gestured towards the rounded eastern end of the building to their right, "that, of course, is the Corona chapel, which was added on in 1220 to house St. Thomas at the actual Translation of the saint to more…appropriate circumstances. Let's go inside. This is the southwest transept door here."

The Archbishop led the way inside through the large arched wooden doors. It was shaded and cool inside this entry. He stopped for a moment and pointed into a small chapel to their right.

"This is the Warrior chapel, or St. Michael's Chapel," the Archbishop explained. "The tomb in the center is of the patroness, Lady Margaret Holland with her two husbands, John Beaufort and the Duke of Clarence on either side. The King will visit here a bit today since Lady Margaret and John Beaufort are his great-grandparents. John Beaufort was, of course, John of Gaunt's son. The King's mother, Lady Margaret, my dear friend, comes here often to visit."

The Archbishop looked with affection at the tomb in the small chapel, and sighed. The boys looked at each other, then looked ahead at the open area of the transept, The group moved ahead up some stairs, and onto the worn brown stone floor. Just ahead, and a little to their right was a lot of scaffolding, and they could look up around into the open unfinished tower.

"St. Thomas was, of course, Archbishop and Lord Chancellor," the Archbishop continued. "He had been great friends with the King, Henry, the Second of that name. But their relationship had run afoul and Thomas had spent many years in exile. He returned in 1170, but the King remained unhappy. The King had his moods, apparently. At one point, frustrated beyond all reason, the King cried out, 'will no one rid me of this troublesome priest?' Four knights…uh…misinterpreted…the King's cry as an order and set off. They came to Canterbury to this very Cathedral, just after Christmas. The third day of Christmas, in fact. St. Thomas had been in the Cloister, over there," he gestured off to the left.

Thomas," the Archbishop continued, "despite hearing of threats, came into the cathedral and, in his pure white habit," he gestured to his own clothes, "Thomas came into the Cathedral and began to celebrate Vespers." Morton gestured to the right, up some very worn grey stone stairs and through the choir to the altar. Morton, with his eyes closed, pointed to their left into the large open gothic nave.

"It was dark and cold that night," the Archbishop continued in a soft voice, "but the candles were lit, and there were about a hundred or so worshippers present for the Vespers." He paused and shook his head a bit.

"Suddenly," the Archbishop exclaimed, "the knights burst in through the door we just entered, and came right across here, disrupting the service, shouting 'where is the traitor to the King?!'"

The boys started at the sudden exclamation, which still echoed in the cathedral, and looked involuntarily back at the door.

The Archbishop continued in an excited voice, "The Archbishop's priests and monks, his friends and servants, tried to hustle him out the back of the church, but Thomas would have none of it."

The Archbishop led the boys across the transept. They looked up the worn stairs across the construction. "These are the same stones, boys," the Archbishop said in a whisper, "that the murderers trod on their way over there." He pointed across the transept to a landing that went down some stairs to the left. He gestured for the three boys to walk over to those stairs.

"The villains started down those stairs," Morton went on pointing down, his voice carrying over to the boys now on the landing, "and you will see that they lead to two adjacent chapels, one at the bottom landing, and the other chapel to the right."

The Archbishop then ascended the ten or so stone stairs to his right, up to the choir and the construction under the middle tower. He turned towards the boys, now halfway down the stairs, and said, "the soon to be murderers cried out 'where is the Archbishop? The traitor to the King?'"

The boys looked up at the Archbishop, who suddenly raised his arms and his golden crozier in the air, crying out in a commanding voice, as he then descended the stairs back to the transept, fire in his eyes like some old testament prophet, "And Thomas came to them, crying, 'the righteous will be like a bold lion and free from fear!" The Archbishop lowered his voice from fury to humility and reasonableness as he added, "'Here I am, not a traitor of the king, but a priest; why do you seek me?'"

As the Archbishop had approached, the boys shrank backwards down the steps. Thomas More tripped a bit on one of the lower stairs, but found his footing as he arrived at the lower landing. This was a grey stone vaulted room. The ceiling was high overhead from the nave, and the stairs, landing, and ceiling created a great open feel for a small room. On the far wall from the stairs there was a simple wooden altar, and to the right a large pillar and then an arched, open entry to a room dark except for a few candles burning inside.

The Archbishop descended the stairs to rejoin the boys in this close chapel. The Archbishop gathered the three boys into a huddle with his arms, and said in a low voice, "This is where it happened, lads. This is the room. "Thomas Becket brushed past his killers, calm as can be, and knelt to pray at that little altar there." The Archbishop stood up, disengaging from the boys, and went quietly over to the altar of Saint Benedict. He knelt, and gestured for the boys to do the same. Two monks in black habits emerged from the small darkened chapel to their right.

Without looking up from his prayers, the Archbishop said in a quiet voice, almost now as if he were talking to himself, the boys forgotten and irrelevant, "the knights, no…the creatures… didn't know what to do, they didn't, of course, want to kill a priest at prayer in a church. Is there a more unforgivable crime? Still, they drew their swords, here in this chapel of Benedict, next to a Chapel of Mary. Thomas said to them, 'Here I am, ready to suffer in the name of He who redeemed me with His blood; God forbid that I should flee on account of your swords or that I should depart from righteousness.'"

The boys each looked at the Archbishop, who had bowed his head in prayer, tears forming in his eyes. Thomas felt a lump forming in his throat.

After a moment, the Archbishop went on, "not knowing what to do, the killers tried to drag Thomas from the Altar, Thomas spun from their grasp, falling to his right." The Archbishop came to a crouch and rolled around to his right, around Tunstall's legs. He stopped his turn at the large pillar, which he hugged closely, his face turned to the left. He continued speaking, "the demons laid hands on the martyr and tried to pull him from this pillar, right here. When they failed to move him, frustrated, they took their swords to him. The first blow opened his skull, here." With his left hand he pointed to the back of his head. "A single, brave monk came to hold his Archbishop. Thomas tried to fend off a blow from the villains, now consumed by blood lust. Several blows from swords wounded Thomas, the Archbishop grievously." The Archbishop went into a defensive crouch.

"Thomas Becket was still conscious after this and, knowing he was to die, said simply in a low voice, 'For the name of Jesus and the protection of the church, I am ready to embrace death.' And with that, the murderer name Rainold swung his sword and cleaved off the top of the

Martyrs skull. Right….here….” He pointed at the floor and he stood up, straightening his white robes, looking, and yet not seeing the still kneeling boys.

The three stood and walked the few steps to the Archbishop and the holy spot upon which he stood. All four made the sign of the cross.

“Rainold swung his sword so hard,” the Archbishop continued in a conversational voice, “that his sword, after killing Thomas, struck the pillar here.” He bent and reverently touched a dent in the stone. “This mark in the stone is from that blow. His sword shattered and he dropped it onto the floor next to the martyr and his sole attendant, Edward Grim.” He paused and nodded to the two silent monks, who came forward bearing a broken sword. Thomas More noticed the dried blood on the side, ancient, brown and flaking.

The Archbishop John Morton took the broken blade from the monks and held it in front of the boys, “this is the murder weapon, boys. This is the blood of the martyr Saint Thomas Becket.”

The boys crossed themselves and each, in turn, reverently kissed the blade. The Archbishop returned the sword to the monks who departed back into the small Lady chapel behind them. The Archbishop knelt to the ground, touching the stones where Becket had died, saying softly, “these, my young friends, are holy stones. The Saint lay here oozing on the floor.” He felt the smooth, worn, brown flagstones. The boys knelt to do the same.

After a moment, the Archbishop stood, made the sign of the cross. The boys did the same. “Come with me then,” the Archbishop commanded. The boys followed along silently, but looking at all the gothic marvels of the church as they went back up the staircase to the transit then, going straight they went along the north aisle of the church for a hundred or so feet.

The Archbishop seemed to have recovered some from the murder, but remained solemn. About two thirds the way up the aisle, the group turned left into a little downward circular stone staircase.

As they were going down the dim stairs, well worn with time, the Archbishop began again, saying, "The knights took Thomas's body down here into the crypt." Finishing the stairs the group entered a large open space, well lit with candles. "This is the oldest part of the Cathedral," the Archbishop continued. It was built four hundred years ago by the Normans."

The Archbishop walked to the east and pointed at a rounded part of the far wall, saying, "that area wasn't there then. It was added by the Archbishop Stephen Langton fifty years later. The body of the martyr was laid here." The archbishop went to the center of the eastern part of the crypt. A candle was burning near a well worn area of the floor. "A tomb was build for the body here and Thomas was laid in it. The body was raised a bit, and the tomb had three arched areas along the side."

The Archbishop smiled and said happily, "Miracles began to occur almost before the martyr's body had cooled. King Henry, realizing the sin that had been committed in his name quickly came to do penance for Becket's murder. The King came as a penitent, unshod, a hair shirt, and on his knees, crawled to the body of his former friend, his Archbishop, his Lord Chancellor, of whom his words had caused murder, martyrdom."

"So many Pilgrims started to come to venerate the Saint that the side arches became a part of the Pilgrimage, one approached the tomb flat, and asking Thomas's help, the pilgrim would place his head in the tomb. I'm told that if one saw the Saint's body, a cure would be forthcoming. King Henry's grandson, the Third Henry, visited here, and placed his own Royal Head into the tomb!"

The boys nodded, each imagining the scene.

Morton let that sink in, then continued, "the problem soon became the crowds, and soon those small stairs became quite an obstacle for anyone. It's very limited access, so the Cathedral was expanded and the Corona chapel was built on the eastern end. That includes the rounded end you see there, which supports the chapel above."

The Archbishop turned to go back to the stairs, saying, "and fifty years after the murder, in 1220, on Tuesday July 7, the first Feast of the Translation of St. Thomas Becket was celebrated by my Predecessor Stephen Langton, with the King, the Chief Justice and the Papal legate all in attendance."

The Archbishop turned just as he started up the stairs, and added, "the bones were placed into a golden box, the sliced off part of the skull, called the corona, separately held. The saint was carried up these stairs, with all reverence and ceremony," He turned and carefully ascended the stairs.

At the top of the stairs, at the junction of the north aisle and the north transept, the Archbishop led the group to some stairs. Thomas perceive people at the top of the stairs, but suddenly wondered if the cathedral had been cleared for the Archbishop. There were some very worn stairs leading up into a large, circular area of the cathedral. Looking up at the high ceiling of the chapel, Thomas saw the arched coming together as a flower button, painted red. On the right side of the steps, there was a tomb with a black iron fence surrounding the black effigy of a knight in repose.

Mountjoy quickly tapped Thomas on the elbow and mouthed the words, "Edward, the Black Prince," excitedly.

The stopped the boys at the base of the stairs, pointing down at the deeply rounded, worn steps. "it is traditional," he said with a smile, "to approach St. Thomas up these stairs with great reverence on one's knees." He paused a beat as he went to his knees on the stairs, before adding, touching the worn steps, "and probably safer as well."

The group ascended the steps on their knees three boys abreast behind the Archbishop. Remaining on knees, the group made a little right turn around the Black Prince's tomb. Thomas's breath left him involuntarily as he encountered the tomb of Thomas Becket as pilgrim's had for nearly three hundred years. There was a golden box atop a tall marble altar. The golden box was open, the top propped open by wires, and a green wooden box was elevated partly out, That box was open as well, and tipped so that bones could be seen in the box.

Even more breathtaking was around the pedestal, where countless gifts to the Saint had been lain for centuries, including large jewels, gold, boxes, papers. Thomas estimated that it would take over two dozen wagons full just to move this great treasure around. The Archbishop stood and gestured with a wave of his right hand towards the mass, saying, "Here is the Saint Thomas Becket now. The trinkets are gifts from the centuries. I am going over here to the Corona now, but I would like to leave you three to pray."

The Archbishop moved over towards the left to the rounded brightly lit chapel at the end of the church. The boys crawled forward.

"I've never seen so much treasure," thought Thomas

*"That is certainly the message the Archbishop wanted you to take from this."*

"No, no, not the message, but look at all this stuff!"

*"I agree that it is a lot of treasure. Think about the donors! Kings have placed jewels there. Somewhere deep in the pile must be a gift from Chaucer."*

"The Black Prince and King Henry the Fourth are buried right here with Saint Thomas.

*"That represents a lot of devotion. The gift of self."*

"This has been quite a pilgrimage."

*"That it has. I'm proud of you."*

"The other night, when I was ill. Was that Thomas in my dream?"

*"You two are connected now. You completed the pilgrimage to Thomas, not just his shrine."*

"I haven't a gift for him."

*"Don't you?"*

Thomas was brought back by the slight noise of Cuthbert and William quietly rising on either side of him and moving quietly over in the direction of the Archbishop. He suddenly appreciated the weight of his precious, rolled up parchments. Smiling, he gingerly unrolled the canvas, now quite dirty, and took one of the two manuscripts of his poem. He gingerly rolled and recovered the other. He quietly rolled up the parchment and gently wedged it into a nook created by a number of other piled up gifts.

Thomas bowed his head and thought, "Saint Thomas, Archbishop and Lord Chancellor of England, martyr, I wish that I had more to offer you, but from this pilgrimage, this is my most precious belonging. Please be with me through my life, whatever I do.

*"Very nice. Anything else?"*

"And please help safely deliver the Queen. Let me help save the Queen."

Thomas looked up at the bones of St. Thomas in their elevated box. The sun had risen enough that it was shining through the great stained glass windows of the rounded eastern end of the church. Remarkable flashes of red, blue and bright white light splashed around the chapel, the nearby raised tombs and, of course, St. Thomas. Transfixed, Thomas watched the light angle off of gold and gems, off the reliquary boxes, playing, dancing around the room. He felt an odd peace come over him. He looked up towards the painted rosette in the ceiling, and noted the light made the stone flower appear to move, as if in a gentle breeze.

In the distance, half a church, yet far away, Thomas heard the soldiers and the Woolers on their tour with Brother Thomas, who was relating the fate of St. Thomas. Thomas flashed to the face of St. Thomas from his dream, and relived the moments of his martyrdom, the blood on the white habit, the bloody sword, the body being held by his Brother. Thomas flashed to Jesus on Calvary, His mother weeping as her son died on the cross.

A sense of light, of well being began to burn in Thomas More's chest. He looked down at the gold and jewels, at the treasure around the box of bones. The light from the windows seemed to have lit the tomb into some great, ancient funeral. Thomas watched the light flames lick up around the bones. He felt the warmth from the pyre feed his own as that warmth climbed to his neck and then face.

Thomas bent over, prostrating himself before the tomb, and the white light reached his brain, his vision.

"It's too much," Thomas thought, white light in front of his eyes.

*"Let go."*

Thomas released the tension in his body, and exhaled. The light reached in and over him, and the light, the fire within him filled him to the top of his head, and then settled down, making him feel warm, atingle, all over.

He took a sharp inward breath, and it was as if he could feel the light expanding out into his limbs. He took a look at his hands, but they appeared normal. His vision continued to clear, to become well lit and acutely sharp, as if all the colors and angles had been drawn with a sharp pen. Shadows seemed no longer to exist.

*"Breath."*

Thomas breathed, at first as an act of will, then more naturally.

"Trust and Love," thought Thomas, concentrating on breathing, but starting to feel lighter and fuller at the same time.

*"Let it fill you Thomas."*

"There is more, isn't there?"

*"Look around you"*

Thomas looked around the circular hall, past Thomas Becket's casket and pile of treasure. To his right, he saw the Woolers and the soldiers come in from the narrow crypt stairs, and to his left he saw the Archbishop, Cuthbert, and William standing in the small corona oriole, with the beautiful, ancient stained glass above them. The three were staring back at Thomas More at the tomb. Cuthbert and William appeared concerned, but the Archbishop, looking intently at him, had a quizzical and happy smile on his face.

Looking across the room, Thomas saw his father and the other men coming up the stairway from the south aisle. They were all there, including the young princes. It seemed to Thomas that most of them had never visited St. Thomas here before because, as they got to the top of the stairs and came around the corner of the tomb of Henry the fourth and beheld the pile of treasure and the open casket, most stopped, mouths agape.

John More appeared to have visited before, because as he came to the top of the stairs, he saw Thomas More and called out, "Son?"

The Archbishop had moved towards the arriving men, with Cuthbert and Mountjoy trailing behind. The Archbishop called out, "wait, John," and the men paused at the top of the stairs, over by the tomb of the long absent King, now looking at the Archbishop.

Thomas looked at his father, and back at the Archbishop. The light that filled him seemed to send tongues out from him, caressing the people in the Chapel. As the light touched his friends, Thomas felt more warmth.

"The light is love," Thomas thought.

*"Yes. Feel it. Look around the room. Feel your love for these people. For everyone."*

"Is this what happened to Becket?"

*"At the end, yes. Everyone is complicated, Thomas."*

"Am I at the end?"

*"Heavens no. You are at a crossroads."*

"Of what?"

*"Of who you want to be. More specifically…how you want to be among others."*

"How others see me?"

*"Not quite. More how are you connected with others. Look at the lights connecting you with everyone. Are they equal?"*

Thomas looked at the tongues of light, they were strongest with those whom he felt the deepest connection, and nearly absent with those whom he either disliked, or had no connection.

"The light is greatest with people whom I already love."

*"That is both normal and not in accordance with your gifts."*

"What do you mean?"

*"You have a remarkable capacity for friendship, for love."*

"I like having friends."

*"Yes, but you also maintain those friendships. Look around the room. See how much light, how much love is going out to so many people that you didn't know a week ago."*

"They were all kind to me."

*"Why do you think that is? You radiate friendship. You even have a small finger of light going to Sergeant Fineaux."*

"I saw that. I didn't particularly like him."

*"And yet... You are still trying with him, still sending love his way. That is extremely unusual."*

"Well. He wasn't having a good day yesterday."

*"Like I said."*

Thomas paused for a moment. Looked again around the room. Noticed the faces around the room, looking at him, mostly concerned. Those closest to him, those with the most light, were smiling at him, waiting.

*"try sending more light to someone who has little."*

"How do I do that?"

*"Concentrate on the light, and on the face of someone you don't know, and love them."*

Thomas looked at John Clement, the young, new doctor, Prince Richard, who was studying Thomas. He looked at his handsome face, and at the sadness in his eyes. He felt in those eyes the pain of a father lost, of the uncertainty, of living a lie. Thomas felt compassion and empathy for him, as he studied him. The light he sent to Richard grew stronger. Richard and Thomas locked eyes, a silent understanding between them, and the light grew stronger. Thomas extended love towards Richard, and Richard smiled.

*"Excellent, now his brother."*

Thomas did the same with Sir Edward Guildford, King Edward the fifth. He was older, and harder to engage, much more wounded, he had seen his Uncle, the Earl Rivers, beheaded in front of him just after his father had died. He had lived through uncertainty, and Thomas felt his pain in his own heart. Thomas felt the light between them thicken. Thomas and Edward connected and they both smiled.

*"See, you can control it. Now use your gift to serve God."*

Thomas looked around the room, smiling. He looked at his father, their connection large, booming.

"Who are you?" Thomas thought.

*"I am, Thomas, and you know that I love you.'*

Thomas nodded. Still smiling broadly, he noticed that the light became progressively less visible, but could still be keenly felt.

Thomas looked up and around the chapel. The light through the great stained glass had become more direct, but still played around the room. He grinned at his father and nodded. The other men with him were motionless, not sure what to do.

Thomas turned to the Archbishop. Still smiling, Thomas stood and straightened his brown, dirty robe and walked calmly to the Archbishop, who was watching Thomas intently. Thomas bowed formally, and said, "My Lord Archbishop, I believe that the Corona over there completes my Pilgrimage, and my contract with you." He felt the connection with the Archbishop swell.

The Archbishop nodded, saying quietly, "yes, Thomas, let us visit that." Then, looking around the chapel, the Archbishop said to everyone, in a booming, happy voice, "Everyone finish where you were on your tour. The King will be here shortly. Thomas, Lord Mountjoy and Cuthbert Tunstall and I have some final business to attend to." He gestured to the group of men led by John More, adding, "since you all just arrived, why don't you join us at the Corona, and then we can all find some place to speak before the King arrives."

The Archbishop turned and led the boys over to the small, marble pedestal in the curved end of the chapel under the stained glass windows. Studying them, Thomas realized that the glass portrayed scenes from the Martyrdom of St. Thomas.

There was a glass box on the pedestal, and looking in, Thomas more saw the face of a golden effigy of St. Thomas's head. The face was peaceful, they eyes open.

The Archbishop resumed his tour, saying, "as I mentioned, Reginault's sword cleaved off the top of Becket's Holy skull and it went off to the side. That was the death blow. The sword broke against the pillar. You've held that. The piece of skull and hair, the Thomas's corona, was kept separately, and a death mask made of gold of the Saint's face and Head."

He pointed around to the back of the head, saying, "and they replaced the missing piece with the actual corona, here, and then built the Corona chapel around it."

Thomas looked at the back, seeing the very old hair and exposed bone of the skull of the Saint. The Archbishop looked at him expectantly, and Thomas caught a vague glance at his father, who seemed amused. The rest of the men all looked vaguely horrified.

Thomas looked at Cuthbert and William, being careful to maintain a respectful smile, and to look back at the effigy between each glance at a person. He consciously avoided seeing the blood matted hair.

Deciding, Thomas knelt at the marble pedestal in a position also at the feet of the Archbishop next to it, and bowed his head, saying, "thank you my Lord, Archbishop." Thomas then stood, and removed the pilgrim's pin, given to him in Rochester by Brother Will. He placed the pin on the top of the glass, murmuring, "thank you, Brother Will," and then,, turning to the people around him, saying in a loud voice, "Thank you all.." a pause, then more loudly, "Saint Thomas Becket!"

The group around him reflexively replied, "Pray for us!"

The Archbishop, smiling broadly, clasped Thomas, and Cuthbert and William around the shoulders, saying, "yes indeed! Pray for us." He studied each boy benignly, adding, "I am so proud of the three of you."

He looked up at John More and the men accompanying, saying, "John, Sergeant Fineaux, all the others of you, thank you for coming down. We have a lot of work to do. But first…" and he bowed, "Edward and Richard, I am so very happy to see you again."

Mountjoy's mouth worked silently, but John More stepped in smoothly, saying, "My Lord Archbishop, I am loath to correct, but I believe you meant to say 'Edward and John,' as I would like to introduce Lord Mountjoy and….I'm sorry…"

"Cuthbert Tunstall, sir," replied Cuthbert.

"Ah, yes. I remember," John More replied with a smile. "Tom Tunstall's son"

Cuthbert nodded painfully, "Your father is a good man," John said kindly. "introduce to Lord Mountjoy and Cuthbert Tunstall two of our young friends, Sir Edward Guildford and Doctor John Clement."

The Archbishop nodded appreciatively, saying quickly, "yes please forgive me, Sir Edward and Doctor Clement."

Brother Thomas slowly approached the group with the Woolers, Thomas Howard and the soldiers, as well as a few additional Pilgrims not before seen who had tagged along. Thomas

Howard, and Godfrey and Mary Wooler approached the group staring at the tall blonde boys in their midst, as if they had seen ghosts.

Before Godfrey could open his mouth, bow, or bend, Thomas More quickly said in an overloud voice, "Godfrey, Howard, Mary! I would love for you all to meet our new travelling companions, Sir Edward Guildford and Doctor John Clement."

"How is this possible?" Godfrey asked in a low voice.

"It's true then," murmured Thomas Howard.

"Clement" and "Guildford" were about to speak when they were cut off by the Archbishop, who blurted, "I think these are enough introductions for this very busy morning! The King will be here shortly. As nearly as I can determine all Pilgrimages to St. Thomas have been successfully completed. I wish you all the joy of your findings." He stopped for a breath and smiled at Thomas More.

He continued at a pace, adding in a stern manner, "the Queen, Elizabeth, has become quite ill after being delivered of a Princess, at Richmond Palace, five days ago on the second. There is significant concern that she may die. The King is coming today to pray to St. Thomas, to beg for her recovery. Our King adores his wife, the Queen. After prayer, we will be accompanying the King to Richmond, to attend to the Queen."

Several in the group started to ask questions, but the Archbishop held up his hand, saying, "we do not have time for questions or arguments. Thomas Howard, Somerset didn't make it down with the King, so you are the Captain of these men, who are now the King's men. I will need you to come and speak privately with me after this conversation. Lord Mountjoy?"

"Yes, my Lord Archbishop!" Mountjoy replied in haste.

The Archbishop continued benignly, "I believe that you will make a spectacular second in command to Captain Howard." He paused and smiled, "particularly with Godfrey Wooler as your Sergeant. While Master Howard converses with us, would you please go with the men and Sergeant Wooler, and prepare yourselves for the arrival of the King from the old Palace?"

"Yes, sir," replied Mountjoy with alacrity, though he looked at his gold and black doublet, which was stained and dirty from the road, and asked, "my clothes sir?"

"They are pilgrim's and a Lord's clothes, sir." The Archbishop replied sternly. "Wear them proudly. Don't slouch when the King approaches." He smiled as Mountjoy went over to the men.

Tunstall looked nervously at the Archbishop, asking in a quiet voice, "and me sir?"

"The King's men," the Archbishop said immediately, "need a priest and a deacon-chaplain. So does the King."

Cuthbert turned bright red and stammered, "but…sir."

The Archbishop laughed merrily, saying kindly, "not to worry young Tunstall." He looked up, and said, "Father John Colet?"

Colet moved around his Father, "yes sir?"

"Ah yes, there you are, John," Morton said happily, "I am making young Cuthbert here your acting Deacon." He paused a moment, saying, "We haven't much time, and Cuthbert, I apologize for the minimalist ordination, but come over here…Brother Thomas and Father John, you as well. Cuthbert please bow your head."

Cuthbert bowed his head towards the Archbishop, and Morton, John Colet and Brother Thomas all placed their hands on his head. Morton then, said loudly, so all might hear, his voiced echoing around the Cathedral, "Cuthbert Tunstall, Will you be loyal to the doctrine, discipline, and worship of Christ as a Deacon, as were Saint Stephen, and Saint Thomas Becket before you?"

"I will," replied Cuthbert, seriously.

"Do you believe that you are truly called by God and His Church to the life and work of a deacon?"

"I believe I am so called," replied Cuthbert.

The Archbishop continued, "Do you now in the presence of the Church commit yourself to this trust and responsibility?"

"I do," replied Cuthbert.

"Will you respect and be guided by the pastoral direction and leadership of your bishop?" the Archbishop asked.

"I will," replied Cuthbert.

The Archbishop then looked up, prayerfully saying, "Father, through Jesus Christ your Son, give your Holy Spirit to Cuthbert; fill him with grace and power, and make him a deacon in your church. Make him, O Lord, modest and humble, strong and constant, to observe the discipline of Christ. Let his life and teaching so reflect your commandments, that through him many may come to know you and love you. As your Son came not to be served but to serve, may this deacon share in Christ's service, and come to the unending glory of him who, with you and the Holy Spirit, lives and reigns, one God, for ever and ever."

The people gathered all said, "Amen!" as Morton, Colet and Brother Thomas withdrew their hands, clapping Cuthbert, all smiles on the shoulder.

"Now," the Archbishop intoned, "Deacon Tunstall, I charge you to serve Father Colet, these men, myself, and the King."

"Yes sir!" said Cuthbert happily, now looking at Colet for guidance.

Father John Colet laughed, saying "All right Deacon Tunstall! Let's get a move on." The two went over to the soldiers, and Godfrey leaned to Mountjoy and whispered, "Lord Mountjoy, we need you to give the order to head outside to muster."

Mountjoy looked to Howard, who nodded, and Mountjoy said, "Men we must repair outside to serve our King."

The soldiers drew up to attention, saying, in unison, "yes sir!" and together with Colet and with Deacon Tunstall at his side, they marched the men out of the cathedral, leaving the Corona chapel the way they had entered, skirting around old King Henry's tomb.

"Next," said the Archbishop, "Mary Wooler, I would very much like for you to join our group to discuss how we may best serve the King and the ailing Queen."

Mary Wooler nodded and gave a little curtsey, but then looked nervously at her children.

Picking up on the glance, Morton said, "Ah, yes…Brother Thomas, would you be so kind as to take charge of the Wooler children, as well as these fine other Pilgrims, to take them outside and prepare them to properly welcome their King to Canterbury Cathedral with the monks?"

"My pleasure, My Lord Archbishop," Brother Thomas said with a smile and a bow. "Come with me you all." Sweeping them up, the kind monk escorted the children out after the soldiers onto the lawn.

Once the children were outside, the Archbishop looked at his remaining group and said, I believe we might talk more discreetly and comfortably in the Chapter House. Please follow me."

Without speaking any more, the Archbishop swept back off down the stairs to his right past the Black Prince, and strode purposely, followed by the group along the South Aisle again, past the construction and down the stairs again to the site of St. Thomas's martyrdom. Once down the stairs, Morton opened a large, arched wooden door that opened to the lawn of the cloister, ringed all around by a covered open walkway. They turned right, and through another large door into the open large chapter room.

The chapter room was where the monks all met daily. It was a big rectangular room, simply furnished with benches. On the far wall from the door, there was a large, arched segmented stained glass window, with seven columns of glass depictions of three saints each. There was beautiful filigreed woodworking around the room with decorative stalls, and an ornate ceiling of carved wood. On the far wall, under the glass, there was a small door leading to the left.

During the walk over, John More had moved to Thomas's side and had draped an arm protectively around him. John Fineaux and his son in law, John Roper had taken a position in the rear, with Edward Guildford and John Clement. Henry Colet, Mary Wooler and Thomas Howard ambled in the middle of the group, each seeming somewhat confused about why they were in this group.

Once the entire group was in the room, the Archbishop moved quickly around them and closed the door with a loud clonk as the heavy wood contacted the stone jamb. Morton then cam back to the group, each one of whom had turned back and was watching the Archbishop expectantly.

Morton smiled, saying, "well….now that most of us are here."

"Most of us?" asked Fineaux impatiently. "My Lord, you need to stop spinning so many webs. What is the meaning of this?"

The Archbishop smiled benignly and made the sign of the cross in the air, index finger and thumb touching, saying, "Peace, Sergeant."

This seemed to make the Sergeant angrier, but since his tormentor at this time was both the Archbishop of Canterbury and the Lord Chancellor of England, he held his tongue, turning instead on Thomas More, saying, "at least share with us, my Lord, why we had to go careening about Kent looking for a fourteen year old boy."

Morton laughed kindly, "you mean my page, young Thomas More?"

Fineaux nodded and Morton laughed again, replying, "why…Thomas is the key to the whole thing."

Thomas More looked confused. His father put a protective arm around him, saying, "My Lord Archbishop, now really…"

Morton cut him off kindly, "No, John More. He is… in many different ways, and it has taken me a long time to figure out how. But Thomas is the connection."

The small side door banged open, and several people came charging into the room, the lead man crying, "connection to what, My Lord Archbishop."

Thomas turned more slowly than the others to the noise, and with his father's bulk between him and the newcomers, he only recognized King Henry when his father bent low in welcome to the King.

Thomas bowed broadly as well, trying very hard not to stare at the slight, pinched looking man in front of him.

"Stand up, all of you," the King commanded, adding, "we haven't much time."

Thomas eyed Edward Guildford and John Clement curiously, but their faces were masks, only smiling when a young man stepped from behind the King. At that point, though, Thomas's smile broadened considerably and he and Edward Stafford made eye contact and nodded happily at each other.

Thinking no one was watching, Thomas mouthed, "why?" to Edward. Edward rolled his eyes and shrugged his shoulders in response.

Morton coughed discreetly, having witnessed the exchange, all while never taking his eyes off of the King.

"My Queen is quite ill," the King said, characteristically without preamble. "I have come to Canterbury to seek the help of Saint Thomas. My Archbishop also persuaded me," he paused and nodded to Morton, "that I require the help of all of you." He paused and looked sourly to his left, adding, "and he persuaded me to bring Edward Stafford, the Duke of Buckingham, at least for now, along with me."

Edward smiled thinly and bowed deeply, his face red.

The King looked at the group in the room curiously, saying blandly, "I know most of you, and I discern a certain lawyerly pattern to the group." His eyes paused on the two blond haired young men. He seemed to start a bit, but quickly recovered, saying, "You two I do not know."

Morton quickly cut in as the two young men started to both bend and speak, saying, "Your Highness, allow me to introduce Sir Edward Guildford and Doctor John Clement."

The young men bowed, keeping their eyes on the King.

The King replied nonchalantly, "your resemblance to my ailing wife is disconcerting." The boys looked up, concerned. Edward's head turned to the King.

The King's lips were neutral, his version of a smile, as he said, "fear not. Perkin Warbeck was a diversion. I knew that. A King..." he paused and looked curiously at Sir Edward, continuing, "a true King, knows that the only real power lies in having more information than everyone else." He stopped again and cast a nonchalant glance at Morton, adding, "though, I suppose that every King must have subjects who can give them a run for their money in that regard."

Morton nodded to his King with a small smile on his face.

The King continued, "you boys were never in exile, never in real danger, you were cosseted, then you were hidden." He paused again, glancing at John More and Henry Colet before saying, "very effectively, I might add. But you visited your mother on her deathbed a month ago." The boys faces blanched.

"Your half brother, Thomas Grey, is also talkative when drunk," the King added blandly, seeing the young men's discomfort.

Guildford and Clement both stole looks at each other, faces reddening. Edward Guildford glanced in the direction of the door, as if measuring the possibility of escape, his heart racing.

"Relax," said the King with a hollow, tinny laugh. "First, very few know your secret – most people think you both murdered years ago. Second, my wife is ill, and finding and executing her brothers wouldn't help her."

Thomas More studied the King, who seemed completely self possessed. He had mirthless eyes, and rotten teeth, which caused him to keep his lips firmly clamped over the blackened stubs. Thomas wondered idly what the Queen saw in him.

The King cast his eyes around the room. He looked at Morton again, asking, "Archbishop, why have you brought all these people here?"

Thomas's ears perked up. The Archbishop couldn't defy the King. The Archbishop looked unfazed. "Sire," he started slowly, "each of these people is part of the puzzle. I… we…

are all at your service, and at the Queen's. Each of us had made vows of one kind or another. We are all sworn, in one way or another to our King and to our Queen. The Queen is ill. I believe that Saint Thomas will help us to aide our Queen, as our cause is just and pure. And I believe that a visit from the Queen's brothers will also be restorative, most especially since one of them is a physician, recently trained in Italy with the great Doctors." The Archbishop stopped and looked at the King, who was listening intently, face neutral and bloodless.

After a short silence, the King replied slowly, asking, "but how is it they are alive?"

The boys blanched again.

John Morton continued, unfazed, explaining, "I'm not yet completely sure, I've only had a month to investigate…" He shot the boys a considerate glance. "But it seems that lawyers were involved." He nodded his head at John More, and discreetly smiled.

"As I recall, My clever Archbishop," the King said sardonically, "you too are a lawyer."

Thomas More started. He had not known that. It stunned him to realize that he had never asked, or even showed curiosity about John Morton. He had been, simply, "the Archbishop," or, "the Lord Chancellor." Thomas was embarrassed that it had never occurred to him that the Archbishop had once been fourteen and had to determine his path in life.

"In many ways, your Grace," Morton replied with a smile, "I remain but a humble canon lawyer."

"I don't know that the word 'humble' could ever really form an appropriate connection with you" the King replied drily, continuing, "but pray go on."

Morton laughed, and made a little bow to his King, then said "Anyway, sir, it would seem that your… ah… predecessor, Richard, had made a vow to his brother, your Queen's father, King Edward, that he would at all hazards protect the King's children."

The King's eyes arched. He looked over and studied Guildford and Clement again, who looked straight back at him. Edward Guildford made a respectful nod to the King."

Morton continued patiently, choosing words carefully. "England was in turmoil after King Edward's death. The Queen's brother, Lord Rivers took possession of the heir," he nodded to Guildford, "and the Queen took the other children into sanctuary at Westminster. Buckingham," Morton nodded to Edward Stafford, "Edward's father, met with Richard, and they met the heir and Rivers. Rivers was an ass to everyone, and basically argued that the Prince of Wales was in his possession, and was a minor, and that he would rule as King himself. Buckingham and Richard could not get him to see reason or law, in fact Rivers moved with troops against Richard's men, which was unfortunate, so Richard arrested him, tried him, and executed him, right there at Pontrefact."

"I was assured that Rivers was an innocent man executed by a tyrant," Henry said quietly.

"That was the story put out," Morton simply replied. "Richard realized that he was in a bind. He remembered the minority of Henry the Sixth, from which neither Henry nor England ever really recovered. The power struggles, the private wars, all to gain control of a child-King."

Morton waited while King Henry processed that. "My Father and Uncle," the King said quietly, almost under his breath, "were half brothers to that King Henry. They told me of those times. It is my greatest worry that I should leave Arthur a young heir."

"That was the situation that Richard faced," Morton said gently, "and he apparently decided that the welfare of his brother's children, at their ages, meant that he must take an unusual path."

"Displace them," the King said abruptly.

"Yes, my Lord," Morton said quietly. "We discussed it at length. I was opposed to such a step, but Hastings was violently so. I was excused from the meeting…Richard sent me to fetch him some strawberries…and while I was gone, tempers flared, Hastings threatening to kill Richard for even discussing it. And so Richard executed Hastings right then. On the spot. Richard was committed to what he saw as his only path forward."

Thomas More listened intently, but watched Guildford and Clement, who stood expressionless.

"The Princes were living comfortably at the Tower,. Richard was crowned King," Morton continued, "and their cousin, young Edward Stafford, frequently in their company. After about a year, though, the Duke of Buckingham, figuring that Richard was weak, decided to make a play for the throne himself. That ended….badly…for him."

The King said simply, "you were, as I remember, implicated in that plot as well."

Morton replied simply, "yes, I was. But not in the way many think. You see, I too had made a vow to King Edward to protect his children at all hazard. I was concerned about Buckingham's potential actions towards the Princes."

King Henry nodded.

Morton then continued, "and shortly after that, the Princes disappeared from the Tower, from London. I tried to reach out to Richard, to their mother, the Queen, but received no answer. I was frantic and in exile…" Morton stopped to collect his emotions.

"And?" Henry asked.

"And nothing…" Morton replied. "Never a word except for rumors that they had died abruptly in the Tower, either from disease or murder. I'm a patient man, your Grace, and so I had kept looking for these past seven years. Never a trace of them. I kept looking though…and last month your mother in law died."

The boys blanched, stiffening their posture.

"And the Princes surfaced," King Henry said, "visiting their dying mother."

"Yes, King Henry, the Princes surfaced," Morton said slowly, "and I took them into my custody, handing them off to Sergeant Fineaux for safe keeping while I sorted it out."

"Perkin Warbeck, the imposter?" King Henry asked. "Related?"

"No," replied the Archbishop, "I think that the family has never believed the Princes dead either, and these are feelers to draw the Princes out of hiding."

"And yet they were never drawn," the King said. "Except for their dying mother."

Thomas thought the King looked impressed. The boys remained standing stock still.

"So what do we do with them?" the King asked thoughtfully.

"I have some thoughts, your Majesty," Morton said with a smile. "but to explain them, I need to finish what I know of the tale."

King Henry nodded his agreement.

Morton continued, "It seems that Richard decided that the Princes would always be in mortal danger. While they were alive, some one or another would always be pushing their claim to the throne, trying to take possession of them or their names…."

Morton let that linger in the air for a bit, since that was also the experience of Henry Tudor, now King Henry and his childhood as bit player in the struggles for the throne. Then he continued, "and Richard apparently decided that the "Princes," the heirs to King Edward needed to be dead, so that the sons of his brother might live."

The Princes smiled a bit. Uncertain, but remembering their Uncle who tried to care for them. They looked at the King.

"I discovered," Morton continued, "that shortly before the Princes' final sighting in the Tower, that Richard had met with several people at the Guildhall in London, including the Lord Mayor," he paused and gestured to Henry Colet, "and an estimable London lawyer named John More." He gestured then to Thomas's father. "And then I found out that, in addition to the Princes, there were two other children at the meeting, Edward Stafford and his friend, young Thomas More." He completed this by gesturing for the King at Edward and then Thomas."

King Henry's eyes bore into Thomas More's face, and Thomas turned red and squirmed a bit. His father maintained a protective arm around his shoulder.

"Now, Thomas," Morton smiled warmly at Thomas, "as it happens has been my page for the past two years, and never breathed a word of this to me, or, as nearly as I can determine, to anyone else." He nodded in respect to Thomas. John's arm tightened a bit proudly on Thomas's shoulder.

"It would seem," the Archbishop said slowly, for emphasis, "that Richard engaged John More for the purposes of effecting his plan." He paused and smiled, "and wanted to ensure that it was done legally." He nodded again at John More. "It would appear that Richard chose well. It took me a while, but I found the papers. It would seem that a very nice minor noble couple in Offington in Wessex had a son Edward's age who, conveniently, had died of a fever just then. John More arranged for the Prince and heir to be adopted by the Guildford's as their son."

"You can do that?" the King asked with a raised voice.

"Yes, your Majesty," Morton replied respectfully, "you can. It's really tricky legal work. But, as I said, Richard had chosen well. The papers, the renunciation, any necessary payments and fines, all of it are iron clad. For all legal purposes this is Sir Edward Guildford before us here, not Prince, uncrowned, King Edward. And he cannot ever legally revert," Morton added with finality, looking at Guildford, who nodded assent.

"And the spare?" Henry asked, bloodlessly.

There was no other nobility who had recently lost a child, but a safe and likely family was found for him in Yorkshire, the Clements. Again the paperwork is iron clad, and this is John Clement who stands before you. Not noble, but obviously well educated. Something of a polymath, really. Has just finished his studies in Italy and is now a physician."

John Clement nodded to Morton.

"So, with that preamble," Morton said officially, "Your Highness with your permission, I should like to present to you two loyal subjects from the reaches of your Kingdom, Sir Edward Guildford of Wessex, and Dr. John Clement of Yorkshire."

The two blond haired brothers came forward and knelt with their heads down, hands clasped as if in prayer, in front of the King. In unison they both stretched their arms up as a position of submission to the King and said, "I promise on my faith that I will in the future be faithful to the King, never cause him harm and will observe my homage to him against all persons in good faith and without deceit."

The King seemed startled, but regrouped. His thin lips nearly curling upwards. He took the hands of each in turn, saying "I accept your fealty."

Morton beamed. The King gestured for Guildford and Clement to rise and return to the group. They did so gratefully backing up from the King.

The King looked again at Morton, who cleared his throat, and asked, "now what?"

Morton replied, "well, to tie up the loose ends of the story, I discovered that there was someone in England who knew the fate of the Princes, and who had never said anything to anybody. Even her husband." He nodded to Mary Wooler. Thomas turned and looked startled at Mary.

The Archbishop continued, "Mary Wooler is the wife of Godfrey, one of the King's men of the Tower for Edward and Richard. She was nurse and nanny to the boys while they lived at the Tower. At Richard's personal request, she took each of the boys by night to their new lives in the country. Mary, thank you so much for protecting King Edward's children."

"How is it that I do not know her then?" asked the King.

"Her husband, Godfrey was with Northumberland at Bosworth," Morton answered, calmly. "They left with their children for the north right after the battle. As it happens they were on Pilgrimage to Canterbury and ran into young Thomas More."

"And where is Godfrey, who was against me at Bosworth?" the King asked patiently.

"The Lord works in mysterious ways, your Highness," Morton replied. "Godfrey Wooler is outside right now as the Sergeant of an honor guard for you that is Captained by young Thomas Howard, here." He gestured blandly to the red haired, red-faced Thomas Howard. They will be greeting you as you leave the Cathedral after praying for your wife's health to St. Thomas."

"The Queen," the King exclaimed. "How does any of this help my Queen?"

Morton replied soothingly, "We shall all pray together to Saint Thomas, then we shall, if the King agrees, of course, travel with the King to Richmond Palace and attend upon our ailing Queen."

"And what help will that bring?" the King asked.

"The Queen just had a baby and is quite ill," Morton said happily, "we will be bringing her brothers, whom she has long thought dead, and one of whom is a physician newly trained in Italy." He paused for effect. "In addition, we would bring her a nurse, her own nurse from childhood, and her favorite cousin, Edward."

"And the need for the rest of them?" asked the King.

"A fair point," conceded the Archbishop, "there is a point in our story that I haven't worked out yet, and I believe that the Queen will want that answered, which is why Thomas More and Edward Stafford were at this meeting."

The King looked at John More and asked, "More, do you know why Richard insisted that you bring Thomas? Or you, Colet? Any thoughts?"

John More bowed and replied, "your Majesty, no idea at all. I thought it was to ensure my cooperation, but I don't think so. I have a thought that it was for the young Duke of Buckingham. He and my son were, are, quite close."

"A Duke and a Common Lawyer's son?" the King exclaimed. "Why?"

The Archbishop interjected, before either Edward or Thomas could speak, "Because the boys lived across the street from each other on Milk Street in London, and they are only three weeks apart in age. Either way, Edward and Thomas were at the meeting. And my sources tell me that Richard was quite taken with young Thomas, in fact they had a conversation that no one was able to overhear."

"W.w.w.here…?" sputtered John More.

The Archbishop cut him off sharply, saying, "I have my sources of information." He paused and looked at Thomas, asking, "are my sources correct, Thomas?"

"Yes, my Lord Archbishop," Thomas said, bowing slightly.

"What did Richard say to you, boy?" the King interjected.

"I swore him an oath never to tell," Thomas replied.

"Well, I am the King and I order you to tell!" the King said impatiently.

Thomas looked at his father and at the Archbishop.

*"Trust and love."*

"I am sorry, your Highness," Thomas said hesitantly, "I swore an oath. I cannot break that contract."

John More said gently, "Thomas, the other party to the contract has died. You are released."

Thomas said firmly, "King Richard said I was never to say. There was no end to the promise."

"But I am King," Henry said, "and Richard was a usurper, illegitimate. I order you to tell me."

"I am sorry your Highness," Thomas said, bowing low. When he stood, he looked at the King and at the Archbishop. The King looked impatient, but not angry, and the Archbishop looked amused.

Finally, the Archbishop broke in, saying, "as I said before, it would appear that Richard chose his people well. Its no matter, I have a thought as to Thomas's presence that day, which is that Richard also swore to the Duke of Buckingham that he would take care of his son." Morton turned to look at Edward Stafford, and asked, "isn't that right, your Grace?"

Edward seemed startled, and hesitated, before saying, quietly, "yes. The night before he was executed, Richard let my father come see me. To tell me goodbye."

The King started. He murmured quietly, "Richard did that for Buckingham?"

Edward nodded sadly.

Thomas felt for his friend, wanted to embrace him. The light from the great stained glass window that Thomas could see behind Edward changed a bit in that moment, giving a small aura around Edward. Thomas watched as the light brightened, expanded.

*"Love, Thomas. Feel it."*

Thomas allowed the light to expand, pulsing out to everyone in the group. Thomas looked at the Archbishop, and at his father, both bathed in the light. With an effort he moved light to each of the people in the room. He looked at the King, saw and felt his sadness, and he felt empathy for him, for his situation.

The image of another King Henry, in his tomb back in the Corona chapel, watching eternally over St. Thomas came to his mind, then he saw other Kings, milling about, as Thomas thought about the unbroken line of Kings. Finally, standing next to Henry, was a smiling King Richard. He was clean and regal looking. He smiled as his eyes met Thomas's.

"Ah, there you are," came Richard's disembodied voice, soft as a night breeze.

"King Richard!" thought Thomas. "How"

*"It's love, Thomas."*

Richard looked over at the two young Princes, now common men, but alive.

"It worked," Richard exclaimed happily.

"Yes, sir." Thomas thought. "It worked perfectly."

"Your father is a very good lawyer," Richard said, impressed.

"Yes he is," Thomas replied, adding, "and a good father."

Richard looked on happily, the room seemed to have stopped around them.

"I don't know what to do about King Henry," Thomas said. "He wants to know what you told me."

"What do you want to do," Richard asked.

"It would be a lot easier to just tell him," Thomas replied.

"Is that what you want to do?" Richard asked again.

"No," Thomas said definitively, "I want to keep my promise to you. I simply said it would be easier to tell."

Richard laughed, "the mouths of babes! I meant that, Thomas"

Thomas slumped back, thinking, "the real puzzle here is how to help the Queen."

*"Everything always works out the way it is supposed to, Thomas."*

"Yes, but I still have to choose."

*"Choose what?"*

"The course that gets us on our way to the Queen with her brothers. I think the Doctor is the key."

*"And"*

"And the King hasn't made up his mind yet. He doesn't have enough information. Enough trust."

*"Why would the King trust you, or any of this? Especially when you don't trust him? At least enough to confide in him what Richard said.*

"What do you mean?"

*"You mostly trust the Archbishop, and your father, and Edward. The rest of the men here you don't trust at all."*

"The men?"

*"Mary Wooler and Godfrey you trust completely. They we're on Pilgrimage with you. You need to learn to trust and love everyone. Only then will your Pilgrimage truly be complete."*

Thomas looked again at King Richard, who still stood to the side of King Henry. He was smiling and had his hands on his hips.

"Is that Mary Wooler over there?" Richard asked.

"It would seem that everyone knows Mary except for King Henry," Thomas replied. "Yes it is."

"She took the Princes to their new home," Richard said, "and like you she never told a soul."

Then he had an idea, saying quietly to the Archbishop, "My Lord Archbishop. K.k….Richard did say that I could ask for help in keeping my promise."

"What does that mean?" the King interjected.

"Sire," Thomas replied, "it means that Richard asked me to ensure that the world never knew the better parts of him… That the world thought him a villain capable of murdering his own nephews in cold blood."

"I am all right with that," the King replied evenly. "And it further protects those nephews, the brothers of my Queen. Let's leave it at that, then." He paused and looked at the Guildford and Clement, adding viciously, "and you two have my sufferance. But if either of you ever step even so much as a toe against me I will have you drawn and quartered as common traitors before anyone thinks twice about it."

"Yes, your Highness," the boys responded, "we understand."

The Archbishop eyed Thomas shrewdly, then turned to the group, saying, let us return to Saint Thomas for the safe delivery of our Queen."

"For our Queen," they all replied, and they turned to the main door of the Chapter house, away from the great saints of the stained glass window, as the King swept past them.

The Mores, father and son, looked at each other and shrugged, moving off the room the was they had come, following the hurrying King back through the North Aisle and up the steps again past the Black Prince. At the top, the group stopped abruptly as the King first beheld the tomb and the pile of treasure. His eyes glinted especially brightly at the treasure.

Thomas still saw the lights playing all over the room. St. Thomas was now atop his tomb, and he gave Thomas a little wave, then pantomimed the act of moving the love around among all the people.

"This is Becket?" the King asked.

"Has his Majesty never before visited?" the Archbishop tentatively asked.

"Never," replied the King hastily, asking, "the box up there is it?"

"Yes," the Archbishop replied evenly, his eyes a mask, "the relics are in the box, there."

"What do I do, Archbishop?" the King asked.

"Pray to St. Thomas for intercession for the Queen," the Archbishop answered. "We can all pray with you, or we can leave you alone."

The King looked uncertainly at the reliquary box. He turned to Thomas More, and said, "You, boy."

Thomas bowed respectfully.

The King said, "I notice you are wearing a pilgrim's robe. Did you pilgrimage here?"

"I did, your Majesty," Thomas replied.

"And what did you see?" asked the King with a curious tone.

"Here," Thomas answered, "I saw, and still see the lights from the window, and I see St. Thomas atop his tomb. I see the rays of love that connect all of us."

The King looked at Thomas. A wave of irritation passed across his face as he said, "I see nothing of the kind, young man." He looked at the group, and asked, "does anyone else see what this boy describes?"

Mary Wooler, alone in the group shyly raised her hand.

"Madam Pilgrim," the King asked, "what do you see?"

"I see the lights that Thomas sees," Mary replied simply, "and a monk in a white robe whom I assume to be Saint Thomas." She giggled nervously as a little hiccup.

"What was that, Mrs. Wooler?" the Archbishop asked.

"St. Thomas waved at me," she said shyly. "And winked."

Thomas laughed a single snort, but then noticed his father staring at him, and stifled it.

"Perhaps it is a function of the Pilgrimage, Sire," the Archbishop said soothingly.

"None of the rest of you?" the King asked icily.

None raised their hand.

"And you, my Lord Archbishop," the King said, "surely you see your predecessor?"

"Alas, your Highness," the Archbishop said, "I have long prayed for such a vision, dreamt it, hoped for it, but it has not yet been given me."

"Useless," the King said. "I knew this was a waste of time." He seemed stricken. "The Queen. What of the Queen?"

The Archbishop came forward tentatively. "Perhaps, King Henry," he said quietly, "If you, Thomas and Mary were to pray together. Perhaps their gift may be extended to you. Perhaps

St. Thomas will use them to intercede for the Queen. Your hopes are, after all, for the Queen and not yourself."

The King had moved around the tomb, the treasure, studying it, staring at it, as if he were trying to will the vision. He appeared to grow frustrated.

"We should leave," the King said, "I need to get back to my wife."

Edward Stafford had moved over near Thomas and had taken his hand. The two old friends looked at each other and Edward mouthed the question, "you really see it?"

Thomas smiled sadly at his friend, and nodded, "yes."

The Archbishop moved over to his King and said, "Yes, Sire, of course, but the arrangements to leave will take a little bit. How about if you, Thomas and Mary stay here to pray, and the rest of us go make ready. It is early yet, but today is the Feast Day, and there will be crowds outside. I would like to make ready and I would like to give you some time in peace."

The King looked up and nodded, saying, "that makes sense. But we mustn't tarry long."

"Yes, Sire, of course," said the Archbishop,

After a moment's thought, the King held up his hand, saying, I would like the boys to stay as well." He pointed at Guildford and Clement, "and Stafford as well."

"Certainly, your Majesty," the Archbishop replied, "may I ask why?"

"Because I don't trust them to emerge to a large crowd and announce that the King couldn't see anything, but they could," the King replied frostily, "Happy Feast of St Thomas."

Thomas saw Saint Thomas smile at that and cross his arms.

Guildford and Clement's faces burned red. Thomas could not tell whether from anger or embarrassment. Edward simply looked amused and gave Thomas's hand another squeeze.

The Archbishop smiled warmly, saying, "as you wish, Sire. The rest of us, let us go make preparations. We shall leave for Richmond shortly." He then turned on his heel and made his way past the Fourth King Henry and out the eastern transept door. Thomas could see a sizeable crowd outside, but the door quickly closed as that group made their way outside.

The King turned to the remaining five – Thomas and Mary Wooler, Edward, John Clement and Edward Guildford. He walked slowly around them, studying them, not menacing, just a keen look like a cat deciding whether a sighting is proper prey or a friend.

Finally, the King spoke, saying "Edward Stafford, what do you have to say for your friend Thomas, here."

"He is my best friend, your Highness," Stafford replied simply. "I trust him completely."

The King humphed, saying, "that would be helpful if I trusted you completely."

Edward reddened. St. Thomas frowned.

Thomas looked at Mary and gave a little shrug.

"I don't know what to do," Thomas thought.

*"What do you want to happen?"*

"Honestly, I'd like to be a ways away from the King."

*"Fair enough…Why?"*

"He frightens me. He could really do anything he wants."

*"But will he? He seems…frightened."*

"He is King. What does he have to be frightened of?"

"Whom do you trust completely?"

"Father, Edward, the Archbishop, Mr. Cheeseman. A lot of people."

*"Who can he trust completely?"*

Thomas thought. Finally it came to him.

"The Queen?"

*"Anyone else?"*

"Maybe his own mother, but she's tough. I met her once."

*"Precisely. If he feels he cannot trust, how does he eat, sleep?"*

"So what do I do?"

Thomas knew though without his own internal answer. He waked towards the King, saying, "Your Majesty, may I speak?"

The King, who was now leaning on King Henry IV, silently studying the writing engraved in the black stone, looked up at Thomas from his thoughts, and nodded for him to proceed.

"Your Majesty," Thomas began hesitantly, "you said that you had never been here before."

The King nodded assent again.

"But you know the story of St. Thomas?" Thomas persisted.

"Of course," the King said. His voice was rising in irritation, but he realized that and controlled it.

Thomas thought for a moment, and decided to continue.

"I wonder, Sire," Thomas asked, "how Saint Thomas Becket's story must look to a King?"

The King looked startled, and first blurted out, "why do you wonder that?"

Thomas held steady, "it would seem to me, your Highness, that the perspective must be different."

The King cast looks at the other four in the chapel, who were studiously examining the ground.

"It is said," the King said finally, "that Thomas Becket and the second King Henry had been the best of friends. That the rupture came over Becket's defiance of the will of the King. It has been assumed that Henry was hurt that his friend would disagree with him so publicly. Then Henry, in anger, was heard to ask, 'will no one rid me of this troublesome priest?' Feeling that license had been given, four idiots came and killed the Archbishop of Canterbury."

The King stopped and looked at Thomas. Over the King's shoulder Thomas saw Saint Thomas looking and listening intently.

The King continued, "I think the story is wrong on a few points… First, a King doesn't have friends. The King is alone. I do not believe that King Henry was hurt over the defiance of a friend, I think he was angry at the resistance of a subject. And I think that he was angry at himself for making that subject so powerful that he felt public resistance was possible. Second, I fault King Henry for not realizing that every word uttered by a King has import. Henry had difficulty controlling his temper, and that served him ill."

The King looked downward, sadly. Saint Thomas watched intently. Thomas More concentrated on the lights connecting everyone in the room. He noticed how thin the connections were to the King.

Thomas More said quietly, "but Sire, you are not alone."

The King looked up.

Thomas continued, "you said before, you have the Queen."

"Perhaps not for long," the King said sadly.

"Forever," Thomas said. "No matter what, you will always have the Queen. Her spirit…Her soul will always be with you, no matter what."

The King sighed, saying, "You are young. And you have never borne the burden of being King."

"Nor will I ever, Your Majesty," Thomas replied in a respectful tone. "But I think that each of us has a person or two whom we can trust absolutely, no matter what. The question is will we trust?"

"And if that trust is mislaid?" the King asked sardonically.

Thomas answered thoughtfully, "I think that I believe, Sire, that trust can be betrayed, but never mislaid. The act of offering trust is Christian, and human."

"How old are you, Thomas," the King asked.

"Fourteen, Sire," Thomas replied.

"What does a fourteen year old know of anything?" the King asked, "Can you even grow a beard yet?"

"I'm trying," Thomas said, touching the back of his hand to his clear face. "I feel like it is just nearly there."

The King laughed a bit.

Thomas concentrated a bit on the connecting lights, tried to move some of that energy to the King, to increase his connection. Oddly, the King resisted.

While thinking about the light, Thomas had maintained a rather fixed look on his face, simply gazing at the King.

After a moment, the King asked, "is there anything else you would like to ask me, Thomas while we wait for the Saint to appear?"

"I wonder, Sire," Thomas asked after a moment. "My father once told me to be wary of noblemen because all they really care about is their own survival."

Edward and the two former Princes stepped forward, saying, "Hey there Thomas."

The King held up his hand and they stopped in their tracks. "That was a statement, Thomas," the King said quietly, "not a question."

"Yes, Sire," Thomas answered respectfully, trying not to look at Edward and lose his nerve. "My question, your Majesty, is whether that is true?"

The King looked seriously at Thomas. Thomas noted that the light between them flickered a bit, like a candle lighting. His thin lips curled a bit, nearly into a smile. After a moment, the King said, "you have been a Page in the Archbishop's court, and your best friend is a rather notable nobleman." He acknowledged Edward ever so slightly before continuing, "what does your experience tell you?"

Thomas thought hard about his answer. "It depends, I suppose" he started out slowly, "upon the nobleman. I've seen great generosity and great selfishness."

"Not the frank answer, I would have expected from the Thomas More that Edward Stafford described as being 'honest to the point of pain'," replied the King drily.

The light between them waned.

*"Love and trust, Thomas."*

"Very well, your Highness," Thomas replied, taking a deep breath. "I am only fourteen, and in that time I have only seen three people of nobility behave in a manner that I would consider 'selfless;' who in an action, a deed or thought, put others truly first, even at risk to themselves."

Edward looked expectantly at Thomas. Thomas gave a small, sad shake of his head in reply. The King caught it.

"I am guessing that Edward is not on the list, based upon that little exchange," the King said with a little amusement.

"My great friend Edward has not been put in a position of having to decide such a matter," Thomas replied evenly, adding "at least in my presence. I can say that he has always been a good friend to me, and there would be no reason for that other than friendship, so perhaps that is evidence of Edward's character."

Edward relaxed a bit, and the King replied, "that is fair enough. Well then who are these three paragons?"

Thomas smiled, "I can't speak to paragons, but I admire each of them immensely. The first is Lord Mountjoy, William Blount, whom I just really met on Pilgrimage. He joined us and has been immeasurably kind and supportive, as I am sure our friend, Mary Wooler, would attest."

Thomas turned and smiled at Mary, who said, "Your Highness, I agree completely, Lord Mountjoy is the reason we were able to complete the Pilgrimage. He even cared for my children when I was overcome with fatigue last evening. He has been…what was your word, Thomas? … Selfless."

The King frowned a bit, eyes wide, surprised, and said, "Mountjoy…That is interesting. I shall remember that. Thank you for telling me. Who else?"

Thomas thought for a moment, trying to decide whom to name next. Deciding, Thomas replied, "your Queen, Sire."

"Elizabeth?" King Henry replied.

"The Queen," Thomas replied firmly, "is endlessly helpful and charming. She is remarkably kind, and has helped me, and Edward, and really everyone I've ever seen come to her. She has, in my experience, always behaved selflessly and kindly to everyone. And, I suspect, it would have been easier for her to do otherwise. Her very nature seems selfless."

"Elizabeth," Henry repeated softly, his eyes a mask. Thomas noticed the light around Henry strengthening. Thomas mentally moved to expand it, as the King pondered his love for his wife.

After a moment more, King Henry looked up, his eyes a tiny bit moist around the edges. He spoke quietly, saying, "you mentioned a third, Thomas. Who was it?"

Thomas hesitated. The light between them flickered.

*"Love and trust, Thomas."*

Thomas still hesitated, looking forlornly at the King.

The King asked softly, "was it King Richard, Thomas?"

Thomas nodded, choking up.

"Don't be afraid of me, Thomas," the King said gently. "How was he selfless? I should like to know your thoughts."

Thomas straightened up, saying quietly, "I was with Edward in St. Paul's when King Richard allowed Edward's father leave before his execution to come to Edward and say goodbye."

He turned to Edward, saying, "I am so sorry, Edward." Edward had teared up, and waved Thomas off."

"Is that it, Thomas?" asked the King.

"No, Sire," Thomas replied quietly, looking round at the Princes. "I made a solemn promise to King Richard not to reveal what he asked me, but I believe he wouldn't mind." Thomas looked up to Saint Thomas, who nodded and smiled. Thomas leaned in, saying quietly to King Henry, "King Richard saved the Princes, you now know that, but he ordered me that no one know that he had. He felt that the Princes would be safer if everyone thought that he had killed them as threats to his own kingship. He made me swear to never speak about the best act of his life – saving his nephews out of loyalty to his brother. The secret that he made me swear was that the King of England protects children."

Exhausted, Thomas slumped. Out of the corner of his eye, he espied his rolled up manuscript, left in honor of St. Thomas. The sight of it strengthened him. He stood up straight again, and glanced at St. Thomas, who was looking solemnly back, nodding.

To his surprise, King Henry was also nodding. Thomas noticed the light between them had thickened and brightened. The King looked at Guildford and Clement, and said, "did you know this?"

The two boys nodded.

"And you accepted it? The risk that your Uncle was taking for you?" they looked confused, perhaps defiant.

"Richard was correct," Henry said, suddenly to Guildford, "you were not ready to be King. You were just a boy, but, I am guessing, not a particularly brave one."

Edward Guildford looked at him, a little anger creeping into his face.

King Henry said, "Don't bother being angry Sir Edward Guildford. You accepted being a humble knight in the country because you valued your life over anything else. Same for you Dr. Clement. I have nothing to fear from either of you. I am King. I won the Crown in Battle, defeating a man far more noble, more Kingly, than either of you. I married your sister, who is now my Queen, and a great credit to our country. Most importantly, I love your sister, I love my Kingdom, my country, my citizens, more than my own life."

The light was now blazing around King Henry. To Thomas's eyes he seemed to grow in stature. St. Thomas watched, his face a mask.

"Thomas," the King said simply. "Thank you."

Thomas bowed to the King, who continued to brighten. As he straightened, he looked back up at St. Thomas, who nodded solemnly.

"Your Highness," Thomas said quietly, "I was wondering if you could see St. Thomas now?"

The King looked startled, and turned slowly back to the tomb and the pile of gifts. Slowly he turned his head upward, and…

"I see him, Thomas," the King said quietly. "Thank you." He sank to his knees, and bowed his head, praying quietly, "St. Thomas, please save my wife. I don't know how I should live without her."

Thomas also went to his knees near the King, praying, "please St. Thomas, intercede with God on behalf of Queen Elizabeth."

There was light around these two. Then Mary Wooler joined them, praying for the Queen.

At the sides, Edward, Guildford, and Clement seemed confused as to what to do, though when the King went to his knees in prayer, they automatically followed suit, and when the King prayed to St. Thomas, they did as well.

Standing up, the King said quietly, "Thank you St. Thomas," and crossed himself. He then pulled a golden ring with a large ruby off of his finger and placed it on the pile at the base of the tomb.

Edward, Guildford, and Clement looked at each other. Edward very quietly asked the other two, "did you see anything?" Small head shakes were his response.

The King turned from St. Thomas back to the group, and said, "Sir Edward Guildford and Dr. John Clement, you have no cause to worry about me. As long as these are your identities, you are safe from any persecution. But Richard was correct, you are safest if everyone concerned believes the Princes to be dead – and legally they are - so let us keep it that way. I think my wife would like her brothers in court – hidden in plain sight, as it were. And Dr. Clement, since my wife is grievously ill, a physician for a brother could be very useful. Will you accompany me to Richmond?"

"Yes, of course, your Majesty," the boys replied immediately.

"Good, then," said King Henry. "I trust you." And he turned and his thin lips curled upward towards Thomas. A smile. "Thomas," the King added, "of course no one must ever hear a word of this."

"No one must ever know of your best act?" Thomas asked impishly.

"Precisely," the King replied, "such is the burden of the good King. We should get moving. I believe we have tied up St. Thomas long enough, and there are plenty of pilgrims outside waiting to see him."

"And their King, as well," Thomas added.

"Ah yes," Henry replied, "their King as well."

With a side glance, a nod and a little salute to St. Thomas Becket, the King of England swept wordlessly past the tomb of the earlier King Henry, out the south aisle, and opened himself the large door leading outside.

Thomas and the rest were right at his heels as the door opened out into the hot July sun. The crowd noises immediately hushed as all saw the King and immediately fell to their knees.

All that is, except for the two rows of soldiers, making a path down on either side of the door. The soldiers were wearing the green of the King's men and were each holding long sharpened poles erect with their right hands. The closest on either side, on the left was Thomas Howard, standing full erect, a sword quickly unsheathed and held up in salute. On the right was a large, hairy soldier, clad in the dirty brown robes of a pilgrim. He held a Sergeant's sword in the air, and bellowed, "All Hail the King of England, Henry, the seventh of that name!"

The King smiled again, still thinly, but definitely a smile. "Please everyone, arise." The King said. "Polemen?!" the King said, surprised, looking at Thomas Howard.

"Yes, your Highness." Thomas Howard replied, unsure of how much to speak.

"I thought the English armies didn't want to adopt polemen," the King said, adding, "thought to be 'too French.'"

Thomas suppressed a smile, looking at Godfrey. Mary looked down, trying not to laugh.

Thomas Howard stepped forward confidently, a soldier now, "begging your pardon, your Highness, your Polemen won at Bosworth. I know, they killed my grandfather and seriously wounded my father. I am your soldier, Sire, and I like to win." He bowed respectfully to the King.

"Where did you learn of the Polemen, Captain Howard," the King asked.

"From my Sergeant, Sir, Godfrey Wooler," replied Howard, gesturing to Godfrey.

"A Pilgrim Sergeant?" the King asked, looking at Godfrey.

"Aye, Sir," Godfrey replied with a salute and a bow.

"And Mary is your wife?" the King asked.

"Aye, Sire, she is," Godfrey replied warmly.

"Then you are a lucky man," stated evenly. "Where is your uniform?"

"I was on pilgrimage with my family," Godfrey answered the King, "when I met Thomas Howard, as he was friends with my travelling partner, Thomas More. I saw the greatness in Captain Howard, and he kindly made me his Sergeant. Obviously pending your approval, Sire."

The King turned to Thomas More, saying, "all roads lead to More?" He giggled a little at what was nearly a pun, then turned to Howard, "we shall need to acquire a uniform for your Sergeant in short order, Captain," the King added, "and by the looks of him we will need to shear an extra sheep."

The Archbishop approached and bowed, saying, "Your majesty, we should probably…"

The King cut him off kindly, saying, "yes of course, My Lord Archbishop, but first I should like to greet the pilgrims, and I am told Lord Mountjoy is here. I would like a word with him."

"Of course, your Highness," the Archbishop replied, surprised.

The Archbishop turned and motioned to Lord Mountjoy and to Cuthbert. Mountjoy was still in his gold and black, though it appeared a little cleaner than before. The two approached the King and bowed, saying "yes your majesty."

The King looked first at Mountjoy, saying, "Lord Mountjoy, I have been hearing great reports of your character, and the estimable Mrs. Wooler says that you even babysat her children last night. When the Queen is better, I would like to speak with you of children."

"Yes, your Majesty," Mountjoy replied, happy, but confused.

"Trust and Love, my dear Mountjoy," the King replied, smiling again.

The Archbishop caught Thomas's eye. Thomas shrugged imperceptibly.

"I don't know you," the King said to Cuthbert.

"I am Cuthbert Tunstall, a student," Tunstall replied.

"Ah," the King replied, "I do know your father. He is a good man, in my estimation. Are ye friends with this group?"

"Happily, I am," Cuthbert replied.

The Archbishop broke in, "he is also a deacon of the church, your Highness, I have claimed him."

"A deacon, eh," said the King. "My Lord Archbishop, does the young deacon have the funds to study in Italy?"

"I don't know, your Highness," the Archbishop replied, and, turning to Cuthbert, asked, "Deacon Tunstall, the King would like to know if you have the funds to study in Italy."

Cuthbert blushed bright red, stammering, "N..n..n..o, y.y.y.our Majesty."

"Please see to it that he does, My Lord Archbishop," the King said kindly.

"My pocket or yours, your Majesty?" the Archbishop asked with a smile.

"You claimed him as one of yours, My Lord Archbishop," the King replied happily, "and we are at your Cathedral, not my palace. So I would say yours."

"As you wish, Sire," the Archbishop said with a smile and a bow.

The King turned finally back to Thomas Howard, who snapped to attention, calling out, "Sire."

"Relax, Howard," the King said in a friendly way. "You have done well with these, my polemen. I am impressed. I suspect that Somerset will be enraged to see how well turned out you all are."

Thomas Howard sagged a bit, "Somerset, Sire?"

"Yes, Howard," the King replied. "Your Captain, sent you off here to see you fail. Weak chin."

"Yes Sire," Howard replied, all the attention in his voice. Then a pause, "sent to fail?"

"Don't worry, Howard," the King replied softly, "we shall teach you Court politics. But from what I see, you are a soldier."

"Yes Sire!" Howard replied happily.

"Your father is up defending the North for me," the King went on. "I believe that you should be joining him with these men, but only after you all accompany me to Richmond to attend to my wife. Then, when she recovers, you may make your case to your Queen and King about why you should be allowed to go forth with your betrothal to her sister, the Princess Anne."

"Sir?" Howard replied, confused but hopeful.

"You have begun to prove yourself to me," King Henry replied. "I think I should like you as a brother in law." He paused, then added with a wink, "but first, of course, you must convince the Queen of your worth."

"Sire," the Archbishop leaned in, "I was wondering. You mentioned Somerset, and you came into the Chapter House alone. Did you leave your guards somewhere?"

The King laughed, forgetting to cover his teeth. "Oh yes. My men. They are, I believe waiting outside the Chapter House door that I entered. Somerset will be pissed."

The Archbishop nodded to the Abbot, who had approached, and signaled to him to go retrieve the men and bring them around the Cathedral to this yard.

The Older men, and the Wooler children had all been attracted to the commotion. The men all bowed, and the King bowed in return, welcoming them into his presence.

John More looked quizzically at his son, who shrugged and smiled.

The King turned to the Archbishop, saying in a loud voice, "My Lord Archbishop, I think that we have kept these holy pilgrims from Saint Thomas Becket long enough. Would you mind if I said a few words?"

"You are their, our, King, your Majesty," the Archbishop replied with a bow.

There were some cheers from the people that quieted quickly as the King cleared his throat to speak.

"My loyal Englishmen," the King began, "today is the Feast of the Translation of Saint Thomas Becket. It marks the movement of the remains of a uniquely English saint into the beautiful chapel you are about to see. You all know that St. Thomas and the King, the second Henry had a disagreement, and that supposed friends of the King came and grievously slew the Archbishop in this very church. You will see where this Holy man, this wholly English man was martyred, where he died for all English men."

The crowd sucked in its breath.

The King continued, "I believe that that King and that Archbishop fell out, not over policy, but over a lack of trust and love between them, and from the stories, where trust and love had once been quite bountiful."

The King paused, debating, "I have just visited with the Saint."

A murmur through the crowd.

"I can tell you," the King continued, "that this is sacred ground, this cathedral, this chapel, the tomb of this Saint. God lives and courses through this place. Take a breath and feel it course through your body. That healing, that trust, that Love! runs straight from Saint Augustine, through Saint Thomas Becket to us here today. Please know that your King prays with you here today and always. And so, like my predecessors, I pause to kneel,"

The King knelt in prayer, quickly followed by everyone in the courtyard. After a moment of silent prayer, the King crossed himself and stood. The rest of the crowd stood up quietly as well.

The King looked at the now arisen Archbishop, and asked in a loud voice, "My Lord Archbishop, would you do us the honor of a prayer for Saint Thomas?"

The Archbishop bowed, then raised his right hand, thumb to forefinger and made the sign of the cross, saying, "*Sancte Deo…*"

The King raised his hand slightly, saying quietly, "My Lord Archbishop, these are Englishmen, not Romans, perhaps, just this once, we could pray in English?"

The Archbishop looked startled, then smiled broadly, crying out happily, "Certainly, your Majesty! And began again *O God, for the sake of whose Church the glorious Bishop Thomas fell by the sword of ungodly men: grant, we beseech Thee, that all who implore his aid, may obtain the good fruit of his petition. Through our Lord Jesus Christ, Who livest and reignest with Thee in the unity of the Holy Spirit, forever and ever.*"

The King and all the rest said "Amen," and crossed themselves.

The doors to the Cathedral were opened, and the King made a "you may go in" gesture to the crowd, and stood happily as they filed past, knuckling their foreheads, bowing or curtseying as they past. All happy to see their King.

Once the crowd had moved into the church, the Archbishop approached the King, saying, "and now, Sire, we really must begin our journey to Richmond to the Queen."

The King agreed with a nod, then said, "I have a ship waiting at Whitestable. That will take us to London, and then we will proceed apace from the Bridge to Richmond by barge." He paused for a moment, then looked at the troops coming around the far corner of the Cathedral, saying, "Ah…here comes Somerset. Howard, you better act smart."

Thomas Howard and Sergeant Wooler snapped to attention and began calling out orders. To the surprise of many, Godfrey and Howard took positions nest to the King, and the soldiers rapidly formed a circle around the King, their Captain and Sergeant, with their sharpened poles positioned out at a low angle and snapping their shields up, with a loud clap as they met.

Several onlookers, stragglers entering the Cathedral clapped.

Somerset, Sergeant Egliston, and their soldiers approached. Somerset was angry, Egliston appeared amused. The King, as was his wont, had a neutral, observing expression.

"What's all this?" Somerset cried as he approached. "Howard, where have you been? You've been missing for days with these men?"

"I am where you sent me, Sir," Howard replied respectfully but firmly, "I am at the King's side in Canterbury."

The King's face remained a mask.

"And what's with these poles? We don't fight French, Howard," Somerset continued, adding, "and who is that person with you?"

The King suddenly cut in, dryly saying, "typically, My Lord Somerset, a soldier in the King's army, upon approaching the King will acknowledge the King before proceeding on to berate a junior officer in front of the King. But I understand your concern for me at my disappearance from your care on the other side of the Cathedral might have outweighed your need for manners. Please allow me to introduce Sergeant Godfrey Wooler…Captain Howard's Sergeant-at-Arms, I believe?"

The King turned to Howard, who nodded, saying, "yes, your Majesty."

The King then said, with studied amicability, "Captain Howard and Sergeant Wooler, as your subordinates have been sharing how, upon your orders, they were able to arrive as an advance party here at Canterbury, on a feast and fair day, no less, to secure our Royal Presence, and to ensure that we are able to swiftly accomplish our tasks here in order to expeditiously return to our ailing Queen in her time of need. I thank you for your diligence and foresight in sending this estimable force for me."

Somerset's mouth moved, but no words emerged.

"I am further informed," the King then continued, "that you have been experimenting with Polemen in our forces, that, while perhaps French in origin, greatly facilitated God's will in my victory over the usurper at Bosworth. You honor us, Captain, thank you."

Sergeant Egliston looked down to avoid laughing. Somerset nodded, and mumbled, "thank you, your Majesty." Looking around, he noticed Guildford and Clement standing off to the side. His mouth dropped a bit, thinking they looked familiar.

The King quickly intercepted that look, and said, "Somerset, I believe you know most of the people around here, except these two gentlemen from the country, recently arrived to our Court. Allow me to introduce Sir Edward Guildford, of Kent, and Doctor John Clement, of Yorkshire."

Somerset nodded greetings.

"Excellent," the King continued, "and now, we must be off, I think, to attend to the Queen."

The King then moved between his soldiers, and made off heading back around the Cathedral to the North.

The rest of the group just stood there for a moment as the King abruptly strode off, as if in a trance. The King abruptly stopped and turned around, saying, "surely the King shall not be allowed to wander off alone a second time in one morning?"

Coming to, the soldiers snapped to attention and quickly made ranks around the King, who continued off to the north.

The rest walked quickly behind their entourage, closing that initial gap.

John More came up next to his son, and quietly asked, "what happened in the Cathedral, Thomas?"

"I cannot say, Father," Thomas replied respectfully, "for that is between the King and I. Bu I may offer the hope and belief that St. Thomas is with us."

John More observed, "the King seems happier than I've ever seen him, and his wife is, I am told, quite ill."

"Love and trust, Father," Thomas replied. "Let's call it a Canterbury tale."

John More shook his head lovingly, and Thomas let out a bounding, delighted laugh that only a 14 year old boy who has just cracked himself up can emit.

The long boats had just arrived at the Thames docks for Richmond Palace. The group exiting from the boats had traveled by ship from Whitestable up the Thames to the docks by London Bridge. They had all boarded a fast river cruiser that worked by both sail and oar at Whitestable, just north of Canterbury in the ocean right at the mouth of the Thames. The boats had sailed for a few hours up and through the Thames, past so many of the spots they had just passed on the southern shore on foot. The group waved at the massing ships in Sittingbourne, and Thomas told his father the story of Brother Will as they passed the large Fort in Rochester. The boat put in briefly and the Princess Bridget, the Queen's sister came aboard. She smiled and waved at Thomas as she alit, but then went into the cabins where the King had set up office.

They passed Greenwich, Edward looking imploringly at Thomas once again. They could see Alicia Percy Stafford on a horse on the lawn, watching the ship pass. Edward waved at her and, to Thomas's surprise, she waved back.

"Better at home, Edward?" Thomas asked.

Edward blushed.

The crowd on deck grew excited as the Tower of London came into view. The lower water gate for traitors to enter ignominiously passed, and Thomas admired the very old stone towers and their domed tops.

The boat turned rightward as the London bridge neared, to the docks between the Tower and the Bridge.

Thomas More and Edward laughed and pointed at the rushing water and their starling. Thomas Howard playfully hit More on the shoulder. Mountjoy and Tunstall were about to join in when the Archbishop came up from behind, and brought the boys back into line with a warning cough.

Fortunately, the King had not heard. After tying up, and visitors from the City arriving to greet the King, the group alighted from the cruiser at the dock, went up and around on the London side, of the bridge, and back down to the water to the King's barges. Sir Henry Colet and his son, John, made their goodbyes, and headed up the hill into the City. The high spire of Saint Paul's towered over the scene, guarding and protecting London as Thomas assumed it always had.

Thomas had seen the King's barges from the shore before, and they were a real spectacle, low slung longboats with a dozen oarsmen in the front, and a red silt cabin with gold dragons embroidered on the roof. In the prow stood a brightly uniformed soldier holding a halberd. Thomas's heart fluttered a bit at the weapon, as it always did.

The King alit in the lead barge. As he entered, his pennant arose, a red dragon on a white field. Others entered barges in accordance with rank, or general desire for company.

Thomas, his father and friends were on the fourth barge to set out upstream for Richmond, but the oarsmen were all strong and, aided by a rising tide, the barges covered the seven miles or so to Richmond Palace quite quickly, one or more of the barges in convoy breaking off at various palaces up the River. There was a brief pause at Westminster where, begging leave, Sergeant Fineaux and his son-in-law Roper disembarked, claiming business at the courts.

Thomas More looked up from the small pier at the landfill and Westminster Palace and Hall, with the Abbey looming off in the distance. His father was able from the water to point out the law courts and Westminster Hall. Looking across the River, Thomas was able to spot

Lambeth Palace, where he had so happily served the Archbishop for two years. In the barge ahead, he saw the Archbishop, made eye contact, pointed to Lambeth and waved. The Archbishop happily waved back.

The barges proceeded upriver, passing Chelsea, which was beautiful as always, with gardens lining the banks in full July bloom. At one point, Thomas was certain he saw a grove of mulberry trees, their white ripe fruit in lovely contrast to the deep green leaves.

It was evening when the group arrived at the docks of the Palace of Sheen in Richmond. The Palace was of white stone with a large footprint but only three or four stories tall. There was a castellated wall and a surrounding moat. Off to the left, Thomas saw Carthusian monks, in their white robes moving about silently in the gardens of their adjacent monastery. Even from a few boats back Thomas was able to see the King's face become radiant as the Palace came into view. He had no doubt that the King viewed this particular palace as his home, and he recognized the look, as the same one he and his siblings got when speaking of Milk Street.

The King bounded off the first barge, and set off apace across the green lawn to the entrance to the Palace. His soldiers, Godfrey included, made haste off the next barge. Thomas and his friends came off later, and looked at each other for leadership in following the earlier group. They all looked at Edward Stafford, who smiled confidently, saying, "the King will have gone that way," and he pointed. "The Queen's chambers are over there." A vague hand gesture to the left side of the building.

As they set off, the Archbishop approached John and Thomas More, saying "John and Thomas, might I have a word?"

Father and son slowed, John answering, "of course."

The Archbishop placed hands on both More's, and said, "I want to thank you both for your help. I think the Princes are safe with the King now, and the King seemed as happy as I have ever seen him. Thomas, did he see St. Thomas?"

"I believe so, my Lord Archbishop," Thomas answered. He held up for a second, chewing on another question.

The Archbishop noticed, and said, "you may ask your question Thomas."

"Yes, My Lord," Thomas answered hesitantly. "At the Cathedral, you said only the people who had seen St. Thomas should stay…"

"Yes," the Archbishop replied kindly, "and?"

"Well Sir," Thomas continued, "on the tour you gave us, it seemed obvious to me that you had seen him."

"And?" said the Archbishop.

"Well," Thomas said, confused, "you excused yourself."

"Why would I do that, Thomas?" the Archbishop enquired.

"I don't know why you would say you hadn't when you had," Thomas blurted out.

"Did I say I hadn't," the Archbishop asked.

"You excused yourself," Thomas repeated.

"Thomas," the Archbishop explained patiently, "I had no idea whether the King would see St. Thomas. I did not want the King to be under the pressure of his Archbishop and Lord Chancellor being able to see something, of being given a Grace, that was not available to him. A couple of commoners, maybe, but not the Archbishop."

"But you left Edward Guildford and John Clement?" Thomas said.

"I wanted the King to see that he had nothing to fear from them," the Archbishop said. "And if the King saw St. Thomas and they did not, so much the better." He let that sink in, then said, "and I have a question for you, Thomas."

John's ears perked up, as his son replied, "yes, my Lord."

"So after the pilgrimage," the Archbishop proceeded, "and St. Thomas, and whatever else you've seen and heard and spoken about internally…" Morton paused and weighed Thomas's startled look at him. "Yes, Thomas. You are not the only one. We all probably have His voice in our heads. But only a very very few of us, like the Prophet Samuel of old, bother to listen."

"You hear Him too?" Thomas asked, while his father had an alarmed look on his face.

"I do," the Archbishop replied. "As you grow, you will find that it is important to make certain that it is the correct voice, but yes. And, your father is right to be alarmed, it must be your own secret. It is both a gift and a burden." He stopped, and added happily, "which I think is the very definition of a responsibility. Which brings me to my question…After everything, do you still wish to attend Canterbury College at Oxford?"

"Very much so, My Lord," Thomas answered excitedly.

John More interjected, "but the Law, Thomas!"

The Archbishop replied, "John, you know I have nothing but admiration for you, but the study of law may wait for two years. He is only fourteen."

John replied immediately, "but he is to study law."

"Two years will make him a better lawyer, open his mind," the Archbishop replied firmly, "And need I remind you John, that I am a lawyer. Oh. Yes.. and the Lord Chancellor of England. I respect you immensely as a lawyer, John. Your work for King Richard was remarkable. Think about why you object to Oxford."

Thomas looked at his father.

John immediately relented, "Very well then, but let me be so bold as to say this to you My Lord, Canon law is different from the Inns."

"I agree," said the Archbishop, who added nothing more, and started to walk off.

John More watching both the Archbishop and the stricken face of his son, abruptly changed his heart, and called out, "My Lord Archbishop, please wait. Of course I believe my son would benefit from time at Oxford."

"Thank you Father!" Thomas cried before the Archbishop had a chance to reply.

They had paused at the outer gate of the castle, and passed into the shadow cast by the building.

The Archbishop turned and smiled at John More, clapping him again on the shoulder, "John, thank you. I think the world of both you and Thomas. And look at the change in him from the Pilgrimage."

John More nodded agreement.

The Archbishop turned again and said, "with Oxford agreed to…'like a contract'…Eh Thomas?" He paused and winked at Thomas, "then we should see to the King and Queen, and how the family reunion is progressing."

He started to turn again, but thought better, and looked at Thomas, asking, "speaking of contracts Thomas, What did you end up deciding about your contract with Richard? Anything you would like to share?"

Thomas looked seriously at the Archbishop, answering slowly, "yes, My Lord Archbishop. In conversation with King Henry, I determined that my contract with King Richard was with the King, rather than with Richard, and so I was honor bound, and contractually bound to King Henry."

"And King Henry," the Archbishop enquired, impressed.

"Has informed me that my contract of silence is to continue," Thomas replied.

John and the Archbishop both laughed, saying together, "Lawyer!"

Their group happily picked up their pace, catching up to the group at the door of the Great Hall of the Palace. The large wooden door was closed, but laughing could be heard from within. Edward shrugged when Thomas gave him an enquiring look. The adults simply stood motionless, listening.

After a brief wait, the doors were opened by soldiers with halberds. The Great Room was still lit from the high oriel windows, but the deep shadows of recesses in the evening setting sun were offset by torches and candles lit along the wall.

The King came forward, leaving the Queen's brothers and sisters, saying happily, "all Praise to Saint Thomas Becket! My wife, the Queen's fever broke this morning. She is quite tired, but taking food."

Everyone shouted their thanks. The King looked at Thomas More, winked, and gave a little nod, mouthing "love and trust."

Thomas saluted back.

"In celebration of the Queen's deliverance," the King continued, "and to welcome our daughter, the Princess Elizabeth, I have created a group of soldiers, 'the Queen's men,' who shall be a Royal guard, and troop for the Queen." The King gestured to Godfrey Wooler and his men. "Of course their Sergeant will need at some point to have different clothing, as his Pilgrim's robe, if not his pilgrim's spirit, will, I am sure, someday wear too thin for modesty."

There was laughter as Godfrey looked down happily red-faced.

The King went on, "I have asked young Master Thomas Howard to continue as their Captain until a suitable replacement may be named. I have great confidence in our young soldier, and I need him in the North." He nodded to Thomas. "Oh, yes, and given Howard's obvious nobility and lineage, my wife the Queen has consented to his marriage to her sister, the Princess Anne."

Cheers around.

"I am also delighted to announce that two fine young men from the country, Sir Edward Guildford and Doctor John Clement will be joining our court. Welcome!"

The two young men nodded appreciatively.

"And with that," King Henry concluded, "I am certain that you are all quite hungry. So, I am told, that dinner is ready."

"My Lord Chancellor," the boatman asked again. "Are you ready to go?"

Thomas More, Lord Chancellor of England started. He stared blankly at the man, saying "yes, of course," and was helped off the pier at the Westminster docks down into one of the King's barges. The oarsmen stood ready, helping to balance the low boat as Thomas climbed in.

Going to a simple chair set up under the red silk canopy, Thomas looked up at the Palace of Westminster, and the Great Hall, with the Courts, and the looming mass of Westminster Abbey off behind. On the Abbey wall, Thomas could see the scaffolding of the chapel, the Lady Chapel, that was nearing completion that King Henry the Seventh had begun for his Queen, and that his son had continued to build for his parents.

Thomas turned his head to the left, and took in the red brick towers of the Archbishop's Lambeth Palace. He thought for a while about Archbishop Morton, dead now for thirty years. He still missed his old mentor acutely every time he saw his palace. He missed the kindred spirit, but wondered if that was what he had truly been, after so much had happened.

Thomas glanced, unsmiling, at the boatman and crew, and took the copy of Ludolph's Life of Christ that Henry Stafford had given him out of his pocket. Thomas glanced at the familiar daily prayers, frowning a bit.

A desk had been brought for him to work at while the men silently oared through the quiet Thames. The River was right at mid-tide so the current was minimal, and the weather sunny. Thomas silently acknowledged the new furniture, and continued looking through the book. He was pleased to find a printers error on the fourth page. Nodding his head solemnly, Thomas turned to the frontispiece, and, taking the offered pen, wrote, "*Liber quonda Thomae Mori ('Book of Thomas More')*."

Satisfied that he had claimed the book, he turned to a hard perusal, first for errors, and then for meaning. The Barge swept past the More estate in Chelsea. Thomas glanced up and saw the mulberry trees in full fruit. In the distance, Thomas heard vague, muffled cries. "That'll be that idiot Tewkesbury," Thomas said under his breath. "Heretic." As with a bad taste, Thomas turned and spit off to the left of the boat.

The crew of the barge looked askance at the Lord Chancellor, and subtly turned to the left so as not to hear the cries from his home in Chelsea.

After a bit, the crew settled into a rhythm and Thomas was lulled into time passing quickly. The new Richmond Palace started to be visible well off in the distance. The old Palace of Sheen at Richmond had burned to the ground in 1496, and had been very expensively rebuilt. The new Palace was quite large, but now also quite tall, with at least twenty high spires, topped with the rounded Minarets which had become popular in Thomas's lifetime.

"King Henry the father had been devastated at the loss of Sheen," Thomas thought.

*"God's blood but he was,"* came the voice from within.

"Truth be told, I like the new palace better,"

*"It is far more luxurious, more appropriate for a King."*

Thomas grew uncomfortable, something gnawing at his brain. He shifted in his plain chair. The boat rocked a bit, but quickly steadied. The Palace grew nearer.

"Love and Trust," Thomas thought, at last, coming to a decision.

*"What is that supposed to mean?"*

"You've changed," thought Thomas, as he espied a smiling King Henry the Eighth standing on the lawn awaiting Thomas More's, his Lord Chancellor of England, arrival.

Made in the USA
Las Vegas, NV
07 July 2021

26060289R00261